# Father PAUL'S WAR

## MARK CHENG

Alliance Publishing Press

# Alliance Publishing Press

Published by Alliance Publishing Press Ltd
This paperback edition published 2013
Copyright © Mark Cheng 2013
Mark Cheng asserts his moral right to be
identified as the author of this book.

ISBN-13: 9 780956 999252

*Typeset in Times New Roman*
*Book & Cover Design by Mark James James*

# Father
# PAUL'S
# WAR

# Mark Cheng – A Biography

Mark Cheng was born in Hong Kong in 1930, the eldest
of nine children. Following the Japanese occupation of
Hong Kong, he and his family fled to China in 1942.
Mark left his family there, and followed his old headmaster,
Father Donnelly, to India where he stayed until 1947.

Back in Hong Kong and inspired by his teachers, Mark became a
Jesuit novice in 1949. But he realised that the life wasn't for him,
and he left the noviciate to train as a history teacher.
He met his wife Irene at teacher training college, marrying in
1957. Realising that Hong Kong would eventually be handed
back to the Chinese, Mark moved once more. He and his young
family came to the UK, where they have remained ever since.

Mark and Irene have a son, a daughter, and five grandchildren.
In his spare time Mark has been a Parish Choirmaster, and Choir
Director of a Gregorian Chant group. He also paints, and in
2005 was a founder member of the Eagle Gallery Artists
group in Bedford.

*To the Cistercian monks*
*of our Lady of Consolation*
*at Yang Chia Ping near Peking*

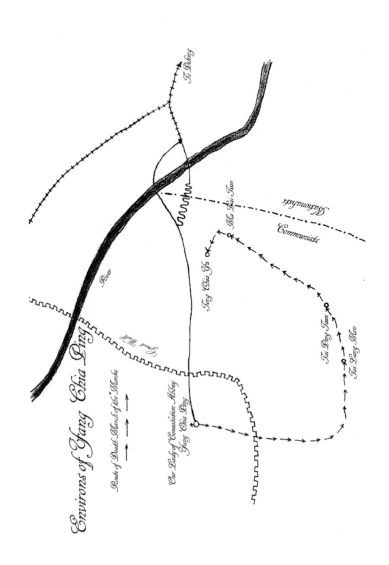

Environs of Yang Chia Ping

Route of Death March of the Monks → → →

Our Lady of Consolation Abbey
Yang Chia Ping

Great Wall

River

To Peking

To Peking

Nationalists

Communists

Ma Chai Tsun

Tong Chia Yu

Tai Ping Tsun

Tai Yang Shan

# Map of China

Some of the Places Mentioned in the Book

Peking

Tientsin

The Yellow River

Nanking

Shanghai

Chengdu

Wuhan

Chungking   The Yangtze River

Shanghr

Liuchow

Canton

The Pearl River

Nanning

Hong Kong

Taiwan

## Old and New Romanisation of Place Names

Peking - Beijing
Tientsin - Tianjin
Nanking - Nanjing
Canton - Guangzhou
Liuchow - Liuzhou
Chungking - Chongqing

# ONE

He had come into the valley, and into its familiar silence, disturbed only by the occasional small sounds of the vegetation. Familiar, too, were the tall, serrated ranks of blue-grey peaks which flanked this barren valley with its rocky soil. It was dotted about with dwarf oaks and small pines which showed dark against the bleached ochre of the steep hillsides. Wild rhododendrons shared the landscape, and in summer flooded the desolate valley with primal colours, but they now also showed dark against the soil. There were apricot trees, too, and in springtime the soft pastel hues of their blossoms briefly transformed the quasi-lunar landscape into an ethereal, soft-edged Eden. The oil from the kernels of their fruit had provided a valuable, if not a substantial, income to those who once inhabited the valley. But this valley, in spite of a fleeting impression in spring, or when the rhododendrons flowered in their glory in summer, was not Eden. The meagre living which was wrested from its unyielding, stony soil was the result of much sweat and toil.

The pines swayed and rustled, and dust rose briefly as a cold wind blew down the valley, for it was already November, and the oaks and apricot trees had shed their leaves. The late morning sun shone pale yellow, without much warmth, in a washed, pale blue sky, made even paler in parts by a haze of marestail clouds. He shivered and wrapped his cotton quilted coat more closely around his spare frame. He was alone in the valley, as he had expected, on the narrow metalled road which he had once helped to build. He was hungry. At least he knew he ought to be hungry, as he had not eaten since the evening before, and that only sparingly, for his supper had consisted merely of a crust of stale steamed bread. He had been very reluctant to use the little money which he had managed to earn and save. He had other plans for that money. He felt for it now, the notes and the coins, which he carried in a cloth tied to his belt. Yes, it was still there. He realised that he had been getting paranoid about his little share of worldly wealth. He must be careful.

He had not far to go now, only another mile and a half, give or take a few yards: not much at all after a week's journey, when he had walked for ten or more hours a day. This was nearly journey's end, for the next twelve hours or so. He picked up his canvas rucksack, slung it on his shoulder, and continued his journey up the valley.

There should have been a pair of simple wrought iron gates at the end of the road, set in the middle of a boundary wall built of the bluish-grey brick that was the universal building material of the country which extended levelly on both sides before rising, following the gradient of the valley sides. However, the gates were no longer there, only the remains of the wall, and the debris left at its base. Two years' weathering had not been sufficient to transform the cruel destruction into an acceptable historical ruin. Some of the brickwork had been washed clean, but in many places the charring caused by the blaze still looked fresh. The brass plaque, which had been a gift of a benefactor and which had been set into one of the gate pillars, remained in place, even though it showed evidence of partial melting and was now discoloured by verdigris. He had been told of the destruction, and had visualised it to be much more comprehensive. Now, he was only surprised that the wall had not entirely disappeared, with the still usable bricks carted away for other buildings. The isolation of the place had something to do with it, he was certain.

He stepped through what had been the gateway into the enclosure. The porter's lodge was only a blackened shell; the interior was full of what had been its roof. Burnt timber lay about the area, some on top of and some under broken roof tiles. Amazingly, there was still soot on the remains of what once had been whitewashed walls, and he could even tell where the crucifix had hung. There was no way in which the little building could be made functional again.

Weeds were rife in what had been a well-tended garden which lined the avenue from the gate to the centre of the enclosure. The lawn was now waist-high grass and weeds. But some of the plants, if bare now because of the season and distinguishable from the surrounding growth only because he knew where they had been, were still there, where they had not been deliberately vandalised or destroyed. The apricot trees and the pear trees, he had been told, had been put to the torch, but many of them, he could see from a distance, had managed to survive and were now in their winter gauntness and still growing in the orchards. The hardy and fruitful apricot trees never needed much tending, anyway. The pear trees, which had been introduced into the valley in the last century, were almost as hardy. However, he might take a closer look later. He wondered what had happened to the oats and the millet, too.

He went on towards the main buildings. The remains of the main buildings. And the watery sunshine and desolation and his memories accompanied him all the way. Yes, his memories had come with him. But somewhere, he had left his feelings behind.

If parts of the four walls of the porter's lodge had been left standing, there was not much in the complex of the main buildings apart from a few jagged remains that used to be walls, and heaps of rubble. In front of him was the huge mound of fallen bricks and wood which was once the bell tower. He walked round that into the nave, and apart from the lower half of two bays in the sanctuary there was nothing left of the Chapel. The top of the stone high altar lay on its side, leaning against the stone supports. He turned right and saw that the cloister garden had not survived the fire. Half of the walls of the Chapter Room were still standing, and the ledge on which the last row of seats had been built had survived. Surprisingly, too, it was almost free of debris. Across from the cloister garden, where the kitchen used to be, the solid brick-built stoves were still in place, but where the dormitories had collapsed on top of the Refectory and the warming room near by, there was only a mountain of rubble. In the other wing, the library and scriptorium had fallen into the study rooms. He climbed on top of the heap there, and under a roof tile he found a book. It must have been the only book which had, perhaps miraculously, survived the night of destruction, and had lain there for more than two years, exposed to the elements but protected by its robust cover and the friendly tile. The title on the spine had been bleached off, but the inside, though damp, was still in reasonable condition and certainly legible. It was St Bede's *History of the English Church.*

He nearly laughed aloud to himself. What use was St Bede to him now? Why couldn't he have found a copy of the Vulgate, or at least St Thomas à Kempis!

However, he put St Bede into his rucksack.

He picked his way through to the Abbot's house. There was nothing left there except for the obligatory pile of rubble. This building had received most attention from the pillagers who had believed that vast amounts of gold had been secreted there, and he could see the holes which had been dug in the floor in the search for that mythical treasure. The guest house next door and the infirmary on the other side had fared no better. Further out, he could see that none of the workshops, barns and granaries had been left with their roofs on. The oil presses would not have survived either. It would be pointless, too, to explore the stables. He wondered if any of the packhorses and mules would still be alive, working for other masters.

Another gust of wind blew down the valley, and he suddenly realised how tired he was. He used to be able to tell the time by reading the shadows cast by the buildings, but he couldn't do that now. He looked at the sun.

It must be about eleven, he told himself.

Time enough for a rest first. He headed for the Chapter Room.

As he stepped over the threshold, somehow the desolation around him seemed to vanish. He felt that the walls were around him again, and that the only light came through the lancet windows on either side of the Abbot's seat, with above it the large crucifix that hung on the wall, the wood black and the corpus waxy-white in death. He was again in his habit, as he advanced and bowed to the Abbot. But the brief vision disappeared as he straightened up. He walked over and sat down where he had last sat in Chapter, in the back row against the wall.

He shut his eyes as memories filled his mind. He remembered when he had first attended Chapter. As a new member of the Community he had sat in the front row near the entrance. But before that…

\*\*\*

He was a southerner from near Canton, where his family lived. His father, a distant, unusually tall, majestic figure, had named him Leung Waihung, and the name had been duly entered into the family archives which were locked up in a safe in his father's room. He was the third of five sons and two daughters, and he was the youngest child of his own mother. He quite early on realised that he was his mother's favourite – being the youngest, he supposed – but his mother never spoiled him. His father had two other wives, both of whom were senior to his mother, but his mother, he learned later in life, had been loved best. That, however, did not seem to have caused ill-feeling among the wives – it was merely a fact of life. Father was a salt merchant, and therefore a wealthy man, and they lived in a big house with a large, formal European garden and three courtyards with a suite of rooms round each, one for each wife and her children. There was an army of servants. He had a special servant all to himself, who shadowed him everywhere. There was a major-domo who practically had authority over life and death – perhaps he did have; he could never be very sure. Two or three times a week, sometimes more often, this man would hang a lantern over his mother's door, and this meant that she would not be with them that night. He always missed her on these occasions. He tried begging her to stay, but his mother would say nothing, would give him a hug and a kiss, and then was gone. At first he was quite puzzled by the connection between the appearance of the lantern and his mother's absence, and people, even his older siblings, would smile but would not answer when he asked. It was not until much later that he learned the significance of the lantern, and then he took it for granted.

They were a happy family; the half-brothers and half-sisters got on well together, and the children mixed at the family meals twice a day. They used to sally forth into the countryside on picnics and for their favourite pastimes, boating and swimming in the river, ignorant of, or ignoring, the political unrest which was devastating the country. The war between the central government and the local warlords, who were no more than robber barons, did not break the latters' hold over individual provinces, and the subsequent war between the government and the Communists only came to an uneasy and inconclusive truce in the early 1930s. However, these events seemed very far away to a little boy, and the place he liked best, when he felt the need to be by himself, was a spot in the angle between two roofs which he got to by climbing through a window in his room. He quite often did this deliberately to annoy his servant, who never discovered his hiding place and would look everywhere for him.

"Master Waihung, where are you?"

"I'm here," he would say softly, with a grin all over his face.

From his hiding place he could see a wide sweep of the countryside, where the colours mutated according to the seasons, and the trees changed their robes as frequently as the seasons changed. Beyond the paddy fields and the orchards, he could catch a glimpse of the big river, and the dark shapes of the barges on it. When the wind was right, he could just about hear the chug of the barges' engines.

He could stay in his hiding place for hours, and he often did.

He did well at school, and decided to go to university as two of his half-brothers had done before him. Both went to the American Christian university of Lingnan in Canton.

"Lingnan's the place," one of his elder half-brothers told him. "It's a great university, and I enjoyed my time there."

He must have done. He had also become a Christian and married a Christian girl in a Christian church. That was the first time Waihung had been in contact with Christians, and he wasn't very sure that he liked being one of them. If his sister-in-law Meiching was typically Christian, then they must be very difficult people to live with, with their taboos and so many things they couldn't share with the family. In addition, Meiching was forever trying to convert people, and he resented that. He decided that he did not want to go to Lingnan, respected though it was in South China. It also had the reputation of being an establishment for the rich, and he realised now that he was developing an incipient social conscience. Besides, he wanted to do engineering, not liberal arts. For this he had a precedent in the family. One of his uncles had been among the first Chinese students sent by the government on a scholarship to America to study marine engineering; he now lived in Hong Kong and worked for a ship-building firm. Although the family occasionally heard from him, the relationship was not close. However, he was not interested in building ships; his interest was in bridges and roads, part of the infrastructure that the country needed to get on a par with European countries.

He heard that there was a good engineering school at the University of Hong Kong. He liked the sound of Hong Kong. Some of his friends went there to do medicine, and he learned from them what a lively, vibrant place it was. ("And the girls are great," one of them said.) Also, his father was willing, and he was very tempted, but then he decided against that, too.

"I don't want to spend an extra year in Hong Kong just to improve my English, which is worse than my Mandarin, and then find that I can't cope with the language," he told his mother, who was rather relieved that he had decided not to go too far away, after all.

And then she burst into floods of tears when he told her that he had got a place at Peking University to do engineering under the great Hasselbach. That was in 1931.

The family, the clan, made a weekend of it at the end of August, in Canton. But before they left home, his mother burned incense on the family altar, and together they put joss sticks into the earthenware pot that stood on it. They went to stay in a really grand hotel, where the floors were laid with marble from Tali and there was a bathroom with an enamel bath on each level, where the doorman bowed to you and 'boys' in uniform carried your luggage for you from the rickshaw to your rooms. There were also ceiling fans which one could make to turn at three different speeds. It was so very different from the country inn in his home village. But wasn't Canton noisy at night!

They went shopping the next morning at the Sun Department Store and the Sincere Department Store, with their garishly dressed windows and bright lights – even in the daytime. There one could buy chinaware and glass and bathtubs and clothes on mannequins. There just was no end to the variety and amount of stuff one could spend money on, and all the goods had come from the United States, France, England and even South America.

"Look, Mother," he kept saying. "I've got enough things to take with me. I don't want any more."

It proved to be a losing battle. It was, in fact, a lost battle even before it had begun. He was, however, thankful when his father bought him a wristwatch.

"Just give him the best you have," he told the sales assistants who swarmed round to serve him. He always had that sort of effect on people.

"You'll need that, my son," he told him in his lofty way.

His mother bought him a pair of American shoes, and one of his half-brothers bought him a tie.

"You'll have to learn to put on a tie, Waihung," he said, "when you meet girls and go to dances, and things."

Then it was time for lunch. They went to a restaurant which belonged to a friend of his father, and they had to have three large round tables to accommodate the Leung clan. They had a complete floor to themselves. After that, the young people went sightseeing in a fleet of rickshaws. They went to inspect the ships on the quayside, to look at the English houses in Shameen, and to gaze up at the tall Gothic facade of the Cathedral of the Sacred Heart. This was one of the wonders of Canton. It was built all of stone, and astonished the locals with its size and its soaring spires. The people of Canton called it simply 'Stone House'.

"How are they different from your lot?" he asked his Christian sister-in-law, and immediately regretted the question. Meiching spent the rest of the afternoon trying to explain the differences to him.

All good things come to an end. The next morning they saw him off at the crowded, busy railway station. The goodbyes were suitably decorous and unembarrassing. His mother held herself ramrod-straight and managed not to burst into tears though he could see that her lips were trembling. But it was his father who surprised him. He had not expected anything more than a curt nod of the head when he said goodbye. But the old man extended his hand for him to shake.

"Waihung," he said formally, "you are the most intelligent of all my sons. So, do well in your studies. You carry the hopes of the family."

He thought that barely twenty-five years ago the resources of the entire family would have been deployed to get him through various stages of education with the ultimate aim of his entering the Imperial Civil Service Examinations. He wondered if he would be honour-bound to commit suicide if he failed that degree examination, though it was an unlikely possibility.

He did not enjoy the journey to Peking much. For one thing, it was too long, even on an express, for he was travelling from one end of the country to the other. He was thankful that his father had insisted on a private sleeper. It gave him his own space, but it also meant that he was isolated from his fellow passengers. He tried to study the landscape with the eye of a would-be civil engineer, but that, too, palled after four or five hours, and thereafter, one paddy field was much like another. The scenery did change as the train made its slow climb up the wide, mountainous and wild watershed which divided the Pearl River basin from that of the Yangtzekiang. The town of Kukkong, which controlled one of the rail routes through the mountains, was passed in the night, and the train wended its interminable way for the next couple of days to Wuhan – he had to remember to call it 'Wuhan' in Mandarin rather than 'Mohon' in his mother tongue – on the Yangtze. Beyond Kukkong, the people spoke, as far as he was concerned, a different language, which, in spite of his being taught it at school, he had difficulty in understanding at first. He was in effect in another country.

The arrival in Peking was a relief. Being confined to a train, even if he had his own private space, was not much fun. He didn't feel as though he could have taken much more. At least, however, he had read all the books he had brought with him from Canton, plus another couple he had acquired en route, while the flat, alluvial plain of northern China flashed by outside his window. He went straight from the railway station to his university hall, where he found he had been allocated a first-floor room overlooking a walkway between grassed areas criss-crossed by minor pathways which connected most of the halls of residence. The spartan, simply furnished bedroom-cum-study, with desk and chair and bookcase, a slightly wobbly wardrobe next to an enamel washbasin on a stand, and an iron bedstead with a rather worn mattress, appealed to him, and he found the idea that it was to be his home for the next four years rather exciting. It did not occur to him until later that this was his first taste of freedom, a sort of coming of age. After settling in, he spent the next few days before term started in the company of some new friends he had made, sightseeing in the city, capital of the country no longer since the beginning of the Republic, but still impressive with its wide boulevards and its cobbled side streets, a mixture of the ancient and modern utilitarian. On the whole, he thought, he much preferred Canton as a city.

Finally, on the second day of term, he and all the other civil engineering first-year students met Dr Michael Hasselbach in the faculty's No. 3 lecture theatre. There were not many Europeans on the teaching staff then at Peking University, and Hasselbach would have been easily picked out. There were reported sightings of him on the first day of term. Waihung was curious, but he had had no luck. And then, the door behind the lecturer's desk which ran the whole width of the platform opened and the great Hasselbach entered. The chatter died, and the freshers, not certain what to do, shuffled to their feet.

Hasselbach turned out to be of shortish stature, and to have a polished dome of a head round which was a fringe of light brown hair. Below somewhat bushy eyebrows were eyes which were grey and expectedly penetrating. He was dressed in a dark suit, a dark red shirt and a brightly coloured tie which clashed beautifully with the shirt. That was his lecture theatre outfit, his new students later discovered. The only thing that ever changed was the tie, and it was always brightly coloured, as though he had little dress sense, or didn't really care how he looked. However, although he might be somewhat reminiscent of the absent-minded professor, he showed, at that first meeting, that he spoke impeccable Mandarin – which was more than some of his new students did.

"Thank you, gentlemen. Please do resume your seats. You are no longer in a middle school, and I do not expect you to stand up for my entrance. My name is Hasselbach, as you all know, I expect, and you can address me as Dr Hasselbach."

Then he did what a teacher always did at the first meeting with new students. He checked the register, outlined the course, and issued a timetable. And that was the end of the first lecture.

Life at the university proved to be congenial. Waihung fitted quickly and painlessly into the academic and social rounds that made up this life, and he was picked for the university basketball team. The new southerners briefly went mad as they always did when they first experienced snow, which this year came in early December. They dived into it, built snowmen, pelted one another with the stuff, and generally behaved as though they were only half their age. And then they regained their sanity.

He was a natural hard-worker and enjoyed the challenge that his new studies provided him. From the grade B which he was given for his first written paper, and for which Hasselbach congratulated him, he progressed to a straight A by the end of December, and thereafter his grades never strayed below that. He was intelligent enough to realise that he was still, in the first semester, at a rudimentary stage of his studies, but was beginning to find that Hasselbach was increasingly seeking his contribution in group discussions and seminars. One day, early in January, he kept to his bed because of flu, and in the afternoon one of his friends came to see him. He had been half-dozing and he felt light-headed. But, having been on his own all day, he was glad to see him.

"You know, Waihung," said his friend, depositing his own pile of books on the floor by the only chair in the room before he sat down, "how Black Broom's eyes sweep the lecture theatre when he walks in? And you know what he asked this morning?"

This friend was another southerner. There were quite a few of them at the university, even among the first-year engineering students. To the more irreverent of them, the professor was 'Black Broom' because that's what his name sounded like in Cantonese.

"No. You tell me. And in the meantime, please do pass me the aspirin."

At home, his mother would have given him a rice bowl full of a bitter herbal brew, the ingredients for which she got from the medicine shop in the village, and wrapped him in a thick cotton quilt so that he sweated out the fever. But, like the majority of his new friends at the university, who professed to be cynics and atheists and believed that SCIENCE had an answer to every question in the cosmos, he believed in the supremacy of modern medicine, and it certainly required much less labour.

"Here you are… and shall I pour you a glass of water? Well, old Hasselbach, after sweeping the room with his white eyes, said, 'And where is young Mr Leung this fine morning?'"

"And what did you say?"

"*I* didn't say anything. Nobody did, because we didn't know where you were. And then he said, 'Should any of you see him in the next twenty-four hours, would you tell him I particularly want to see him about his last paper.'"

He groaned. "I knew I shouldn't have put that in the paper!"

"Why? What did you write?"

He sat up to explain, but had to close his eyes until the dizzy spell had passed. His friend was concerned, but he persisted.

"Well?" he asked when his friend had finished. "What do you think?"

"You want me to be honest?"

He nodded. And winced when whatever was inside his head decided to start knocking.

"It won't work." His friend then took fifteen minutes to tell him why it wouldn't work. "It's the mass and the weight. And now, shall I bring you some soup? Or do you prefer noodles?"

"Soup, please. And a bit of that steamed bread." He was not to know that steamed bread was going to play a rather important part in his life.

Two days later, he felt well enough to go back to class, although he still felt somewhat unsteady on his feet. He followed Hasselbach to his rooms after the lecture.

"Are you better?" asked the professor as he ushered his pupil into his office.

"I'm much better, thank you, sir."

The simplicity of the furnishings of the professor's room no longer surprised him. The rooms of his other teachers were much more plush. Nor was he surprised when Hasselbach offered him green tea from a thermos flask instead of English tea or American coffee as some of his Chinese colleagues would do.

"Now, Waihung." They had settled on what he wished to be called at their first meeting. "About your paper... Have you heard of this man?" Hasselbach handed him a volume from a pile on his desk.

"No."

"Read from page 147."

He looked up, rather embarrassed. "I'm sorry, I haven't got enough English."

"No matter. Well, this what he is saying..." Hasselbach translated. "Sounds familiar?"

"That's what I wrote," he stammered. "Almost exactly the same."

Hasselbach smiled. "Let me congratulate you, Waihung. What you wrote isn't new, but that you should have been able to work it out for yourself independently, that's something. More than something. We'll make an engineer of you yet! By the way, you should learn English, you know, to read the journals and books, and German too, if you can manage that."

Then, as he rose to go, Hasselbach stayed him.

"Are you going home for Chinese New Year after the exams?" he asked.

"No. It's not worth it. By the time I get home, it will be almost time to start back again. Some of us are going to stick together and we'll see what we can do."

"Yes, I think I have an idea who they are. Will you come to a party Black Broom holds every Chinese New Year's Eve for homeless strays from Canton and other places? I've asked some of them already, and they are going to come. By the way, they are not all from engineering."

Then he suddenly realised that Hasselbach had spoken in Cantonese.

"Oh, yes, I'll come!"

"Well, then. This is the address. Some of you know it."

*** 

It was not difficult to find the address on Maple Street although he had not been able to meet anyone yet who was familiar with it. He arrived with a number of fellow guests who had decided to come along together, and having pressed the large brass doorbell they were waiting outside the whitewashed, functional two-storey building. It did not look like a private dwelling.

"It looks like a..."

They could not make up their minds what it looked like. The door opened and a face peered short-sightedly at them from behind thick lenses.

"You must be Father Hasselbach's guests," said the white-jacketed man. "Do come in out of the cold."

They were in a spacious entrance hall, as simply decorated as Hasselbach's college room. The only furniture was two upright chairs, one on each side of the double front door, and both covered by a mountain of overcoats. On the wall opposite was a large crucifix. (Very much like the one in the Chapter Room, he recalled.) Four doorways led into the entrance area, and they all had double doors. The partially open ones on the left wall led, he could glimpse, into some sort of church. Two doorways flanked the crucifix on the wall opposite. The doors to the left were closed, and above them was affixed a wooden panel on which was painted the word 'Private'. The doors to the right were open, and through them he could see a lighted corridor with a number of rooms off it. There were stacks of chairs and tables in the corridor, as though they had been cleared from another room. The last pair of doors, those on the far right, were open and through them he could hear the chatter of conversation and the clink of glasses.

"You can leave your coats here, and it's through there." The man then disappeared through the doors marked 'Private'.

It was a largish room, with a movable blackboard pushed into a corner. He was now sure that those desks and chairs had been moved out from in here. A good effort had been made to transform the room for the festive occasion – crêpe paper streamers hung from the ceiling, and there were balloons everywhere. Someone had written 'Respectful Wishes for Spring Happiness' on a large sheet of red paper and this occupied an honoured position over a fireplace where a cheerful fire was blazing. On either side of the fireplace were long tables loaded with bottles and bowls of drink and plates of food. There were already perhaps twenty people in the room, both men and women, and they turned to look at the new arrivals, glasses in their hands, before resuming their conversations.

Hasselbach, no longer disguised as a layman with an appalling dress sense, was now encased in the sort of black gown which Waihung knew from what he had seen in photographs was the normal attire for Christian priests. He advanced to meet them. His manners were far too hearty, he thought. He felt resentful. He felt betrayed by one whom he had respected and learned to trust.

"Welcome, all of you."

He reluctantly put out his hand to be shaken, and he could tell by the quick glance Hasselbach he threw him that he immediately felt his hostility. The priest then turned to greet the others who had come with him.

"Meet some of my friends," said Hasselbach. Two other men, both dressed like Hasselbach, waited to be introduced. "Father Tauziat, our Superior." This was the tall, ascetic-looking man with a wild mane of near-white hair. "Father Liu." This was the Chinese man, about his own height.

Waihung and his party shook hands with both men.

"This," said Hasselbach, "is Mr Leung Waihung, my star pupil in this year's intake. He's obtained an A-plus in the end-of-semester exam he's just done. If he's not careful, he'll make an excellent engineer."

"We've heard a lot about you," said Father Tauziat. "Congratulations."

They were then introduced to the other group of guests. Some he had known well, others he had by sight only, and still others he had not known at all.

"And this is Miss Margaret Siu."

Hasselbach was introducing him to a slim, pretty girl, dressed in a plain blue silk ankle-length gown edged with some sort of silver embroidery punctuated with tiny pearls. Her eyes were almost on a level with his, but then she was wearing high-heeled shoes.

"How do you do?" he said formally. They shook hands.

She had short, lightly permed hair, framing a gently curved, pear-shaped face and ever-so-slightly slanting eyes that made him gasp.

"I've seen you about," she said. "You have to be in engineering, if you know Dr Hasselbach so well."

"I don't really know him at all, apart from his being my professor," he said, his resentment now surfacing. "I certainly didn't know he was a Christian missionary!"

He could feel Margaret stiffening.

"Look, I'm not a Christian myself, neither Catholic nor Protestant, but I think you are not being fair. The Jesuits run this place so that people like us who come from other parts of China can meet and socialise. I've been coming here now for four months, and I've never had Christianity preached at me."

"Jesus Society! That says it all, doesn't it?"

Margaret threw him a withering look.

"You are ignorant, and suspicious as only the ignorant can be!" She pointedly turned her back on him, walked away and spoke to someone else.

For the rest of the evening, he wandered listlessly from group to group, always taking care to avoid Margaret and Dr Hasselbach, but he was unable to become a part of any group. He fancied that after the preliminary greetings he was politely excluded. He thought of leaving the party and going back to his room except, he realised, that would be even worse. Eventually he found himself with the Chinese priest.

"How do you find Peking, Mr Leung?"

He didn't want to say that he preferred the glitter of Canton.

"An interesting city," he said noncommittally.

"Apart from the historic parts," said Father Liu, "like the Forbidden City, I much prefer Shanghai, where I come from. It's much more... international, and it's so alive! Have you been to Shanghai?"

"No. I hope to go one day." He actually wanted to ask: Why did you become a Jesuit?

"I did my training and my university studies at Zikawei near Shanghai. Have you heard of a man called Zi? He gave that place to the Jesuits."

Waihung shook his head.

"He was a Confucian scholar in the last years of the Ming Dynasty. He is credited with being the first modern Chinese to have been converted to Christianity. He took the name of Paul when he became a Catholic."

"That would have been" – Waihung made a quick calculation – "at the beginning of the seventeenth century? I thought that Christianity came in with the Unequal Treaties in the last hundred years."

"No. Do you know that Christianity first came to China in the sixth century in the form of a heretical sect called the Nestorians? And then again in the thirteenth century in the Yuan Dynasty? And it did well on both occasions. So, you see, Christianity and China are old friends. You may also like to know that the mother of the last Ming emperor was baptised Constance."

He wanted to know why the Nestorians were heretics, and what happened in the thirteenth century. He was surprised that he was no longer angry. This polite, casual conversation had dispelled the resentment.

The party came to an end soon after ten, and the guests decided to visit the traditional New Year's Eve Fair and watch the fireworks which ushered in the New Year. They went in a body, but the girls were sticking together, and he was far too shy to approach Margaret in public. But the fair was good fun and the fireworks noisy and brilliant.

"You can tell me more about the Jesuits another time," he had said to Father Liu half in jest, but only half, as they said goodbye.

"So perhaps I'll see you again? You can come any time. Oh, and do you play chess?"

\*\*\*

This first Chinese New Year away from home passed uneventfully. In fact, there was scarcely anything to do. Everything was shut down for three days, and the red litter which was the debris of fireworks and firecrackers grew at a terrific rate. Shops and restaurants only reopened reluctantly, it seemed, on the fourth day. He was beginning to enjoy his independence and his freedom and did not mind the solitude. While most of the country made the obligatory rounds of visits to relatives and superiors, he was quietly – yes, quietly, for the university campus was almost entirely deserted except for those who had chosen to stay – learning English. He found that he was assimilating vocabulary without any difficulty, which was what he wanted for reading. Speaking the language, he knew, was another matter.

Halfway through the holiday, he felt that he needed a break, and he went for a long walk round the city, and somehow found himself in Maple Street.

"Why not?" he said to himself, and knocked on the door.

\*\*\*

The new semester had begun, and he had not seen Margaret again since the party when they all wished one another Happy New Year as they parted to go their separate ways after the fireworks. She had said goodbye stiffly, refusing to look him in the eye.

And he had neglected to ask her which of the women's residential halls she was in.

Then early one morning, she came down the walkway which led past his window, clutching an armful of books and files, her head bare in the freezing air, her footsteps making deep imprints in the thick snow left by the previous night's heavy fall. He struggled with the window, which had frozen to its frame, but managed to throw it open before the girl went past.

"Margaret!" he called, his voice hollow and dead amid the softness of the snow.

She heard him, however. She turned, looked up and recognised him, then smiled and waved, hostility forgotten.

"Wait! Just a minute!" He got into his coat, grabbed his books and raced down the stairs, then at the bottom he remembered that he had forgotten his scarf. And so he had to rush back upstairs to get it.

"Hello," they said at the same time.

"Are you always this early?" he asked.

"No. It's just that today I've to see my tutor before the morning lecture, about something I wrote."

"What actually do you do?"

"I never told you, did I? I do Chemistry, under Professor Tsao."

"And then... research?"

"Maybe. But I want to go into pharmaceutics eventually."

Then conversation flagged, and they walked on in silence. He thought hard of things to say but his mind would not respond.

"I heard that you played chess with Father Liu," she said after a while, turning round to look at him.

"Oh, yes. I needed a break that day." He was pleased that she knew.

"Are you any good?" she asked. "At chess, I mean."

He laughed, and regretted it. He swallowed a lungful of cold air, and went into a paroxysm of coughing.

That made her laugh, but it did not make her cough. She thumped him on the back.

"Are you all right?"

"Yes. I'll be all right in a minute. Anyway, Father Lau... I mean Liu... beat me twice. I won the third game, but I suspect that was because he let me win."

And that was utterly ego-deflating. He had been champion chess player at his school, with an unblemished record.

Too soon, they arrived at the Chemistry building.

"Well," she said, "here I am. Nice of you to walk with me."

They shook hands. But he wanted more than that. He took a deep breath, for he had never asked a girl for a date before – in fact, he had never met a girl before.

"Can we... meet for lunch?" he stammered, and he could feel his face colouring. Later he could swear that her face coloured too, ever so slightly. "In the canteen?"

"Yes."

"About half past twelve?"

"Fine." And then she hurried into the building.

***

No man could forget his first date with a girl. And even now, eighteen years and another life later, sitting on a hard stone seat amid the ruins, the memory of that first lunch with Margaret still stirred him. People said that one never married one's first love, and in his case, it had certainly been true. Without regrets, and true. He wondered what had happened to her.

He was glad that his feelings had come back to him.

***

The harsh northern Chinese winter rolled into spring, and the cherry blossoms added another dimension to the landscape. He and some of his friends became frequent visitors to the Jesuit Chaplaincy, for that was what it was, and there he quite frequently ran into Margaret. Most of those who made use of the facilities there had come from the Canton area, but there were also others from the Cantonese-speaking areas of Kwangsi. They came to chat and to exchange gossip, to play table tennis in the lecture room after they had cleared it of desks and chairs and set up the table, or sometimes to dance to records on a gramophone which one of them had to wind every three records or so. In another room were less active activities such as ludo and Monopoly, and even snakes and ladders. Many were the games of chess he lost to Father Liu, sometimes with Margaret sipping tea and watching, and going into distracting fits of laughter when an important piece was taken.

One day, they were setting up for another game when Father Liu stopped.

"Wait," he said. "I'll show you something."

He returned a few moments later with a rectangular wooden box and a large board divided into black and red squares.

"You know what this is?" he asked, as he took the carved pieces from the box and arranged them on the board.

"I know," said Margaret. "That's European chess. I learned to play when I was at school. It's not that different from Chinese chess."

They played a trial game, with Margaret guiding Waihung successfully through the moves, then he lost the next game to Father Liu.

"You two have a game," said the priest. "I'll watch."

In spite of Father Liu's frequent prompting, he lost to Margaret too.

"You didn't mind losing to me, did you?" she asked later.

"Why should I mind?"

***

"Your protégé and that very attractive girl, Margaret," Father Liu remarked to Father Hasselbach that evening over their after-dinner pipes, as trails of tobacco smoke wafted slowly and picturesquely to the ceiling. "They seem to get along."

Hasselbach threw him a look, grunted, but said nothing, and continued pulling on his pipe.

***

Waihung went for bicycle rides into the countryside with his friends, and watched the maize and the wheat and the barley being sown, and then returned to chart the progress of its growth, simply out of interest and curiosity. Often the party had their meals in country inns or at wayside foodstalls, and as often they took picnics with them and ate them under shady trees. Their occasional boisterousness caused the country people to mutter into their hands. On other days, he and Margaret went for long rides on country buses, and did not mind, or care, where they took them, just as long as they were able to sit companionably together and watch the scenery go by outside the dusty windows.

On one such bus trip, an old woman who had got on with a cage full of chicks, and who appeared to ignore everybody on the bus, said to him as she went past on her way out after several stops, "The little young lady is very pretty."

Caught by surprise, he didn't know what to say, but grinned. Margaret turned pink. They looked at each other: the old lady had assumed too much.

Sometimes, especially when it rained, they went to the cinema to watch Charlie Chaplin and the Keystone Kops, and once or twice they went to the Peking opera, but as Margaret did not particularly care for the music they stopped going together. When asked, he went with his other friends. And Margaret, who had gone to a convent school in Hong Kong, offered to help him with his English.

"Why didn't you go to Hong Kong University?" he asked her one day. "You wouldn't have had trouble with your English."

She looked at him as though to say: We wouldn't have met if I had done that. But he was probably overrating himself.

*33*

Then, one day, they decided to go to the Chaplaincy.

"I'll watch you lose to Father Liu again," she said.

"I want to show you something else," said Father Liu when he came out to meet them. "Come with me."

He took them into the room at the end of the corridor, and in a corner of this seldom-used dusty room, under a window, was an upright piano.

"Do you play?" asked the priest, looking from one to the other.

"No," said Waihung, shaking his head. There had been a piano in the primary school he'd attended, but apart from the teacher no one was permitted to touch it. One of his friends had explored its shiny surface and left a finger mark, and he could still remember the painful afternoon when the teacher was determined to find the culprit. She had, he remembered gleefully, failed to do so.

Margaret said nothing, but walked to the piano, opened it and played several exploratory scales. Father Liu drew up a chair behind her.

"Here's someone who can play."

"No. I'm not very good. I haven't touched a piano for eight months."

But Beethoven and Chopin flowed from her fingers. And soon, he added Brahms and Mozart and others to the music he learned from Margaret.

***

The academic year drew to an end in June, and he finished as top of his class in the end-of-term examinations. Before he left for home, he had a meeting with Hasselbach, who handed him a pile of journals.

"By the autumn I would like you to read the articles I have marked, and I would like to see some notes made as well. I understand you've acquired sufficient English to deal with the reading?" The professor peered at him in the best professorial manner.

He was sure Hasselbach enjoyed doing that, pretending to try to put people off.

"I hope it's been a good year?" Hasselbach added, almost not as a question but as a statement.

"It has, indeed, very much. And thank you, sir."

He saw Margaret and a number of his other friends to the railway station. She was heading for Shanghai, to spend a week with friends before going home to Canton. And then, all of a sudden, he realised that he was going to miss her. He left on the long journey to Canton the next day.

\*\*\*

Home was pretty much the same as it had been nearly ten months ago. He had written so much about his life in Peking that he thought they would probably no longer feel the urge to ask him any more questions. But they did, and he told them again what he had done since he went away, and the two half-brothers who had gone to Lingnan sounded as though they rather envied him going to Peking. He met Margaret only a couple of times in Canton, where they went to the cinema and had lunch or dinner. Sometimes they simply had tea in a European-type café and walked about, content in each other's company. But after a while, he longed to be back in Peking.

They travelled back together, and managed to secure adjacent cabins on the train. He did a lot less reading this time.

And it was almost with a shock that he realised that he was no longer a freshman, and that there were people who were going to experience for the first time what he had done twelve months ago. Then, one morning in December, as he and Margaret took their short walk to the Chemistry building, which they were now doing regularly, they burst out laughing at what they saw. A new group of southerners were pelting one another with their first snowballs, as they had done the year before.

One day, at the beginning of the second semester, Hasselbach detained him after an unusually long lecture. He had been hoping to dash off to meet Margaret, who would be waiting in the canteen. He was annoyed, and only reluctantly followed the professor to his room.

"I won't keep you long," said Hasselbach. "I know it's lunch time, but I've been trying to catch you in the last few days."

*And I always shot off like an arrow.*

"Have you had any serious career plans yet?"

"Not really," he said. He shrugged. "I don't really know what's on offer."

"We can talk about that another time. But I would like you to keep in mind the possibility of a higher degree in England, perhaps, or in America?"

"You… you think I'm good enough for it?"

"You will be in another two and a half years if you are not going to fall away."

He thought for a moment. "I'll have to ask my father, you know."

"You think there may be a problem with money?"

"No… It isn't money."

"If there is, there are ways of getting round that. There are research fellowships and such that will allow to you pursue your studies. Anyway, think about it."

The problem was not so much his father. Or money.

"I thought you weren't going to come," Margaret said as he took the seat next to her. The two girls who were sitting opposite chatting with her rose to go.

"See you at the lecture," Margaret called, and they turned round to wave before disappearing through the canteen doors.

"Sorry to be late," he said. "Hasselbach wanted to see me."

"Something exciting?"

He told her, and they both fell silent.

"Well done," she said. Her voice was barely above a whisper. "Congratulations."

She felt guilty: she should have been so happy for him. Was she becoming possessive?

A shadow had fallen between them, which only slowly lifted, but by spring, things had returned to normal. Then, one day, in summer, she was packing up after a picnic in the forecourt of a desolate, disused temple in the countryside that they had cycled to. The altar was empty; the statue of the Buddha had been taken away. Grass and weeds were growing between the flagstones. He suddenly became very still. She looked at him.

"Anything the matter?" she asked.

"No," he said. "It's just that I'm going to be a Catholic."

"Would you believe it if I said I could see it coming?"

"Could you?"

Margret ignored the question, but had one of her own. "But why? What did Father Liu say?"

"I don't think I was ever an atheist." He grinned. "In spite of Meiching, my sister-in-law. I reckoned that there has got to be something more than this world around us... Oh, I can't really explain! I only know that unless I take the step now, I shall probably regret it. A lot of what Father Liu stands for makes sense," he concluded.

"And Father Liu?"

"Caution, he says. I'm to think about it and tell him when we come back in September. Also, I'm to read some of the books he's given me. And you, did you never think of becoming one with all your years with the nuns in Hong Kong?"

She shook her head. "Can't say I did. It's funny, isn't it, that it should be you."

***

That summer, they travelled back to Canton together, and he stayed with her family for a few days in their modern flat overlooking the Pearl River before returning home. He met her parents and her two brothers. They took him to a recital given by an Austrian pianist from Hong Kong. Their families couldn't have been more different, he thought. And then he and Margaret made a short visit to the Cathedral of the Sacred Heart, the 'Stone House', this time not just

*37*

to gaze at its architecture. The building was beginning to mean something more than just stone and mortar now.

"Are you going to tell your people?" she asked when they left the church.

"I've been thinking about it," he said. "I've got a half-brother who is a Protestant, and his wife is also one. I wouldn't be sure he didn't become one just to get married, actually. Anyway, you see, my people are used to the idea of having a Christian in the family. But, somehow, I feel this is more than just... just becoming a Christian."

He was by no means certain, in fact, he had no idea at all, what else the step might lead to. It was perhaps much wiser not to mention it until it was a fait accompli. And for a moment, he was oblivious of her. She gave him an anxious look, and then deliberately, and perhaps symbolically, took possession of his arm. That brought him round, and he looked at her and smiled.

At home, they found him somewhat withdrawn, and they put it down to his vacation work. But he was with them on their usual outings, and went with his mother to lay flowers on the family graves, as he had missed the Ching Ming visit to the cemetery because he was away. Then Margaret came and stayed for a few days, and they were at first very polite, but soon she had captivated them.

"Why are you called Margaret?" Meiching asked her one day. "Are you a Christian?"

"No. I just fancied the name. It means 'pearl', which is what my Chinese name means."

His reception into the Church in the baroque Chapel at the Chaplaincy took place a few days before Christmas, and it was attended by some of the friends he had made there. And, of course, Margaret.

"I baptise thee, Paul," said Father Liu as he leaned over the baptismal font.

Margaret had asked him why he took 'Paul' as his Christian baptismal name.

"I like the idea of the Road to Damascus, where the original Paul was converted by a flash of light. You know, Father Liu is the 'flash of light' for me! Also, I want to be called after Paul Hsi, or Zi, the one Father Liu told us about last year."

There was a small reception afterwards, in the lecture room across the entrance hall.

"Welcome into the fold," said Hasselbach.

"Thank you, sir."

"And when is it going to be your turn?" one of Margaret's girl friends asked her.

"I don't know," she said seriously. "I don't know if I'll ever be."

But she went to Midnight Mass at Peking Cathedral with him and the other Catholic students. Afterwards, they returned to the Chaplaincy where they celebrated Christmas with the traditional chicken rice porridge and Christmas cake provided by the Jesuits. Then he walked her back to her hall of residence, and there, standing in the snow under the light over the door, to her surprise, he kissed her for the first time.

"Happy?" he asked her.

She nodded. "Very. And you?"

And she kissed him again.

***

It was strange how things turned out. That Christmas night, with Margaret in his arms, he was prepared to give up his chance of going for a higher degree abroad. In the event, he did give up that opportunity, but for a very different reason. The turning point came a year and four months later, in the spring.

Father Liu always arranged a three-day retreat in Holy Week for both students and staff of the university. Normally the retreats were given at the Chaplaincy, but because of the lack of facilities they had to be non-residential, and the participants returned to the hustle and bustle of ordinary life each evening. This was obviously unsatisfactory. Occasionally, they were able to use the

Franciscan convent, but this year Father Liu had been able to secure accommodation for male students at the Reformed Cistercian, commonly known as Trappist, monastery of Our Lady of Consolation near the village of Yang Chia Ping in the mountains eighty-five miles west of Peking. The place was ideal for a retreat, and it would also give the undergraduates a taste of contemplative life, and give them the opportunity to attend some of the monastic Hours in addition to St Ignatius' Spiritual Exercises.

"Unfortunately," he said, "the ladies will still have to come to the Chaplaincy."

Margaret was, of course, not involved. In any case, she had gone to Shanghai for the short spring or Easter break.

They went up in a hired bus, on a cold, misty day. As the driver carefully nosed the bus into the mountains, Waihung – or Paul, now – was reminded of some lines from a poem he had once read:

Into mountains far and cold
The stone path rises steep,
And in the deep of shrouding mists
Quiet homesteads sleep.

It was that first sight of the monastery in the mist which, he decided later, was the turning point. That's where I want to be, he said to himself. Another 'flash of light' moment.

Everything else followed.

The guests were given a guided tour of the monastery on arrival, and, after settling in and a quick tea, the retreat began with an introductory talk in the late afternoon.

"We follow our own timetable," Father Liu told the ten retreatants. "However, I am posting the monastery's timetable on the notice board, as some of you may wish to sample the life here. The Guest Master told me that you are always welcome to join the community in their Office Hours. Provided, of course, they do not clash with our own schedule. However, we do join the monks at their conventual Mass each day. And, by the way, I shouldn't advise anyone to go to the Night Office: it's at three in the morning. And even Prime is at five thirty. Still, it's up to you…"

Two of them did go to the Night Office, and one of them was Paul. While his friend went back to bed afterwards and did not get up again until half past six, with the others, Paul went to the Chapel for Prime. He was somewhat bleary-eyed when Father Liu gave them their first lecture of the day. Later on, he could recall little of the Spiritual Exercises that Holy Week, but plenty of the monastic Hours he attended. And what he found particularly attractive was the Silence.

"How was the retreat?" Margaret asked when he met her at the railway station. "And what was the monastery like?"

He started to tell her what the monastery was like on the way from the station, and he was still at it when they were having dinner that night in their favourite restaurant.

"It was the best three days in my life," he concluded, but he was not referring to the retreat.

They did not see less of each other this spring and summer, but Margaret noticed that he was frequently very quiet, and even absent-minded.

"Is there anything wrong between the two of you?" one of her friends asked her one day. "You look… pensive, somehow."

"Oh, I'm all right, and there's nothing wrong. Not at all."

He and Margaret again travelled back to Canton together at the end of that third year. This journey was hazardous, as there was active warfare again between the ruling Nationalists and the Communists not many miles from the railway line, in the mountainous region of Kiangsi. Again they were able to book adjacent cabins, and after depositing his suitcase in his own he joined her in hers. After supper, she told him that since Easter she had been seriously exploring the possibility of going on to further studies in America when she graduated.

"I didn't want to tell you until there was something concrete, one way or the other," she said, not looking at him.

"And...?"

"Michigan is going to give me a place if I get a decent degree."

"That's good. I'm happy for you."

"And you? Will you be going to England, then? Durham, is it?"

He looked out of the window and did not answer for a long moment.

"I don't know," he said slowly. "Probably not. I don't quite know how to tell you this, after all that we have shared together. Sometimes I feel like rather a heel. I think I am going to be a monk at the Cistercian monastery."

Why!? Why!? Why! she screamed in her mind.

"Congratulations," she said, trying to sound normal. "I have been half expecting you to do something like it all this time."

"Really? Since when?" He was curious, but he was also unsure whether she had said it to absolve him.

"Ever since you first went to play chess with Father Liu. You know how much alike the two of you are?"

He shook his head.

"I must admit, though, that I thought you were going to become a Jesuit. This is, I must say, rather surprising. Though," she added after a short pause, "less surprising if I really thought about the enthusiastic way you told me about the monastery after the retreat."

"Well, you knew more than I did!"

"What does Father Liu say?"

"What he said two years ago when I asked him about becoming a Catholic: 'Think carefully' – which is what I have to do now."

"And your people? Have you told them yet?"

"No. I don't know how to either. It might have been easier if my father had been a Catholic, but he isn't, and that makes it impossible."

It was now dark, and they had not switched on the light in the cabin, so he did not see the tears which fell. She was glad when he put his arm round her shoulders, and she sought his hand and held it until it was time for him to go back to his cabin to go to bed.

He did see more of her this summer. He went up to Canton whenever he could. And they also went back to Peking together. He still had not told his father what plans he was thinking of making. His father did ask him once, though, if he was considering going on to further studies.

"It will depend of how I do next year," he prevaricated.

He was pleasantly surprised by his father's reaction when he eventually wrote to tell him what he was planning to do.

"My son," his father wrote back, "you must make of your own life as you think fit, although I have to admit to a certain disappointment in your decision. Perhaps becoming a Catholic monk carries more prestige than becoming a Buddhist one. However, it is your mother you must convince that what you are going to do is right."

He graduated in the summer of 1935 with a first-class degree in civil engineering. Hasselbach, he could tell, was extremely pleased. The professor was seated on stage with the other members of the university's teaching staff, and was observed to be grinning from ear to ear when the dean of the Engineering Faculty summoned Waihung to receive his diploma, presented by the President of the University. At the same time, Margaret received her diploma: she too had obtained a first-class degree, in Chemistry.

"So when are the two of you going to tie the knot?" the more curious of their friends asked.

Their close friends knew their plans. The others had not been informed.

"We've got our careers to think of first," they replied.

Margaret spent a month at home and then went to Hong Kong to join the ship which would take her to America. He saw her off at the railway station in Canton.

"Goodbye," she said, bravely, as they shook hands. "Good luck, and pray for me."

She kissed him, on the cheek.

"I will," he said, "if my prayers are worth anything."

And then, at the beginning of September, he headed once more for Peking. By now, the fighting had shifted far to the west.

*\*\**

"Pax Intrantibus," the letters above the double gate declared in welcome. He had learned enough Latin from Father Liu to understand that it said: "Peace to those who enter." He pressed the brass knob that was the doorbell. A brother came out of the Porter's Lodge and opened the gate.

"They're never locked," he was told.

He stepped across the threshold and knew somehow that he had come home. If the brother had not been watching, he would have fallen on his knees and kissed the ground. This was 17 September 1935. It was the feast of the Impression of the Stigmata on St Francis of Assisi.

"I'm the new postulant," he informed the brother.

"We know. We've been expecting you. Just knock on the door of the monastery."

And that night, his first in his new home, with the note of the 'Salve Regina', which all monks sing as a sort of 'goodnight' to Our Lady, echoing in his ears, before he fell asleep he thought of Margaret. How was she adapting to her new life in America? Could she forgive him for the hurt he must have caused her?

*\*\**

He stirred and looked up at the sun again. It seemed to have scarcely moved. Perhaps memory did flash by without account of time. He picked up his rucksack and walked over the stump of wall to the sanctuary of the ruined Chapel.

# TWO

Paul settled into his new life without much trouble, although it wasn't easy to get used to rising at two in the morning to sing the Night Office, and at first all he wanted was to go back to bed. He learned to pray, he learned to meditate, he learned to sing the Office and he learned to live in a community: he learned to follow the Rule of St Benedict. And from being a townsman, he learned to be a countryman. He herded the goats of the monastery, learned to milk them and breed them, and learned to make goat's cheese. He tended the vegetable garden, pruned the apricot trees and extracted oil from the fruit which helped to provide valuable income for the monastery: a monastery had to be self-sufficient to survive. And the monastery's tractor was his particular delight.

The months of postulancy passed, and at the end, with his four fellow postulants, he was invested with the white habit of the Cistercians. Father Liu came to attend the occasion.

"You look great in your habit, Paul," he said. "You're a real monk now."

"Not quite," said Paul with a laugh. "I've still got my noviciate to do."

"Of course." And then Father Liu looked quite hard at him. "You are settling down all right?"

"Yes," Paul replied. "It's a great life. I can't wait to make my vows."

"May I offer you a little word of advice?" said Father Liu.

"Yes, please."

"Festina lente. Make haste slowly. Don't spoil things by being over anxious. But, hold firm: I'm sure you are called."

These, as we have seen, were difficult years for China. There had never been peace since the founding of the Republic twenty-five or so years before. Things might have progressed smoothly, with developments in democratic ideas and practices, if an old imperial general, Yuan ShiKai, who had been chosen President of the new republic had not fancied himself in imperial robes instead and decided to turn the clock back by claiming the imperial throne for himself. He didn't last, but he wasn't the last to be dazzled by regal glory. Some years later, the secessionist warlord of Paul's home province of Kwangtung harboured similar royal pretensions. In the meantime, local strong men with their personal armies made casual alliances, and just as casually repudiated them. Singly and in blocs they fought each other as well as the central government under Chiang Kai-shek, who succeeded Dr Sun Yat-sen, the founder of the Republic, as head of state. One interesting character among the warlords was Feng Yu-hsiang, the 'Christian General', who reputedly christened his troops with a hosepipe. He had been converted to Methodism, and ruled his fief and his army according to his ideas of Christian socialism. He was greatly admired by a leading Protestant missionary, and he, in fact, wasn't the first leader in China to claim to fight under the banner of Christ. The leader of the Taiping Rebellion in the nineteenth century had claimed to be the brother of Jesus Christ.

This was the time when the mighty bickered and tried to outplay each other, and the urban middle class aped the lifestyle of the wealthy in Europe and America, and all they seemed to be concerned with were mail-order purchases from Sears and Roebuck, the fashions in Paris, and which were the best nightclubs to go to in Shanghai. This was the time when the common people were being ground under. Their crops were ruined, abandoned or stolen by the warring troops, and they were robbed of their meagre possessions, and even their modest trinkets and their clothes; their women were violated, and their young men forcibly enrolled in a warlord's army, where they starved and died while their leaders gadded about resplendent in tailored uniforms gleaming with the medals with which they had decorated themselves, and riding on their war horses which were better fed than their troops. Some of them even had imported automobiles as their chariots.

Japan then played a part in the middle of the warlord problem. The Japanese invaded Manchuria, in the north-east, which with its well-watered, fertile agricultural land was regarded as the breadbasket of the country. They set up the puppet state of Manchukuo, and installed the young deposed Manchu emperor Puyi as nominal ruler. Puyi lived a privileged and flamboyant life until the Communists put him in virtual captivity. He spent the rest of his life as a gardener, tending flowers in the old Imperial Palace which had once been his home.

The loss of Manchuria pretty well made Peking a frontier town.

This was the picture of China in the mid-1930s , as Paul was starting his new life. He lived the simple, austere routine of the Cistercians, under the guidance of the ever patient Master of Novices. The memory of Margaret had faded into the background. By the end of the noviciate, he was ready, prepared and eager to enter fully into the life that he had chosen. With two of his fellow novices – two had dropped out – in front of the entire Cistercian community and friends, he made his vows of 'stability, obedience and conversion of manners before God and His Saints'. He would have liked his parents to be there, as the parents of his fellow novices were there to witness their sons take the momentous step. Unfortunately, it was not to be, and in any case they probably wouldn't understand what it was all about, but his father had written to offer his congratulations, and his mother had written to tell him that she would be praying, and offering incense on the family altar for him to be a good monk. Father Liu was there, and his old professor Father Hasselbach, who had travelled up especially for the day. Father Hasselbach had borrowed the university delivery van for the purpose.

Paul met them at the simple reception afterwards.

"Now you really are a monk!" said Father Hasselbach, as he shook Paul's hand.

"Thank you," said Paul.

"It's interesting how things can turn out, isn't it?" Father Hasselbach went on. "When I first met you, I thought I was training a first-class engineer! And now, look at you... as far from building bridges and aqueducts as one can get!"

"Surely you don't think it's wasted," laughed Paul. "As a matter of fact, I have been using the skills you taught me and am building a road, over the hill there."

He turned and pointed towards a narrow ribbon of white on a distant hillside.

"That will be taking our tractor to our new field on the other side. We are planning another apricot orchard."

"Where do you send the oil?" asked Father Liu.

"Some abroad. A lot of it to Shanghai. I don't know much about it, really. Father Matthew, over there, he's in charge of things like that. You know," he continued after a pause, "we've been praying for the Church in Spain... but Father Abbot doesn't say very much."

"Oh," said Father Hasselbach, "it's a bad business there."

"The Communists have been killing priests and nuns and emptying monasteries and convents," said Father Liu. "Mind you, from what we are told, Franco's lot aren't exactly angels, either."

"It's a topsy-turvy business. Franco's accepting help from Hitler and Mussolini, and that has turned world opinion against him. With friends like those, as they say, who needs enemies!"

"People are thinking that the Germans and the Italians are up to something," said Father Liu. "And Japan..."

The Axis Powers that aimed to dominate the world.

"Let's hope not," said Paul. "We've enough on our hands as things are."

We may try to keep the world from us, he reflected, but the world has a way of getting to us. Being a monk is not a way of escaping the world.

Just as Father Hasselbach was starting the car for the long ride back to Peking, Father Liu turned to Paul.

"Oh, I nearly forgot. I'm supposed to be passing on Margaret's best wishes."

"Thanks," said Paul. "So you keep in touch?"

"Oh, yes. We correspond regularly."

He had a feeling that Father Liu hadn't nearly forgotten. He just hadn't been sure if he ought to pass on the best wishes. Especially not to a new monk? But why not? Margaret was a part of his life, a happy part of his past.

\*\*\*

Paul's future in the monastery was partly marked out for him. He was going to be trained for the priesthood, like a number of the monks at Our Lady of Consolation. So after his vows, he embarked on the long road to ordination through the years of Philosophy, which taught him to think and which he enjoyed, followed by Theology, which taught him to 'know' God. He discovered that the deeper he delved into the mystery that was God, the more there was to discover. He was to find that it all left him with as many questions as answers.

His mornings were devoted to his studies, and his afternoons to manual labour, from which his intellectual occupation did not excuse him. He had to admit to himself that he was perhaps happiest with the tractor, a rather ancient piece of machinery, donated by some American benefactor who had little idea of how difficult it was, in the backwaters of the barren hills behind Peking, to obtain spares. The machine now required fairly constant, loving attention, although when it did work, it almost performed miracles. And then, whenever the monastery needed anything done with concrete and stones and rubble, he was the man they called on.

In addition to their own cloistered life, the monks of Consolation, at the behest of the bishop, also ministered to the surrounding areas. There were a number of villages, some large and some small, scattered around the monastery, with a Catholic population. There were even whole villages whose population was Catholic, and one of them had suffered martyrdom less than a hundred years before during one of the endemic periods of persecution under the Manchu emperors. The monastery's priests would take turns to go out on a Sunday to say Mass in the villages, some of which had a small church or Chapel; and where there wasn't one, Mass would be said in the home of a villager with a room, or a barn, large enough to accommodate a dozen or so worshippers. If the distance to travel was long, the priest would stay at the home of a villager the night before. Monks would also be sent out to prepare people for baptism, for First Communion, for Confirmation or for marriage, and not infrequently to perform weddings. Therefore, in fact, the community of Consolation also did the duties of parish priests.

Initially, Paul was assigned a small catechetics group which met in one of the spare rooms in the monastery. And then, one day, Father Michael, the Prior, summoned Paul.

"You are being assigned to Father Stephen for the Sunday Masses rota around the villages. Father Stephen will start saying Mass at the church at Lungchuan again this coming Sunday. We're re-opening the little church there. Do you know where it is?"

"Not really, Father… Well, no."

"It's further up in the hills, and it's a longish walk." The Prior looked sidelong at Paul. "You are fit, aren't you?"

"Yes, Father." Paul smiled. "I've just been passed by Dr Kung." As 'A1', he thought to himself, but he'd not say that.

"I'm sure you are all right. If Mrs Chang could make it down here to Mass with her bound feet, and at least twice your age, you should be all right."

Paul wasn't sure if Father Michael was being a little facetious, but Maria Chang was a real character. Like many women of her generation, she had had her feet bound for a time when she was a tiny girl, and though they were no longer bound, it had permanently damaged her feet. By all accounts she was a beauty, and had many suitors, especially as she came from a well-to-do family. It took her a while to make up her mind, and she eventually picked a young army officer, Chang, who happened to be a Catholic. So to marry him, she became a Catholic herself. And she didn't just become a Catholic, she became a very devout and active Catholic. She used to walk down to the Abbey, on her damaged feet, to attend Mass at least three times a week; the monks always wondered how she managed it.

"It's like walking down the mountain on stilts, but more painful," someone said. "And then going back up, all on the same day!"

"And three times a week!"

Then just before Paul entered Consolation she offered to become a catechist, and she spent even more time at the monastery. By then, sadly, her husband had died, of malaria, while on campaign against the Communists in the mosquito-infested jungles of Yunnan in south-west China.

When Mass started being said at Lungchuan again, Maria Chang stopped coming down to the Abbey on Sundays, although she was still a frequent visitor on weekdays. She also had her duties as catechist, and she held classes when it was convenient for her pupils to attend. With the opening of the small turn-of-the-century church in her village, Mrs Chang had assumed the duty of sacristan, laid out the vestments, and loaded the ciborium and filled the wine and water vessels. She was so reliable that the priests decided to leave the vestments and chalice in her care. As she came to know Paul better, she started to take an interest in his progress, and she told him often that if the Abbot knew what was good for the monastery, he should ordain him right away! Maria Chang wasn't afraid of speaking her mind. Paul found her a little overpowering.

Another friend Paul made was the monastery's doctor, Matthew Kung. The doctor came from a wealthy, old Catholic family, going back perhaps three centuries or more to the end of the Ming dynasty, when the Jesuits first came to China. He had received his medical training in France, and could have stayed on in the West, but he elected to return home to serve his own people. Some wondered if his name 'Kung' had any significance, and there were rumours that he was a direct descendant of Confucius, in Chinese 'Master Kung'.

"Look," he would say, when anyone brought the subject up, "everyone in China can claim to be descended from some duke or other in the Shang, or the Chou dynasty, two and a half thousand years ago. 'What's in a name?'" he'd conclude, quoting Shakespeare.

Shakespeare was 'big' in China. Everyone knew about him, as they knew about Beethoven. 'Sar-si-pei-ah', they called him.

Dr Kung drove up twice a year, and whenever he was needed, to check on the health of the community. He'd stay several days, as there were nearly a hundred monks in the monastery. While he was at Yang Chia Ping, the villagers around would bring their sick to the monastery, where he would treat them for free. Some of his patients insisted on paying him: quite often, he would be returning to Peking with a couple of well-fed chickens in the back of his bus-sized Citroën in lieu of payment. Not infrequently, he also carried some sick person to the hospital in Peking.

Dr Kung used to say to Paul every time he gave him his physical, "In spite of your slight frame, you are as strong as an ox. How do you manage it?"

On 8 July 1937, not long after Paul had made his vows, the monks as usual gathered in Chapter for their daily conference. The Abbot, instead of dealing with matters arising from the concerns of the monastery, began Chapter by delivering startling news.

"I have been told," the Abbot, who had the reputation of being unflappable, informed the community, in his usual quiet manner, "that as from yesterday China and Japan are, as it were, officially at war. Japan opened hostilities on Marco Polo bridge near Tientsin."

China had been on a virtual war footing with Japan since 1931, when the latter invaded Manchuria, arousing strong anti-Japanese feelings in the country. These feelings were exacerbated by Japan's bombardment of Shanghai in the following year. The incident resulted in the Japan's isolation of Japan on the international stage, and for a while she held back, biding time. Some people blamed Chiang Kai-shek's preoccupation with the Communists for his not taking a strong line with Japanese aggression. In addition to all this, there had already been long-term resentment against Japan since Peking's port, Tientsin, had been assigned to Japanese control at the beginning of the century after the trouble of the Boxer Rebellion, when China had defied the world and failed dismally. So no one in the community was surprised at this development, but the news was no less startling for all that.

Then Paul had a letter from his mother. This was nothing special, as she had been writing to him almost every week. She could not write herself, and so all her letters came in the hand of one of Paul's half-sisters. This letter, however, screamed panic.

"Are you all right? Are you safe? Will you be coming home? Your brothers are talking about joining up!"

Paul wrote back: "I'm all right. I'm safe. No, I shan't be coming home. Things are pretty quiet around here." He wasn't at all sure that the letter would calm his mother's nerves.

In the next few weeks, Japan had taken control of the area around Tientsin and Peking, and was making a drive for Nanking, the then capital of China on the Yangtze River. Shanghai was again assaulted, with European troops, mainly British, looking on and cheering the Chinese from the neutral zone of the International Settlement, and refugees flooded into the foreign enclave to escape the fighting. Chiang Kai-shek, however, had reserved some of his best troops for the defence of Shanghai, and the Japanese troops did not have an easy time. Eventually they broke through, and then made for Nanking. But the Chinese government had moved to the safety of the vastness of Szechuan, in the upper reaches of the Yangtze, in south-western China. Chungking was now the wartime capital of China.

Then came news of the fall of Nanking. And the horrific massacre that followed.

"They beheaded people for fun," Father Abbot told Chapter.

At the beginning, life went on as normal in Yang Chia Ping. They saw no Japanese and the villagers continued to till their fields. The monks carried on with work on their farms, and Paul and his fellows students applied their minds to their philosophical studies. They held debates and symposia on Aquinas and Aristotle and modern philosophers like Nietzsche. Paul became interested in the rather discredited Plato. He accompanied Father Stephen to Lungchuan and elsewhere on Sunday mornings, and as time went on, he was given the task of supervising Maria Chang, whose theology was sometimes shaky.

One day, while Paul was on his way to one of the monastery's outlying farms, he fell in with a young couple he recognised. They had been coming to Sunday Mass at the monastery for as long as Paul remembered.

"Morning, Father," said the man.

It wasn't much use telling the man that he was some way from being a 'Father'. For most people, anyone in a monk's habit, or in a cassock, was a priest.

"Morning, Simon," he replied. "Morning, Magdalene."

"Yes, Father," said Simon, answering Paul's unspoken question. "Actually, I told Father Seraphin on Sunday. We finally made up our mind to leave."

"But where are you going?"

"Well, almost anywhere. We reckon that we can't live here anymore," said Simon, half waving his arm at the landscape. "I've a cousin who lives down Yangchong way. Yangchong's still free, and we'll stay there for a while. We're heading for Lichuan tonight... that's about fifteen miles away, then Wuling the day after, then..."

Paul understood. So far, the ruling hand of the Japanese on the area had been light, but most people felt uneasy living under alien occupation.

Paul looked at the suitcase in the man's hand, and the lighter bundle in the woman's. Simon also had a heavy-looking backpack slung over his shoulder.

"What about the rest of your stuff? And how are you going to live?"

"We live in a rented house, anyway," said Simon. "We've left our furniture with Magdalene's parents. They say they are too old to move away."

"Simon's a carpenter," said Magdalene. "And I can always wash clothes."

"We'll find work. And we've got some savings we are taking with us. You know, our neighbours already left. They are heading for that Communist place in... Shensi, I think. We are heading for Szechuan. The Japanese will never get there."

"But we'll be back!" he called as they moved away. "When we've won the war!"

Paul wished the couple luck, for, he told himself, they needed luck. He also said a quiet prayer for them.

Paul discovered that more people were moving away. Some of them were young couples, like Simon and Magdalene. But there were also families, couples with children. Some travelled lightly, others wheeled their belongings in a wheelbarrow. Every Sunday, the number of people who came to Mass went down, slowly.

Then one day, the Abbot sent for Paul.

"Your old mentor, Father Liu," Father Abbot told him, "will be coming up from Peking in a couple of days with five people. They will be staying for a while with us before going on. What I want you to do, since you know Father Liu well, is to take care of them while they are with us. They can stay in the guest house. Make sure that the rooms are made ready. Father Liu may, if he wishes, stay with the community, so get one of the empty cells prepared. On the other hand, he may wish to eat his meals with his group. In any case, make sure that meals are sent over."

Paul waited to be dismissed.

"I'll leave things in your capable hands," the Abbot said.

Father Liu and his group did not arrive the next day, nor the day after. However, the group appeared the day after that, a little before Sext. They had come up on the familiar charcoal-burning bus with the rickety chimney exhaust, and looked weary after the long ride.

Brother Porter brought them to Paul, who showed them to their quarters.

"Would you like to use the washroom before lunch?" he asked. "Lunch will be sent over after Sext which will be starting about now."

The group wanted to attend Sext.

"I hope you won't find it boring," Paul said. "It will take only about twenty minutes."

He led them into the Chapel just as the Abbot intoned, "*Deus, in adjutorium meum intende*" – *O God, come unto my aid.*

Paul was given permission to have lunch with Father Liu and his group, and to spend the afternoon with Father Liu.

"You know," Father Liu began, "that because of the situation the university was not reopened after the summer holidays, and it seems that it won't reopen again as long as the Japanese are in occupation. In fact, a lot of the professors simply disappeared. A number of the students came to me because I was involved in the Chaplaincy, as you know." He broke off from what he was saying. "And you know, Paul, that Father Hasselbach has gone back to Shanghai."

They were worried about their future, and even if the university reopened, few of them wanted to carry on under Japanese occupation.

"I for one," said a second year medical student, "don't want to start every day singing the Japanese national anthem!"

"That's what they have to do now," said another, who should have been starting his third year in Chemistry, "in primary and secondary schools."

"And they have to learn Japanese!"

They discussed the problem long and hard, and made their momentous decision. They would head inland, perhaps to Wuhan on the Yangtze. Surely it was far enough inland to be secure from the invaders. They consulted Father Liu.

Father Liu had plans of his own. So far, the Japanese had been leaving religious organisations and places of worship alone. But, like other Chinese people, he was not by any means comfortable living under occupation. Eventually he discussed his problem with Father Tauziat. The Superior was sympathetic, and in fact suggested a role Father Liu could play. Why did he not go to Wuhan, or perhaps Chungking, to establish a Chaplaincy for refugee students not just from Peking, but from Shanghai, Nanking, and other Chinese universities? To this Father Liu readily agreed. And started to make plans.

"What sort of money will you be planning to take with you?" asked Father Tauziat.

"Chinese," said Father Liu.

"I suggest you take American dollars as well. I'll authorise the withdrawal."

This was when the five university friends visited Father Liu, who persuaded them to aim for Chungking rather than Wuhan. They decided to stay for a few days at Consolation, to gather strength, as it were, before launching themselves into the unknown. Their one worry was how to get across Japanese into unoccupied China, but in this they were helped by the sheer size of China, and Japan's preoccupation with the drive on Nanking. They had hoped that once Nanking, the seat of the Chinese government before the war, fell into their hands, Chinese resistance would collapse. However, Japan never had enough troops to patrol properly even the areas under their control, and travellers seldom had any difficulty passing from occupied into free territory, or the other way round.

Four days after their arrival at Consolation, the guests said goodbye to the monastery.

On the morning of the departure, the travellers rose before daylight. Father Liu said Mass in the guest house, which was also attended by Paul, who had, of course, been up since two. They had oatmeal porridge for breakfast, and then they were off.

They aimed to do thirty miles that first day.

The late September morning broke rain-washed pale, bright and cold, but it was a good day for walking. While similar groups often hired porters, this company carried their own luggage, a suitcase or a haversack each, for they needed to be careful with their limited resources. It had been a wrench to leave their books behind, but their hope was that their parents would post them on when they arrived at Chungking. The surprising thing about those war years was that the post was never interrupted and passed freely through the country. Neither warring government wanted to disrupt it.

So they set off, though not with a song on their lips, or in their hearts. The mood was sombre. They were not unique, nor were they the first, for they were only five among thousands, maybe even millions, of secondary, college and university students who traversed wartime, and war-torn, China with their teachers and their schools, braving hardship, danger and the possibility of death, seeking intellectual and political freedom. Many sold personal possessions at a fraction of their real worth to finance their journey, and not unusually, families uprooted themselves for the education of their children. The Japanese despised the Chinese for what they considered to be a lack of martial spirit. They were much mistaken, and that was why they failed to subdue China, which stood alone against them for four years.

And so it was that Paul, that autumn morning, said goodbye to Father Liu. Would they meet again? Paul wasn't at all sure.

Father Liu promised to write.

***

"I've heard from Father Liu," Paul told Father Abbot in early spring. "They've arrived in Chungking."

"That's good news," said the Abbot.

"The bishop's appointed him Catholic chaplain to the University of Chungking as well as to the University of Chengdu."

"And the boys?"

"They've settled in, apparently. Three of their parents have managed to send them money, but for how long, before the Japanese get wise to it, no one can say."

"How about the other two? How do they get by?"

Paul smiled at the ingenuity of it.

"They sell blood to the hospital, which pays very well, it seems. They do it every other week, and they live on the money, and in the meantime the body replenishes the lost amount."

Father Abbot was concerned. "How long can they keep it up, though?"

"I don't suppose anybody knows."

Father Abbot changed the subject. "Does anyone know how many Peking boys have followed?"

Paul spread his hands. "I couldn't say, Father."

"I've kept a count," said the Abbot, "from my sources. It seems there have been another twenty or so from Peking, alone."

"Oh," Paul just remembered to add, "Father Liu is learning to ride a motorbike, so he can get between the two towns more easily."

Father Abbot raised his eyebrows. "I hope he knows what he is doing!"

That evening, at Vespers, the community said a thanksgiving for the safe arrival of Father Liu and his group. The Chapel rang with the simple melody of the *Te Deum.*

\*\*\*

Paul looked from the ruins of the Porter's Lodge to the ruins of the monastery Chapel. There wasn't much of it left. As he made his way there, he came across the rusted remains of his beloved tractor.

Somehow it had got moved from its shed to the herb garden, which of course was now overgrown with weeds. Then his mind went back to those war years...

*** 

One day, the occupation forces discovered Yang Chia Ping.

They came on a windy late October afternoon, during the hour of post- prandial siesta for the Cistercian community, which was meant to compensate for their early rising in the small hours of the morning. Most of the monks, however, used the time for reading, or study, or for catching up with work. Paul was preparing for the discussion on Kant he was to take part in. He was, in fact, struggling with Kant, whom he found difficult to comprehend.

On this day the wind came whistling down the bare valley, across the fields and pastures and the orchards of the monastery, through the main street of the village, whipping up mini dust storms and what was left of the dead leaves from long-bare trees. The troop carrier rolled into the village square, with its complement of twenty soldiers under the command of an officer, and halted in front of the temple. It was watched by adults with trepidation, from behind windows. A few children, as yet unacquainted with fear or caution, and full of curiosity, watched from open doorways. Some of them were called back indoors by anxious parents.

The officer alighted from his place by the driver, and the troops jumped down from the rear of the carrier. They were confident, at ease and unsuspicious. Some of them carried their long rifles with them, others came down without. They wandered about the square, looked through doorways if they were open, calling to each other in their staccato language which no one in Yang Chia Ping understood. Except for one man, who was obviously Chinese, in civilian clothes, who was willy or nilly their interpreter. On this occasion, he had nothing to do.

One of the soldiers decided that he needed to relieve himself. He went behind a bush next to the temple. His friends laughed at the noise he made.

Then they all got back onto the carrier, which was driven up the road to the monastery gates. The porter saw them coming and came out to watch. The officer stood up in his place, and peered through the wrought ironwork at the buildings. Then he noticed the metal cross on top of the gate.

The interpreter was summoned from the back of the carrier. He listened to the officer, then turned to the porter.

"The officer wants to know what kind of place this is."

The porter pointed to the metal plaque on the gatepost.

"This is a Catholic monastery," he informed the interpreter, keeping an eye on the officer. "Cistercian."

The interpreter passed the information on to the officer. The porter wasn't sure whether 'Cistercian' meant anything to him.

"How many are you inside?"

"Seventy-six."

"Are they Chinese?" The interpreter translated the next question.

"Mostly. There are a few Europeans. And one Canadian." Brother Porter was meticulous.

Without another word, the officer sat down; the interpreter got back onto the carrier. The driver made a three-point turn and drove back down to the village. The porter watched it take the turning to the next village.

"Hm! They are full of themselves," the porter muttered to himself.

This diminutive force made its circuit of the surrounding villages, confident that it would not be interfered with. The Chinese had no guts. They did not have the courage or the will to fight back. If they did, how was it that the Japanese imperial forces were able to conquer Manchuria without resistance, could control so much of the country in so short a time? Apart from the battle of Shanghai. They did show some guts then, but they did not last long, did they?

Still, it was better to be safe. So the occupying troops made a weekly circuit of the district. They did not do it on the same day each week, in case the locals were going to be up to something. Just to be safe.

They did it for a joke. Every time they came to Yang Chia Ping, one of them would be detailed to relieve himself behind the bush by the temple. That was good for a laugh. And then they would pass on to the next village.

***

The symposium went well. Paul held his own, in Latin, as Kant, and St Thomas Aquinas, represented by one of his fellow philosophers, did not have an easy time. He was nearing the end of the accelerated philosophy course, and he was looking forward to starting his theological studies, again accelerated, so that he would complete the normal seven-year course in four. He was going to have Father Augustine again, which was an excellent thing. Though he did go on a bit at times!

In addition to helping Father Stephen on Sundays, Paul had been given the task of visiting families in Yang Chia Ping. Every two weeks or so, we would pay a visit, usually rather brief but occasionally extended, to a family in the village, whether the family was Catholic or not. In those harsh years of the war, he learned about their life, their work, their joys and sorrows, and their problems. Quite often, he found it difficult to stand back, to look at their hard life dispassionately. Where he could, he would help, or at least the monastery would.

In time, the Japanese took to entering people's houses. Most of them were still polite, but certain others demanded to see the family jewels and other objects a family deemed precious. These might be of a pair of silver earrings, or a jade statuette of the goddess Kuanyin, passed down through the family for generations. Others openly demanded money.

At one visit Paul made to the village the day after the Japanese had been, he found the family in distress. The man, who was usually reticent, was even more so than normal, but he also looked angry. His wife, with their three children about her, was in tears. At first, they refused to tell him what the problem was. But at last...

"They took all our money."

"They? How many of them were there?"

"Actually, just one."

Just one, or a thousand, the result would have been the same.

"Did he threaten you?"

"No, he didn't. He just said: 'Give me all your money.'"

And the soldier took all their money, including their small change.

"Did many of the other soldiers know?"

"I don't know. Perhaps."

Another thought struck Paul. "Have you any food?" he asked.

"We've still got some rice, and some cabbage. And a bit of salt fish. We were going to do some shopping today, but..."

Later in the day, Paul brought some food and some money for the family, but he knew that these would not solve the problem.

When the Japanese came for their next visit, Paul, with the permission of the Abbot, was ready for them. He had also managed to find a brother who spoke some Japanese. He was Brother Hilary. Paul had posted a villager at a spot which overlooked the approach road into the village. He was to run up to the monastery when the Japanese troop carrier was sighted.

The warning came during the hour of the siesta, but Paul was ready. His heart was beating faster than he liked, but he forced himself to calm down.

Paul and Brother Hilary reached the village square just as the Japanese drove into it, and they waited at the entrance to the temple, because that was where the vehicle usually stopped.

When the officer saw the monks, he and his interpreter came up to them.

"We don't normally see you in the village," he said. "Is there anything I can do for you?"

By then the troops had all come down off the carrier, and were standing about with their long rifles, almost as tall as most of them, in their hands.

"I have a complaint to make," Paul said through his interpreter.

The officer raised his eyebrows in question.

"The last time you were here," said Paul, "one of your men entered a house and robbed the family of all the cash they had."

The soldiers suddenly stopped their chatter. The officer folded his arms, then spread his right hand.

"So where is the man who was robbed?" he asked.

"He's too scared to come out; so I am speaking for him."

Paul did not really expect any worthwhile response from the officer, and he was surprised when he fired a series of questions at his men. They shifted uneasily, looked at one another, and then began to edge away from one man. Eventually, this man was standing alone.

"So you are the one? LOOK AT ME!"

The man looked up, and nodded.

"I want to hear you say it!"

"That was me," the man stammered.

"You are a disgrace to the Japanese Imperial Army! Which house did you rob?"

The man pointed.

The officer strode into the house and brought the family, the man, his wife and their children, to the door. The soldier turned to face them.

"Is this the man?" the officer asked.

"Yes."

The officer took his revolver from its holster and shot the thief in the back of the head. Blood and brain sprayed the dust of the square. The man fell forward amid the screams of the woman and the children, twitched, and was still.

The other men fetched a tarpaulin from the troop carrier, wrapped the body in it and put it in the carrier. Then they all got back on board.

The officer turned to the shaken monks, bowed, and got back on the vehicle, which then drove off. They had left the blood and the brain in the dust for the villagers to clean up.

Paul couldn't sleep that night. He kept seeing the dead man and the blood and the brain in the dust. He sang the Night Office in a dream. He prayed for the repose of the dead man's soul. How responsible was he for the man's death?

Justice? Was it for justice that he did what he did?

If he managed to keep awake in the morning, if he managed to keep his mind on the intricacies of Aristotle and St Augustine, it was because his conscience, at the back of his mind, refused to let him doze off. However, time was a healer, and so was the calming wisdom of the Abbot, who understood what he did better than himself.

Peace of a sort had returned to Yang Chia Ping when Paul began his theological studies, again under Father Augustine. The Japanese made their usual round once a week, but what was unusual now was that the soldiers were much subdued; they no long barked questions at each other. The offensive ritual relief of the bladder stopped. After they had got off the troop carrier, the soldiers would stand in small groups, rifles in their hands, and speak in soft voices, as though they had become more wary of the villagers.

"It's almost worse than before," one of the villagers who came to Mass at the Abbey confessed one Sunday. "They're going to kill us, you know."

"You can see they don't trust us anymore," said another, when Paul paid him his own weekly visit. "Not that I expect them to trust us: I never trusted them anyhow, what with all those rumours about them we hear. Tea, Father?"

He had tried so many times to explain that he was not yet a 'Father'. They seemed never to have heard!

"'Brother'. Don't let it escalate into something worse, though," said Paul, as he sipped his scalding cup of tea. "Don't let it get worse."

In reply, the man tousled the hair of his small daughter, who was leaning against his knee.

"You haven't said 'good day' to Father Paul yet," the man told his daughter.

"Good day, Father," the little girl said quietly.

"Your son," said Paul after a short pause. "How old is he?"

"Daniel, he is eleven. He should be going to school. But in times like these, I don't want him walk the two miles to the high school in Hanlei. But he is going to Mr Gao at the end of the village."

Mr Gao was an old scholarly type who gave lessons in the classics for a pittance. He had a good reputation, Paul heard. He was a real conservative and traditional type and thought learning Science was a waste of time. Nor did he approve of Christian missionaries. "What do we have to learn from them? What can they teach us?" he used to say.

Paul was determined that, one day, he was going to meet Mr Gao.

Then one Sunday, in the depth of winter, after Mass at Lungchuan, Maria Chang came up as he was helping Father Stephen to put away the vestments and the chalice and the Missal.

"Brother Paul," she said, "we are in trouble."

"Yes?"

"We, the village, I mean, are going to run out of food, some time, if something isn't done, somehow."

"How?"

Life was hard here in the mountains north-west of Peking, in the province of Hopei, at the best of times. The lack of flat agricultural land, the shortage, generally, of water, the scarcity of pasture, made it a difficult place out of which to make a living. The monks were able to cultivate the land profitably because they had the means to organise their resources, because they diversified and had more useful contacts than the local farmers. And every autumn, the harvest was crucial. It had to be carefully hoarded, carefully doled out, if it was to last the winter.

And then groups of strangers came among them. They came with rifles on their shoulders and revolvers in their belts, and some were even armed with old sabres. They declared themselves to be the Resistance.

"Do you love your country?" they demanded. "We are fighting the Japanese. We are, in fact, fighting for you, for us all. It is your duty to give us your support. We'll need arms, and food, and perhaps even recruits."

"So what do you want now?" asked a rather suspicious villager.

"At the moment, we need food. We'll welcome anything you can spare."

The grain was held in a communal granary in the precinct of the village temple. The village elder was fetched.

"We need to hold a meeting to decide how much we can spare for you. Come back this afternoon."

The strangers duly returned in the afternoon and were given a generous measure of barley, which the villagers had harvested earlier in the year. For the winter. A couple of the younger members of the village also decided that they should join the freedom fighters. Unfortunately for Lungchuan, this wasn't the only group which demanded their support. Nor so politely.

"But we have already given a lot of our food to the group who came last week!" the village elder protested.

"Are you sure they were a genuine patriotic group?" the leader of the new group asked, hefting his rifle.

"We can't keep giving our food away!" wailed the village elder.

"Look! I don't care if you can or not, we need food. Some of us haven't eaten for a couple of days. So where do you keep your rice? Or barley? Or wheat?"

This second group, though smaller in number, actually went away with more than the first.

"It's not just us, this village. It's happening all round the countryside. The other day, Hsichiachuang, five miles down the road, was actually robbed," said Maria.

"Yeah," said a man who was putting the chairs away. "They not only took food. They went through every house in the village looking for money and valuables."

"They're as bad as the Japs."

"Worse! They're supposed to be our own people!"

"What can we do? If we fight them, we'll be accused of helping the enemy. If we don't, we'll starve."

To the surprise of most people, the only group that paid for their requisitions were the Communists. Their reputation rose. But they also introduced a scorched earth policy in areas they did not control. One day, one of the Communist groups came to the monastery. They demanded to see the Abbot.

"We know you have firearms," the leader said.

That was no secret. They had been donated to the monastery to fight off bandits. Somehow the villagers felt safer because of it. What they didn't know was that none of the monks could use them, and some of them were beginning to rust.

And before the Abbot could say anything...

"We want them."

They were handed over. This in fact proved to be a piece of luck.

The situation rapidly worsened for the villages. What they lost most, of course, was what they needed most: food. The demands grew more frequent; the amounts demanded also rose, often to unbearable levels. In the barren time of winter, they saw their hard-saved stores dwindling. Nor was it just food they lost: implements were requisitioned, clothes were taken. And there was nothing that the ordinary people could do. Eventually, many communities became dependent on the monastery for subsistence.

Although the country round Yang Chia Ping was quiet, and the occupying power had an easy time, there were guerrilla activities in more remote areas. Here, a small Japanese outpost had been attacked. There, a Japanese column on the move had been ambushed. Elsewhere, a lone Japanese soldier who had strayed had been lynched. The Japanese began to be jittery, and the local population learned to keep their heads down. The patrols increased in frequency, and in strength.

One grey, cold January day, a Japanese patrol in two troop carriers stopped briefly as usual at Yang Chia Ping before moving on to the next village. The road led into a narrow, dry valley, overlooked by steep banks on either side. The patrol was ambushed. The first shots slightly wounded several of the troops, but neither driver was hurt, and they were able to get to the end of the valley where it broadened out. The carriers were stopped and the soldiers fanned out along the valley. By the time they moved back to where they were first attacked, the ambushers had melted away into the bare hills further up the valley. News of the attack quickly spread over the area.

"They will come back," everybody predicted.

And they came back, the very next day. They came back in punitive force, in several troop carriers, with mounted machine guns next to the driver and others facing aft. The company was no longer commanded by a lowly lieutenant, or even a captain, but by a major. Accompanied by the usual interpreter.

This time they turned everyone out of the houses. Stoically, the villagers lined up in front of them. The men were then separated from their families and led to the centre of the square, and children started crying, desperately hushed by their mothers.

"The Japanese Imperial forces," the major began through a loudhailer. His words were translated by the interpreter. However, as the interpreter did not have a loudhailer, the words were not as impressive as they were intended to be. "The Japanese Imperial forces have so far been extremely lenient and considerate to you, but this kindness, this consideration, was obviously misplaced. It is most fortunate for you that, in spite of the attack yesterday, none of my soldiers has died."

He paused, and signalled to his sergeant, who in turn barked an order to his men. Three of the villagers were pulled out and made to stand on their own.

"Look at them," the officer ordered his men. "Remember their faces."

He then turned to the villagers.

"Next time my men are attacked, within five miles of this village, these three men die. And," he continued, "from now on, every time we come, I want you to stand outside your houses. If there is a man missing, I shall want to know where he's gone."

The men of the village were sent back to their families, and a count of each household was made before the villagers were allowed to go back into their houses.

But the Japanese had not finished with Yang Chia Ping yet.

The convoy left the village, but instead of taking the road to the next village, it again drove up to the monastery. The officer demanded entrance to the monastery grounds. The porter opened the gates and the convoy streamed in. The Abbot, accompanied by Brother Hilary, met the officer at the entrance to the monastic buildings.

"I have to search the monastery and the surrounding countryside," said the officer without preamble, "for terrorists. As the search will take some time, I shall need to set up camp here for the night. Perhaps we shall cause least disturbance to you if we set up our tents over... there." He indicated the apricot orchard, where the trees were bare of leaves in the winter, and where there was also a well.

The Abbot signified his consent.

"My men will search the grounds," the officer went on, "and one of you will show me round the buildings."

"I'll show you round the buildings," said the Abbot. "Where would you like to start?"

The officer waved a hand to indicate that he had no preference.

The Abbot led the officer, accompanied by two of his men, through the hallway into the refectory. This was empty, and obviously there was no hiding place, and after a cursory glance around the party went through into the kitchen where the Brother Kitchener was preparing the midday meal with the assistance of the brothers who had been detailed to help. Brother Kitchener was made to open all the cupboards and the storerooms as well as the dumb waiter which carried food from the kitchen up to the infirmary. The officer made certain that no one was hiding there.

Then the party went upstairs to the infirmary. This too was empty. There happened to be no sick monks. The linen cupboard was opened for inspection. Next the dormitory was carefully examined; every cell was inspected, all cupboards and wardrobes opened. The party was then taken through the scriptorium and study where a number of the monks were working; then the toilets, the bathrooms. After a tour round the Chapel, the group was led into the Abbot's house.

"Here is the Abbot's parlour."

"Thank you." The officer bowed, and was shown out of the building.

The night passed without incident, although the monks could hear the troops singing in their tents.

At Mass the following morning, the monks were surprised to find the officer standing to attention at the end of the Chapel. He made the sign of the Cross where it was customary to do so, but did not approach the altar at Communion. The Abbot was intrigued. Afterwards, the Abbot got the story out of him.

"Seminarians and theological students in my country are not exempt from military service. There are a number of us, and life is not easy."

"Don't some of the things you people do bother you?" the Abbot asked.

He officer looked at him, and shrugged. "I have my duty to do."

But he said it in Japanese.

Later in the morning, the company left as they had come, having found nothing suspicious in the monastery's grounds or in the countryside around.

Thereafter the visits of the Japanese were more frequent, and always in some strength, and for a good while, the situation was quiet. The villages were, at least, not harassed by the invaders even if their situation got progressively worse, and they came to rely more and more on the monks for relief. There were rumours, however, of disturbances farther afield, and of stern reprisals. Life in the monastery went on in as normal a fashion as possible.

"War has broken out. England and France are at war with Germany," the Abbot told the community one autumn day. "Belgium succumbed to the Germans. Japan and Germany are now allies."

The Abbot was told by a Japanese officer that he was now an enemy alien and was under house arrest: he must not leave the monastery without permission even if he needed to see a doctor. The same rule applied to all the monks who were French. Not long afterwards, when Petain surrendered to the Germans, he was told that he was now an honoured ally, and restrictions on him and the few French monks of the monastery had been lifted.

Meanwhile, Paul was drawing to the end of his theological studies. He was first rapidly ordained through the four minor orders and then admitted to the order of sub-deacon. He now assisted at the celebration of High Mass, not as a server at the bottom of the altar steps, but in the company of the celebrant and the deacon at the altar. One of his jobs was to chant the lesson. However, he had to wait until he was ordained deacon before he could chant the Gospel, or give a homily.

And so, clad in the purple vestments for the season, this was what he did at High Mass on the snowy First Sunday of Advent. That Sunday, one of his fellow monks accompanied Father Stephen to Lungchuan instead of him. Maria Chang would have preferred to come down to the Abbey that day, but she had to be at home for Father Stephen.

"Sorry to miss your first Mass as deacon," she told Paul the next time they met, "but I couldn't leave Father Stephen."

So impressive was his chanting that the Abbot decided to train him as assistant precentor. He was glad that he still had the duty of looking after the monastic tractor.

Problems similar to those suffered by outside communities at large, though to a different degree, beset the monastery also. The apricot extracts which had provided to a large extent the monastery's income now found few buyers, and went into storage rather than generating funds. The grain crops the monks cultivated became the main source of food for people of the countryside around as well as for the monastery. The milk from the monastery's herds went to supplement the diets of the children.

"The situation cannot," Brother Cellarer told the Abbot, "last forever. There will come a time when there won't be enough to feed both us and the people outside."

Father Abbot did not hesitate.

"Do what you can, Brother. If we have to have short commons, we'll have short commons. We cannot allow our friends in the villages to starve."

Communist groups had been most active in fighting a guerrilla war against the Japanese. In fact, most of the trouble that the Japanese experienced had usually been caused by them. But when Hitler and Stalin signed their famous, or infamous, pact, the situation changed. The Communists made only a token show of resistance to the invaders. It they had not done so, they would have lost all credibility with the people they had been so keen to profess they were protecting from tyranny. Other groups, however, were active. Their activities consisted chiefly of disrupting communications and destroying military supplies. The guerrillas always managed to melt away at the approach of the Japanese and were never caught. The occupying authorities showed their frustration with more and more stringent regulations. Identity papers were issued and movements were restricted, and making a living became difficult. Villagers had to provide proof of identity to come to Mass. Even monks travelling to say Mass in their habits were not exempt. Several times, Father Stephen and Paul were turned back on their way to Lungchuan 'because of an emergency'.

In the middle of all this, Paul passed his final theology examination, and he was advanced to the diaconate. He felt a real thrill when his turn came to chant the Gospel of the Sunday at High Mass: he was almost 'there'!

And then the day of his ordination to the priesthood approached. At one of his visits to the monastery, Dr Kung asked him:

"Is there anything you would especially like, Paul, to celebrate your ordination?"

It was customary for diocesan priests to receive a chalice as an ordination present from their family or friends. Not infrequently, some of them ran into serious debt to pay for the present: it was almost like paying for the wedding of a son of the family. But Dr Kung, surely, knew that a monk had no personal property. A gift to him would be a gift to the monastery.

Paul politely declined. A couple of days before the ordination, however, the Abbot sent for him.

"Dr Kung," he said, "has sent you a present. Why don't you open the box to see what it is?"

It was a chalice, delicately simple in design, gold-plated on silver, with 'To Father Paul on his ordination' etched round the base.

"It's beautiful," Paul whispered. "But he shouldn't have. I asked him not to."

"You can thank him in person tomorrow," said the Abbot. "He's coming up with Mrs Kung for the ordinations if he can and the Japanese are not closing the roads. They won't be going back till the day after the ordinations."

It happened that the Japanese had imposed no travel restrictions on the big day, and there was a sizeable congregation from the Catholic population around. There was even a Protestant missionary among them, who had come with his family. He was in fact a frequent visitor to the monastery. However, apart from Dr and Mrs Kung, and the Protestant missionary and his family, there were no visitors from Peking, or Tientsin, as there had been in previous years.

The monastery laid on what in those hard times could well be described as a sumptuous feast after the long ordination ceremony. The refectory was somewhat overcrowded with the community and the large number of guests present, but it was an enjoyable and cheerful occasion. When the guests had dispersed, the normal routine of monastic life was resumed.

And for Paul, another threshold of his life had been passed. He was now an ordained member of the clergy, with the privilege of celebrating Mass, and the power of loosing and binding. But above all, he was a monk, vowed to stability, obedience and conversion of manners before God and His Saints. In a very uncertain world.

Then one day, Brother Porter hurried up the driveway to the main building to report that something really serious had happened. Three miles or so out of Yang Chia Ping, a Japanese convoy had been ambushed, and a number of the troops killed by sniper fire, and the guerrillas had as usual disappeared before the Japanese could redeploy and go on the offensive.

"The villagers are frightened," he told Father Abbot. "Very frightened."

"Do you know if anyone from Yang Chia Ping was involved?"

"Not as far as I know. I don't think they're likely to have been involved."

"Ah." The Abbot shook his head. "There are other ways of being involved than toting a rifle."

His own seventeen-year-old niece, he knew, although the family had not said so openly in their letters, was being involved in the maquis as a messenger. He prayed daily for her, but was quite proud of her, really.

The Japanese arrived the next day in strength at Yang Chia Ping. The vehicles stopped in the centre of the village square, and the soldiers spilled out to form a ring of steel around them. The sun glinted on the bayonets of their rifles held at the ready, and the interpreter relayed the order of the soft-spoken officer through a loudhailer. The villagers emerged from their houses and were lined up in front of them. At a sign from the officer, the men of the village were pulled out and stood to one side of the square. Some of the women started to wail.

"Silence!" they were ordered through the interpreter. The wailing ceased.

One of the soldiers pointed up the road leading to the monastery. There, where the road met the square, stood the Abbot and a number of his monks, watching.

The officer walked up to the Abbot and saluted.

"Do not interfere," he said quietly in English. "This is none of your business." He then strode back to the centre of the square.

The children were sent back to their families, along with a couple of the old people. The rest were ordered to kneel in a line, facing away from the centre of the square. Two of them whimpered in fear; some others defiantly straightened themselves to kneel upright. The officer walked across behind them, and then walked back.

Three shots; they sounded hollow in the open air. Three dead men fell forward on their faces. The officer returned his revolved to its holster. This time, he did not bother to stop the wailing of the women.

The soldiers got back onto their vehicles and the convoy headed out on its way to the next village. The monks knelt by the dead men and said a prayer over them before helping their families to carry them into their homes for the funeral rites.

Then things went quiet for a while. There were no attacks on the enemies for several weeks. Life slowly returned to what could be called normal, except for those who had lost their men. The monks tried to help them as much as they were able. One of the murdered men was Mr Gao, the village schoolmaster, and one of the monks, Father Raphael, went into the village every morning to fill his place until a new teacher was appointed. Eventually they found an old scholar who had got tired of living under occupation in Peking. Since his requirements were modest, the village was able to pay his wages, in kind. A lot of village schoolmasters were paid this way.

Paul now joined the group of monks who were priests in taking turns to say Mass in the surrounding villages. He found that there was a tangible atmosphere of fear and unease everywhere since the killings at Yang Chia Ping. People dreaded another outburst of patriotism. And they dreaded even more the prospect of Japanese retribution. They were caught, they were trapped: not everyone wanted to be a hero. He also became responsible for various people who grew interested in becoming Catholics, which meant that he was also working more closely with Maria Chang. When, almost inevitably, she got to know him better, she became more and more of a mother to him, and this worried him. He took his worries to Father Abbot.

"The point is," said Father Abbot, "you are aware of the situation. Situations like this happen, so what you need to do now is to keep an eye on it, to make sure it doesn't cross a boundary." He looked up at Paul. "You understand what I mean?"

"Yes, Father."

When Hitler decided to revoke the Soviet pact and invaded Russia, the Chinese Communists again became active. One day, there was news of another guerrilla attack on the Japanese, who suffered a number of casualties. The retribution was again savage. This time, it fell on a neighbouring village, and one of the village elders was beheaded. Then there was news of an even more savage incident. Although Father Abbot had come to know about the massacre at

Nanking and he had in turn informed the community, not many people of the villages were aware of the atrocities committed there. So this new incident generated absolute horror.

There was in a small town called Lushan, about ten miles or so from Yang Chia Ping, a small hospital run by Dr Chandler, a British medical missionary. He was supported by his wife, who was also a doctor, as well as several local nurses and kitchen staff. Although to the Japanese he was an enemy alien, he was left alone, and continued to run his hospital. Dr Kung knew him, and had frequently supplied him with the drugs that he needed. Then one day a company of troops burst into the hospital, accusing Dr Chandler of sheltering guerrilla fighters. In spite of the doctor's protests, they went through the hospital, and when they could not find any, they accused Chandler of hiding them in secret places.

That night, Brother Porter opened the gate to a young villager in a blood-soaked jacket, and with traces of blood on his face.

"They started screaming," the young man told the Abbot, "at the doctor, and at everybody. I came out of the kitchen to look."

And the horror of what he had seen made him pause, before he was able to go on.

"And then, the officer drew his sword... and cut off the doctor's head. It... it dropped on a chair before falling on the floor... and the doctor was still standing... There was blood on the ceiling."

"And then?" the Abbot prompted.

"Two of them went for the doctor's wife with bayonets. She doubled up and fell... there."

The speaker pointed with his finger, as though he was describing what he was witnessing.

"Then they all went mad, and bayoneted everyone, including the patients. A couple tried to run, but they were shot down in the garden."

"I was lucky. My friend fell on top of me, and I played dead until I heard them drive away."

Instead of cowering with fear now, the people decided that they had had enough. At the approach of a Japanese patrol, able-bodied men of a village would melt away, so that only the elderly and the very young were to be found. Women were regarded as being below suspicion, for, being country people, they were thought to be unpolitical, and therefore harmless. The Japanese had not, it seemed, noticed that there were now, almost suddenly, a large of number of village women on bicycles in the countryside. Some of them even appeared to have become quite friendly.

One wintry day, when a half-frozen patrol tumbled off their open-topped carriers, a couple of women brought them steaming pots of tea. One of them even managed a few words of Japanese. One smiled shyly at the officer, who had the good manners to smile back.

I wonder what they are at, he thought to himself. But in the next few minutes, in a conversation held in broken Japanese and still less fluent Chinese, the woman learned that the soldiers were not due back for four days. Small matter. But the newly formed local guerrilla group was made aware of the information within half an hour.

Some of the monks became involved as messengers. Paul quite often carried messages from village to village, as he made his weekly rounds. He had no illusion about the risks he was taking, certainly for himself if he was caught, even though his monastic habit gave him some protection. He knew that some of the brothers were also involved, but as they never talked about it, he had no real idea who they were or what in fact they did. And Father Abbot? Surely he knew?

The Japanese tried to impose a news blackout in the territory they occupied, and no radios were permitted on pain of death. A number of people were executed for possession, but news did manage to be disseminated through the few radio sets that were successfully hidden. And through the post which, surprisingly, the occupying power never managed to control. But there was good news, and there was bad news. News of the unsuccessful Japanese assaults on the southern key stronghold of Changsha boosted everybody's spirits. The lack of progress in South China was another encouraging situation; the Japanese had occupied Canton and the coastal strips of the south-eastern and southern provinces of the country, but made practically no advance inland. For a couple of years it was stalemate chiefly because the Japanese had their hands full elsewhere in Asia and the Pacific, where they were, it seemed, unstoppable. They were not shy about telling people about Pearl Harbor, for example. They could not stop telling everybody who would listen that they were going to bring down imperialist America. They took Hong Kong in eighteen days. And they had defeated British Empire forces in the jungles of Malaya and outwitted them over Singapore. Now they were on their way to India, and Australia wasn't safe from them. China could wait.

Paul often wondered about his family. He had letters from his mother, who told him that everyone was safe and that they did not have a problem living under occupation. Some of his brothers – half-brothers, strictly speaking – had joined the national population migration to south-western China. She did not know where they actually were, but they had been heading for Chungking or Kweilin, or even Kunming, on the way to Burma and India.

One June day in 1944, when China had been at war for seven years, and Europe for four, Father Abbot told Chapter:

"The Allied forces have successfully made a landing in Normandy."

But this news was counterbalanced by a Japanese push into unoccupied China. This in turn sparked off another huge population movement in southern China, always staying just ahead of the Japanese advance. There was a two-pronged military movement. One prong drove through Changsha, which had held them up before, into Kwangsi, to be joined by the other prong advancing up the West River and the south coast. The combined forces then pushed north into the mountainous province of Kweichow, aiming for the last bastion of Chinese resistance, Szechuan. The wartime capital of China, Chungking, was probably not so secure after all.

And Paul. He had lost all contact with his family during this Japanese onslaught. All he could do was pray.

Again the invaders were held up. They were overstretched, and the mountains of Kweichow were defeating them. At the same time, their European allies, Italy and Germany, were in retreat. Italy changed sides and Germany was alone. Japan had always, practically, been on her own, in spite of the Axis connection. When Germany surrendered to the Allies in April 1945, she was truly alone.

Eight long years of suffering, hunger and privation for the people of China eventually came to an end with the surrender of Japan to the Allies, after Hiroshima and Nagasaki were devastated by atomic bombs in August 1945. There were endless, unresolved, discussions and debates regarding the justification of the use of the atom bomb, the echoes of which some people claimed were felt across the Yellow Sea in North China.

The monks celebrated what they hoped was the coming of peace with a solemn Te Deum, intoned by Paul, who was now the fully fledged new precentor. He still had charge of the monastic tractor, though.

As the situation settled, and crops were grown again, a delegation of village elders from the surrounding countryside presented the monastery with a plaque to thank the monks for the service they had rendered to their people. They were thanked for feeding the hungry, comforting the sick and the dying, filling in where there were gaps for necessary tasks. Solemnly, the plaque was placed on the gatepost at the entrance to the monastery. The village elders were then treated to lunch at the Abbot's table in the refectory.

***

But now the refectory was no more, nor the kitchen beyond. Paul crossed what used to be the cloister garden, now waist-high with weeds, and arrived at the Chapel.

# THREE

The area of the Sanctuary in front of the ruined altar was relatively free of rubble. He hunted round for suitable pieces of masonry and built a hip-high one-foot-square column over which he placed a piece of weathered, charred wood that he had found under a window to the left. This was as much as he could do. From his rucksack he brought out two small tea cups, the Chinese sort, not European ones with handles. He also placed a saucer on what was now the table. He found the tin in which he kept homemade communion wafers and put one on the saucer. Last, he put a small stone bottle on the table. This contained the wine he had managed to save for just this day. There wasn't too much of it left, but there was enough.

He then went, with one of the tea cups, to the old Kitchen. Surprisingly, the tub which used to be fed by a drainpipe before the building was destroyed was still in its place and had not been taken away. There was some water in the tub and he filled the cup and brought it back to the table.

Everything was now ready.

He took a big step back, this thin, gaunt man, with his unkempt hair prematurely streaked with grey and a week's growth on his chin. He was dressed in an old serge jacket he had been given and loose trousers, with over all a faded, padded knee-length coat, and on his feet the old leather shoes he had been given by a dying comrade. He stood up straight, closed his eyes to collect his thoughts, and, still with his eyes closed, he made a deep bow, and then straightened himself again. He paused a moment before raising his hand to his forehead to make the sign of the Cross.

"*In nomine Patris, et Filii, et Spiritus Sancti...*" he said softly. "*Introibo ad altare Dei... I will go in unto the altar of God, unto God who giveth joy to my youth... For Thou, O God, art my strength...*"

He knew that today was Sunday, 13 November, but he had not been able to work out which Sunday after Pentecost it was. In any case, it didn't matter, as he could not recall the Mass for whichever Sunday it was anyway. He knew it was also the Feast of the young Polish Jesuit Saint Stanislaus, who trekked over the Alps to Rome, in spite of opposition from his father, to join the Order. He had then thought long of which Proper to use for the Mass. He first thought he might say the Requiem, and then decided it would be more appropriate to say a Mass of the Martyrs. Yes, μαρτυρεω: 'I bear witness', which was what the community had done. He had been able to recall most of a Mass of Martyrs, which he had carefully written down. He also decided to say Corinthians 13 as the Lesson and the Beatitudes for the Gospel. They seemed apt enough, but, in any case, he knew he was unable to recall any other passages from the New Testament with anything like real accuracy.

"*Salus autem iustorum a Domino...*" He began the Introit from the right side of the altar. "*But the salvation of the just is from the Lord...*"

\*\*\*

The martyrdom had begun in July two years previously, with the prelude a year before. The euphoria which pervaded the country with the conclusion of the Second World War and victory over the Japanese soon evaporated. Any hope that might have existed of the two sides co-existing and co-operating vanished, and the Nationalists and Communists were at war again, this time to the death. The Communists had used the period of truce well and had perfected a policy with which they were able to win the hearts and minds of the impoverished peasantry. The Nationalists, on the other hand, were confident that with superior numbers and, more important still, the superior armaments with which they were supplied by the Americans, they would be able to annihilate their enemy once and for all. Battle was joined in Manchuria, which had been returned to China by a defeated Japan.

Within months, the Monastery of Our Lady of Consolation found itself in an unstable no-man's-land as the front line swung one way and then the other and back again. For a long while, the monks were never quite certain who was going to be in control of the area from one day to the next. Something, however, was certain. Whenever the Red Army, that is, the People's Liberation Army – the PLA – was in control, the countryside was put to the torch to prevent its enemies from getting local supplies, and the people were left to starve. The other side, however, was not much better, and whatever the peasants had managed to hide from one was inevitably taken by the other. But as the Communists made it a policy, generally, to pay for what they took, they were slightly less unwelcome. Neither side, however, interfered with the monastery, and the community carried on as well as it could and adhered to centuries-old Cistercian traditions of feeding and clothing the starving and destitute, and helping those in distress. Memorial tablets recommending the community for their assistance and generosity were presented to the monastery by grateful villagers, as has been seen. But what eventually happened was not unexpected.

One day, Dom Alexis, the Abbot, decided to give voice to the community's concern in Chapter after the normal business of the day had been dealt with. The community had had an inkling of the extraordinariness of the occasion, and there was a definite change of atmosphere when the Abbot, instead of standing up to dismiss the gathering with the accustomed prayer, settled back in his chair, and paused as he surveyed the seventy-six faces looking back at him, before continuing.

"We are all aware, I am sure, without exception, of the situation that China is in today, and as a consequence the uncertain future we in the monastery will be confronted with. The country is facing the prospect of being taken over by the Communist Party, whatever the Nationalist Government may say. This is my personal view, and it appears to me the only realistic view. And, of course, there will be drastic changes.

"The Chinese Communist Party has repeatedly stated that religious freedom is guaranteed, but history has also shown us that wherever the Communist Party comes to power, religion suffers. Church property is appropriated, and religious houses closed and communities dissolved; priests and religious are imprisoned and perhaps killed. In Yugoslavia, two of our great monasteries, Mariastern and Our Lady of Liberation, were closed and the monks imprisoned when Marshall Tito took over the country. These are the realities we have to face."

He then continued as calmly as he could in spite of the turmoil and pain in his own mind.

"If this community is forced into dissolution, by closure, dispersal or other means, the six of our brothers, including myself, who are European, will perhaps have an easier time than the rest who are Chinese, as we are likely to be expelled rather than suffer other forms of persecution. If I am to be taken from the monastery, then Father Augustine will, of course, take over the authority, to be assisted by Father Michael, the Prior. I dare not attempt to forecast what may befall you, my Chinese brothers. But one thing is certain: you will have a very difficult time."

In which case, he continued, those who were able should make for the nearest city which was still in the hands of the Nationalists, which, at the moment, was Peking. There they should make their decision as to whether they wanted to move further away or stay. He knew that Dom Paulinus Li, the Prior of the other Cistercian house in China, had spoken of plans to move to a safe haven. Szechuan, perhaps, which had served as China's wartime capital: the Nationalists might be able to hold out there, as they had done once before. Or even Hong Kong or Macau. Maybe, they thought, the two houses might consider joining forces.

"Personally, though Dom Paulinus may disagree with me, I believe we can only find a safe haven outside China, and my choice would be Hong Kong. Perhaps those of us who are able should try to make for this tiny British colony. The journey will be far from easy. It will, I suspect, be a long and painful pilgrimage."

\*\*\*

Then, one day in 1946, the PLA, in one of their periods of control of the area, drove up the road to the monastery in a military lorry. Like Paul when he first came as a postulant, the officer, with grenades on his belt and his hand on his revolver in an open holster, had not realised that the gate was never locked. He demanded to see the 'person in charge'. The porter led him and his troops to the monastery building where he was shown into the guest room. Almost immediately, the Abbot came through to greet the officer.

"What can I do for you?" he asked, but he encountered naked hostility in his visitor.

"You are the man in charge of this… this place?"

"I am the Abbot of the monastery."

"You and one of your people are required to come with us to answer questions at Headquarters."

Dom Alexis knew better than to argue, or even ask questions. The problem was which of his monks he should ask to accompany him.

"Will you please wait a few minutes while I find the other person?" he said.

His mind went to Father Odilo, a big Shantung man from south of Peking. He was tough and cheerful and not easily rattled. He came from Weihaiwei on the coast, which for the last fifty years had been administered by Britain. A number of Weihaiwei-ese had been recruited to serve in the police force in Hong Kong. Odilo was one of them, but after one tour of duty he returned home to join the monastery.

Dom Alexis found him and explained the situation.

"He said he was leaving it entirely to me," Odilo later told the community. He was too modest to say that he was honoured to accept.

Dom Alexis and Father Odilo were ushered into the lorry at the gate, and that was the last time Dom Alexis was seen by the community. Headquarters was a school house in which the normal furniture was made to serve different functions, and the two monks were put in different rooms in an upper floor as they arrived. After a short wait, Odilo was taken to a room downstairs to face an officer. He was badgered aggressively with accusations for long hours until he lost count of the days.

"It wasn't an interrogation," Odilo reported, "and that's something we must learn to face."

When he realised that neither he nor the Abbot was likely to be sent back to the monastery after the first day's 'interrogation', he did the best he could to turn his room into a temporary home by putting the desks together to form a bed. After the first night, he preferred to sleep on the floor. He never saw Dom Alexis, but he heard him being taken out of his room for what must have been the interrogation, and then, many hours later, returned, and then it was his own turn.

At the end of six weeks, Odilo, tired from the interrogations and weak from near starvation, was told that he was free to go. The PLA forgot to provide transport for the long journey back, and he walked through the night to return to Yang Chia Ping. Dom Alexis was forbidden to return to the monastery, and in order to avoid aggravating the situation and causing unnecessary trouble for his brothers, he made his way to Peking (Odilo conjectured), from where he would probably be evacuated with other foreign nationals. Perhaps, thought Paul, he was able to get to Hong Kong to prepare for the arrival of his brothers.

The community had not, in fact, expected to see Father Odilo again, and had been certain that the end might come any day and very soon. The monks had all surrendered their personal papers for safe keeping on their admission to the monastery, and now Father Augustine decided the time had come to return them.

"Keep your personal papers, such as your identity cards, always on your person, even when you are sleeping," warned Father Augustine. "I suggest you sew a pocket to the inside of your habit or your shirt to keep the papers in."

To the surprise of the monks, they were not molested again. Apart from the realisation that their Abbot had been taken away from them, life carried on as normal. The liturgical year came to an end and Advent began on the first of December. Bitter winds blew as usual, and snow fell during that first week of Advent. The older members of the community made use of the Warming Room next to the Kitchen and were issued with extra quilts. Christmas was celebrated with the accustomed solemnity and joy, and, in time, Easter and Pentecost, too. Father Augustine, a quiet and gentle man, in contrast to the much more autocratic character of the Abbot, and already much revered as Master of Novices, proved to be as caring a head of the monastery as Father Alexis had been, and some of the brothers began to hope that the monastery might survive after all.

June came to a normally glorious end, when the valley had long assumed its summer garb. The cereals were growing contentedly, it seemed, in the fields up-valley of the monastery. The calves and kids were making good progress, and some of the villagers had come to view the young animals and had picked the ones they wanted to buy from the monks. July opened with two great feasts, the Feast of the Precious Blood and the Feast of the Visitation.

The blow fell on the first of these two days. The blow seemed even more cruel, as the community had been lulled into a false sense of security.

The monastery bell tolled, as it did every summer day, at nine o'clock to summon the community from the various tasks which had been occupying them since half past six – the young monks from their studies, the workers from the fields and barns, and others from pastures further up the hills – to a period of private prayer before Terce and High Mass. As the rest made their way to the cloister, and Brother Andrew, who was on porter's duty that day, was on the point of leaving his lodge for the main building, the entrance bell jangled.

"The sun no longer shone," he told Paul a long time afterwards, while the two of them were breaking rocks for the building of a dam two hundred miles into the mountains to the west. "And I suddenly became very cold."

***

"It's his shoes I am wearing," Paul reminded himself, moving towards the centre of the altar. "*Kyrie eleison... Lord, have mercy...*"

***

"Open up," an officer of the People's Liberation Army, with what seemed to be a platoon of troops behind him, demanded when Brother Andrew came to the gate. "I have business with the two you call Father Seraphin and Father Chrysostom."

"They would be in the house," Brother Andrew informed him as he swung the gate open. He was roughly pushed aside as the officer led his small troop up the path. The monks who were converging on the building from the fields and the barns gave way to them and waited for them to pass.

"I have business with the two whom you call Father Seraphin and Father Chrysostom." The officer reiterated his demand to the monk nearest to him.

By the time the soldiers arrived at the open front door, Father Prior and the two monks they sought had already come into the hallway. Paul, who was following his students, some of the young monks who were studying for the priesthood, down the cloister on their way to the Chapel, had heard the noise from the outside and decided to investigate. He was on the point of entering the hallway when he heard the PLA officer questioning the two monks, his voice pitched unnaturally high, jarring in the place of silence. This was a man full of authority, but with little sense of humanity, Paul thought.

"You two call yourselves Father Seraphin and Father Chrysostom? Grave charges have been laid against the monastery. You are to come and answer them in the People's Court."

Father Seraphin was, at the age of thirty-eight, a well thought-of member of the monastery. Father Chrysostom was younger, only thirty years of age; he was the Cellarer, in charge of farms and buildings. Because of their frequent dealings with the public, they were the best known of the community to people outside, and that might well be the reason they were singled out by the Communists.

By now, Paul was not the only witness to the incident. Other monks had appeared in doorways, obscuring the view of those behind.

The officer made a sign to his followers. Two of his troops came forward and tied the wrists of the two prisoners behind their backs. Paul saw the less robust Father Seraphin wince as the thin cord was pulled tight. And then they were led away, watched now by most of the community, down the path and out through the gate, but not towards the village of Yang Chia Ping. The monks were being taken further into the mountains, and in their white habits they showed clear against the darker colours of the valley until they disappeared with their escort round a bend in the road.

The stunned community attempted to gather its wits as the significance of the morning's event sank in.

"What's going to happen?" Their eyes sought those of Father Prior.

"Let's go into the Chapel," Father Augustine said quietly.

Before the monks started to move, Brother Andrew, against all customary rules of a Trappist monastery, spoke out.

"Father, may I follow Fathers Seraphin and Chrysostom to find out what is happening to them? I shall be back as soon as I can."

Father Augustine agreed after some slight hesitation.

"Thank you, Brother Andrew. But get out of your habit first, and put on a hat to cover your tonsure. And, please, be very careful."

The Mass for the Feast of the Precious Blood of Our Lord was celebrated by Father Michael. Joy was in the words the monks spoke and sang, but there was little of it in their hearts that day. Father Michael abandoned his planned homily and tried to lift the spirits of the community with words of hope. But they sounded empty even to his own ears.

"Let us pray for both our brothers, and for the community,' he concluded.

Brother Andrew missed dinner, but returned at one o'clock when the bell summoned the monks from their sleepless siesta. He was breathless, having run most of the distance on his way back, dust-covered, and hungry. He was made to eat, wash and change before facing a special session held in the Chapter Room to hear his report.

"The Fathers were taken to Hsing Chuang," he reported.

This small village where the monastery had some pasture land was about half an hour's uphill walk from the monastery. Although he had started five minutes or so behind the party with their prisoners, Brother Andrew was able to catch them up without much difficulty, but he was careful to stay well back and not to attract attention. The stage for a trial had very obviously been prepared, for there were banners strung round the centre of the village, and placards nailed to doors and trees, proclaiming death to traitors, foreign spies, cruel exploiters of the peasants and the proletariat, dishonest traders, hoarders of the treasures of the People, and various others. It was clear that someone had exercised his imagination considerably. In the middle of the village square were three tables put together, covered with red cloth, and seated behind the tables were three grim-faced officers in PLA uniforms, one of them a woman, and standing behind them was practically everyone from the village, the old people sitting on chairs or squatting on stools. Brother Andrew also noticed that mixed with the villagers were men in PLA uniform and the distinctive cloth caps.

"Even old Mr Ho was brought there in a camp bed," said Brother Andrew. He had forgotten his Cistercian brevity.

The two Fathers were pushed forward when they arrived and made to kneel on the ground before the court. Behind each was a soldier with his rifle permanently raised as though ready to bring it down on the prisoner's back for any unsatisfactory answer.

"You call yourself Father Seraphin?"

"Yes."

The soldier's rifle wavered.

"Speak up! The People can't hear you!"

"Yes!"

Father Chrysostom identified himself in the same way.

The charge against the monks was one of oppression of the people through high-handed and dishonest dealings. Several villagers came forward to give evidence. They had overcharged one for a calf they had sold.

"You overcharged Comrade Yin, there, for a calf he bought from you in April last year! Do you admit that?"

And before the monks had been given time to respond, one of the PLA men raised his arm as though conducting a choir.

'That's the truth!" the villagers all shouted. "That's the truth! That's the truth!"

Silence fell as the woman judge raised her hand.

And then other charges. They had underpaid someone for chicks they had bought. They had used short measures when selling the villagers grain. As each charge was brought, the villagers all shouted "That's the truth!" until the woman judge raised her hand and silence fell again.

"Then they pushed James Tsao forward," Brother Andrew continued. "The man appeared to me to come reluctantly, and he kept looking at the presiding judge. I believe he was under pressure."

He reiterated the same charges which everyone else had been making, but because he was also a known Catholic, his witness was considered to have more weight.

"Father Seraphin and Father Chrysostom were given no chance to answer any of the witnesses. In fact, they were not allowed to say anything. They just knelt there, with their arms pinioned to their sides, their eyes on the ground. One of the soldiers hit Father Chrysostom with his rifle butt for looking up."

"They are guilty, are they not?" the chief judge asked the assembled crowd. "Do you agree?"

The reply was deafeningly clear. "Yes! We agree!"

Again the woman judge raised her hand for silence.

The monastery's cows and goats were then confiscated as compensation as well as punishment for oppressing the People. The People, however, did not benefit from the fines. The livestock was passed on to the Red Army.

"Then one of the villagers saw me," said Brother Andrew, "and looked away. I think he was pretending not to recognise me. I thought it was time to leave."

Silence, not the normal Cistercian silence, fell, broken again a moment later by Brother Andrew.

"I can go up again tomorrow and see what is happening to the Fathers."

"No," said the Prior. "That would be too dangerous, both for you and for the Fathers."

The next day, the two monks were moved to another village called Lichia Wantze, this time south of the monastery, where they were again put on trial. The charge this time was that the monastery was built with the indemnity which the foreign governments had exacted from the Chinese government to compensate for the damage done in the Boxer Uprising in 1900.

This time the monks were allowed to respond.

"May I point out to Comrade Judge that the monastery was built in 1883," Father Seraphin offered reasonably, "and therefore it could not have been built with money from the indemnity. Besides, we weren't even born when the indemnity was paid."

Rational explanations did not work. There was the usual guidance from the bench on the last, the sixth, day of the trial. "These monks are guilty. Do you agree or don't you?"

"We agree!"

"The monastery is hereby fined fifty blankets!" The bench of judges handed down the sentence.

Father Seraphin, who had dealt with reasonable people most of his life, was still trying to be rational. "If we must pay, we must pay. But please be reasonable," he said.

The community waited. Towards the end of the afternoon, the two priests staggered into the enclosure. Both were covered in bruises, and Father Chrysostom had to have his back bandaged by the Infirmarian. This had been the overture, and that night the words of the Compline sounded particularly apt. There was nothing the community could do. The monks settled down stoically to await their fate.

*"In manus tuas, Domine, commendo spiritum meum... Into thy hands, O Lord, I commend my spirit."*

\*\*\*

In the next two years this had become Paul's constant prayer.

\*\*\*

That was the last time, too, that the community sang the *Salve Regina* at the conclusion of the last office of the day.

Paul dreamed that night. He was a student again, and was walking with Margaret on a beautifully sunny day along the edge of a cliff, and they had a long, long view of the calm blue sea, and seagulls circled and swooped down to the narrow beach below. In the dream he was aware that he had never seen such a cliff before, and... what was Margaret doing in the dream? Then all of a sudden, the sky darkened with rolling, lowering storm clouds, and drenching rain fell, as thunder and lightning broke from the blackness overhead... He woke up with a start.

There was shouting and calling, both men's and women's voices. There was the heavy thud of footsteps outside his cell and downstairs in the cloisters. There was the sound of breaking glass and the crash of heavy objects. He was still in the dark, and just sufficiently awake now to put on his habit and shoes, when someone burst into the cell and threw him bodily into the passage outside, where he found his fellow monks in the same situation. They drew together while the invading mob ransacked the dormitory cells, emptied the mattresses of straw and took the cloth as well as the blankets. The people from thirty villages had come to collect the fine imposed at Lichia Wantze.

"You're finished!" one of the mob informed the group of brothers Paul was with. "Everybody knows that!" And the villagers had decided to participate in that finish.

By two o'clock the mob had gone and silence descended again on the monastery. The monks returned to their cells to inspect the damage. They were littered with the straw from the mattresses. The rooms were picked clean, including of any clothing. The laundry, too, had been raided. There would be a lot of villagers walking about in monks' habits, Paul remembered thinking at the time. It meant, however, that all the clothes the community had were what the monks were wearing. Cloth, Paul remembered, was a precious commodity in this deprived area. Surprisingly, the looters had left the rest of the monastery alone, including the Chapel. In any case, the monks hoped that the looters were satisfied with what they had taken, but they had to wait till daylight to assess the damage.

It was obviously hopeless to get back to sleep, and at three o'clock the community gathered in the Chapel for the Night Office. This was sung, as was the custom, by candlelight, scarcely sufficient to read by but the community knew it by heart, and as the cadence of the chant rose and fell, peace and the quiet were returning. It was followed, as usual, by Masses said, in several 'relays', by the eighteen monks who were priests, and the silence was broken only by the low murmur of the celebrants and the responses of the acolytes. It was

Paul's turn this morning to say one of the Masses, and as he was reading the last Gospel, the monks were distracted by low voices and the padding of more footsteps in the cloister. The looters had again invaded the monks' quarters, although in smaller numbers, to carry off whatever they had inadvertently left behind. This time they entered the infirmary, ejected the sick from their beds and carried off the mattresses. The invaders still, however, left the Chapel alone. Paul suddenly felt a sense of total unreality together with an overwhelming desire to escape.

The sacred Hosts were consumed. The Tabernacle was left empty every Holy Week from Maundy Thursday to Holy Saturday. But this time it was empty for a very different reason, and no one knew when, and if, it would house the Blessed Sacrament again. The community sat and waited in the Chapel.

Father Augustine ordered bread and drink be brought into the Chapel.

"We should eat now," he said. " We don't know what is going to happen, and whether we shall be allowed to eat later in the day. We need to keep our strength up."

The PLA returned at dawn with the mob. This time, under direction from the officers, the latter removed everything it had missed in the night: the millet and the corn and the lentils and the precious salt and the cheese and apricots and other foodstuffs from the storerooms and granaries, as well as agricultural tools from the workshops and sheds. These were stacked on lorries to be taken to the Red Army. Somehow, they left the tractor alone. The mob then indulged in the almost total destruction of the library, which contained the works of the Church Fathers and Philosophers as well as volumes on modern agriculture. This time the Sacristy was not spared. Chalices were taken away and vestments were cut up. While the crowds were enjoying themselves, an officer, the same one who had arrested Father Seraphin and Father Chrysostom a week ago, strode into the Chapel ahead of some of his troops. Father Augustine rose to meet him.

"You are all under arrest," he said, so that everyone heard and so that there was no mistaking what he said.

"Where are you taking us?" asked Father Augustine.

"You are not going anywhere. You are going to be tried by the People." But the Chapel was clearly too large, and perhaps too comfortable, a place for the monks, and anyway, it needed to be searched and its contents confiscated for the benefit of the People. At first the officer was at some loss as to where to put his prisoners, but he soon decided on a fairly big room just down the passageway. A glance into it had convinced him that it was only an empty room without any furniture. And so the community were incarcerated in their own Chapter Room.

It took five days for the trial to be staged. In the meanwhile, the community were at least together, and although there was a constant guard outside the door, there was little interference, and they were able to say their office – Father Augustine had wisely decided not to have the office sung – without interruption. Requests for blankets – for nights were chilly in the mountains, in spite of the fact that it was summer – at least for the older members of the community were refused, and it must have been hard for Brother Bruno, who was eighty-two, and Father William, who was seventy-five. Illness began to afflict the other older monks also. Father Alphonsus was developing a form of dysentery.

The monks were fed on one roll of steamed bread a day.

*** 

His mind was so centred on the Mass now that he was again no longer aware of the ruin around him. He recited the Gradual after he finished the Lesson.

"*Clamaverunt iusti, et Dominus exaudivit eos, et ex omnibus tribulationibus eorum liberavit eos... The just cried, and the Lord heard them, and delivered them out of all their troubles...*" And after he had said the Alleluia and the accompanying psalm verse, he bowed over the centre of his small altar.

*"Munda cor meum ac labia mea... ut sanctum evangelium tuum digne valeam nuntiare... Cleanse my heart and my lips... that I may worthily proclaim Thy holy Gospel."*

***

On the morning of 13 July 1947, the monks were marched down the path through their garden, out of the gate to the open space in front of the monastery. From the clamour they could hear from inside the enclosure, they guessed there was a large crowd outside, but they were not prepared for the spectacle that greeted them.

There must have been over a thousand people around the open space, many of them squatting on the hillsides for a better view, and Paul recognised many faces. They were not just people from Yang Chia Ping. The crowd had been gathered from villages from miles around, from villages deep in the mountains and those lower down the valley, and among them were also a number of strangers who wore the distinctive cloth cap with the red star. Their prosecutors had organised this well.

Paul flinched as though someone had lashed him, and he stumbled. His mouth felt dry, and he tried to swallow.

"Courage, mon frère," said Father William, who happened to be walking next to him, making his voice heard above the din.

"Thank you, Father. Pray for me." He took a deep breath and looked deliberately about him.

Banners in their dozens fluttered in the breeze, almost all of them listing the 'crimes' of the community. The largest of them all proclaimed: "The Grand Assembly of All the Villages for the Common Judgement Against Yang Chia Ping." The community was marched into the centre of the open space amid the escalating clamour and herded to one side of a group of tables taken from the Refectory. The tables were draped with a red cloth, and behind them were seated a row of PLA officers – at least Paul took them to army officers. It had now become obvious that their arch-persecutor was

Li Tuishih, a prim, pale young man with immaculately Brylcreemed hair and gold-rimmed spectacles, who was never in anything but his quasi-military uniform: the fanatical ideologue and chief judge, who organised, directed, orchestrated and conducted the hate campaign against the community. Paul was convinced that this man was so motivated by a deep detestation of Christianity that it affected his reason and his action. As if by instinct, the monks cast their eyes on the ground, scarcely having to remember how Father Chrysostom had been beaten for looking up.

"Exploiters!"

"Traitors!"

"Foreign spies!"

These were some of the names called that Paul was able to distinguish, but very soon the words just merged into a roar of sound.

Father Augustine had deliberately marched at the head of the column, with Father Michael, the Prior, who had volunteered to march with him at his side. As superior of the monastery, he was ready to answer the charges on its behalf. This was also an attempt to shield Father Seraphin and Father Chrysostom, who had suffered enough during the previous week, from any further attention. He thought at first that the ploy had succeeded, as his name was called and he was pulled forward and thrown to his knees in front of the judges.

"Are you the one who calls himself Father Augustine?"

"Yes."

The assembly, however, also helped to identify him. "Of course he is! He can't deny it!" the crowd roared.

And then Father Augustine realised that the ploy was not working after all, for Father Seraphin, ill from the previous week's barbarous treatment, was summoned, as was Father Chrysostom. The three monks were now kneeling in a row in front of the judges. Father Seraphin was again called. He inched forward on his knees.

"Are you Father Seraphin?" asked one of the judges, though they all knew perfectly well who the priest was.

"Yes."

"We cannot hear you!" shouted another.

One of the guards raised his club for a blow, but was stayed by a gesture from Li. That could wait.

"You are to answer," the chief judge declaimed, "three grave charges this morning."

There was a murmur from the crowd. Li waited for complete silence before continuing.

"The first charge is that the monastery was responsible for the repression of our heroic brothers, the Boxers, by foreign powers."

This was an extension of the charge laid against the monastery at Lichia Wantze previously. Father Seraphin tried to explain.

"The monastery had nothing to do with either the Boxers or the foreign troops."

His attempt was swept aside. "Do you plead guilty?"

Father Seraphin straightened and looked at the judges. He was getting tired of the repeated nonsense.

"Not guilty," his voice rang out.

He was floored by a swipe of a club wielded by one of the guards. As he struggled to rise, he was felled by another blow. Paul could feel, palpably, the concentrated venom which was directed at this gentle, learned and saintly man. On his back were visited all the imagined crimes of the monastery since its foundation in 1883, this man who was not born until 1909. Paul watched with anguish. It was a long, long time before the beating stopped, and Father Seraphin pushed himself to his knees again, eyes closed to steady himself.

The judge appealed to the assembly.

"Guilty!" they roared back.

The second charge was read out. "The monastery had received arms from the French government to use against the people of the region."

In spite of the pain inflicted on his body, Father Seraphin's head was clear.

"Those rifles were sent to the monastery in the twenties to protect it against the warlords who were the enemies of the People," he pointed out with particular emphasis on the last word, "but they were never used. You people took them away to use against the Japanese during the war."

The argument for the defence was not accepted. This time it was the other man with the club who swung it first. Again it was some time before they had finished, and Father Seraphin had to answer the third charge.

"The monks," the charge went, " had hidden many precious things in the hills to keep them from the People."

So, Paul thought, are we coming to the real reason for the show? The plunder of the monastery last week had obviously yielded little of real value.

"Not guilty," pleaded Father Seraphin for the third time that morning. They clubbed him again and again. If he rose too slowly from the ground, he was beaten back to it, and if he rose too quickly, he was beaten down again, and all this amid cheers, applause and jeers from the crowd. Any of the men there would have been in trouble if they had not joined in the cruel charade.

***

He recited the Gospel passage he had chosen for this Mass.

*"Beati pauperes spiritu, quoniam ipsorum est regnum caelorum... Blessed are the poor in spirit, for theirs is the kingdom of heaven... Beati estis cum maledixerint vobis, et persecuti vos fuerint, et dixerunt omne malum adversum vos, mentientes, propter me... Blessed are ye when they shall revile you, and persecute you, and speak all that is evil against you, untruly, for my sake..."*

If one was blessed when one was reviled and persecuted, then Father Seraphin, who was highly regarded by the community as well as people outside, and who was tipped to be the next Abbot after Father Alexis, must surely be thrice-blessed.

He finished reciting the Gospel and bent to kiss the altar. He turned round to face the congregation, if there had been one. And there was one. The woman must have been there for a while. She was now getting down on her knees after standing for the Gospel. Her head was bowed beneath the black lace veil which all women wore in church, and in her hands were a missal and a rosary.

"*Dominus vobiscum... The Lord be with you.*" He opened his arms in greeting.

She looked up, and there were tears on her face. He could see her mouthing the response silently in Chinese.

"*Et cum spiritu tuo... And with thy spirit.*"

And then her jaw dropped. She had recognised him.

***

Paul knelt there, his head throbbing from the noise, reeling from the long exposure to the summer sun. He glanced at Father William. The old man was motionless, leaning back on his heels, head upright, eyes closed and mouth slightly open. He appeared to be relaxed, almost detached. Paul wondered if he was in fact asleep, and envied him. He made an effort to pray, but his mind refused to respond. So he emptied it of all fears, all expectations. That, perhaps, was a measure of peace.

But there was no peace. The agony was beginning afresh, this time for Father Chrysostom. Father Seraphin had somehow managed to drag himself back to where the other two priests were, and was now sitting on his heels, lips compressed and eyes closed against the pain. Father Chrysostom took his place in front of the judges.

"We have found Father Seraphin, and the monastery, guilty of the crimes against the people," he was told as preamble, "and if you do not assent to our verdict and confess them yourself, you are as good as dead. Do you assent?"

The priest later told his brothers that he never felt that first blow. He was just very surprised that he found himself on the ground. But he did feel the blow that came after.

"Do you assent?" he was asked again.

Blows fell again. Then someone yanked him back on to his knees.

"You are in charge of buildings and farms, are you not?"

Father Chrysostom said that he was.

"The monastery is herewith accused" – Li raised his voice so that all the one-thousand-strong assembly could hear the charge – "of usurping the best land in the area for itself and living off the people, and you are responsible."

There was not much point Father Chrysostom explaining that the monastery's land was 'best' because the monks had been painstakingly labouring hard to improve it. If the ears of corn were full and the fruits from the orchard were soft with juice, it was because the monks had toiled long with their hands. So he simply pleaded, "Not guilty," and the stalwarts with the clubs went to work on him. Finally, he crawled back to join the other two.

And he, and the monastery, were found guilty by the acclamation of the assembly.

Father Augustine, too, was found guilty, and a fine was laid on the monastery.

"It would take more than ten Yang Chia Pings to give you what you demand, even though we are not guilty of what you say," he said. His age was no safeguard, and the seventy-five-year-old priest was beaten for protesting the innocence of the community and for pointing out the severity of the unjust punishment.

For all the noise and show and all the acclamation from the People, it was in fact surprising that no sentence was passed. The president of the tribunal simply declared the trial adjourned and the monks were escorted back into the monastery. The villagers dispersed, and presumably they went home, many of them trudging many miles into the mountains in the gathering darkness of the evening. The monks were herded into the Chapel, and they did their best to care for Father Augustine and Father Chrysostom, and especially for Father Seraphin, who had suffered so cruelly.

Several days passed. Although they were still held prisoner in their own monastery and were existing on short rations, for their captors were by no means inclined to generosity or charity, the bruises slowly healed, and even Father Seraphin was mending. No one knew what would happen next. They did know that the Cistercians in Yugoslavia had been tried and imprisoned, and many slaughtered, although a number of them had been able to take refuge in Cistercian monasteries in Germany. And that seemed to be following a pattern created in the Spanish Civil War. Here in the mountains of Hopei there was no Germany for them to escape to. The nearest non-Communist country, Korea, was a sea away, and so was Japan.

By now Paul was beginning to be convinced, if he thought about the matter at all, that Hong Kong, a British territory, was the only place that could provide sure refuge. Even if the Communists succeeded in taking over China, as Father Alexis seemed so certain that they would, they would still not be in a position to challenge the might of Britain yet. Perhaps in that faraway place the communities of Our Lady of Consolation and of Our Lady of Joy, mother and daughter houses, would be reunited.

The monks were moved out of the Chapel at the weekend and placed under heavy guard in a dormitory. Then on the following Wednesday morning they were told that there was to be another trial.

"This time," they were told, "there will be a conclusion."

On 16 July, at about the time when they would normally process into the Chapel for the conventual Mass, the monks dressed for the last time – although they did not know it – in full habit and filed out of the dormitory, down the cloister and into the choir in the Chapel, because that was where their new public trial was to be held. The trial in the open had been a frightening occasion for many of them; but there was poignancy in the venue of their second trial. This was where practically all of them had given themselves to their Master by solemn vows. Whatever was going to happen to them was a fulfilment of the promises they had made. They had promised to be victims with Christ. They should fill up in their bodies the sufferings of Christ for His Church. They had dedicated their lives to God in a total, uncompromising abandonment of their whole beings. They had vowed to lay down their lives as holocausts, as testimony, as witness to Him. And here, now, as they lined up between the choir stalls in front of the High Altar, they were living out their promises.

Paul did not know what his brothers felt, but the thought of this gave him a certain measure of courage. Again, he found himself next to Father William, who because of his age was bearing up less well, it seemed.

"Courage, mon père," he murmured.

"Merci," the old monk replied. "I'll need it."

Father Alexis had been wrong on one thing. The foreign monks had no privileges, and because a number of them were old, their suffering was more acute.

The choir stalls were filled with soldiers of the People's Liberation Army as well as with representatives of the people from the villages, and the judges were seated behind tables set up in front of the altar. Behind the monks, in the main body of the Chapel, were the rest of the assembly, the villagers.

The trial began with a strange demand from the tribunal. The prisoners who wore glasses were told to remove them, and they were declared to be confiscated. It was thought, Paul found out later, that the wearing of spectacles gave the wearer a certain authority of learning, and as illiterate peasants respected learning and scholarship, this respect would cloud their judgement, and give the accused an unfair advantage. All things, it seems, had to be seen to be done fairly.

By now, there was not much doubt in the community which of them was going to be singled out for special treatment. As they expected, Father Seraphin was again called before the bench of judges. The usual identification process was repeated, accompanied, without much surprise, with the usual beating. Father Seraphin was, however, not required to answer the same old charges. There was a new one this time.

"It has come to the attention of this court that during the Japanese occupation of this area you went to a certain village, and into the homes of certain villagers, to obtain information for the enemy. Do you plead guilty or not guilty?"

The charge was so preposterous that the priest was for a few seconds dumbstruck. Then, "Not guilty!" his answer rang out.

The plea was sufficient. Blows rained down. Father Seraphin fell forward on the stone floor, adding a knock on his forehead to his other injuries. The beating this time was particularly savage and long. At last, as he writhed on the flagstones and the blows still fell, it became unbearable, and the victim cried, "Show a little mercy! Show a little mercy!"

Li had his moment.

"Now is not the time for mercy." He spoke for all in the Chapel to hear. "Now is the time for revenge!"

When the tribunal considered that the accused, his putative crime still unproven, had had enough, they called their witness.

A middle-aged woman, her hair gathered in a bun on the back of her head in the fashion of country women, walked up determinedly from the nave and stopped by the priest.

Maria Chang. Mrs Chang.

The witness identified herself to the court.

"Will you swear that Father Seraphin is guilty of obtaining information for the Japanese in your village?" It was not so much a question as an order.

A number of the monks watched her. Had this faithful friend of the monastery, who had done so much for them, been turned? This woman, who was to Paul almost like a second mother?

What she did then astounded the gathering.

"Let's stop this nonsense!" she said, her voice loud, and clear.

This was followed by a stunned silence. She went on:

"Father Seraphin certainly isn't guilty of obtaining information for the Japanese," she said, amid a growing swell of sound from the back of the Chapel. Her voice rose still higher to counteract the noise. "It wasn't he who came to our village when you said he did."

"Who then?" one of the judges shouted. Very few witnesses had ever contradicted the bench. How dare this insignificant woman contradict the court!

"It was Father Paul…"

They did not let her finish. "Come forward, Father Paul!"

Paul went forward and was thrust to the floor.

"You are Father Paul." Before he could respond, the judge went on, "Do you deny going to the village on the occasion in question?"

"No."

"Then you don't deny that you obtained information from certain villagers to pass on to the Japanese."

Before he could plead not guilty, Maria Chang spoke.

"Father Paul came to our village to help a dying Catholic. He gave the man Extreme Unction and the Blessed Sacrament. He did not obtain information to pass on to the Japanese."

One of the judges was so infuriated at the interruption that he leapt out of his chair and ordered the witness to be tied to the post of a candelabra. "Let this woman have a taste of the lash!" he screamed.

But Maria Chang would not be silenced. Even as she was led to the candelabra, she called out, "Father Paul is a good man, and he helped us when the Japanese made trouble for us, and…"

She never finished her sentence, for the first blow landed, and she had to bite her tongue to stop herself from calling out in pain. The guards beat her again and again until she slumped, hanging by her tied wrists from the candelabra. She was cut down, and one of the guards examined her.

"She's dead," he told the judges.

They threw a red banner over her and continued with the trial.

"Do you plead guilty?" Paul was asked.

Like all his brothers, he was beaten when he pleaded not guilty to what he was accused of.

"Guilty!" the crowd roared in the usual manner, at a prompt from the bench.

Other monks also underwent the ordeal of trial and beating. Brother Roch was beaten so mercilessly by three guards that some of the monks threw themselves forward in an effort to shield him from the blows and were themselves beaten. When at last it was asked what punishment should be meted out, the crowd shouted with one voice, "Death! They must die. All of them!"

The judges solemnly stood up. "We can only take the People's decision as our decision," the chief judge declared, "for the Communist government is the People's government. But we raise one question." He looked round the Chapel, and the assembly waited. "Do you want all the monks to suffer or only those most responsible?"

"All must suffer!"

The monks expected to be taken off immediately for execution, as was the custom, either outside the monastery, at the scene of their previous trial, or in the cloister. They had their belts, scapulars and medals stripped from them. Eight of them were shackled, hand and foot. Then they were marched down the cloister but, to their surprise, not to their deaths. They were led to the refectory and placed under a strict guard. Maria Chang, who was discovered not to have died, shared their imprisonment.

But the trials were by no means over. For the next two weeks, various monks were individually interrogated and punished, either by beating or by solitary confinement.

Would it be totally unrealistic to ask if there was some sort of subconscious admiration for this group of stubborn men, whose lives and attitudes were so incomprehensible to their persecutors? Or was there some innate sense of justice that deterred their judges from ordering their instant death, for after all no crime had been proven? Or were these judges inhibited by directions from above? No one could understand why the executions were not carried out, least of all the condemned men themselves.

In an effort to show the community how the other half lived, fifty lay prisoners were moved into the monastery, perhaps as a first step towards the secularisation of the community. The only effect of this ploy was to double the number of bodies, making life more cramped and more inconvenient. Then, they were divided into groups of seven, four monks and three civilian prisoners, and put into various rooms. Maria Chang shared her prison with other women. The new prisoners were in no mood themselves to do anything to advance the cause, and they found the monks' life totally alien. They perhaps realised, more than ever, that monastic life was not all roses when the monks got up at two o'clock to say Matins. There was a certain amount of grumbling, but the monks would not be put off. The two groups remained apart, and the experiment to introduce the monks to secular life came to nothing. The lay prisoners were withdrawn. And Maria Chang, fortunately and perhaps surprisingly, was sent home.

This period was only an interlude. What was to come was the Via Dolorosa of the community, ending in their Calvary.

\*\*\*

"*Nobis quoque... famulis tuis... partem aliquam et societatem donare digneris cum tuis sanctis Apostolis et Martyribus... Vouchsafe to grant us, Thy servants, some place and fellowship with Thy holy Apostles and Martyrs: with John, Stephen... Cecilia, Anastasia...*"

Paul was no longer in doubt where in the Canon of the Mass he should remember his brothers. He felt it could not be right to do so in the commemoration of the dead: these dead did not require his prayers. He was not trying to forestall their canonisation in any way, but there was nowhere else they should go. Their place had to be here, with the martyrs. So he recited the names, each face vivid in his mind as he said the name.

"Brother Bruno.

"Father William, Father Stephen, Father Alphonsus, Father Augustine and Father Aelred...

"Father Emile, Father Michael, Father Bonaventure, Father Odilo...

"Father Seraphin, Father Chrysostom, Father Maurus, Father Simon, Father Theodore...

"Brother Conrad, Brother Mark, Brother Aloysius, Brother Bartholomew, Brother Clement, Brother Jerome, and Brother Philip...

"Brother Anthony, Brother Malachy, Brother Amadeus...

"Brother Alexius, Brother Roch, Brother Eligius, Brother Hugh, Brother Irenaeus and Brother Martin..."

All thirty-one of his brothers. There might, he thought, be even more, as there were others still unaccounted for. And... of course...

"Brother Andrew.

"... *et omnibus sanctis tuis... and with all Thy saints. We pray Thee admit us into their company, not weighing our deserts but bestowing on us Thy own free pardon...*"

\*\*\*

One day towards the middle of August, the Communists, still apparently keen to have the monks on their side, took them out for a stroll. For whatever reason, it seemed to have been Li Tuishih's idea. Shackles and wires were taken off, which surprised the community, but it was for a very good reason, as they soon discovered. They thought they were being taken out for another show trial. Well, not this time – but it was certainly not a pleasure jaunt either. Li prepared the monks for their educational tour by giving them an address.

"You deluded company of men," he began. Then he told them how they had been duped by their religious superiors, how their religion had blinded them to the truth, and how their view of the world had been warped by their life in the cloisters. Gone was the corruption of the old order. "I shall now show you how things have changed under our enlightened rule," he promised them. "I shall take you to Chang Ko Chuang."

On the night of 12 August, the community were marshalled on the path leading down to the front gate for the start of their outing. The monks did not go empty handed. Each one of them was loaded down with heavy weights of supplies, mostly foodstuff, but there were also tools and ammunition and other necessities of the People's Liberation Army. The PLA served the people, so why should the monks not serve the army? Paul reckoned that if they had put another kilo on his back, his legs would have buckled and he would have collapsed. All the other monks were similarly loaded. Age did not spare any of them. Then they set off.

In the dark, and sometimes by torchlight, they walked and stumbled on the narrow paths, downslope and up, in the wild mountains. Progress was slow as they stumbled over cols and passes, and when progress was slower than their escort liked, they were prodded with rifle butts. It seemed as though the guards had decided that there should be no beating on this trip because it was not meant to be punitive. Perhaps they were concerned that once anyone collapsed under his burden, they themselves would have to share it. Their rifles were as much as they wanted to carry.

They marched through the night and halted only infrequently and briefly, and during these periods of rests some of the monks dared not sit down in case they would not be able to get up again. They took their rest leaning with their packs against a tree or on a ledge by the roadside. Morning was welcome, for it brought daylight which made their progress less hazardous. A halt was called at noon, when they were allowed some cold plain boiled rice.

Paul took off his pack, and helped Father William to take his down. The old man was white with exhaustion.

"I'm all right, Brother," he gasped. "Go and look after someone else."

Brother Bruno was eighty-two, but his pack was only fractionally lighter than those of the others, and certainly far heavier than any eighty-two-year-old ought to shoulder. Father Chrysostom had taken his pack off for him. He was now sitting on the ground, leaning against it, eyes closed, his face ashen.

"Is he all right?" Paul asked.

Father Chrysostom shook his head. He started to load some of the old man's burden onto his own pack.

"No. Don't do that," said Brother Bruno. "I'm all right. Truly."

It was late afternoon when they approached Chang Ko Chuang. Bent double under his load, Paul could only catch a glimpse of their destination out of the corner of an eye. In front of them was a large homestead which used to be the property of a rich landowner, but the Communists had established a commune there after they had taken it over.

"I shall show you what we have achieved," Li Tuishih announced proudly.

Paul saw cultivated, well-tended fields of ripening millet and barley on the floor of the south-facing valley side, and terraces cut into the hills. There was a large threshing floor in front of the house, empty for the next few weeks until harvest time, across which some of those who had been working in the fields, carrying the usual mattocks and hoes, were walking to the house. It was a peaceful scene, reminiscent of the community's own life which terminated so suddenly six weeks ago. The landowner's house was large, with three courtyards, and built with the same universal grey bricks that reminded Paul of his own home on the other side of the country. And this, even in the present circumstances, reminded him that in the last letter he had received from his mother before the invasion of the monastery she had told him that the family had been considering moving to Hong Kong in view of the troubles which, some people had told the family, were bound to come to their area. She said that she would write to him again once the family had made up its mind. Paul hoped that they had made the right decision. And there was only one that was right, he thought.

The landowner and his family no longer occupied the house. Paul wondered what had happened to them.

"We've taken over the homestead," said Li, "and turned it into a commune."

"What happened to Mr Tzu and his family?" Brother Roch could not help asking.

"They got what they deserved," Li told him seriously, with no attempt at humour, "and they deserved what they got." Which could only mean one thing. He thought for a second, and then added, gratuitously, offensively, ominously, his good intentions entirely forgotten: "Like you."

The monks shed their loads on the open courtyard in front of the house, and it was clear that the older men were entirely exhausted. Several of them could no longer stand and had to be helped inside. They were crowded into three rooms where they were kept under close guard for the next three days. Li did not keep his promise of showing the monks what the new order had achieved in this little corner of the world.

Word had, however, been passed round that Brother Bruno had collapsed. The Feast of the Assumption on 15 August was the Golden Jubilee of this humble monk's first vows, and Brother Bruno celebrated his day by going Home.

The monks borrowed a couple of spades, carried the body up the side of the valley and buried him. Then they were marched back to Yang Chia Ping.

So what had they seen of Chang Ko Chuang? Nothing.

Back in Yang Chia Ping, the monks were put in chains, and when their warders had run out of chains, their wrists were tightly bound with wire.

Elderly Brother Clement died next, and almost immediately afterwards Brother Philip. The community suspected that they had died of grief at the loss of all that they had known for most of their lives, and of shame that their own countrymen should treat them so. They had no way of explaining this to their brothers from other lands.

***

The Via Dolorosa.

Two weeks later – Paul was afterwards able to date it as 28 August – again at night, the monks were told that they were being taken on another walk. The community very quickly realised that, like the last one, this was no pleasure jaunt. They were roughly lined up in the cloister, and the guards went round making sure that the chains and wires with which they were shackled were secure. A few fortunate ones had their wrists tied in front of them, but many had them tied behind, which rendered them totally helpless. Paul was lucky in that his hands were tied in front of him, but he soon discovered that the tight wire manacles cut into his wrists, making them feel as though they were on fire. His mouth went dry, and he began to feel light-headed.

He thought, he almost hoped, that they were being taken out to be executed. At least then the agony would be short.

They retraced part of their steps of two weeks ago but now were being taken deeper into the inhospitable mountains. This time they were made to understand that they were not allowed even the occasional and necessary word.

"You are under no circumstances to communicate with each other," they were instructed. Then the officer in charge of the column remembered that his prisoners were not in the habit of speaking aloud: "Neither by mouth nor by gesture!"

Father Augustine again led the column. He set a slow pace to suit the older members of the community, and for once, at least at the beginning, that did not seem to annoy their escort.

"Take a last look at your monastery," a PLA officer told the prisoners, with, Paul thought, a certain amount of relish.

They looked back up the path, for their way lay generally

downhill. Already the monastery buildings looked ghostly in the dark. If the officer had meant to taunt and hurt, he did not understand the detached mind of the Cistercian. Then they lost sight of the monastery when the road dipped, and for most of the community that was the last glimpse they had of their home.

Often they walked in single file, for the path was narrow, but sometimes when it widened the guards hurried the tailenders forward and they walked in pairs. They walked through the night, as they had done last time, without halting. Towards mid-morning, without warning, one of the guards struck Brother Malachy hard with the butt of his rifle. The monk fell, grunting with pain.

"We told you not to communicate! So why were you talking?"

Brother Malachy struggled back to his feet.

"I wasn't saying anything to anybody! I was saying my prayers!"

"I don't believe you! We know you people can communicate just by lip-reading! Next time, whether you're praying or not, keep your mouth shut!" And the guard smashed the butt of his rifle into the ribs of Father Maurus, who happened to be watching. "Move on! What's the point of your praying? Your God isn't coming to your rescue, you know!"

After what seemed hours, Paul looked at the sun and guessed it must be about noon. He was beginning to feel hungry, but what was worse he was thirsty, and his tongue had, it seemed to him, swollen to three times its normal size and acquired the texture of sandpaper.

They stopped just before entering the next village and sat on the roadside. Curious onlookers, some of whom the monks knew, came to watch while the guards went off to buy food at the foodstall. This was, however, for themselves: the monks were not fed. Paul begged a child for some water. The child was on the point of going away and fetching it when he was stopped by his father. Some other monks were luckier, and were surreptitiously given a little water to drink.

When the soldiers had finished eating, they resumed the march. At the next stop for meals the monks were fed on dry balls of boiled rice, and they realised that they were to be given food only once a day. Quite a number of them had to feed like animals, for their hands were tied behind them. These had the worst of things, and their already soiled habits were further soiled with urine and faeces.

Just before dark they entered a small village on a spur of the Great Wall called Ta Lung Men. The older monks collapsed where they stopped, and some of them went into a swoon-like sleep. And they slept that night on the cold and stony mountainside. The weather changed in the night and rain clouds gathered, and by morning a fine drizzle was falling, steadily soaking the monks as they lay or sat in the open. There had been no question of rousing the community for Matins or Lauds or any of the Hours. Most were too exhausted by the previous day's march, and in any case needed to rest as much as they could in order to survive. A few did wake up out of pure habit, and these few managed to murmur the Office without fear of attracting the wrath of their guards: so certain were they that their prisoners would make no effort to escape that they posted no sentry and all found beds indoors.

When the guards were ready, they started to move off again. Today the road climbed steeply south-eastwards into the broad belt of wooded mountains which stood between Peking and the Great Wall. The fine drizzle that fell in the morning at Ta Lung Men had become a torrent of freezing rain, whipped up by howling winds so fierce that few could stand without having to lean into them to stay on their feet. But the monks were driven on and were not allowed to rest. It became obvious that the older men were beginning to lag behind. Some were totally exhausted; others were becoming ill and developing fevers which made them shake violently. There was little the guards could do to hurry them along.

"Where's Father Alphonsus?"

For once the guards could not manage, in the debilitating rain, to enforce silence on the community.

Another brother pointed downhill.

"We'll carry him," a brother bawled into the ear of one of the escort, "if you will let us make a litter." He held his wrists out for his shackles to be removed.

With the aid of a machete and wires from the wrists of some of the monks, a rough litter was built, and Father Alphonsus rode on the shoulders of four of his younger brothers.

In time, most of the other elderly and ailing members of the community were carried in this fashion. On the second day of the climb, they arrived at Tai Ping Tsun where they were put in pigpens for the night. The climb continued the next day, still in the icy, driving rain. There was no easy ride for the old monks, for the paths were slippery, and on many occasions the passengers were nearly spilled or dropped.

On the night when they were making their way towards the little village of Ma Lai Tsun, this was what happened to Father William. One of the carriers of his litter fell in the slippery mud of the path they were climbing and Father William hit his head on a jagged rock. The wound started to bleed profusely. The carriers realised what had happened, but there was little, it seemed, they could do. Paul, who had been carrying a litter and had already arrived at the village with the leaders for their short halt, saw that something was wrong when Father William's litter came in. One of the carriers was making frantic signals with his eyes to attract attention. Paul went over to examine Father William. Blood covered the old monk's head and face and soaked his habit, and was still oozing from the wound. The old priest was dead. They buried him, and then they were hurried on.

*** 

Teng Chia Yu. It was only one of many mountain villages but, with Mu Chia Chuang, it should go down in Cistercian history as a place of infamy. They had come into it by a mountain path, the young – themselves hobbling on blistered and lacerated feet – carrying the old, and it did not seem much of a place, with the usual blue-grey brick-built houses of different sizes lining the road, and the forbidding mountains looming behind. The monks were kept in this mountain village for twenty-five days. They were housed in several buildings, quite close together, that were broken down and decrepit; tattered, torn strips of rice paper covered the windows instead of glass, roofs leaked to admit the freezing rain, or were non-existent, and walls had cracks that let in the icy draughts. The nights were bitterly cold but no blankets or covering of any sort were issued to the monks, who lived and slept in their habits, minus the scapular which might have provided some little protection. Paul and some of his brothers were housed in a disused temple where there was minimum cover. They put the oldest and the weakest in the roofed area around the altar, and the rest slept with the rain on their faces.

The show trials started again, which huge numbers of villagers from the surrounding area were obliged to witness. Again, Father Seraphin and Father Chrysostom were singled out for special treatment. Father Seraphin was tried and beaten more than twenty times in those twenty-five days. He never spoke of the savage treatment, but each time he was brought back to the others his body shook with pain, and an occasional groan escaped him. But he was not to be broken, and the persecutors could not make him plead guilty to the trumped-up charges he was asked to answer for on behalf of the community. Then, one day, they wired his thumbs together, and then his big toes, and thumbs and toes were wired together so that he could only kneel or lie on his side.

Father Chrysostom was put into solitary confinement in a pigsty, where his habit, already soiled, was now stained with ordure and acquired a permanent stench. He asked for a blanket.

"You don't think right," was the answer to his request. "So you sleep with pigs." And, of course, Father Chrysostom did not get his blanket.

Other monks, too, were put on trial, and suffered the beatings which invariably followed the show, though it had to be admitted that their sufferings were not to be compared with those of Father

Seraphin and Father Chrysostom. Paul's back and neck were sore with bruises. By the second half of September, he was no longer aware of the passage of time. He was scarcely aware of being alive. He was permanently cold, and was always hungry, and he tended to go into a trance, with snatches of psalms and prayers fading in and out of his consciousness. But there were also long stretches when he was lucid, and that was when he found that his wrists were perpetually on fire, the flesh almost meeting over the wire that bound them. At other times, his bodily functions performed without his consent, much to his amazement afterwards. But, eventually, the terrible shows came to an end – in late September, as he worked out much later – when the Communists began to realise that they were drawing fewer and fewer spectators, and all the shouting and beatings were becoming monotonous.

But not before Death had come to Teng Chia Yu and claimed a number of lives.

They had arrived at Teng Chia Yu on 7 September, and eight monks died within the first ten days. Among them were Father Stephen, Father Emile and Father Alphonsus. Father Emile, at sixty-five, was one of the fittest and hardiest men in the community. Paul reckoned that, like Brother Clement and Brother Philip, he died of grief. Father Alphonsus had been suffering from dysentery, and for some reason or other had been kept in isolation so that no one could give him the little care they could provide. His death was reported to the community by one of the young guards. "He looks like that man on the Cross," he said in awe.

The other five were Brothers Conrad, Jerome, Mark, Aloysius and Bartholomew. The guards would not allow the burial parties to dig deep graves, and when the lightly piled topsoil was washed away by the rain, their bodies were stolen by wolves.

Then, one day, the commander of the column announced to the monks that the monastery had been burned down.

"We burned it down the day we left Yang Chia Ping," he told

them. "And soon there will be no Christian churches left in China!" he exulted.

The monks refused to believe him. It was not possible, they thought, for it made no sense to destroy a building which could be so useful to anyone who took it over. These men, who had forsaken the world, were more practical-minded than the dogmatists who were trying in their way to improve the world. A detail of guards was then ordered to escort three luckless young brothers all the way back to Yang Chia Ping to prove to them that the devastation had indeed taken place. They returned that evening.

"Yes, it's true," they reported, with tears in their eyes. "The monastery has been burned down."

Then in early October the community, reduced by death, was moved on to Mu Chia Chuang. The very thought of the name later sent a shiver through Paul's guts and pain through his soul. Then, his mind did its best to obliterate thought of the infamous place, and sometimes he wondered if he was not in fact in the middle of a nightmare and would wake up, relieved, in his cell, the crucifix spreading its comforting arms from the wall above his bed.

This was the community's death camp, its Golgotha. Here they were kept in buildings no different from those at Teng Chia Yu. At first the monks were deluded into hoping that their persecution was coming to an end. It was obvious that Li and his henchmen were waiting for orders from above. These came in the shape of an American jeep captured from the Nationalists, its twelve-rayed star hastily covered with red paint and adorned with yellow stars. The officer who came did not stay long, but next morning, to the surprise of the monks, they were fed. They were given stale steamed bread and water to wash it down. Their meal was witnessed by the whole platoon of guards, with Li sitting in a chair, relaxed and smoking. Paul thought he saw disappointment in his face.

The monks were grouped roughly according to where they came from. Then from one group five young monks were indicated. They were pulled out to stand before the officer. Paul wondered what brutality was now being planned for these innocents.

And as innocents they were treated. The brothers were told that they were not so much to blame as the old monks.

"You have been deceived. These old monks have taught you to think incorrectly. Now, I hope, you have learned some sense!"

He paused to gain maximum dramatic effect.

"Go home. Go home to your families. Get married. But," he warned, "don't make the mistake of entering another monastery or a seminary, and don't allow yourselves to be made into priests. We will soon have all China under our control. We'll eliminate Christianity, and if we catch you in another monastery, we won't be so gentle with you!"

With that the five brothers were ushered out into the road. It was too much to expect that they would be given a chance to say farewell to their brothers.

Four days later, seven more young monks were released with a similar warning, and others were sent away in the same manner. So by the middle of October only the older lay brothers and the priests were left.

Then Father Anthony and Father Augustine, the Novice Master and temporary Superior of the community, died by poisoning.

***

Paul bowed low over the makeshift altar.

"*Panem caelestem accipiam... I shall receive the bread of heaven...*"

He broke off half of the consecrated wafer and put it back in the saucer. This was for Mrs Chang.

"*Corpus Domini nostri Jesu Christi custodiat animam meam in vitam aeternam... May the Body of our Lord Jesus Christ preserve my soul to life everlasting...*"

He straightened up and turned, holding the Host with his right hand and the saucer under it with the other. Mrs Chang came and knelt to receive Communion.

"May the Body of our Lord Jesus Christ preserve thy soul to life everlasting."

When he had recited the last Gospel, from the first chapter of John, he came and knelt with Mrs Chang to say the Prayers after Mass together. These were set prayers for the conversion of Russia. The Church should also devise a set of prayers for the conversion of China, he thought.

Then Mrs Chang helped him to dismantle the altar.

# FOUR

Paul was back on his seat in the ruins of the Chapter Room, with Maria Chang and her basket next to him, their backs against the remains of a wall which sheltered them from the occasional blast of cold wind. The mid-November noonday sun also provided just enough heat to prevent them from feeling cold. Mrs Chang had brought a lunch of bread and roast pork in barbecue sauce and hot tea in a thermos flask, and had offered to share it with Paul.

"You need feeding up," she said, seriously.

This meal was so superior to the half crust of stale steamed bread that he had been carrying about that he accepted the offer without qualms. Even a monk, even a vegetarian Cistercian monk, he told Mrs Chang with a smile, was entitled to some luxury occasionally.

He said grace, and then took a sip of the still scalding tea and bit into the sweet roast pork.

"This is good! Excellent!" he sighed, and Maria Chang was pleased.

They ate, each restraining an almost overwhelming desire for news. Paul noticed, however, that she scarcely touched the food, leaving most of it to him, and he felt very ashamed. He ought really to know better. But it would hurt her feelings now to refuse the food. He didn't quite know what to do, but took care to slow down so as to compel Mrs Chang to have more of her share. Her own food.

Then they settled back and talked. He had the first question.

"I hope you're not still suffering from the beating you took on account of Father Seraphin and me?" he asked solicitously.

"No." She didn't want to say more.

"How come you are here today? Your village is a long walk away."

Mrs Chang hesitated, as though reluctant to answer.

"I come down here almost every Sunday," she admitted. "There are no priests around anymore, so I come down here to pray when I can and when the weather is all right." She looked up at the sun. "It's good today, and not too chilly. Guess my surprise when I found you here this morning! Of course I didn't know it was you, or what you were doing, at first. And then, I knew."

She turned to look at him again.

"You're a lot thinner, and very sunburned. Were they hard on you?" She almost raised her finger to touch him, and then remembered not to.

Paul shrugged. "Well... could be worse, a lot worse. I was lucky, in a manner of speaking. So they shut down the little church in your village, did they?"

"Yes. It's the Party Headquarters for the area now."

Then she asked her question.

"What did happen at Mu Chia Chuang, Father? We heard a lot about it, but it was all rather confused. The young monks came through my village on their way to Peking. Seven of them, I counted. By the way, those young men did make it to Peking. I checked, and they joined with other Cistercians, and I heard that some of the monks got away to Hong Kong, before the city fell to the Communists. They were led by a senior monk, Prior Paulinus Li, from the other monastery."

"Thank God for that!" he said.

"But there are still some from Yang Chia Ping left there, living on a dairy farm – I'll give you the address when we get home. Why didn't they get away, too?" Then she returned to her question. "And... what really happened to the rest of you? And what happened to the French monks?"

***

Things did not get worse after the young monks were released, or at least sent away. Things had always been bad, and there was no way they could have got worse. The days turned cold and the nights began to freeze, and the inadequate buildings in which they were kept were no protection. And while things were bad for all of them, they were far worse for the old monks. Soon after the death of Father Augustine, the Novice Master, the last of the Europeans, a Dutchman, Father Aelred, also died.

"They were all pretty old, you see," he said, as though in explanation. "We tried to shield both Father Augustine and Father Aelred and Father Emile from the elements by placing them as far away from the weather as possible, but what with the exertion and the lack of food... and no blankets..."

He waved his hand in a helpless gesture.

"We were all regarded as dangerous criminals, we from Yang Chia Ping and twenty-odd Cistercians from the other monastery, and every morning or afternoon there was someone being beaten, for hours at a time, until the poor man was half dead. They usually did it outside, for all the village to see how criminals, I suppose, were punished."

They could all hear the thud of the falling blows and the grunts of pain and not infrequently the cries for mercy. These did not make any difference. Quite the reverse.

"Where's your God now?"

A lot of them died in October.

"I think fourteen of us died in that month, including Father Michael, our Prior."

"Someone who lives in the next village from Mu Chia Chuang told us," said Mrs Chang, "that a number of you were horribly murdered."

Paul would have preferred not to remember that day, but he could never forget it. That Wednesday, 28 January 1948. As near as he

*127*

could make it.

It had snowed quite heavily during the night, and those who slept near the open courtyard woke up shivering towards the morning under a blanket of snow. The streets were all white and quiet.

"Father Seraphin, who had suffered and survived such a lot, Father Chrysostom with him, and Brother Alexius, and the generous, impetuous, brave Brother Roch... you remember him, don't you?"

Mrs Chang nodded. "If his hands hadn't been tied that day in the Chapel, he'd have floored the guards. I'd just come round to see him being beaten."

"And Brother Eligius. They took them out. At first we thought it was going to be a new kind of show, a mass beating. So we started praying for them."

"And then?" prompted Mrs Chang.

In his mind, he saw them, their hands pinioned to their sides, as they were led out into the snow-covered street, all sound deadened by the drifts. The guards drove them, stumbling and slithering in the slippery snow, round the corner of a house and they were lost to the view of their brothers.

"They killed them," he said quietly. Then he shook his head.

"No matter, Father Paul," Mrs Chang said gently. He would tell her in his own time. If he wanted to.

"They then came and told us to go and look at the bodies. And, there, on the mountainside, they lay... amid... amid... pools of blood which stained the snow. Brother Martin broke down. He said, 'Did you have to do that?'"

"And what did they say?"

"Nothing, of course. They didn't have to justify their actions." Then he added bitterly, "We were merely condemned criminals awaiting execution. Then... then, you know what they did? You didn't know... You wouldn't know. They threw the bodies into the village cesspit." He managed to hold his voice steady.

Mrs Chang broke the subsequent silence.

"Come on, Father, drink some tea."

He took the mug gratefully.

"And you, were you all right, Father?"

"Yes. I'd got over the wounds on my wrists." He held them out to show Mrs Chang. They were healthy apart from a scar right round both of them. "And, curiously enough, I didn't get as many beatings as some of the others, like Father Seraphin, for example. One day, the officer sent for me. Not Li. Li had gone away temporarily. Someone said he'd been summoned to Headquarters to answer certain questions."

The officer had set up house across the road. The owner of the house and his family had to move in with the family next door. Li had been much more ascetic and lived with the troops. The officer had been told by one of the monks that Father Paul was an engineer by training, and he had a proposition for him. Paul thought that the officer was being unusually polite.

"We are building a dam in a place about two hundred miles west of Yang Chia Ping and I've been asked to find an engineer. I've been told you are one. It will be a position of some responsibility," he added.

Paul concluded that things had to be pretty desperate for them to look for help from the community. "Do I have a choice?" he asked warily.

"Do you seriously mean that you actually want to stay here?"

After the murder of the five monks barely three weeks before, Paul felt that he had nothing to lose.

"I'll let you know in half an hour," he said, and left.

Father Simon was the most senior member now of the community. Paul told him what had been proposed, and added his own plan.

"I'm going to ask for four or five other brothers to go with me. I'm not sure he'll say yes, but I'll lose nothing by asking."

There was no hesitation in Father Simon's response.

"You must go," said the older monk, who was so weak now that he could scarcely rise. "I believe it is everyone's duty to get away from this hellhole if possible. See who you can manage to take with you. You must take the fittest ones. The weak and the sick aren't any use. Then, when there's an opportunity, make for... Hong Kong, or wherever... Now, why are you hesitating?"

"I don't want to leave the community while we are in this predicament."

"Then I'll order you to go. Go with my blessing... our blessing, brother."

So Paul knelt by the older man's litter and received his blessing.

This, he was determined then, was to be the beginning of his long march to Hong Kong. It was a pity that he would not be able to take many more of his brothers with him.

"Anyway, I went back to the officer with a list of five names, and I bargained with him for nearly an hour." He resumed his story. "At times he was so angry that I was afraid the whole deal might be off. At the end, I got Brother Andrew. Only one, but still one. A lorry came for us next day, and we got to our new prison after nightfall. It was a long journey. The place was called Shang Chuan. It was merely a row of small brick-built houses and cottages set under the steep hillside on a path which had been widened to take motor traffic, and then there was a fairly gentle slope down to the small stream. There was no shop, or temple. And above the village was the camp."

They nearly died from the cold as they were taken across the frozen mountains. It was a sunny day, but it was a pale, heatless sort of sun, and the two monks huddled together in the lee of the driver's cabin for warmth. There was one stop for lunch, but the monks were not allowed to get off the lorry to stretch their legs. They were not even allowed to stamp their feet on the floorboards of the lorry to beat some warmth into their limbs and bodies. However, the armed escort did throw them a roll of steamed bread each.

They were put into a hut with seven other prisoners for the night, and for the first time since they left the monastery six months before, they slept under a quilt, and, miracle of miracles, they were actually warm. For the first and almost the only time in their Cistercian life, neither Paul nor Andrew woke up at the right time to say the Night Office. They were sent for by the commandant at reveille, in the still dark hour before dawn, when the other prisoners trooped off to their work without breakfast. The authorities did not seem to believe in feeding their prisoners more than once a day, at midday.

"You are Liang Weishung?" The commandant, between sips of steaming tea, pronounced his name in the northern speech.

"Yes. Leung Waihung." Stubbornly, he let regional pride take over; his answer was in his native Cantonese. He felt angry. He was tired of being pushed around. The commandant looked at him but said nothing.

"And Wang Rupin?" This was directed at Brother Andrew.

Andrew nearly missed the question. He was gaping at Paul, open-mouthed. Not quite the Paul he'd known the last ten years.

"And you are the engineer?"

Paul nodded.

"And this one?" The commandant waved his hand at Brother Andrew. He was right to be suspicious. The man was correct up to a point, and only up to a point, for Andrew did build roads while they were at Yang Chia Ping, and was an experienced bricklayer. In any case, Paul was not going to yield without a fight.

"My friend has experience in building roads and houses and other structures." He looked the commandant in the eye. "I need him as my assistant."

The other man nodded, without saying anything. Then he looked at the monks again.

"You can't go out in these," he said, indicating the tattered and grimy Cistercian habits which had been their only clothes since the midnight invasion of the monastery by the mob. And their sandals which had been repaired with strings. He walked to the door and bellowed into the snow.

As a result, they were issued with shirt, trousers, jacket, padded overcoat and socks, fur hat and earmuffs. There was a pair of leather shoes which were too big for Paul, and so they went to Brother Andrew. Paul got a pair of cloth shoes, like those worn by most country people. When they had changed they went back to the commandant.

"Are you sure you are an engineer?"

"I have a diploma from Peking University to prove it."

Paul wasn't sure if it was the right thing to admit, even if the university was where Mao Tsetung was a librarian before he went seriously into politics – worse luck!

Paul handed over his degree certificate, which he had managed not to lose in the terrible times in the last few months but was now sweat-stained and badly creased, for inspection. The commandant looked at it, then handed it back without saying a word.

"Well. Come and see what the problem is."

The village and camp were in a valley which looked very different from the one at Yang Chia Ping, but it had the same feel, though possibly even more desolate and more stony, and had fewer trees, and the dwarf oaks which grew on the steep mountainsides were even more stunted. But, as at Yang Chia Ping, someone had turned a part of it into perfectly adequate agricultural land, with a dam and modest pumping station which must have dominated the village which had now become almost a part of the camp. It used to supply water not only to the farming land immediately below, but to other villages down-valley as well. The dam, however, had disappeared, and in its place were heaps of rubble. Without the lake behind the dam, the pumping station had become useless. Peeling paint and rusted ironworks advertised its desolation. The only source of water for the village was the stream which had somehow managed to navigate itself round the rubble of the dam and followed its ancient course down the valley. It wasn't a stream of any large volume, but at least it was supplying fresh water.

"Who did this?" Paul asked.

The commandant looked embarrassed. He cleared his throat noisily before replying.

"Er... we did. We did it to stop the Nationalists from having access to the water."

He's an honest man, perhaps, Paul thought, and waited for the rest.

"The fighting has moved far to the south, and we're now in control in this area, and we decided we ought to rebuild the dam because the people can't do without a proper water supply. So we set up a work camp here. That was last summer. We used our prisoners – many of them were soldiers in the Nationalist army – and the villagers helped. We thought we were doing a good job. But a flash flood two months ago..." He opened his hands expressively. "I reckoned we'd done too good a job blowing it up."

Paul scrambled through the snow-covered rubble to inspect the damage, followed by the commandant and Brother Andrew. The demolition had indeed been too perfect. It had torn absolutely everything out, and the repair had been done without due regard to the foundation. One couldn't just pile rubble and stones on top of one another to make a dam.

He beckoned Brother Andrew to him. He was determined to convince the commandant that Andrew was indispensable so that he could ensure reasonable treatment for both of them. For himself, he had little doubt that he was going to be treated adequately, for he was beginning to believe that the commandant was a reasonable man. And they needed him.

"Well?" the commandant asked. "What do you think?"

As they walked back to the commandant's office, Paul told the man what he needed.

"I need a site office. I can convert one of the dormitory huts if I can have one. Or a room in one of the houses, but I don't want you to throw anybody out for me. I want a large table to work on, and plenty of paper, pencils, rulers... the usual stationery stuff."

He glanced at the commandant. He was nodding.

"You can get the men to start clearing the rubble right away. By the time it's done, I should have the plan more or less ready. I hope." The engineer in him was starting to take over. "And we'll require..."

By the time they got back to the commandant's office, Paul was told that he could have one of the two spare huts.

"That one over there. It's empty. Unless you want the other one."

Good, thought Paul. He picked the one at the upper end of the row of prison dormitories, right under where the old dam used to be, and it also happened to be the furthest away from the commandant's office. Whoever had designed the original camp had put the prisoners' huts by the stream, which bubbled its way healthily and boisterously between vertical banks overhung with ice and snow. The designer of the camp had not reckoned on the flash flood, and what Paul saw were recent replacements, sited exactly where the old ones had been: this was a situation that might sometimes turn dreams into nightmares. The water by his hut would be clean, however, unless someone soiled it further up. There appeared to be little chance of that as the village was below the camp. In any case, the water should be safe at least in the winter, when people were not likely to be wandering in the inhospitable mountains to pollute the stream.

Paul was pleased with the way the situation was developing. Dangerous prisoners though the monks were described to be, the commandant appeared a rational sort of person, or at least pragmatic, and, what was more important, they were seen to be trusted by him right from the very beginning. The result of this was that the guards, who could be so cruel and brutal to their prisoners, were actually civil to them. Whatever else might happen later, this provided a breathing space and time for them to recuperate.

They used part of that first day moving the bunk beds out of the hut and searching for appropriate furniture. Basically, it only meant finding a table large enough for engineering drawing purposes, and some shelves. They took great care not to commandeer anything that was being used by their fellow prisoners, or that belonged to the guards. They found a long, snow-covered refectory-type table behind the kitchen, and installed it in the hut. They kept the chairs which were already there, and they built shelves with the rubble and planks which were lying about. When the meal-time gong sounded, they had completed the transformation.

Paul studied the hundred or so of his fellow prisoners as they shuffled in line for the dollop of rice and couple of strands of vegetables and the diminutive brown speck, meant to be meat, which passed for their daily meal. In the six months since the camp – a work camp, and not a punishment camp – had been set up, a group of reasonably healthy men had been reduced to little more than leathery skin wrapped round sticks of bones, made more grotesque by the apparent oversize of the skull. Of course, he and Brother Andrew were possibly in an even worse condition. If the authorities were serious about building a dam, even a small-scale dam, then they had to have better nourishment. The alternative would be a succession of skeletons that passed for a workforce and an ever extending graveyard. He decided that, if it were up to him, he did not want a workforce larger than the number of prisoners already in the camp. More people would only get in the way in the relatively narrow space.

There was no such thing as a dining hut, and prisoners took the food from the kitchen block back to their own huts where they ate it sitting on their bunks or on chairs, or squatting on the floor. The monks joined the seven men in their dormitory.

"You are not new prisoners, are you?" said one of them, called Mang, after they had introduced themselves. "Where were you, then?"

"Mu Chia Chuang," said Andrew. "East of here, over the mountains."

"Isn't that where they keep a load of Catholic monks?"

Paul had planned not to divulge their identity immediately as he had feared it might erect a barrier between them and their fellow inmates. However, it would now be wrong to hide. He looked at Andrew.

"Yes," he said. "We are two of the monks. Lucky, for the time being, I suppose."

"How the world has changed!" Mang commented.

"How did you get to know about us?" Andrew was curious.

Mang shrugged his shoulders. "Word gets around. Don't ask me how, and I'm not trying to be mysterious. But it does." He looked hard at them. "You had a really hard time, didn't you? You poor buggers!"

Paul and Andrew looked at each other, and neither could suppress a smile. But they hid it well. Mang's heart was in the right place. By then their cellmates were showing real interest in them.

"So you're *shenfu*, Catholic priests?"

"He is," said Andrew. "I'm not. I'm only an ordinary brother. And what were you, then, before all this?"

Mang, Paul decided, was a cheerful and possibly loveable rogue, but could probably be vicious when crossed. He found out later that Mang had been a small-time crook, guilty chiefly of thieving, and that he had the sense to reckon he was fortunate not to have had a bullet through the back of his head.

"They decided to send me here because they thought I'd make a good labourer. I am big, you see." He was still tall, of course, but his size had been greatly reduced by the inadequate diet.

Four of the other six had been soldiers in the Nationalist army.

"He's an officer."

Paul was looking at a young man of about twenty-five, no different now from the others.

"I don't spread that about," he said. "It's not safe."

Of the remaining two, one had been a primary-school teacher, and the other a farmhand who had refused to testify against his employer at a show trial.

All dangerous criminals.

In the afternoon he and Andrew, accompanied by a guard, went for a really good look at the site to try to work out what the situation had been before the old dam was demolished. It was too much to expect to find surveying equipment in the camp, so they devised their own. After an hour or two, when their guard showed irrepressible signs of boredom, Paul decided to co-opt him.

"Write down these numbers when I call them out," he told the man. "You can write?"

That evening, he went to the commandant with preliminary ideas and certain demands. Well, 'propositions', he decided to call them.

"I've roughly worked out the capacity of the old reservoir. Was it really adequate? If it was not, I can increase the capacity by constructing a higher dam, and this will channel water to a larger area. We're on the edge of a very dry area, so I believe a larger irrigation area would be a good idea. I don't know how much larger without a proper survey and studies of the area, though. Do you want me to build a higher dam in any case? But even if all you want is to rebuild the old dam, it is more than just a repair job, and I think you ought to put it to your superiors."

"Do you want more men?"

"No. Unless you can send a number of real engineers, then no. Besides, we'd only get in each other's way."

There would not have been a problem if he had asked for another hundred men. Manpower was never a problem. But the authorities might baulk at what he was going to demand. "No. Propose," he told himself.

"We're all going to work extremely hard at this job, whether we're building the big dam or the small one, so I want better food for the camp. Two proper meals a day, with meat, or at least soya beans, and decent vegetables... and a lot more rice. A reasonably healthy man could eat two bowls of rice at a meal, not the measly one small bowl you give them now. Unless you wish to keep replacing men who die, and have half the men spending their time digging graves. And then most of the time the newcomers won't have a clue what they ought to be doing. And I want dynamite for blasting," he added.

The commandant's eyebrows rose. But, he was almost going to say, that's more than what some of our troops are getting!

"I'll see. But, no promises."

"Besides," Paul added, "the new dam is going to be a very good thing for your future promotion."

The commandant gave him such a look that Paul realised this had been the wrong ploy to use. There were men of integrity on both sides, after all.

They waited. In the meantime, Paul worked on two sets of plans. The rubble of the old dam was being cleared away slowly, which suited his plans anyway. He did not want his men to be overworked before they were adequately fed.

Paul and Andrew were also working out a system by which they could fit a common monastic life into their new one. They found that they were able to say most of the Office together, though seldom at the appropriate times, and they found great comfort and strength in that. It had turned out to be a good thing to reveal their monastic identities, as they were never disturbed when their new friends found them reciting the psalms together. *Shenfus* did things which ordinary people didn't, and they respected that. It was a pity, however, that there were no facilities for saying Mass.

Mang woke up one night while they were saying the Night Office, and for a moment was disorientated by the murmuring of the monks.

"Oh heck!" he said, then turned over and went back to sleep.

"Do you fellows really get up to say your prayers in the middle of the night?" he asked the next day. "So when the heck do you sleep?"

\*\*\*

"That," Paul explained to Mrs Chang, "is an expurgated version of what he said."

"I thought so." Mrs Chang laughed.

***

They waited a week. Then Paul was summoned to the commandant's office.

"I don't know how you did it," said the commandant. "The stuff is on its way, I've been told, including the pump, cement and the dynamite. And I am authorised to buy the sort and quantities of food which you asked for. Did you pray, or something?"

"Of course I prayed!"

Paul didn't say it, but he reckoned that someone high up in the Party had some sense. Common sense seldom won with dogmatic totalitarianism, but occasionally there was a glimmer of hope. In any case, a new daily routine was worked out which made room for two mealtimes, and the diet immediately improved. His fellow prisoners gave him full credit.

"Tinghau!" many of them said to him, raising their thumbs. "Very good! Excellent!" It became rather unbearable when some of them took to thumping him on the back as they said it.

He set his workforce to divert the stream, re-routing it round the old reservoir and bringing it down to a point below the old dam and just above his hut. With the spring thaw already in its initial stages, this was more than necessary work. He was able to persuade the commandant to restrict the working day to nine hours, giving the men a certain amount of time for recreation. Unfortunately, it also meant that the men had to spend a part of their non-working time at political re-education. On the first evening he made an excuse to stay away, claiming that he needed to look over some plans for the dam. However, he was sharply reprimanded, and he began to realise that the commandant was also constantly looking over his shoulder. One of his underlings was probably a political commissar who wielded more real power than he did.

He must learn to tread carefully. For that reason, he and Andrew decided that they must share in the physical labour of the camp.

He had been in danger of overreaching himself, and he was glad that he had learned his lesson in time. However, the commandant himself took these re-education sessions, and he was careful not to involve the two monks in discussions. He needed the engineer and his assistant.

Paul divided the men into two gangs. One was allocated the task of preparing the foundations of the dam, while a smaller group, entrusted to the charge of the ex-Nationalist officer who said he'd had experience with explosives, had the work of quarrying for material for the foundation. Paul was, however, a little suspicious of the motive and the enthusiasm of this man and was not sure that he might not be tempted to sabotage the operation. Andrew was therefore appointed as his second to supervise the activities of the group. Mang, too, he had originally attached to Andrew, but the man seemed incapable of sticking to one group, and Paul often found him at his shoulder offering advice. At first he found him a nuisance, but Mang's own cheery, unintentionally irreverent nature made any annoyance he harboured for more than a few seconds feel churlish. Besides, it helped to remind him that he was in no special position as a priest and a monk. In any case, he was never sure where Mang was. If he was not with him, he must be with Andrew. Or somewhere else.

Spring turned to summer, and desert flowers bloomed further down the valley. Here in the mountains, as in Yang Chia Ping, dwarf oaks donned their dark mantle of leaves, but Paul missed the rhododendrons. The dam grew from its new foundations and he was finalising plans for the pump house. Also, the suppliers had not been able to provide metal sluice gates, and he was working on the idea of constructing them out of wood. But where was he to find the sort of wood he required?

He and Andrew got on well, too, with their fellow prisoners. Some of them began to come to him with problems, for advice, and even with requests to write letters for them.

"I can't write," said one of the ex-Nationalist soldiers. "I never went to school."

And he discovered that writing letters for these unlettered fellow prisoners was like being in a confessional.

"Sorry, am I too fast, *shenfu*?"

"No. It's all right. I'm getting there." Whereas in truth, he had had to get a grip on himself. Many of those who had been soldiers in the Nationalist army had sad histories. They had come from really poor homes, had been forcibly enrolled in the army, had been half-starved as serving soldiers. A lot of them were probably better fed and treated in a Communist prison camp.

One evening, as they were chatting in the cell before turning in, Mang wagged his finger at him.

"Hey, *shenfu*. I've meant to tell you for the last few days, but you've kept us so busy I kept forgetting. You know that man called Teng in Hut 3?"

"Yes. What about him?"

"He's a Christian. Not the other lot. Your lot, making the sign of the Cross and that. He said I'm not to tell you, because he's stopped believing."

"It hasn't stopped you from telling me, has it?"

"No. But he's in a bad way. They just shot his father for being a... reactionary. The family used to own a small plot of land down in Honan. I thought you might want to help him."

"I do, Mang. But it doesn't work the way you think, and I have no magic wand. I'd prefer him to come to me. But don't you go and tell him that either."

"No, sir." Mang gave him a mock salute, the sort he had seen the Americans give in the cinema.

He and Andrew kept the anniversary of the 8 July. That was the last time, twelve months ago, when he had said Mass. There was no reason why, he began to reason, he could not use just any bread. And as for the wine... That was a real problem. Where was he to get communion wine? Could he use the local fire-water made from grapes? Or perhaps even rice wine? He agonised over the issue for a week or so, and still could not make up his mind. The celebration of Mass was a privilege, not a right... Well, why not? He was, he told himself, beginning to reason like a five-year-old.

"What do you think, Andrew?"

"I've been waiting for you to bring that up," Andrew said. "Do you want to hear what I think? Shall I be Devil's Advocate, first?"

Andrew, who had not studied theology, nevertheless proved to be as good a theologian, as well as historian, as any he had come across. His reasoning was lucid and cogent, but unfortunately it was on both sides of the question. The two sides were too finely balanced for there to be an easy solution, but it was useful to hear the argument from somebody else.

"Well, there you are. Now it's up to you."

He took a deep breath and said, "Right!" But still he hesitated.

The months passed. Paul and Andrew were growing so used to life at the camp that they almost could not imagine another existence, post-Yang Chia Ping. Monastic discipline, which they endeavoured to preserve, was followed without much difficulty. At the same time, the dam grew, as did work on the related conduits and channels. The commandant did not interfere with Paul's direction of the work, but did ask, on several occasions, "When is the dam going to be finished? You have been on the job for several months now."

This was towards the middle of July.

"The dam itself, as you can see, is nearly complete. Another week, I think, and then the pump house, another two weeks or so. Three weeks, I think... I'm sure."

And then he asked a question which had been on his mind for a while.

"What happens to us when the work's done?"

The commandant lit a cigarette before replying.

"The people here have been promised amnesty when the work is done. You may or may not know that they are all, more or less, volunteers from other... er... camps, and it was a condition of their volunteering. Besides, this camp will close."

Paul nodded. He knew that, although he was not by any means sure that the authorities would honour the promise of amnesty. If the promise was kept, however, it would, he thought, be a pity. There was now an experienced workforce for dam-building which would be lost. Then he caught himself: what in heaven's name was he thinking? He was in danger of turning into a cog in the machinery!

"Does the amnesty apply to the two of us?"

"No."

It was disappointing, but he was not shocked. He had been expecting that.

"What will happen to us, then? Will we be sent back to Mu Chia Chuang?"

"There's no one left in Mu Chia Chuang."

"So what's happened to the monks there, then? If I'm not mistaken, there should be at least four of us there."

"All I know is, they've gone. As for you and your friend, you will be sent on to another camp. But I've been proposing that you two should be kept in this area to improve the irrigation system, which is dependent on this reservoir, and it is possible, just possible, that my superiors will listen."

Then he paused for a short while before continuing. "But you won't be under me anymore."

***

"This was as close as he came to showing friendship," he told Mrs Chang.

***

A week later, Andrew went up-valley to supervise a minor blasting operation, while he oversaw the final stages of the building of the dam. There was nothing, in fact, for him to do, but it was good to see the final basketful of cement being laid and smoothed over the causeway that was the top of the structure before he turned his attention to the pump house. The commandant came to join him. He looked pleased. Paul reckoned that the completion of the dam would mean another rung up on the ladder of promotion in the Party. He would be pleased.

There was a muffled roar from up-valley, and the two men turned to watch a column of smoke and dust rising clear against a bright blue, cloudless sky behind a spur round which the valley changed direction. A minute or so later, he saw a figure come bounding down the slope, gesticulating wildly and urgently and calling, but the steep mountainsides distorted his words and Paul could not understand what the man was saying.

"It's Mang," said the commandant. Mang had followed his own initiative and joined Andrew and the ex-Nationalist officer this morning.

Something's wrong, Paul thought, and began to run up to meet Mang, with the commandant following him at a slower trot.

"It's the brother." Mang was almost incoherent, gesticulating and pointing up the slope.

They found Andrew lying on his back, head down slope, in the middle of scattered boulders of various sizes. He was bleeding from cuts and bruises on his head, but the front of his shirt was also staining fast with blood from his chest. Paul felt light-headed, and his mind did its best to refuse to accept the reality that Andrew was dying. Then he knelt by Andrew and gave him absolution.

"Sh..." he said as Andrew, still conscious, struggled to speak. "Lie still."

Andrew found and gripped his hand.

"Paul, take my shoes. They'll fit if you wear two pairs of socks." He made an effort to smile at his own joke.

He was quiet for a short while, and then said, "Will you write to my mother?"

By then, the rest of the workforce had come up, and they stood round, numb at the death of this man whom they had come to like and respect.

The commandant turned and told them, "Back to work, all of you." And then he said to Paul, "Take all the time you want. We'll prepare a grave. Where do you want it?"

Still kneeling by Andrew, and still holding his hand, Paul tried to pray, but the words would not come. He had prayed over the dead Japanese soldier, he had prayed over the three villagers of Yang Chia Ping executed by the Japanese. He had prayed over his dead brothers at Mu Chia Chuang. Monastic rules did not encourage special friendships. But Andrew... he was different.

Mang later produced a cup of red wine, which saved Paul a crisis of conscience.

"Ask no questions," Mang said to his enquiring look.

Paul made an unleavened biscuit to use as communion wafer. That evening, Mang, the Nationalist officer and James, the lapsed Catholic, attended the Requiem Mass he said for Brother Andrew.

\*\*\*

"I heard James's confession the next day. He'd come to me of his own free will. I'm sure Andrew had something to do with it."

He sat still and silent, and Maria Chang looked at him but did not disturb him, allowing him to take his time. She was sensing the loneliness in him. Not the Cistercian solitude, but real loneliness. He was gazing across at the ruins of the Chapel, but was not seeing anything. His mind was still dwelling on the burial of Brother Andrew and the Requiem Mass. Then he pulled himself together.

"You see, Ren, the Nationalist officer, laid the explosives and lit the fuse, and they waited behind a large boulder for the explosion. When the dynamite did not go off, Ren was going to investigate. Andrew called him back and went to check himself. That's when he got it full in the chest."

He stopped again.

"Mang somehow took over Andrew's place as my assistant. I was really grateful for that, because for a few days I was totally useless.

The dam and the pump house were finished on time, and the camp was closed and the other prisoners were freed. Mang was going back to Shanghai, and he said he was going to go straight, as he didn't want to run the risk of another spell in a labour camp, or even being executed for stealing a few pence. He gave me an address and said I should look him up some day. Ren shook my hand solemnly and went off. And James. Surprisingly, he put a bunch of flowers he had picked on Andrew's grave before he, too, went off in the truck.

"A new camp was set up two miles down the valley. In fact they simply transferred everything from the camp they closed. But there was a new commandant, and I got on reasonably well with him although he wasn't as sympathetic as the other one. For a while he tried to get me involved in political discussions at these sessions, and when I refused to be drawn, he used to get angry and accuse me of all sorts of things. I thought that he was going to send me back to a real prison camp, and that scared me. But it was nothing new, actually. The community was accused of all those things, and many more. However, he did, as he had been ordered, put me in charge of improving the irrigation system, and, as before, I had my own office and certain privileges which the commandant was pragmatic enough to grant. It also meant that I made frequent visits to the village, where they treated me as an old friend, and I was able to tend Andrew's grave. You might say that I was a privileged prisoner, which under the system was quite unusual.

"Well, they kept me for months, and only released me in the amnesty before the first of October although the work was not complete. I might have come back sooner before I made my way to Peking, but I had no money. I thought of begging my way, but that meant risking arrest and further imprisonment. So I stayed around and earned some money. And so, Mrs Chang," he said, trying to sound light-hearted, "here I am."

Mrs Chang looked him over.

"You must come back with me, Father. Look, you need new

clothes, you need a proper bath and a good shave and a haircut. I know my village is two hours in the wrong direction for you, but you aren't in a hurry, are you?... Are you?"

Hong Kong was a long, long way away. Perhaps a lifetime away. There was time yet. So he helped Mrs Chang to pack up her lunch things and they set off. At the bend of the path, he looked back down towards the monastery and recalled the last time he had done so. There had been buildings, then, though not for long.

"Did you know," asked Mrs Chang, "that two hours after you were taken away that morning, a Nationalist column came in jeeps and lorries to evacuate you? The buildings were still burning, and they stayed around for an hour or so, and couldn't find anybody, and then they left."

Paul chuckled ruefully. However, history was what was, not what might have been.

"No. I didn't know." He was beginning to have a glimmer of understanding as to why James Teng had ceased to believe, at least for a while.

"By the way, they forced the villagers to help them destroy the monastery," Mrs Chang added.

They climbed steadily, along a path which he had known well in the years when, as the monastery had responded to the bishop's request to help out, he used to go to serve and say Sunday Mass at Lungchuan. In spite of the irreparable injury done to her feet, which when she was young were bound for two or three years and which therefore never became normal again, Mrs Chang's disability did not seem to have limited her range of activity. She bounded up and down mountain paths, which made a normally able-bodied, reasonably sure-footed person hesitate, with an agility that could only be described as phenomenal. The evil, unnatural custom of footbinding was eventually abandoned when the Manchu emperor was driven off the throne and China became a republic in 1911 under a forward-looking government, eager to bring China into the twentieth century. As she led the way, she told him news of her village. Several times, when she realised that she was talking to herself, for Paul had fallen behind, she stopped and waited for him.

There used to be about thirty people at Sunday Mass. More than half of this number had travelled from nearby villages, and some walked an hour each way, and not many of these stayed away because of the weather, unless the roads and paths were blocked by heavy snowfalls. There was no Gothic church with spires at Lungchuan, and the church was only a converted dwelling. The local congregation had whitewashed it and a local artist had painted a simple set of the Stations of the Cross with the figures dressed in traditional Chinese costumes, which was hung round the church and of which the villagers, even the non-Catholics, were immensely proud. The monks at Yang Chia Ping had believed that the situation was hopeful.

"Some of us were forced to testify against the Fathers during those trials, and now they feel ashamed. Some have given up altogether. Of the fourteen of us at Lungchuan, there are only eight, sometimes fewer, who still call themselves Catholics. I don't blame them too much. It's getting more and more difficult, what with all these political discussions in the evenings when everyone has to attend. Some of what they tell you sticks, you know, Father. Besides, there are people in the village who keep an eye on everybody else – these nosey snoopers! – who report everything they think is not right, according to them. And that includes prayer meetings."

· She waited for him to catch up.

"But we do meet sometimes, to say the morning prayers, or evening prayers, or sometimes a decade of the rosary."

"Don't you get reported, then?"

"Well, we are careful. And… sometimes I don't care."

"You should, you know."

Lungchuan came into view, after a series of stone steps and a path which rose gently to it, about a quarter of a mile away. Mrs Chang paused at the top of the steps.

"I hope you don't mind, Father, if I say you're my nephew from Wangshi who's brought me news of the death of my cousin. Then they'll leave us alone, you see. In spite of all the talk about there being no God or spirits, there's nothing that scares them like Death. And I'll be calling you Weishung. That's your name, isn't it? But only when there are people about."

"Call me anything you want, Mrs Chang!" Paul laughed.

"I like that laugh! It's the first time today you have really laughed. Oh, you've got to call me Number-Two-Aunt-on-my-Mother's-side… I hope you don't mind." Then she remembered to add: "Only in public."

"Yes, Number-Two-Aunt-on-my-Mother's-side."

"I don't think people will recognise you. As I said before, you're thinner, darker, and your hair's grown, and you have a little… beard? And without your monastic habit… No, they won't know you."

Also, the fact that Maria Chang's house was at the near end of the village, and that they did not have to travel the length of the main street, made things easier.

Lungchuan, lying in a shallow upland basin surrounded by what were in fact tops of mountains, was as he remembered it. The path they were on joined a road which had at one time been widened to accommodate motor traffic such as lorries, and led past houses on both sides of it to a small open space where there used to be a general store and a millinery shop which never seemed to be patronised. Some of the houses were the more modern types, with front windows overlooking the street. Others were more traditional, and all one saw was the front wall, broken only by a doorway, behind which was the courtyard leading to the house proper. The building which used to be the Catholic church was on one side of the square. The road then continued to lead out of the village. On this mid-November day, the landscape was dusted with a light covering of snow.

There were still flags everywhere, the red flag of revolution customised with yellow stars as the new national emblem, flags hoisted to celebrate the establishment of the Chinese People's Republic, as Mao Tsetung had declared it, six weeks ago, on 1 October, in honour of which he had been granted his freedom. There was one over every building, and every one of them fluttered in the stiff breeze that had risen since they left Yang Chia Ping and now blew the powdery snow around. It was an attractive sight unless one happened to be in the open in the path of that freezing wind.

The wind and the snow had kept the population indoors, and Maria Chang and Paul made it to the former's house without meeting anybody, so they did not have to make use of the fiction Maria had invented.

She stirred the brazier at one end of the family room and added more charcoal. The room, too, was as he remembered it. There was the light which came in through the courtyard window, lighting up the round marble-topped mahogany dining table which stood in the centre of the room with barrel stools of the same material and design nestling underneath, and the dark mahogany chairs and side tables with legs shaped like bamboo stalks that lined the walls. These were hung with scrolls of calligraphy and watercolour paintings, and one wall was devoted to family photographs. The large one in the centre of the group was obviously of her husband. Paul had never known him, for by the time he first met Maria she was already a widow. Another one was a wedding photograph, with the groom stiff in winged collar and tails and the bride not less stiff in a white lace wedding dress: Mrs Chang was a lot younger then. The other photographs were of their children at various stages of their development, and one of them showed a young man in mortar board and academic gown holding a beribboned scroll. It was almost like his own graduation photograph. And in the position of honour, between two vertical scrolls of calligraphy, was a framed picture of the Sacred Heart above a small shelf – one might call it an altar – on which was a red sanctuary lamp with its white candle burning in front of it. And underneath were two priedieux, on one of which Mrs Chang had placed her veil, the missal and the rosary.

Paul was left in the room while Mrs Chang busied herself in another part of the house.

"I'll be a little while," she said, "so do make yourself at home. You know the place: you've been here before." And indeed he had been, quite frequently, as she always invited him to lunch after Sunday Mass.

"What's happened to Mei?" he asked.

Mei was an orphan whom Mrs Chang had brought up from about the age of seven when her parents were killed by a mine planted by retreating Chinese troops in the first year of the war. She used to help Mrs Chang with the housework, and Paul had given her lessons in the 3Rs after the Sunday lunch.

Mrs Chang answered from the other room. Her voiced stayed steadfastly neutral.

"She decided to join the Communist Youth about a year ago. I believe she's in Peking still celebrating the founding of the People's Republic."

He thought he should say Vespers, for the evening was bound to be busy and he would have little time for himself. So he sat himself in a chair opposite the homemade altar, shut his eyes, and began.

*"Deus, in adjutorium meum intende... O God, come to my aid..."*

Mrs Chang returned when he was halfway through Psalm 110, but when she realised what he was doing she quietly retreated before he was aware of her presence. She returned again ten minutes later, when he had finished, with a folded bedsheet, a hair clipper and some shears.

"I'm giving you a haircut," she announced, and would not take no for an answer. "Besides," she said, "with practically everybody wearing a crew cut these days, your long hair will make you stand out. And your hair needs washing, too. You monks aren't too particular about hairstyles, I hope! I used to cut my children's hair, and I'm afraid I have only one style."

She wasn't a bad barber, he decided later, as he looked at himself in the bathroom mirror while shaving with her husband's old razor. It was not an easy task, the mirror repeatedly misting over because of the steaming hot bath which she had prepared for him. On a chair were laid out some of Mr Chang's old clothes. As an alternative, there were her son's more modern versions of the same. He chose the latter, as being less conspicuous. To be exact, they would not make him stand out. There was also a robust pair of shoes to replace the ones he had inherited from Brother Andrew, which were entering the last stages of their useful existence.

He hadn't had such luxury since before he entered Yang Chia Ping. He'd better not get used to it! But he now felt clean, and perhaps more human again. He was tempted to keep Brother Andrew's shoes as a memento.

"That's not the Cistercian way," he reminded himself. He dropped them into the waste bin, but he nearly went back to retrieve them.

Mrs Chang looked at his new appearance with approval. Over dinner she said, "Some of us meet on a Sunday evening to say the evening prayers. The number varies, as I said before, but there won't be more than six, usually. I think everyone in the village knows we meet, but so far nobody's interfered. We don't know how long we can carry on doing it. Someday, one of these snoopers is going to make a big thing out of it, and we'll have to stop..."

Paul was aware of what she did not say. "And some of us will be going to prison." In particular Mrs Chang. There was also the very real and more immediate danger from wolves which sometimes prowled the village streets and lanes in winter.

"You don't have to meet them. In fact, they don't know you're here."

Father Abbot had once reminded them, when the situation had become difficult during the fighting and some of the community were inclined to be somewhat reckless, "Everyone of you must be careful of your personal safety at all times, because you are valuable, except when it involves the cure of souls, in which case, obviously, your personal safety does not come into the question."

If these people were taking risks for the love of God, for it could be nothing else, how could he do any less? "If you can make some bread without yeast, and some grape wine, red or white," he said, "I'll say Mass for them."

"But you said Mass already today." There were only two days in the year when a priest said more than one Mass. One was Christmas, and the other was All Souls' Day.

"These are extraordinary times, Mrs Chang. Yes, I'll say Mass, if they want me to. And you can forget the Eucharistic fast, too. It doesn't apply today."

Mrs Chang was pleased. "And I'll have been to Mass twice today, and it's not Christmas yet, or All Souls!"

Then she beamed at him. "I've a little surprise for you. Wait." She left the table in the middle of the meal, but returned in a few minutes, carrying a basket. "I nearly forgot."

She put two bottles of communion wine on the table, and a tin box which was full of the familiar small white wafers as well as several large ones which priests used for saying Mass.

"I retrieved these from our church after I came home from your trial in the Chapel. I knew they were going to close it down after they'd taken you all away. You can still use them, can you not?"

The wine might be sour by now, and the stale wafers must be rock hard. "Of course I can!"

"And something more." Mrs Chang brought out a small Latin missal which he used to carry in his field Mass kit.

"I remember forgetting to pack it the last time I said Mass here."

Mrs Chang sighed. "It wasn't so long ago. How the world's changed."

Practically on the dot of seven Paul heard the front gate creak as it opened for someone to come in – on Sunday evenings, Paul learned,

Mrs Chang never locked it until her last guest was leaving – and footsteps crossed the courtyard to the door. This, too, was unlocked. Mrs Chang rose to greet her guest.

"Mr Yuan. Come and meet an old friend."

Mrs Chang had made Paul sit in the shadow. "Give them a pleasant surprise," she had said.

"Recognise him?" Mrs Chang asked Mr Yuan.

The recognition was immediate. "You look thinner, and sunburned, but it's you, Father Liang." He then became serious. "I'm glad you've survived."

Mrs Chang then told him how she had met Paul that morning. "I told you that you should come down to the monastery with me today," she added. "It's got to be a lucky day, the thirteenth!"

Paul, too, remembered Mr Yuan. The only change in him was that now he was wearing the new, universal uniform of blue jacket and trousers, and he was carrying a cloth cap in his hand. Gone, it appeared, was the long gown he used to wear to Mass in the old days. Mr Yuan sensed his scrutiny.

"You get picked out if you don't wear this," he said, "and some eager youngster will report you for being a reactionary. We're supposed to be all the same now. Dressed the same, behave the same, think the same. One big happy family."

"Come, Mr Yuan, stop being so bitter now." Mrs Chang was on the point of offering him a cup of tea when she suddenly remembered. She turned to Paul. "Is this all right?"

"Perhaps we could wait till afterwards," he suggested.

"Father Liang is going to say Mass for us," Mrs Chang explained.

"This is marvellous! We haven't had a Mass since you were… er… taken away."

The outer gate creaked again, and a young couple came through the front door, Vincent and Teresa, whom he had received into the Church barely three years ago. And in Teresa's arms, well wrapped against the cold, was a child. Both, like Mr Yuan, were in the same egalitarian uniform, which, however, did not diminish Teresa's good looks, though Paul noted that she now had straight hair when it used to be curled.

"Father Liang!" They would have fallen on their knees to him to kiss his hand if he had not stopped them.

"No, please, no! I'm still flesh and blood, and, as Mrs Chang says, bones!"

Teresa indicated the child in her arms.

"Father, you'll have to baptise him properly, now that you are here. We did that ourselves when he was born. We called him Paul."

And forthwith, Paul baptised his namesake with water from the urn in the kitchen, just in case it had not been properly done by his parents.

"*Ego te baptizo, Paule, in nomine Patris, et Filii, et Spiritus Sancti... I baptise thee, Paul...*"

"Father Liang is going to say Mass, and so I'm not giving you tea now."

"I should have brought my missal and my veil!" said Teresa.

There was only one other arrival after that, a young man whom he had not met before. He introduced himself. "I am a Catholic, but I also work at Party Headquarters in the village."

There was a distinctive pause. Then Mr Yuan asked, "Would you hear my confession before Mass? I haven't been to confession for more than two years."

"Of course. May I use the kitchen?"

And squatting on a low kitchen stool, he heard their confessions, his penitents kneeling on the hard stone floor, and he humbly gave each of them absolution.

Afterwards he met them back in the front room. Mr Yuan, who had been an altar server in his youth, before Paul even dreamed that he might become a Catholic, made the necessary preparations. Instead of the broken cups and saucers he had used for the Mass in the morning, Mrs Chang had contributed some of her best crockery, and the marble-topped dining table became the altar.

He looked at his small congregation as they, heads bowed in concentration, made their own internal preparation for Mass. And he thought: *Lord, it is good for us to be here...* Maybe I should stay and help. He had worked out from the missal what Sunday after Pentecost it was. This find was a treasure, but perhaps he ought to leave it with Mrs Chang, for whoever might come along after him? Then he made a real effort to concentrate.

So he said the Mass of the Twenty-third Sunday after Pentecost, the dark room lit only by a pair of candles on the altar and a lone paraffin lamp. The communion wine had turned really sour, but only he knew that. He was touched by the devotion with which they all received Communion: Mrs Chang with bliss on her kind features (Paul, having assured her that it was all right for her to receive a second time that day, was himself was by no means sure); tears coursing down Mr Yuan's weathered face; Vincent and Teresa radiant and content. And the young Party worker, too, received the sacred Host.

Normally, Mrs Chang had told him, they would not linger long after the evening prayers or the rosary, ending with an invocation on behalf of absent brothers, which reminded Paul of the similar monastic last prayer for *fratribus absentibus*, absent brethren. There should have been another couple present, but the husband had become ill and the wife had not wished to leave him on his own. Tonight the company lingered, unwilling to end this special occasion. They were anxious to learn news of the rest of the community, for though Mu Chia Chuang was not many miles away as the crow flies, there seemed to have been a news blackout, and apart from knowing that something like fifteen or twenty of the young monks had been released and had been making for Peking, they could only guess at their fate. Mr Yuan, ever sensitive to other people's feelings, however, resolutely steered the conversation away from what he knew must be an extremely painful topic for their honoured guest.

After a little while, Mrs Chang left the room to busy herself in the kitchen. She returned with a tray on which were bowls of steaming rice porridge and hot steamed bread.

"Come," she said. "Let us celebrate Father Liang's return to us today!"

"You know," Vincent said, "this is like Christmas! And special steamed bread with fillings!"

And indeed it was, for people used to go home after Midnight Mass to celebrate with a meal of rice porridge and sweets and cakes, a custom they probably learned from the White Russians who came to live among them after the October Revolution. And tonight, outside, snow gently fell.

"Yes," concurred Teresa, nursing young Paul in a corner of the room, but very much a part of the conversation. "It feels like Christmas."

There was a long moment of quiet while they tackled their food. Then Mr Yuan broke the silence.

"What are your plans, Father?"

Paul looked round the circle of eager faces and hesitated.

"I wish you could stay here, Father," said Vincent.

"That's thoughtless, Vincent," Mr Yuan said sharply. "Let Father Liang talk."

"Yes. I realise that. I'm sorry."

Paul explained carefully. "It is very possible that a number of the monks who survived from both Yang Chia Ping and Our Lady of Joy are now in Hong Kong. I want to make my way there to join this combined community."

"But it's such a long way!" said Teresa.

Paul nodded. He was not exactly sure how many thousand miles away.

"I was on my way to Peking when I decided to make a detour to see Yang Chia Ping. Do you remember Dr Kung, who used to come up from Peking twice a year to give us our medical check-up?"

Everyone knew Dr Kung. He used to drive this great ambulance of a car, even during the period of the Japanese occupation, taking patients who needed special treatment into Peking, and bringing them home again. Twice a year, the sick of the area would converge on the Cistercian monastery, where he spent more time treating the sick from the surrounding villages than examining the health of the monks.

"I wrote to him after I was released, and he said," Paul read from the letter he had taken from his rucksack, "'I shall be happy and honoured to have you stay with us if you are able to make it to Peking.' I was hoping, when I was in Peking, to explore the possibility of taking a passage on a boat to Hong Kong."

He found Mr Yuan looking hard at him.

"Excuse me, Father. You keep using the past tense about your plans. Have you got new ones now?"

Paul gathered himself together before he spoke.

"I think perhaps I ought to stay around here."

Vincent's face lit up. Teresa's did too, but she seemed to see beyond the immediate situation. Mrs Chang frowned, and Mr Yuan shook his head.

"That, Father," he said, "is not a good idea."

"Why?" This was from Vincent.

"Look. Being a Catholic priest is almost a criminal offence in China now. Father Liang will have at least another long spell in some labour or punishment camp if he is caught saying Mass or doing his priestly duties. He might perhaps survive longer in a city like Peking or Tientsin, but in our little mountain villages, where everyone knows everyone else, there is no hiding place. What if some nosey informer asks to meet Mrs Chang's nephew from... Peking? And how many of us have a large enough house to accommodate his own family and Father Liang as well? And it's only a matter of time before – Mrs Chang, excuse me for saying this, but I'm only being realistic – before even dwellings of modest size like this one are taken over for housing three, four families. You may not think so, but this house no longer belongs to Mrs Chang. 'The People' own it now. In Russia, I read somewhere, you'd be lucky to be able to keep a room to yourself. Well, it's not fair to Father Liang."

The rest said nothing. Vincent nodded vigorously to compensate for his previous thoughtlessness.

Mr Yuan looked at Paul and spoke again, attempting to sound hopeful.

"We'll make out somehow, Father. Don't worry about us too much. Maybe another priest will come along one day." He turned to the rest. "Isn't that right?"

They murmured an agreement which they scarcely felt.

*I will not leave you orphans...*

"So," asked Teresa, "what are your plans now? Are you still heading for Peking?"

"Not for another day," said Mrs Chang firmly. "You may not know it, but Father has walked seven days, living on a crust of bread, to get to Yang Chia Ping, and he needs rest as well as a couple of decent meals. You must stay another day. Go the day after tomorrow, or even the day after that."

"You're not walking to Peking, are you?" Mr Yuan asked. And when Paul hesitated, he said, "You are not!"

"I'm trying to save what money I have for a passage on a boat," Paul explained.

The young Party worker spoke for the first time that evening. "I can get you a free pass on the railway into Peking if you would let me have your full name in Chinese. I'll bring it here tomorrow morning. I'm sorry, but I have no authority to take you any further. And... I've got to go now: I've got to be in by ten. Goodnight."

"Can we trust him?" Vincent asked when he had gone.

"He's been stationed in the village since March, and he's always come to these meetings," said Mrs Chang. "I don't know who told him, and I still don't know his name. Nobody knows anything about him, and he never says much, but so far he's been all right."

"He probably can come in very useful, like tonight," Mr Yuan said.

"Can we come again tomorrow night?" Teresa asked, looking from Mrs Chang to Paul.

Mrs Chang seemed to want him to decide. So he said, "Fine, if it's all right with Mrs Chang." He knew they were all taking a risk. But, he, too, was looking forward to it.

# FIVE

Paul looked at the free pass again and wondered at the unfathomable ways of Providence. This document stated quite without equivocation that Liang Weishung was an official messenger of Party Headquarters at Lungchuan and District, and that the railway authorities were requested to provide the aforesaid person a free ticket to Peking as the aforesaid person was on official business for the aforesaid Branch Office of the Party. The impression which one gleaned from the document was that he had been a long-term, loyal and faithful member of the Party. In order to substantiate the claims made in the document, two letters stamped with the Party emblem had come, with the travel pass, to Mrs Chang's house, with the request that they should be delivered to Party HQ in Peking. So he was now employed by the Party, more so than when he had stayed on after discharge from prison and worked as clerical assistant to the commandant. Yes, the relationship between the two men had thawed towards the latter part of his imprisonment.

He stowed all three documents away carefully, in a separate pocket from his other, personal, documents: his identity paper, his degree diploma, and his discharge paper. The last described him, with as much fiction as Mrs Chang's role for him as her nephew and a great deal more hope, as a reformed and re-educated character, no longer addicted to unpatriotic and erroneous opinions. The official fiction was, he knew very well, a necessary part of his release, for it was totally unthinkable that the State would let back into society a still dangerous criminal and traitor, especially one who had been a Catholic monk and a priest. However, he also realised that, if he were to be discovered as a recidivist, his punishment would be that much more severe.

He shouldered his rucksack and met Mrs Chang in her front room. She had wanted to give him one of her son's old suitcases, but he preferred his battered and threadbare bag. He had never liked carrying cases, and the shoulder-slung rucksack or knapsack suited him best if there was any long-distance walking to do. However, he did not expect to do a great deal of it today. With Mrs Chang were Mr Yuan, Vincent and Teresa, and young Paul. There was also Mr Huang from the next village, about a mile away, who had come on the second night of Paul's stay at Lungchuan. They had abandoned all caution to come to see him off. He could see that they were trying hard to hide their distress and disappointment, and he felt he was deserting them. He didn't know what to say. But the others solved the dilemma by all going down on their knees. He blessed each one, individually, making the sign of the Cross on their foreheads, Mr Huang, Mr Yuan, Teresa, Vincent and Paul, and courageous Mrs Chang, who had nearly died defending him.

Maria checked that he had the lunch and the thermos flask of hot tea she had prepared for his journey. The rucksack was now fuller and bulkier than when he arrived; he was carrying an extra change of clothing. He had decided to take only half the communion wafers, and only the opened bottle of communion wine, but in a rice wine bottle. He had the St Bede, and he had also decided to keep the Latin missal. They were all in his rucksack now.

Then he was on his way. He did not return through Yang Chia Ping, for there was no need for him to do that. He went through the village, past the square and the old Catholic church – or, to be up to date, the Party HQ. The road then led him, after a long, twisting descent, to a railway station from where he caught the train for Peking. It was an all-stations slow train, on a line which had been built originally, eighty years before, to carry supplies and building materials to the mountain areas and bring country produce to the capital city's markets and canning factories. But it had always carried passengers too, in basic carriages with few frills or luxuries. Hardy country people did not need to travel above third class, some bureaucrat seemed to have decreed.

However, he soon discovered, there was 'third class' and there was 'third class'. On the strength of his official pass, he was put into a carriage meant to carry only fifteen or so people, the only access to which was through the doors from station platforms. On the doors of this carriage was emblazoned the warning 'Private' in large characters to deter other would-be third-class passengers from joining these third-class passengers. The less privileged scarcely had time to pile into the other three carriages before the engine hooted, and the whole train juddered and began to slide away from the short station platform. At the beginning, the train travelled in long loops along the contours of the mountains, stopping at every designated station to pick up or disgorge passengers with their suitcases and bags, basketfuls of chickens and vegetables, but eventually, some time in the afternoon, it descended to the plains north of Peking, where it chugged contentedly towards its destination. If there was constant activity and change in the other carriages, there did not seem to be any Party member or official travelling today, and Paul had his carriage to himself throughout the journey, which suited him very well indeed.

The train drew into Peking station just before it got dark. He was pointed in the direction of Party Headquarters by a person in uniform, and he soon discharged his obligation to the Party. In fact, he had arrived after the office was closed, so he dropped the letters through the letter box. Then he made his way to the address which Mrs Chang had given him.

"I'm not sure this is right," she had said, "but it's all I was given."

***

Dr Kung pressed the bell on his desk to tell his receptionist-cum-nurse that he was ready for his next patient. There was a soft knock and the door opened. Miss Hsueh ushered in a well-dressed old lady on crutches, who, the doctor guessed, had fallen over in the icy conditions out on the streets today. She settled the patient in the chair by the side of his desk, putting a couple of cushions round her to make her comfortable, and lifted a bandaged foot onto a footstool before turning to leave the surgery.

"Thank you, Miss Hsueh," he said. Thank heavens, he breathed silently, that they hadn't forced nurses into the universal blue jacket-and-trousers outfit which he was wearing under his white coat.

He was starting to undo the bandage on his ancient patient's right foot when there was another knock on the door. He looked up, expecting Miss Hsueh again to enter the room, when he realised that the knock had been on the other door, the one which connected the surgery to the private section of his house. The knock was repeated, a little louder, and the handle turned. The door opened a fraction and his wife, without looking into the room, spoke through the slit.

"The guest has arrived," she said. "Can you come through for just a minute between patients?"

"Yes. When I've finished with Mrs Wen."

He then turned his attention back to the elderly lady who was also an old private patient. "How did you get here, Mrs Wen?"

"I came with my son. He's outside." This patient only lived round the corner.

Dr Kung used to work in the city's General Hospital in the morning and run his own surgery in the afternoon. In the last year or so, the authorities had directed him to work full time at the city hospital. Three times a week, however, he still ran his private surgery at home, but only for patients who lived in the same district and who found it hard to get to the hospital in the first instance. He took very good care not to ask his patients to pay for his services. If they offered a remuneration, it was another matter.

Mrs Wen tensed when he touched the foot, but relaxed when

she discovered his touch was gentle as well as sure. After a couple of minutes, he released the foot and stood up to tell her the result.

"There's no real injury, Mrs Wen. I believe you sprained it when you fell, but fortunately no bones were broken. Keep it comfortable, and don't walk on it for a few days and you should be all right then. Take an aspirin if the pain keeps you awake. And, please, don't wear your high heels until the weather gets better."

"They are my only shoes," said the lady. Before old age, and the New Order, finally overtook her, Dr Kung recalled, she used to be known for her good looks and her elegance. Surprisingly, her feet did not seem to have been bound. "I don't have to have… ointments and things?"

"There's no need, Mrs Wen." And, he thought, even if there's need, I wouldn't know where I can get any. He pressed the bell and Miss Hsueh returned to help Mrs Wen out. Through the half-open door he caught a glimpse of her businessman son who had exchanged his American-made suit and homburg for a blue cotton padded jacket and cloth cap. As far as the doctor knew, he still ran his business, in partnership now with his workers.

It's perhaps not a bad thing, he thought.

"Mrs Wen was the last patient," Miss Hsueh told him. "But the surgery still has half an hour to run."

"I'm closing now," he said. "You may as well go early."

To the guest who was waiting for him in his sitting room, there could not have been a greater contrast in style between this and the Mrs Chang's traditionally furnished front room. There were still calligraphic and watercolour scrolls on the walls, but there were also Monet's *Water Lilies* and Cezanne's *Mont St Victoire*, and he knew they were originals. Along one wall was an upright piano with a pile of music on top – Mrs Kung was regarded as quite an accomplished amateur performer – and a gramophone on a side table next to it. There was a mahogany coffee table in the space created by a leather sitting-room suite. The guest, with a half-empty teacup in his hand

and trying to hold a conversation with Mrs Kung, was balancing on the soft, unstable edge of one of the two single chairs, aware that if he was not careful he could topple back and be forever lost unless someone came to his rescue.

Paul stood up when Dr Kung entered the room and held out his hand. The two men, who had known each other for a long time, greeted each other warmly.

"Thank you, Matthew, and Susannah, for letting me stay."

Matthew stood back to take a good look at the monk in mufti. Paul laughed.

"Everybody does that to me these days," he said. "Standing back and looking at me. I might have been a ghost from the next world. Well, I'm still flesh and bones."

"A lot more bones and a lot less flesh than when I saw you last, nearly three years ago. And you know, Paul, people could well take you as a ghost from the next world, and who can blame them! We thought you must have died from ill-treatment and hard labour, and guess what a pleasant surprise it was to receive a letter from you a month, five weeks ago? You seem to be the last one to have survived."

"I was pretty desperate," said Paul, "to talk to somebody, and the only one I knew in Peking, in North China, who could help me was you."

"Paul was telling me about the dam-building at Shang Chuan… and about Brother Andrew," said Susannah.

Matthew became sober. "How was it there? You didn't say very much in the letter."

Paul told him all, and concluded, "It wasn't bad. I was lucky to be in a responsible position, and in that camp we were reasonably well treated. It's just unfortunate about Andrew. But any place had to be better than Mu Chia Chuang."

Matthew had heard about Mu Chia Chuang from the monks who had survived, and they all had their own stories to tell. He realised that Paul, like the others, was reluctant to talk about his experiences, and so, considerately, he did not press him for his own version.

"Susannah was telling me about the phone call you had from Lungchuan," Paul said after a pause. "I'm sorry it gave you a fright, Susannah. Actually, I didn't know the man was going to phone. And I wonder how he got on to you."

"I was absolutely petrified when the caller said he was from Communist Party Headquarters. What do they want, I thought. We hadn't done anything!"

"Well, that's no excuse." Matthew laughed mirthlessly. "In any case, all that the man wanted to say was that you were on your way, and should be with us in the evening. Then he rang off. But that was three days ago."

"Who's this man?" Susannah asked.

"An unusual character." Paul told them how they had met. "I still think it's Providence. I'm sorry I arrived a couple of days late. I was at the dairy the last couple of days."

The dairy farm housed a remnant of the community of Our Lady of Consolation, of which Matthew was now the medical adviser. The young monks who had been released from Mu Chia Chuang, and who were quite ready to risk their lives to stay with the reduced community, had to be sent away as the resources of the farm were insufficient to support them, and they, presumably, had made their way back to their home towns and villages.

"If we are not mistaken," Paul was told, "they have formed small communities of five or six in their own home areas. The monastery is not dead."

The four priests and two lay brothers who remained were all elderly, and these had elected not to go with the monks of Our Lady of Joy to Hong Kong and were now living a life of great poverty, trying to survive on the meagre proceeds of the farm. They had welcomed Paul with joy, and Paul felt he was home again, and for two days he relived his community life. These days, they had had to give up chanting the Office, so as not to arouse suspicion, and the Office was said instead. However, the monks had kept one chant, the *Salve Regina*, which all monks sang when they went to bed. A sort of 'good night' to Our Lady.

The Cistercians from both Our Lady of Consolation and Our Lady of Joy were helped on their arrival in Peking by the Marist Brothers who lodged them at their college. They later found a dairy farm on the edge of the city and lived under Dom Paulinus Li as prior. Father Paulinus had been planning to take his own people to a new refuge in Szechuan in the mountains of south-western China, reckoning that if the Chinese Nationalists had been able to defy the Japanese from the mountains there, they should be able to do the same to the Communists. But events overtook his plans and proved him wrong. The rapid Nationalists collapse and the overwhelming Communist victories obliged him to consider plans for a home in Hong Kong, for even offshore Formosa (or Taiwan nowadays), the refuge of the Nationalists, might only provide very temporary safety. Father Alexis's instinct, or foresight, had been proved right after all, Paul thought. Father Paulinus now included those from Yang Chia Ping in his plans.

Then the twenty young survivors of Our Lady of Joy in Peking departed, but those from the older monastery elected to remain. Now, one and all, they urged Paul to accept Father Paulinus's invitation to join his new community in Hong Kong.

"We didn't go because we're all too old. But you are still young."

"I'll have to get there first," Paul had said. "And it's..."

"Don't tell us it's too far. It may be true for us, but not for you! Go to Dr Kung and ask his advice as to the best way to get there."

\*\*\*

"Really, they should have gone with Dom Paulinus," said Matthew. "But you can't force people... not even monks. Especially not monks," he added with a laugh.

"Now tell me how it has been with you under the new regime,"

Paul said.

Matthew indicated his clothes.

"As you can see, we all dress differently. Susannah would not dare go out dressed like she is now, in the updated traditional style. No, there's no law about it. In fact, we're supposed to have more freedom than when the Nationalists ruled the country. In any case, the government hopes, I'm sure, that clothes are the outward sign of an inward grace, as we say in our catechism. We've been all right, so far. Fortunately our children are off our hands, and they are both settled with good jobs in America, so that's one less worry. They have, in fact, been trying to persuade us to join them – but honestly, I'm not at all sure I want to go…"

The long pause at the end told Paul the stress that Matthew was subject to. Paul hoped that his friend, whom he had met in his first year at the monastery when the doctor made his six-monthly visit to check the health of the monks, would make the right decision. And Susannah… he could see, and feel, her unhappiness, her worry about the uncertainties of their life. Paul and Matthew also shared another past: they were both alumni of Peking University, although the doctor was the senior by many years. Several times he had accompanied fellow monks to Peking for specialist treatment, and he had stayed with Matthew and Susannah overnight on these occasions and had come to be friends with the family. He had also come to understand Matthew very well, better than Matthew himself realised, and he knew that the doctor was, in spite his long training abroad and his cosmopolitanism and the universality and catholicity of his tastes, proudly Chinese. But this pride appeared now to be somewhat shaken.

And the chalice that Matthew had given Paul at his ordination. Paul wondered who had it now.

"I wish we had gone," Susannah said quietly. "Paul doesn't know what happened in the summer."

Matthew looked a little reluctant.

"What happened?" Paul prompted. "Was it that you had to work full time at the hospital?"

"No," said Susannah. "Tell him, Matthew."

"When I saw what was happening to some of my colleagues, I knew my turn would come sooner or later," Matthew said sombrely, eyes cast down, sitting with his elbows on his knees and rather nervously rubbing his hands together. "Then on the twenty-fifth of June, they came for me at the hospital. They must have spent a lot of time staging the trial. But the worse thing was that I could not let Susannah know what was happening to me."

It took place, as the others had done, in the hospital dining room. The only charge the prosecution brought was that he had collaborated with the enemy during the War. The only evidence they could produce was that he had been able to continue driving his big car around. Where did he get petrol for the car? How did he get petrol for this thirsty car if he had not sold his soul and his country? Various witnesses testified to his visiting Japanese Military HQ.

The prosecution failed to make the accusation stick, and Matthew was released at the end of the long, gruelling and frightening day with a dark warning that he had better watch his step. How ironic, Paul thought. Without his constant badgering at the occupying forces, Matthew would not have been able to run his car, which he used as an ambulance, and a number of patients would probably have died because of a reduced hospital ambulance service.

"I'm glad you came through," Paul said. But Matthew was also a marked man.

"It's late now," Matthew said after a short silence. "We'll talk some more tomorrow night. I start work early in the morning, but there's no evening surgery tomorrow. By the way, when I get home in the afternoon, I shall give you a physical. Then you'll know what shape you're really in. And in the meantime, why don't you take a look around the city tomorrow, and see how much of it you can recognise?"

And Paul found the idea strange that after nearly two years of quite intensive physical labour and a week's hard journeying, there should be days when he had little to do! But, he knew, too, that although he had always been fit, he was more tired than he had originally thought.

He left the house with Matthew the next morning. The doctor was on his bicycle, and Paul was given one which had belonged to his son. In spite of his reputation, Matthew spent more time on two wheels than on four. The doctor and the monk went in different directions. Paul headed first for Tienanmen Square. Before they parted, however, Matthew said, "One thing good about this government is that it's made Peking the capital of the country again! And by the way, take this old watch of mine: you'll need it to keep the time. And please keep it – I no longer need it."

After a short distance, Paul found himself in the middle of the morning rush-hour traffic, most of it heading roughly in his direction. His control of his machine was at first somewhat rusty and uncertain, but the old skill and familiarity soon returned. He alighted at the end of one of the boulevards which led into the large square while most of the other cyclists swept on to their different destinations. This ancient, imperial square was already full of people – sightseers, it seemed to Paul – who had missed the Great Day on 1 October when the Great Leader proclaimed his new dynasty. There were an extraordinary number of men and women in uniform – not just the egalitarian blue suits, but military and paramilitary uniforms. There were also large parties of schoolchildren, most of whom wore the red neckscarves which showed that they belonged to one of the many Communist Youth movements. And then there were just ordinary people, some in family groups. They had come to wonder at, to participate in and to savour, although belatedly, this Great Occasion, this celebration of new freedoms, and the Liberation of a People from oppression and foreign encroachments in their territories and their affairs. It's a pity, Paul thought, that in the exercise of these freedoms those in power had decided to withhold them from a lot of innocent people. And to shed their blood.

It was not just little provincial villages like Lungchuan that refused to take down the new National Day displays. It was the same, even more so, in the capital city. The multi-coloured flags and buntings, blood red, celestial blue and Chinese yellow, were still there, in much greater profusion than in Lungchuan, and draped over the battlements of the great gatehouse was the pronouncement itself, in large gold characters on the crimson banner. Paul made a slow circuit of the vast square. He had come in an attempt to understand and to see how, and if, it related to his own experiences. He could not deny the apparent joy and hope which he saw on most faces, unless one belonged to the wrong set; and the system also in fact, though not in theory, denied everything he believed in and stood for.

He cycled across the city along familiar roads to the university. Nothing external had changed. The old schools buildings were there, and the dormitories or residential halls. Somebody else was occupying his old room, not that it mattered who. The students seemed to be ardent supporters of the new regime, and there were banners to proclaim their allegiance, in addition to the uniformity of dress. But, from what Matthew told him, in spite of the near-normal appearance, Peking was scarcely a university anymore. Gone were the arts, in which ideas germinated and grew and threatened the State. The only faculties permitted to survive were those which promised benefits to the New Order: medicine, for example, and his old school, engineering. Of course there would be no visiting professors from abroad, no one like old Hasselbach or Stephen Mellor, the Englishman who was Visiting Professor in Gynaecology, while Paul was up. If there were foreigners about the capital city, they would be either embassy personnel, reporters for foreign newspapers or sympathisers of the regime keen to sell China's New Order to their own countrymen. He also wondered briefly where Margaret was. He couldn't even remember her family name without an effort.

Siu. That was it. Interesting, that his heart still missed a beat when he thought of her.

The Jesuit Chaplaincy was now a school, and the Marist Brothers' college which had given his brothers shelter was now some sort of youth training place. The Franciscan convent, too, had been taken over, and there was an armed sentry outside its gates. So it must have become another government building. Not many buildings, he thought wryly, had actually been turned into apartments for the people, many of whom still lived in crowded conditions in the less salubrious areas of the city. The Catholic Cathedral, to his surprise, was still open, and as he remembered it. The sanctuary lamp still burned in front of the altar in the dim, cool baroque interior, lit by stained-glass windows which had sustained no damage that he could see. Cardinal Tien, Archbishop of Peking, an almost unknown prelate who to many people's surprise had been chosen by the Pope as China's first Prince of the Church, was in exile. But there was a bishop in his place, and there were notices for Sunday Masses and marriage banns. The Catholic Church in China was obviously not defunct. What he knew of the Church in European countries under Communist control provided the answer. Matthew could tell him if he was right in his conjecture. In the meantime, he knelt in a pew and said a prayer. It was the same Lord who dwelt in the Tabernacle.

He chose a route back to Matthew's house which took him past the old business centre of town. The shopping areas were almost entirely deserted, although some people did stop to look, but there did not seem to be much in the way of merchandise in the shop windows. The old names had all but disappeared. However, Paul had not come to assess the retail industry. What he looked for was more personal to his own requirements: shipping line offices and travel agencies. Again, the international names had gone, although China Cargoes was still open, and the China Steamship Company. Both operated shipping between home ports. There did not seem to be anything which ran to Hong Kong even though it was also on the

South China coast. He was reluctant to ask at the desk. A request for information for foreign travel might perhaps draw attention to himself. After his experiences in the last couple of years, Paul realised he was probably becoming paranoid about the new regime. He was not at all sure if someone on the counter might not in fact be attached to the Office of Internal Security.

Matthew asked Paul that afternoon while he was giving him a comprehensive physical examination whether he had had found Peking much changed from what he had known. Paul took the opportunity to ask him about the Cathedral.

"That was closed down for a while, you know. In fact, most of the churches, Catholic and Protestant, were closed, or at least left without priests or ministers: so much for freedom of religion. Some priests were placed under house arrest but most were in prison. Cardinal Tien managed to stay one step ahead and escaped to America. But recently, the government possibly realised that Christianity wasn't something they could exterminate easily, and there is a rumour that they began to negotiate with some of the clergy. Now this is only hearsay, I reckon, but some priests were returned to their parishes after promising that they would co-operate with the government, that they would not attempt to proselytise... and that they repudiated Papal authority."

Matthew was silent for a while before continuing.

"I went to Mass a couple of times, almost out of curiosity. I was also anxious to find out if anything was really different. But it wasn't, apart from not mentioning the Pope. Frankly, I don't know what to think."

"A schism is developing, I believe," Paul said. "It will tear the Catholic community in two."

Then Matthew concentrated on his work.

"You're fit, Paul," he said at the end of the lengthy examination.

There was more talk over dinner, which Susannah, now without maid or cook, had produced herself, as she had done the night before. Again she apologised. "It's only something simple, Paul." She seemed to be genuinely pleased when he told her she should not be apologetic, and that the food was as good as any he had eaten. He was nearly going to say that anything was better than stale, rock-hard steamed bread, but he realised it would be the wrong comment to make, and bit the remark back.

"So, how do you plan to get to Hong Kong, Paul?" Matthew asked later as they sipped their tea in the sitting room.

"It would be ideal to be able to take a boat all the way to Hong Kong," he said.

Alternatively, he could take a berth on a boat headed for Shanghai or Amoy or any place on the coast, and then do the rest of the journey on land. The chief – in actual fact, the only – obstacle was the cost of the journey, but he was hoping to get some sort of job either in Peking or in Tientsin to make sufficient money for the passage.

"Going on a ship may in fact work out to be cheaper than going overland, as I won't need to worry about buying food."

Or, he could work his way on board a ship in any capacity, from stoker to steward or whatever. This would have been a perfect solution, as he would be travelling and earning money for the next stage of the journey at the same time.

"Don't you need an exit permit under this government?" asked Susannah.

"No, Paul doesn't, at least for the time being," Matthew said. "There have never been travel restrictions to Hong Kong, and under the terms of the 1898 treaty there are no border barriers for travel either way, and so he is free to enter Hong Kong, unless there are new developments we don't yet know about."

"But with hundreds or thousands of people flocking there now," Paul said, "is there not a likelihood of Hong Kong applying some sort of entry restrictions, Matthew?"

"They could be thinking about doing it, but so far as far as I know, entry's still free. Don't forget, Hong Kong is obliged to keep its border open."

"True. My friends who went to study in Hong Kong never spoke about permits and visas." Margaret used to talk about going to Hong Kong as though she was going shopping in the next town. "Actually, I went to make sure this afternoon."

If he had thought of it, he should have gone to the British Embassy that morning before he went sightseeing, but fortunately it was still only early afternoon. He'd had to wait a while, for there were others before him, most of them anxious that when they got to the border they might be turned back. Eventually he got to the head of the queue. He explained who he was to the rather bored-looking Englishman on the counter, what he had been doing in the last two years, and backed up his statement with his identity papers and his release document. The man sat up: not many people spoke to him in French in Peking.

"I want to join the monastery," he concluded, "if it's re-established in Hong Kong."

"Excuse me a moment," the man said and disappeared through a door. Almost immediately, he returned with another man.

"You dealt with those monks before," Paul heard the man say. "It seems we've got another one."

"Oh. I thought most of them are dead."

"Not this one."

Paul was invited to go into the office, and had to tell his story all over again. What finally convinced the embassy officials was the unusual nature of the request, and the incredible story of the applicant. The interview took nearly an hour, but it was worth it. He emerged from the Embassy with an assurance that there were no plans to close Hong Kong's border against the Mainland and a letter which, he was also assured, would work as a visa in case circumstances changed.

"Well done," Susannah applauded.

"And what is your other plan?" Matthew asked after Susannah

finished clapping.

"On land all the way. I can follow the railway lines and head for Wuhan first, and then to Canton. The beauty of this plan is that I can travel on a limited budget. I can find work when I run out of money. And then, from Canton it's only a hop to Hong Kong."

"But eighty miles make a very long hop, Paul. Now, what will you say if some officious youngster in a PLA uniform asks why you are wandering around the country with very little luggage and very little money?"

"I thought about that. I could always say that I was going home to my village near Canton, following the advice given me when I was discharged: go home, find a job, get married. Well, I am going to make a quick visit to the ancestral home."

He smiled at his own attempt at flippancy. Neither Matthew nor Susannah seemed to have noticed it.

"Weren't your family thinking of moving to Hong Kong?" Susannah asked. "I remember your telling Matthew that."

Paul opened and shut his hands, suddenly sombre. "I don't know where they are. They may still be in China, or they may be in Hong Kong. I had no chance to find out before... before what happened. I wrote to my mother at our old address the same time that I wrote to you, and I waited for a month, but there was no reply."

"I'm sorry, Paul," Susannah said.

He wrenched himself out of his mood. "What do you think, then?" he asked.

"I don't know if there is much of a choice between them. Going by sea will take you a long way, slowly. But finding a place on a boat may prove to be difficult. Your plan for travelling overland is almost like begging your way across country – I don't know if I'd dare to try it myself. But, Paul, whichever way you choose, if it's merely a matter of money, I'd like to contribute."

Paul intercepted the look of anxiety which Susannah directed at her husband. It confirmed what he had suspected since he arrived.

The Kungs had been living frugally, and what was even more, cheaply. As a Cistercian, he was in the business of food production, and he knew about the quality of food. What Susannah had done for the meals was excellent cooking with what he would describe as very cheap ingredients. The objects in the house might be expensive, and in normal circumstances would fetch good prices at a sale, but under the present conditions they had no market value. Not many people would want an upright piano, or even an original Cezanne or Monet. And he guessed that whatever money they had in the bank would be frozen, although, from what Matthew had just said they probably had some savings somewhere that they were able to use.

"That's kind of you," he said. Refusing outright would hurt Matthew's feelings, but he knew what he would do.

At his hosts' insistence, he stayed another day. Matthew offered to accompany him after he finished work to the shipping offices to see if there were boats going south, and Paul suspected that he might buy him a passage on the spot, but fortunately an emergency had arisen which required Matthew's presence until after the offices were shut. He imagined that Susannah, too, heaved a sigh of relief. That evening, Paul told Matthew and Susannah what had happened at Mu Chia Chuang, but afterwards, they were able to lift their mood and had a last pleasant evening together, recalling happier times.

"Here's something you may wish to have," Matthew said, taking a small volume from a bookshelf. Thomas à Kempis! "Susannah thinks I ought to give you this to remember us by."

"Thank you!" He was moved. "You must write something on the flyleaf."

Matthew did, ending with "Remember us!" And then he said, using almost the same words as Mr Yuan, "Would you hear our confessions? We haven't been for over a year."

Next day Paul was on a train to Tientsin. If he was hoping to find work on board a ship, it had to be where the ships were, and that meant Tientsin, which was Peking's port, a hundred or so miles away. This city stood on the estuary of a river which emptied into the North Sea, the outsized lagoon guarded by the two horns of the Shantung Peninsula on the right and the Liaotung Peninsula, the southernmost point of Manchuria, on the left. Beyond was the Yellow Sea, which then became the China Sea. Although there were no hills of any significance for the train to negotiate, the number of villages between the two cities made a long day's journey.

He had kept monastic hours that morning. After the confessions the previous night, he had asked Matthew and Susannah if they would mind him celebrating Mass in the house, and they both asked in turn if they could attend, and so he decided to say the Mass at the late time of half past six. When he got downstairs he found that Susannah was already up, and making ready to prepare breakfast. Matthew, too, Susannah told him, was up, and was in the surgery putting together what he needed for the day. Mass was then said in the dining room, and afterwards breakfast was a quiet and somewhat sad meal, for they all realised that they might never see each other again. As he was saying goodbye, Matthew did what Paul thought he might do.

He pressed a thick envelope into his hand. "This should help you a little, I hope," he said, in a characteristic understatement.

He had been ready for this generous gesture. He put it into his pocket, and said, "I'm sorry, I think I left my hat on the bed," and returned to his bedroom. There he picked up his hat, and left Matthew's envelope on the bedside table next to the clock, and by it he left a letter he had written the night before. By the time Susannah found the two envelops, it would be too late.

This was as hard a parting as the one he experienced when he said goodbye to Margaret, or when he left home for the last time to go to Yang Chia Ping. But perhaps, he thought, time had a knack of dulling pain.

He could smell the salt tang of the sea from many miles away, and a while later, he knew he would have been able to see it if there had been daylight. However, he did not know Tientsin, as he had been there only once when he was at university, with Margaret, in fact, when they went to see what the port which everybody had heard so much of was like. There wasn't all that much, he recollected, but there were miles of docks, jammed with medium-sized ocean-going ships and boats of all descriptions. Because of the silting, really big ocean liners could not use Tientsin, but there were enough of the smaller sort to make it one of the busiest harbours in North China. But that was years ago.

The train pulled in to the terminal at about seven in the evening, and he was not looking forward to tramping the streets in search of accommodation in the dark. However, he was fortunate and found a hotel by the station. It didn't look expensive, and on enquiring he found that he could afford it for perhaps a couple of nights. He booked in.

When he made his way to the docks the next morning, he noticed that there were many fewer boats, or ships, in harbour than he remembered from the last time he had been there, and there did not seem to be as much activity. There were few foreign vessels, apart from a couple from Japan and one from Korea. What there were at berth or riding at anchor were small to medium-sized Chinese-registered freighters which plied the Chinese coastal trade. The whole area was dotted about with warehouses, and gateways allowed access. There were dingy teahouses and sleazy diners, most of them also advertising accommodation upstairs. Any night spots there once were had been closed by the present puritan regime. Dock areas, he had always thought, had an inbuilt feeling of desolation, and Tientsin Docks were not different this morning.

He found the streets of shipping offices. Many buildings were empty, and some were boarded up and had 'vacancy' signs plastered across the windows, and there were advertisements for empty office accommodation. Some of the previous tenants had not taken the trouble to dismantle their signs when they evacuated the premises, and on the front of one building was still a neon sign saying 'Messageries Maritimes', and the sign 'Butterfield and Swire' still hung across the front of another. Paul found the China Steamships Company between two empty office buildings. He was a little surprised at the modest size of the office, for he had somehow expected the premises to be larger and grander as befitted a well-known shipping line. The sign which ran the width of the premises could do with some repainting, too, he thought.

He looked through the window into the office. Behind the empty counter he could just see the tops of the heads of two men at work, and on the back wall was a large chart with names of vessels, and information on ports of origin and registration and destination, and dates of arrival and departure in appropriate columns. There were no ships destined for Hong Kong, but there was one whose destination was Shanghai. That ship, however, had departed two days before. Not, he thought, that it mattered: he would not have been able to pay the fare.

One of the two men looked up at his entrance and came to the counter.

"Do your ships go to Hong Kong?" Paul asked.

"Not anymore. Are you looking for a passenger carrier?"

Before Paul could make up his mind how to answer this query, the other man, who was obviously the superior, spoke from his desk, resting the point of his pencil to mark a spot on a closely written page in a ledger. "We carry cargo now, and don't carry passengers regularly anymore, except as supercargo. Everybody goes by train, you see: it's much cheaper and quicker. You're the first one to ask for a place in three months!"

Cheaper, Paul thought, if one had the cash to pay the whole fare. It wasn't so easy for someone who had to work his way on the journey.

"Yes and no," said Paul. He decided to be as open as possible. "First, I want to know how much it will cost. Second, how long will I have to work to save up enough to pay for it. But, really, I'm looking for a job on board a ship to pay my passage."

"Well, friend," said the man, "since our ships don't go to Hong Kong anymore, and we don't take passengers anymore, I can't answer either of your first two questions. As for a job on board ship, we haven't a vacancy at the moment. Sorry." Then he tried to be helpful. "China Cargoes, down the street, may still do business in Hong Kong, so why don't you go and ask them?"

Paul thanked both men and set off.

China Cargoes, he discovered, still did business in Hong Kong, but he would never be able to save enough money for a berth on one of their ships. Shanghai was more of a possibility. He almost regretted not accepting Matthew's money.

"No," he reminded himself. "I couldn't do that!" That would have been selfish and uncaring, especially for a monk.

Paul stood at the counter, trying to make up his mind. The clerk waited, surprisingly patiently.

"Have you any jobs on any of your ships?" he asked.

The clerk looked at him quite hard for a while before he turned and put his head round a door through which came the sound of a typewriter and said to someone inside: "This man wants a job on a ship."

"What sort of man is he?" said a voice. The clerk shrugged. "All right. I'll have a look."

The second man came out. He was short, and tending to obesity, the result of much self-indulgence over long periods, Paul suspected. Before the New Order, he would probably have dressed quite differently. He scrutinised what was visible of Paul above the counter with the practised eye of a shrewd employer.

"What sort of job have you in mind?" he asked.

"Anything you have. Steward, work in the galley, stoker, jack-of-all-work…"

"Have you been to sea before?"

Paul shook his head. He hadn't even seen the sea properly before. But he was not going to say that.

"I heard what you wanted. You want to get to Hong Kong. The trouble is, after we've trained you to work, you're going to jump ship in Hong Kong. It's not on."

That meant that there was work on board a ship, he thought, possibly one that went to Hong Kong.

"What if I sign a contract that binds me to your company for... two Hong Kong voyages? And a half." He wanted to be accurate.

The man watched him as he considered this offer. "Come back tomorrow." He turned abruptly to re-enter his office. His underling watched Paul with an expression akin to pity.

Paul continued down the street and found three more shipping firms. These proved, however, to be minor companies which operated small coasters on short trips, and although one of them was so shorthanded that it actually offered him a place on a boat which was due to sail that afternoon, he did not think it worth his while to go just round the horn of Shantung, taking him further away, in fact, from a direct route to the south. He retraced his steps. If he was not able to find work in shipping, he would have to hunt round in the city, or even return to Peking. He would approach Matthew again as a last resort to see whether he could find him a job in the hospital. In the meantime, he had to wait, and further reduce his funds. The fare from Peking and last night's stay at the hotel had already cut his capital down by a quarter. Another night at the hotel was in fact more than he could afford, but it was worth it if he could get on a ship for Hong Kong, and reach there eventually.

He spent the afternoon in his hotel room reading St Bede.

In the middle of the next morning he was back at China Cargoes, giving his prospective employer time to make up his mind. He had obviously been awaited, as the clerk at the counter immediately went in to announce his arrival when he pushed open the outer door. The clerk then returned to the counter, raised the flap at one end and invited him to step in. Paul found himself in a comfortably furnished office. His prospective employer was sitting behind a large rosewood desk with all the paraphernalia which were probably considered necessary adjuncts of a successful shipping boss. There was even a model of one of the company's ships in a glass case to one side. Next to the door of the room was a girl at a typewriter who was checking through something she had apparently just finished typing. In the old days, neither would have been in blue trouser suits. There was a chair in front of the man's desk, but Paul was not invited to sit down.

"I didn't reckon," the man said without preamble, "that you would survive as a stoker or even as a cook's assistant. But we do need a purser's clerk on the *Fukien* which does the Hong Kong run. It leaves port tomorrow. Judging by the way you speak, you're an educated man, and it's probably the best job for you."

Paul refrained from telling the man that he had survived much worse. "Thank you," he said.

"Will you now sign this contract? We hold you to two round trips, and then you will be discharged in Hong Kong when you get there on the third run." He pushed the contract, in triplicate, across to Paul and held out a pen. "Ink there." Paul took the pen.

The man leaned back in his chair, his right elbow on the armrest. He looked impatient as Paul began to peruse the terms of the contract. Yes. He was bound for two full runs, and to be discharged when the *Fukien* docked in Hong Kong on the third trip. While on board ship he had the right to a bunk and meals and all the recreational facilities. There were other terms which outlined the behaviour expected of him while on board... and others delineating the employer's obligations to him.

"Put your name on the top where it says, and sign at the bottom, if you're happy with the terms of the contract." The man was impatient.

Paul looked up from the contract. "The contract does not mention wages."

The man sighed. Without lifting his elbow from the armrest, he waved a couple of fingers impatiently.

"You have had no sea-going experience, and we are kind enough to give you training as a minor ship's officer although you are way past the normal age, and you are, as I said yesterday, going to leave us when we have trained you. You get free bed and board. No, my friend. We do not talk of wages."

Wasn't this supposed to have gone out with the old regime, and wasn't the New Order supposed to get rid of people like that? He felt anger welling up inside him. He held his breath to get a grip on it. What he did next he believed he did coldly and rationally, by no means under the stress of anger or disappointment. He put the unused pen carefully on the desk and laid the sheets of the unsigned contract next to it. Then, his mind in a daze, he turned and walked out, through the front office, and into the street.

So near! So very near!! And did he have to throw the opportunity away? By now he was only half convinced that he had done the right thing in rejecting the offer of the job, and he half wanted to retrace his steps and beg for it, and then he knew that he mustn't do it. His mind was still in a turmoil as he started walking automatically back towards the hotel and the railway station. There was scarcely any point for him in staying on in Tientsin now, and there were bound to be more job opportunities in the capital city.

He was about to go past China Steamships Company when the second, apparently more important man in the office emerged suddenly and nearly collided with him. He looked at Paul with a sign of recognition.

"Hello, friend! Any luck at China Cargoes?"

He shook his head. For the moment he was incapable of speech. The other man scrutinised him.

"Are you all right? You look white. Shocked."

"I'm all right. Thanks."

"I don't think you are, you know. Look, I'm going off to lunch. Why don't you join me? A bite may do you good. Just there, two doors down."

Paul was grateful to the man. "Thanks," he said. "I can't afford a restaurant. Or even a teahouse. Well, not really."

"Bad as that, eh?" Paul wished the man would go away. "Come. I'll buy you a bowl of noodles. And you can tell me about it."

They found a table near the front of a modest teahouse which, as it was still early, was empty but for two other men at separate tables, eating and reading the newspapers. The best thing about the place was that there was a fire in a brazier in the middle of the room, with a vent in the ceiling which drew the spiralling smoke through the roof. The menu was basic, almost a matter of either noodles with sliced pork or noodles with pork sliced, and there was no choice on tea. They ordered two noodles with sliced pork, and five minutes later the waitress who took their order returned with their lunch.

"So you didn't find a berth on one of their ships? And you need to get to Hong Kong. Are things that bad?"

Paul looked at this total stranger who was showing such concern.

"I do want to get to Hong Kong. I'm not desperate to get there in the next ten days, or whatever, but I want to get there eventually. If I can't get there by sea, I'll try to get there on land. My trouble is," he laughed mirthlessly, "a lack of funds."

He then related his adventures with China Cargoes.

"You know," his new friend said at the end of his story, "you should, I think, count yourself lucky." He paused, as though unwilling to speak ill of a fellow employer. Then he went on. "Tsien has always had a reputation for treating his people badly. His employees were always too poor or two ignorant or even too scared to take him to court. A couple of them did, though, soon after the war, but got nowhere. So no one tried afterwards. You see, the man is too well connected, previously with big shots in the Nationalists, and, amazingly, now with the Party."

"I suppose you are right," Paul said gloomily. But his new friend had not yet finished.

"You see, you aren't even safeguarded by your contract. Not really. He could terminate it at any time and there's nothing you can do about it. And if the contract ties you to the company, what's to stop him from putting you on a Shanghai run, for example, or if it ties you to the ship, he can send the ship on a run to... Weihaiwei, just a couple of hundred miles down the coast, perhaps, and you haven't got very far from here, then. The boss is still almighty, I'm afraid. I should say you're lucky, mate."

There was nothing more to be said. Paul sipped the weak tea which came with the noodles while the other man smoked a cigarette.

"I think I'd better go to the railway station," he said. "I may as well get back to Peking, because I do need a job."

The other man stubbed out his cigarette in the bottom of the empty noodle bowl, exhaling smoke through his nostrils. "I don't want to pry into your personal affairs. You seem, you sound, as though you are an educated man, and I don't think you were a labourer, though" – he was looking at Paul's calloused hands – "you might have done labouring jobs recently. Please don't think I told you about China Cargoes out of malice. I have a proposition. I may not have a job vacancy on a ship, but I do need a shipping clerk in the office, one who learns the ropes quickly, to work alongside me and the other fellow, Chun, and a typist who comes in four days a week. We'll be on monthly terms, and I'll pay you the going rate. You should be able to save something for your journey unless you blow your wages every time you get them. And, tomorrow being Sunday, you can start on Monday. Well, how about it?"

In answer Paul took out his release paper and passed it across the table. The other man read it.

"That's no concern of mine. And does it mean your answer is 'yes'?"

Paul nodded. "Is there somewhere I can stay?"

"Chun may be able to help. You will find him an interesting man. You may even share a similar past history."

Back at China Steamships, he was introduced to Chun. "Welcome aboard," said the latter, "as we say in the trade. No pun intended."

He was also introduced to the typist. "Mrs Wu."

"By the way, Mr Liang is looking for somewhere to stay while he's working with us. I understand you have a spare room, haven't you, and are looking for a lodger?"

Chun scrutinised him, then said:

"You can come home with me to look at the place when shop closes today and see if you want it. It's nothing great, but convenient for things."

"Thanks," Paul said. "I'll collect my bag from the hotel and have a look round the town, and I'll meet you back here at…?"

"Half past five."

Outside, the autumn sun had disappeared behind a lowering layer of clouds and there was a smell in the air which promised snow. He settled his bill at the hotel, shouldered his bag and wondered where he could shelter for the next four hours or so. He thought of the town library.

He found his way there. It was a large, impressive, modern-style civic building with tall double doors set between symmetrically arranged windows on either side. There was a notice on the door, however, which told the visitor that by order of the Tientsin City authorities it was closed for reorganisation until further notice. There was no light or activity Paul could see through the dusty and grimy windows. The building was simply closed. He thought of the Catholic church he had visited the last time he had come to Tientsin. Sacred Heart, he recalled the name, the same as the one in Canton, and it was an attraction because of its Jesuit origins and its baroque decorations, although it had long been taken over by the diocese. He found the church open, but the notice board in the porch was empty. Inside, an old man who might well be the live-in sacristan was carefully dusting the pews. He glanced up at Paul without much interest and then returned to his task. There was even a bunch of flowers in a little pot in front of the statue of Our Lady of Lourdes, but the sanctuary lamp was not lit.

"Where is the priest?" Paul asked.

The man straightened up from his work and rubbed his temple with the back of his hand.

"What do you want the priests for? Confession? There won't be any confessions anymore now. Or Masses either. They came and took them both away last month."

"So why isn't the church shut, then?"

"Who knows. They may come back one day. One may, perhaps. That happened on the other side of town, at St Thomas's. There were three priests there originally. They all got taken away, and now one of them is back. Some people say that if they signed a bit of paper they were allowed to come back. I went to St Thomas's the last few Sundays and things looked the same as they had always done. No difference. So I don't see why our priests can't just sign the bit of paper and come back. Something to do with the Pope, they say."

The man chuntered on, ignoring Paul. After a while the latter made up his mind. It might be a risk, but he was willing to take it.

"Look, I'm Father Liang, from a village the other side of Peking. Can I come and say Mass here, early, tomorrow?" Then as an inducement. "You won't have to go all the way to St Thomas's then."

The old man looked at him suspiciously.

"How do I know you're a *shenfu*? How do I know you're not going to mess about?"

Good questions! He was not dressed like a priest or a monk; he did not look like one. He showed the sacristan the Latin missal. The man's suspicion began to give, but he was obviously far from convinced.

"Are you a Mass server?" Paul asked.

"I've been one since I was a boy." Like Mr Yuan.

"All right then. *Introibo ad altare Dei.*"

The man responded automatically. "*Ad Deum qui laetificat*

*juventutem meam...*" A smile creased his face.

"All right? Now, I want no fuss. Just let me in at six, and you can serve Mass."

"Can I bring my wife?"

"Of course."

"And her sister?"

By the end, Paul reckoned that he would have a congregation of ten: the sacristan and his wife, his wife's sister and her husband, a couple of neighbours...

***

He was back at China Steamships Company just before half past five, having taken the precaution of eating his meal before returning. The typist was putting the cover over the typewriter, and Chun was tidying his files and ledgers away while their employer watched, an impressive bunch of keys in his hand. Mrs Wu left first, nodding goodbye to Paul, and then Chun came from behind the counter.

"Ready?" he asked rhetorically.

Paul got up from the chair he had been waiting in, and his future employer waved the bunch of keys. "See you on Monday, Liang. Half past eight."

"What's his name?" Paul asked Chun once they were outside. "He never told me and at the end it became a bit embarrassing to ask."

"I know the feeling," said Chun. "He's Wang Mintung." Paul saw in the yellow streetlight that Chun's grin was friendly, and he reminded him of Brother Roch. But soon they were trudging through unlit lanes.

"And you are?" Chun asked.

"Liang Weishung," Paul said. "And you?"

"Chun Mu. I understand you used to do other things?"

"I... was an engineer. I was in a labour camp in the mountains until about two months ago. And you? Mr Wang said we might have similar past histories. Were you an engineer, too, then?"

"No. I was a schoolteacher. I used to teach history at the No. 2 Senior Middle School here. Well…" he continued cautiously, "history isn't the same anymore. So, with a wife and two children to support, I decided, wisely as it turned out, to get out of teaching."

He answered Paul's unspoken question.

"My two colleagues were sent away to be re-educated – somewhere in Shensi, I believe. That was after they were accused by their students of teaching imperialist and decadent history, whatever that might mean." Shensi was more than halfway towards the source of the Yellow River. "Our new masters have an aversion to historians, I'm afraid."

After a twenty-minute walk, they stopped in front of a house in a quiet lane over the green front door of which there was a light with a dark metal shade. At eye level, on the right-hand side of the doorway, was a ceramic tile embedded in the brickwork. It bore the number '8'.

"Here we are," said Chun, waving his arm in a half-comic gesture of welcome, and taking out his key at the same time, "at number eight, Greenleaf Lane. Home. Ancestral home, really, as my family has lived here for three generations."

For some inexplicable reason, Paul had imagined Chun's home to be a flat in a modern block which divided into a number of units. This one was much like Mrs Chang's house in Lungchuan. The front door led through a short passage into a courtyard, beyond which were the family rooms. On either side of the passage was a room. Chun threw open the door of the one on the right, reached in to turn on the electric light, and waved Paul through.

It was a larger room than Paul had expected. Along the far wall was a bed with a bedside table and a reading lamp and a chest of drawers. An empty bookcase stood against the left wall, and between it and the window, which was lit from the courtyard, was a desk with another reading lamp. There was also a paraffin heater. The furniture was all modern pieces which contrasted oddly with the traditional building, but the room was certainly adequate. It reminded him of his cell in the monastery.

"A student's or a scholar's room," he said.

"Not far wrong," said Chun. "He was one of the two from my old school who got sent to re-education camp in Shensi. By the way, I'll ask Lingyi – that's my wife – to put the curtains back on the windows; Lingyi took them down to wash."

He led the way out of the room to the one on the other side of the passage. Again, after switching on the light, he invited Paul to precede him into the room. It was a kitchen which, with the large washtub on the floor to one side, could double as a bathroom.

"Since my parents died, I had these two rooms fitted up for renting to lodgers, in order to supplement my income as a teacher. You see, my wife, who was also a teacher, had to give up work because of the children. I fitted out the kitchen in case the lodger preferred to do his own cooking. By the way, you'll have your own front door key, so you can come and go as you please."

He watched as Paul looked round again. "Well?"

"It really is very good," Paul said. "How much are you charging?"

Chun told him. He could afford that, but it would mean that he might have to live extremely frugally until pay day. In any case, he thought, he had been through that before, and was quite able, if necessary, to live on steamed bread and tea and the occasional soya-bean sausage.

"Yes," he said. The two men shook hands to seal the deal.

"Now, come and meet the family. And you're having dinner with us tonight."

Mrs Chun, drying her hands on the apron she was wearing, came from the kitchen to meet him. She was rather small, had straight, unpermed short hair, the de rigueur hairstyle these days, and a pleasant smile. She appeared to be some years younger than her husband, and Paul placed her at round about thirty years of age. Certainly meeting the seven-year-old son first helped with the guess. The daughter was a year or two younger.

"Meet our new lodger," Chun said. "My wife, Lingyi."

"Mrs Chun. Your husband said that you were a teacher, too."

"That was before Shiyu was born." She indicated the boy. "That's a few years ago."

"You were not a history teacher also, were you?"

"Heavens, no. I used to teach home economics. It was a new subject, and parents used to come and argue with me about what I told the kids. These new ideas were all right for places like Shanghai and Canton, they used to say, but not for Tientsin. They thought it was a waste of time. Children could learn cooking and sewing and house-management from their parents, they argued: it was a waste of money to hire a teacher to do that at school. Usually Chinese parents are so deferential to teachers, but all I encountered was hostility. Mind you, things were difficult under the Japanese, anyway, who were always inspecting the school to make sure that we were not teaching anti-Japanese propaganda. Mu had a bad time too with his history! In any case, I was glad to give it up."

Paul had not heard of home economics either, but if it included cookery, Mrs Chun showed herself a mistress of the craft. There was certainly a professional touch to the meal which she produced. It was a pleasant time, and afterwards, when the children had been put to bed, they sat round an open fire drinking warmed rice wine, and conversation continued. Both Chun and his wife told him much about their early life, and themselves tried politely to probe his past history, but Paul was not very sure how much of it he should reveal. He let them know that he had been an engineering student at Peking, and that he had been responsible for the repair of a dam and the planning of an irrigation system 'somewhere out west'. They also learned that he had been in trouble with the present regime, with which they expressed sympathy.

"That's really bad luck," said Mrs Chun, aware, obviously, that her husband might have been at this moment with his old colleagues in a camp somewhere.

The clock struck eleven without any of them having been aware of the flight of time.

"Sorry we've got to drive you away," said Chun. "We have to get up early tomorrow, and we think we'd better go to bed now."

Paul was also thankful that he was able to get away. He remembered that he, too, was to have a short night. Chun had given him a small can of paraffin for lighting the heater until he could get some himself, but he decided he could do without the heater tonight. He said Compline and turned in. Before sleep came to lull him, he told himself that he must get a small alarm clock so that he could wake up in time at three o'clock to say the Night Office, then do his meditation and his reading. He must get himself properly organised now that he was going to live a regular life for a while.

Three months, he thought he would give himself. Then he should be able to make a part of the long journey south.

***

He got up at three. His sleep had been much broken because he was too anxious about waking up at the right time. He realised that he would probably pay for it during the day, but it was Sunday, and he'd have time to rest.

He let himself out of the house at five. Thank God, he thought, the lock was well oiled, as he did not wish to disturb Chun and his family. It was bitterly cold, and his nose felt totally exposed and defenceless, and he shivered. The first step he took as he turned away from the front door nearly caused his downfall, literally. The cold had turned the surface moisture on the cobblestones to ice during the night. He managed to steady himself and thereafter proceeded cautiously. He did not know the direct route between Greenleaf Lane and the Church of the Sacred Heart, so he had to go back to the docks before he could find his way to the church. However, he got there with a good ten minutes to spare. The door of the church had already been unlocked, and a fire had also been lit so that to someone who came in from the freezing cold outside, the building felt pleasantly warm.

The sacristan had everything ready for him. He had even thoughtfully laid out a cassock for him to put on under the alb. The customary invocations came back to him, and he recalled the last time he had put on vestments, alb, stole, maniple, chasuble, for Mass: that fateful 8 July, the Feast of St Elizabeth, Queen of Portugal, peacemaker and carer of the poor, two years ago. Most of those who had celebrated Mass that morning were now dead. Martyrs.

Through the half-open sacristy door, he could hear people enter the church and take their places in the pews. How many were there who were supposed to come to Mass? Ten, did the old fellow say? He had, rather rudely, not asked the man's name.

The man returned to the sacristy to put on his own server's black gown and white surplice.

"What's your name, please?" Paul asked. He used the polite Chinese phrase: What is your honoured name, gentle sir?

"Peter, Father. Peter Shen."

"Thanks, Peter, for all your work. But, no bells, please. No bells at all."

"No bells at the Sanctus or at the Elevation?"

"No," Paul said firmly. "Please remember. We don't want to draw attention to ourselves."

He could see that Peter disapproved. He was disappointed.

"Shall we begin?" he asked.

And Peter led Paul, the acolyte leading the priest, out of the sacristy into the sanctuary of the church to celebrate the central act of their religion, the Mass, for which many had lost fortunes, gone to prison, and even died. Paul could not see how many there were at Mass, because the body of the church was in darkness, but he guessed there must be many more than ten. He had decided, prudently, he thought, not to give a sermon after the Gospel, but he did turn towards the congregation to say a brief word of welcome and to ask for their prayers. He could hear Peter pick up the bell when he was approaching the end of the Preface in readiness for the Sanctus, and he braced himself for the piercing jangle of the five little chimes. But Peter had obviously remembered, because he put the bell down again without ringing it. As far as he could work out, the whole congregation received Communion. He had consecrated thirty hosts, but he had to divide some of them towards the end as the congregation kept coming up.

And he was very surprised when Chun and young Shiyu approached the communion rail together, followed by Mrs Chun carrying the little girl, Suhan, still asleep, in her arms. He remembered that Chun had said the night before that they had to get up early this morning. And this must be what Mr Wang said he and Chun shared.

# SIX

They walked back from church to Greenleaf Lane together, Paul carrying little Suhan, warm in her brocade padded jacket and multi-coloured wrap. It was light now, though the dawn was still grey, with the merest hint of rose tinting the sky over the sea to the east. They stopped at a small, open-fronted, cooked-food shop, where steam rose invitingly from rice porridge bubbling in a huge iron cauldron. They were not, however, interested in that. On a table next to the stove were deep-fried fluffy twisted sticks of soft breadlike pastry, an obligatory treat after Sunday Mass.

"We don't want those," Mrs Chun, or Lingyi, told the cook. "They're already half frozen! Fry us some fresh ones."

"Have a heart, Mrs Chun," the man moaned good-naturedly. "If everybody's as choosy as you, I won't make a living at all! Well... if you don't mind waiting in this cold."

They all packed into the tiny space behind the stove to escape the cold, for the frying could take a while. There were a couple of small tables there where customers could eat if they chose to. Conversation was at first muted and desultory amid the sizzling of the boiling oil, but the cook decided to start a conversation.

"A friend?" he asked. He indicated Paul by a nod of his head.

"My new lodger," said Chun. "Mr Liang."

Paul smiled a greeting, and the cook went back to the frying, and there was silence for a few seconds.

"Your old lodger went away, didn't he?"

Chun grunted a reply.

"Have you been to church?" he asked. "It's very early, isn't it? Have the *shenfu* come back?"

"They haven't. Have you nearly finished? I think that's enough."

The return journey from the church took a mere twenty minutes, including the stop at the food shop. There was no need to go anywhere near the docks at all.

"You must have breakfast with us, Father," Chun said, as he unlocked the front door. "We've bought your share as well."

"Thank you, Mr Chun. I can't keep scrounging on you," Paul said.

"Just this once," Chun pressed. "Sunday mornings," he added. "Please honour us."

There was a welcome smell of rice porridge as they entered the family front room, for Mrs Chun had started the cooking before they went to Mass. "Breakfast in five minutes," she announced as she went into the kitchen.

Paul was a little disconcerted by the deference shown by Chun. It was, though, by no means an unusual attitude among Catholics: one might even say it was normal, but, in addition to his innate dislike of deference to himself, it also had the danger of making the present situation untenable. Yesterday, there had been the normality of the relationship of lodger and landlord as well as colleague, and, as a bonus, there was a real possibility of friendship, for he liked Chun and his family. Now he was being put on a pedestal, and a barrier was being erected, and there was an awkwardness which must not be permitted to develop further. The pedestal and the barrier must be demolished.

"Please," he said to his landlord. "I'm not *Father* Liang to you and your family. To you and... Lingyi, I am Weishung or, better still, just Liang. And at work you are my senior; tomorrow you'll have to teach me office skills, and I may or may not be a good pupil. So forget I am a priest. Treat me as a friend – and I'd be very honoured if you did – who happens to say Mass without official permission."

Chun thought for a moment, then put out his hand. "Yes, Liang."

Halfway through breakfast, Paul asked the question that had been intriguing him since he walked into the sanctuary in church.

"I'm really curious to know how you got to hear about Mass this morning."

Lingyi answered, "It was a woman I used to see at Mass. She came by yesterday afternoon to tell me."

"And you took a chance? That was brave."

"There will be more people next Sunday," Chun said. "You can bet on it. Some of them will come from St Thomas's as well. That is, if you're going to say Mass again."

*If it was a matter of the ministry, then your own safety does not enter the equation.* Not the exact words, but close enough. But he was honestly more worried about the effect a discovery by the authorities would have on these people. They did have to enter the equation.

He was ready the next morning when Chun knocked on his door at eight o'clock, and they set out together for the docks. On the way, Chun told Paul something about the man they worked for and the history of the firm. China Steamships had been founded by Mr Wang's grandfather, who was among the first batch of young Chinese to have been sent abroad by the then government to learn the ways of the West. China had lost every war and encounter with the West for thirty years, and had finally realised that having justice on one's side was no guarantee of victory. Flintlocks were no match against the modern rifle, nor sailing junks against dreadnoughts. Young men were therefore sent abroad, to Europe as well as to America, to acquire the skills and the technical knowledge that would propel China forward into the nineteenth century. Then old Mr Wang came home from America with a degree in marine engineering, and in addition to working for the government started his own steamship business, which had eventually passed into their present employer's hands. Mr Wang himself had also been trained in America, but more in business administration in the field of shipping than in engineering.

"Unfortunately, the war against Japan made life very difficult, and the company soon shrank to its present state," Chun told Paul. "But Mr Wang soldiers on."

"There can't be any real future in this business anymore," said Paul. "So why doesn't he pack up and leave? A lot of his kind have gone to Hong Kong or America."

Chun spread his hands. "You'll have to ask him. Maybe he has the same reason to stay as your friend you told us about yesterday, Dr Kung. We are Chinese."

"Would you leave China," Paul asked his new friend, "if you had the chance?"

"No. Would you?"

"No. But I am. You know I am."

Chun introduced him to the world of shipping, of keeping ledgers and making timetables and meeting deadlines. The work was not very different from what Father Seraphin used to do, and Paul had been the older priest's assistant for a while. Ledger work, however, he found rather uninteresting, and he had been glad when he was released from working in the monastery office, and was able to work outdoors unless his duties as precentor required his presence at singing practice indoors. Mrs Wu did not come in to work on a Monday, and when Mr Wang discovered that Paul could use the typewriter as well, he was put on it for the afternoon.

"But," Paul said, "I'm not very good at all. I type with two fingers, and I am slow."

"That's all right, provided you don't make mistakes in the typewriting."

"How good is your English?" Mr Wang also asked him.

"I can read it, and write it, to a certain degree, but I can't really speak it."

"That's all right. I'll do the correspondence in English, if there is any, and you can check it for me when Mrs Wu isn't in."

Mrs Wu usually did all the correspondence in English when she was in, and all Mr Wang did was sign the prepared letters.

At the end of that first day, when he was waiting for his employees to put the day's work away, Mr Wang, swinging his bunch of keys – as was, Paul discovered, his habit – told him, "You're coming along very nicely and you're picking up things quickly."

"He used to do a bit of that, you know," Chun informed Mr Wang.

"That's excellent. Maybe, Liang, if you want a permanent job, I could have one for you. But we'll see."

By Saturday, Paul was almost convinced that he had never done anything else in his life except enter items in ledgers, fill timetables and make up lists. Perhaps, he thought wryly, he was a natural pen-pusher after all. Life settled into a routine, the two divergent personae of his existence happily complementing each other. He had discovered that he was able to modify his monastic routine to accommodate the demands of his work at China Steamships, and Chun and his family were the real support he knew he needed and on which he could depend. They were understanding, too, and generally let him be, knowing that he would take the initiative if he needed them. He very soon came to realise that his relationship with the Chuns could never be merely that of lodger and landlord. Lingyi, too, quite often left food in his kitchen for him during the day, so that all he needed to do was heat it up again.

After a while, although his dreams continued to be haunted by the horrors of the past two years, he no longer woke so frequently in the night in the midst of a nightmare. The feeling that he now recognised as anger gradually disappeared, and he was finding peace again. However, he missed community life and the support that his brothers were able to give him by their presence. The aspect of monastic life that he missed most was the singing of the Office. He'd tried to do it on his own, but it wasn't the same.

"Have you got in touch with your friends, the doctor and his wife?" Chun asked him one day as they were walking to work through a snow-covered Tientsin a week or so after he had started his new job. "Surely they want to know what's happening to you."

"Not yet," he said. "I wanted to wait till I was really settled down first."

"Don't you feel that you have settled down yet?" Chun sounded slightly hurt.

"Of course I do. Thanks to you and Lingyi."

"Why don't you give them a call from the office? Mr Wang wouldn't mind, provided you ask him first, and you don't do it too often." He added, "And if the call isn't too long."

As Chun had said, Mr Wang did not mind him using the telephone occasionally, and it was Susannah who answered the call when he rang.

"We thought you might have got to Hong Kong by now! By the way, Paul, you did a very naughty thing, you know!"

Paul knew what she meant. "I'm sorry if I hurt your feelings, but I really couldn't take your savings… when you probably have more need of them than I do."

There was a pause at the other end. Then Susannah said, "Yes, we actually do need the money. Well… do you think you may have time some weekend to come and see us again?"

"Look, Susannah, I'm ringing from the office, and I must stop now. But I'll write. I'll write tonight."

Word went round that the 'new' priest was going to say Mass again at Sacred Heart the next Sunday. Peter was asked about it some time during the week, and he honestly said that he was not aware of the possibility. "But, who knows, he might," he said. In the next twenty-four hours, this possibility become first a probability, and then a certainty. Peter was really concerned when Paul did not get in touch, and he did not know how to contact him as he did not know the connection between Paul and the Chuns. He was relieved when Paul finally asked if he could come again.

The congregation started to arrive a long while before Paul got to the church, slipping in quietly and filling the pews, so that the church was more than half full on that First Sunday of Advent in 1949. Before he began Mass, however, some of them came into the sacristy to ask if he would hear their confession, and Mass was put back by twenty minutes. Next time, Paul realised, he would have to allow time for confession as well. He decided to give a short sermon that morning, and he spoke of the season of Advent as one of Hope.

"Let us, with God's help, never lose hope." He did not qualify this, but his congregation knew what he meant.

"Have they definitely changed the time of your Masses, then?" the man at the cooked-food shop asked when they stopped by for their usual purchase. Paul, Lingyi and Chun exchanged glances. The man's interest appeared to exceed the need for casual banter. Then Paul wondered if they were being unduly suspicious.

"We ought to change the time of the Mass, you know," he told Chun and Lingyi afterwards as they were continuing on their way home. Suhan, who was getting to be quite a favourite of his, was perched on his shoulders. "Perhaps we can have the Mass in the evening."

"Can you do that?" Chun asked.

These are not normal times, he told his friends.

One evening that week, Chun knocked on his door. Behind Chun was the silhouette of another man against the white of the floor of the courtyard. The man moved forward to reveal himself as Peter Shen, the sacristan.

"Yes?" Paul said. "Do come in out of the snow."

"Father," Peter asked, "do you do other things than saying Mass and hearing confessions?"

Paul raised his eyebrows in a question of his own.

"There is an old man – older than me, that is – who has been very ill for a long time, and he used to be visited by our parish priest. His wife was at Mass last Sunday, but she was a bit shy about asking you to bring him the Blessed Sacrament, knowing that you were not the regular priest."

"So she'd like me to bring him Communion?"

"He's dying, Father. The doctor has been and he said he only has a few hours."

He hesitated for a moment. He had nothing with which to give the dying man Extreme Unction, the Last Rites. But Peter had come prepared. He opened the small case he was carrying.

"I've brought the holy oil and the stole, but there are no consecrated hosts."

Chun volunteered to go with Paul, although it was late, and Peter was sent home. It proved to be a long night, as Paul chose to sit with the old man and his wife until the end, and it was almost three when they returned to Greenleaf Lane.

"Why don't you take the day off tomorrow," Chun suggested as they said good night. "I'll tell Mr Wang. He's very understanding."

"Oh, no. If you can go in, so can I. Besides, my Novice Master once said that if one couldn't do without sleep occasionally, one had no right to be a Cistercian."

That was the first of the evening house calls he made. He was finding that he was becoming more and more involved as unofficial parish priest. On average, he was making house calls twice a week. He often wondered if the priest at St Thomas's was aware of his activity. He knew that in performing his priestly duties, he was merely following in the footsteps of the Cistercians in Yugoslavia who had been ejected from their monasteries and who were unable or unwilling to seek refuge in Cistercian houses in neighbouring countries.

The question now began to arise in his mind, as it had done briefly at Lungchuan, as to whether he should not stay on in Tientsin to minister to those Catholics who preferred not to use churches staffed by clergy who had come to an understanding with the regime. He was so obviously wanted here. At the same time, however, his personal needs as a monk were pulling him in another direction. In spite of this internal conflict, he was largely at peace and he left the future in the hands of Providence.

One day, he received a letter. It was, to his delight, from Matthew. The letter was very short. "Stay home next Sunday." And next Sunday was the Fourth Sunday of Advent, the Sunday before Christmas, which that year fell on another Sunday. In short, Matthew had somehow succeeded in convincing the hospital authorities that his presence was needed in Tientsin to oversee the arrival of some vital medical equipment and supplies. He came down on Saturday, and Susannah came with him. Chun persuaded Paul to persuade the doctor and his wife to be his house guests, and the doctor agreed over the telephone.

Matthew and Susannah stayed the weekend, and came, with the Chuns, to Mass which was in the morning on this Sunday. They also brought Paul his Christmas present.

"You will not say no this time," said Matthew, "and you can't do the sneaky thing of leaving it behind in your room!"

Paul did not know how much Matthew had tried to give him the first time, but the envelope this time was less bulky, although the amount was still generous, and this in spite of what Paul had told him, that he might consider staying on in Tientsin after all.

"Look, Paul," Matthew said, holding up his hands and pretending to sound gruff. "What you do with your own money now is your business." And so Paul stowed the envelope away.

Christmas came and went, and so did the New Year which ushered in the Holy Year of 1950. Paul celebrated Midnight Mass quietly in Chun's front room with only the Chun family and Peter Shen and his wife in attendance, but he said the other two Masses in the morning for those who came to the church. He did not want his congregation to wander about the streets in the middle of the night and run the risk of arrest. However, Peter and some of the parishioners set up a crib to one side of the sanctuary, the figures of the Holy Family in a cave made out of papier mâché, the shepherds outside facing the main figures. The scene was decorated with evergreen branches and twigs.

"We always put up a crib,' said Peter, "in the old days."

At the end of the Christmas period the crib was put away, perhaps for another year. Towards the end of January, his people – he was now tempted to think of them in such terms: how else should he think of them, now that he had baptised some of them, given others their First Communion, and seen a few to their ends? – were making preparations for the Chinese New Year.

And Paul had really settled into his job. It was almost inconceivable that he had been anything else other than a shipping clerk. He and Suhan became firm friends, and at weekends he often took her on walks.

Was this the life he had missed?

***

It snowed heavily one grey afternoon about a week before the New Year and continued into the evening, but the temperature suddenly turned mild, and Paul and Chun trudged home through slush. It was a very agitated Lingyi who opened the door to them before Chun was able to insert his key into the lock. She stood aside for them to enter, and Paul noticed the almost theatrical glance she cast up and down the street before shutting the door. She ushered them both into her front room.

"Mrs Shen came about an hour ago," she said.

Mrs Shen had bound feet, which made walking in normal conditions a task. That she should have done the twenty-minute walk on her own through snow and slush meant that something serious had happened. Paul could hazard a good guess.

"They took Mr Shen. They went to the church in the afternoon when it was snowing and asked to see Mr Shen. Mrs Shen was able to overhear the conversation. It was, she said, conducted by one of the visitors at the top of his voice, anyway."

Someone, Mr Shen was told, had informed the authorities that a clandestine priest had been saying Mass and hearing confession at the church.

"It's no use your denying it, because the informant was actually at one of the Masses, and you were actively assisting at these religious ceremonies."

They wanted to know who this priest was, and where he was to be found.

"He just came and showed himself to be a priest," Peter said. "So I let him use the church."

"You must think we're idiots," said the officer in charge of the soldiers. "You can do better than that."

"I really don't know anything."

"Come on, old man. Think for yourself. You won't last very long in prison at your age. If you tell us, we won't bother you again. So now…" The interrogator decided to be systematic. "His name. He has a name, hasn't he?"

"Father Lin, Liu, Lu… How do I know?"

"Where does he live?"

"Don't know." Mrs Shen knew the inflection when her husband decided to be stubborn.

"What does he look like? Tall, fat, small, thin…?"

"Much like you, officer."

So they took him away.

"Mrs Shen's really worried," Lingyi said. But she came to warn the priest.

"Do you think it might be the man in the food shop?" Chun asked his wife. "If it was him, he won't ever have my business again!"

"Hard to say," she replied. "But he did show a certain curiosity, didn't he?"

"There was time for him to get into the church at the beginning of Mass and then quickly go home to open the shop."

The enigma was unsolved. Not that it mattered. Paul's mind was already made up.

"Look," he said. "I must leave this house. I am a danger to you. No, don't say anything. Don't be brave, and you must think of Shiyu and Suhan. And please give my apologies to Mr Wang. Thank him for me... I'll write to him. He has been a very kind man, and I am sorry to be unable to give him the required notice."

He was packed and ready to move in less than ten minutes. Lingyi insisted that he take a woollen blanket, and pushed something into his rucksack.

"It's only steamed bread," she said. "And a bottle of water; there's no time to make tea." Then she was in tears, and the three stood for a moment, heads touching, with their arms round one another.

Paul took half of the money from the envelope Matthew had given him. "Give this to Mrs Shen. She'll need it if Peter doesn't come back." Chun was going to refuse it for her, but then accepted the money.

"I'll pass it on to Mrs Shen," Chun said

"And, another thing," he said. "I'm going to take the train south, to Canton if I have enough cash, or at least to Wuhan. I think I've got enough for a ticket all the way. If they ask you, either of you, tell them that. Promise me: don't try to be brave."

He waited an hour at Tientsin railway station, and then boarded the night train with a ticket which would take him all the way to Canton.

Providence did have a way with one.


Next morning, Chun felt a loneliness he had never experienced when, once again, he made his solitary way to work. The two months which the priest had spent with him and his family had given him and Lingyi hope and courage. Mr Wang looked up with a question when he saw that Chun had come on his own. Chun had been thinking to himself what he should reveal to his employer, and in the end he told Mr Wang a complete version of the events. Mr Wang had always known that Chun and his family were Catholics, so that wasn't revealing anything really damaging. Besides, Mr Wang was a good man.

"And he asked me to thank you for your kindness and good will," he concluded. "He'll try to write."

Mr Wang was quiet for a long moment. "I owe him a month's wages," he said. Then, after another pause, "If you had let me know, I could have given him free passage on the *Cormorant* which sailed for Swatow this morning. But Canton is nearer Hong Kong, I suppose."

\*\*\*

Wuhan. It was made up of the twin cities of Wuchang and Hankow that stood on the south bank of the mighty Yangtze River which flowed from Tibet to Shanghai. Its skyline was dominated by a forest of factory chimneys belching out black smoke that showered soot on everything, and one coughed every time one entered the city. It reminded Paul of what Father Aelred, who was Dutch, once told him about the Ruhr district in Germany and the so-called Black Country in England, both of which he had visited in his youth. Paul recalled this, as conversation for its own sake was such a rare event in a Cistercian monastery and one tended to remember every word spoken for a very long time. One just avoided wearing white, Father Aelred had said, and people never hung their washing out in the open because it would be covered with black very quickly. Wuhan was a bit like that, Paul thought. Wuhan was going to be worse than that.

The Chinese, however, were very proud of Wuhan. It was one of the places that would, they hoped, drag China, whether willing or screaming, into the nineteenth and then the twentieth century. It was the home of China's industries, both heavy and light, for peace and for war. It was fed by the rich deposits of coal and iron from neighbouring areas which were carried on its vast system of rivers and their tributaries as well as the developed transport network which had been built by a native engineering genius, a sort of Chinese Isambard Kingdom Brunel, whom Paul had read about when he was at Peking. All roads, one might say, with the necessary modification of a quotation, led to Wuhan.

Wuhan also had a proud place in China's recent history. It was the mutiny of its military garrison that precipitated the 1911 Revolution which overthrew the decadent Manchu dynasty, which had ruled the country so corruptly, so inefficiently and so disastrously in the previous century, and established a Republic. Unfortunately, according to the version of history taught by the present regime, the country fell in turn into the corrupt, inefficient and disastrous hands of the Nationalist Party, headed by its arch bogeyman, Generalissimo Chiang Kai-shek.

Whatever history the city might enshrine, and although he had passed through it nine times before in his life, Paul had never been remotely tempted to break his journey to see Wuhan. The significance of the city for Paul on this journey was that it approximately marked the halfway point between Tientsin and Canton, and that, beyond its hinterland of the Yangtze's southern flood plain, the terrain rose in easy stages towards the foothills of the forbidding watershed that straddled the borders of the provinces of Hunan and Kiangsi, Fukien and Kwangtung. These mountains might have finished the Communists who traversed them at the start of their long trek to safety in the country's north-west.

Just think of it, he told himself. He would be in Canton in a couple of days, and, perhaps, Hong Kong was only another half-day away. And the long, two-and-a-half-year journey would be over in… another week?

As Paul's train drew in to the city, the passengers were informed that the train was going to stop for approximately an hour and a quarter to allow it to take on coal and water and catering supplies. Passengers were permitted to leave the train, but in order to be allowed to re-board they must make sure that they had their tickets with them. Passengers were also advised to take their belongings with them as the compartments were not secure while the train was at the station.

This time, Paul decided that he might as well have a look round the famous city. It would be a change from being cooped up in a crowded, noisy railway carriage, and he needed to stretch his legs. Besides, the sun was shining, or at least it was making a reasonably successful effort to stab through the cloud cover over the city. He shouldered his bag and followed a large number of his fellow passengers – many of whom, he noticed, were taking a chance by not taking their possessions with them – out through the station gates into the centre of the city.

From the inside he found, to his surprise, that the city was not as unattractive as he had anticipated. Whatever old history there might be, and the two cities which made up this one were ancient, it had been clothed in a modern dress. The architecture of its buildings had a certain faded grandeur, and palely reflected the wealth it had accumulated as the leading industrial city of the country. It was not a pretty city, but it was not revolting either. There was a university, one of a number, like Peking, which had been founded in the last fifty or sixty years. At one time, the shops might have been well stocked, but now they looked sorry and empty, and the universal blue of people's dress accentuated the drabness which was evident everywhere. A very few, very brave souls, however, still appeared in public in western jackets and trousers. There was even a man who was wearing a tie!

Most of his fellow passengers headed for the central business district and, for want of anything better to do, he followed them. Then, just ahead, there was a row of public buildings, over which were flagpoles were flying the new national flag. A small crowd of local people had gathered in front of one of the buildings, and Paul was half-curious as to what they were interested in. A number of those from the train joined the crowd. He paused on the pavement on the other side of the street, and noted that the building housed the law courts, the *yamen*. He was then about to pass on when some of the crowd raised a shout.

"They're bringing him out!"

Two soldiers came out first, rifles slung on their shoulders. Then came the man the crowd had been waiting for, his arms trussed to his side, who stumbled down the steps onto the pavement. A long piece of wood had been jammed through the rope which bound him, and it towered over his head. On it was written the crime with which he had been charged, and for which he had presumably been condemned: theft. In any case, Paul was in no doubt that this was an execution, because he had seen it before.

He was a biggish man, but he was also a frightened man. There was severe bruising on his face and a trace of blood in a corner of his mouth. Beneath matted hair and behind an unshaven chin, there was desperation and fear in his restless eyes, and Paul thought that perhaps there was more than just the fear of death. Whatever he had done, whatever crime he had been condemned for, this was the man's Via Dolorosa.

Then, he thought, I should know him.

At the same time, from across the street, the man caught his eyes. And suddenly, there was recognition at the same time that Paul recognised him. "O God, it's Mang!"

"*Shenfu*," he could see Mang mouth the words. Somehow, Paul was convinced that the man had been looking for him.

The fear was still in those eyes, but there was something more now. There was pleading, and that, between Mang and himself, could mean only one thing. Paul raised his hand in a small gesture of absolution, making the sign of the Cross. "*Ego te absolvo, in nomine Patris... I absolve thee, in the name of the Father...*" he recited quietly. Mang understood, and his features appeared to relax. He gave Paul a small nod, and then he was hurried on, followed by a large section of the crowd. The officer who walked behind him was already undoing the buckle of his holster.

Paul had a moment of sudden, wild, panic. He was back in the mountains north of Peking, and he was seeing just such an officer, and just such soldiers, marching him and his brothers to their eventual deaths. He shut his eyes and made an effort to breathe evenly. Reason returned.

He could not leave Mang now. A priest always followed a condemned man to the scaffold. He was doing that now for Mang, keeping pace with him and his escort on the other side of the street. He wondered what Mang – a friend of a sort, and his lieutenant after Brother Andrew's death, although he could never trust him completely, wayward and self-willed as he was – had actually done. He remembered that Mang had said he was going to go straight, and that he was going home to Shanghai. But it was always difficult for an ex-convict to make an honest living, although he himself had been fortunate. Paul said a prayer for Mang.

The Via Dolorosa was not very long. A ten-minute walk brought them to a playground where, as in most public parks and playing areas in China, there had been set up basketball posts, and some boys were playing the game.

"Go away!" the officer told them.

The boys stopped their game, but stayed to watch. This was a public spectacle, after all.

Mang was led on to the basketball court. When they arrived at the centre, he was told to kneel on the ground. Fear seemed to have returned, and he looked round, searching. Paul circled so that he was in Mang's line of vision. And then Mang saw him, and Paul held him with his eyes. And almost at the same time, the officer fired, the front of his throat opened, spurting red, and Mang sprawled forward, half-turning sideways, and the ground under his head began to pool with blood. The officer approached the body, looked to make certain that it was dead, replaced his revolver and left with his men. Paul waited for the crowd to disperse. Most of them left quickly, but some lingered, not doing anything, just looking at the corpse from a distance. Later on in the day, some official would come with a dustcart and remove the body.

The boys were still under one of the basketball posts. Afterwards they might boast to their friends that they had witnessed an execution, but now, they were definitely frightened, and one of them was sick. Paul ignored them, and approached Mang's body. He put his bag on the ground, opened it and took out the bottle which Lingyi had given him. There was still some water in it, and he only needed a few drops.

He knelt by Mang and poured some of the water on the side of his head.

*"If it is possible and you wish it, I baptise thee in the name of the Father, and of the Son and of the Holy Ghost. Amen."*

He then made his way back to the railway station.

There was no train on the platform. He had a moment of panic, but then, he decided, maybe he could still use the ticket. He asked at the ticket office, and was told that the train had left five minutes ago. When he asked if he could use the same ticket on the next train, the man held out his hand for the ticket. Paul handed it over, and the man studied it for a while, and could not make up his mind. He took it into the inner office, and was away for a few minutes. Eventually he re-emerged, followed by someone who by his deportment appeared to wield more authority. This man came to the window.

"You missed your train," he told Paul, stating the obvious.

"I want to know if I can get on the next train to Canton on the same ticket."

"No, I'm sorry. You see, your ticket doesn't allow you to break journey, which is what you have done. You'll have to buy another ticket from here to Canton. But the next direct train isn't until tomorrow."

The world collapsed around him and he was cast into the depths of despair. He felt emptied. And then he felt cheated. He felt resentful. Blind rage was rising inside him, and he was yearning to cry out: "How could You do that to me!"

Paul found a seat and numbly sat down. He was already under shock from seeing Mang die, and his present problem paralysed him. He had spent almost all of his cash on the through ticket, with little more than enough left to buy food for the time he was on the train. What he was going to do when he arrived in Canton he had not thought out, but that question, in any case, had become academic. It was imperative now for him to find work again, although, with the imminent holiday season of the Chinese New Year, which could last fifteen days or more, it would be difficult to find anything at all. Alternatively, he could start walking the rest of the way to Canton, doing odd jobs to support himself, or begging. At least, even if it was the middle of winter, Wuhan was more than halfway to Canton already, though the distance was still over a thousand miles, as he had measured on an atlas. He took a couple of deep breaths. But this Cistercian monk was now finding it difficult to pray. He was so absorbed in his own thoughts, his own misery, he had to admit later when his mind was clearer, that he had not noticed that someone had sat down on the far end of the bench, and he was therefore startled when this person spoke.

"*Shenfu.*"

This man who was looking at him appeared not much older than himself, and was dressed in about the same way: a padded overcoat over a blue jacket and shirt. But he wore a fur hat with ear pieces turned down against the cold, although it was comparatively mild today. His hands were thrust into his pockets. Paul raised his eyebrows in a question.

"You are one, aren't you?" the man persisted.

Paul was resentful at this intrusion into his privacy. He was overwhelmingly tempted deny it. "What makes you think that?"

"I was standing next to you when that man came out of the *yamen*. He knew you, didn't he? And you gave him absolution. And afterwards I watched you baptise him. That was a brave thing to do, Father."

Paul scrutinised the man, and could not make him out. He obviously knew a fair deal about the Church. But he seemed to be walled in, giving nothing of himself away. However, Paul decided, he was not malicious. He still did not like him, though, he told himself stubbornly.

He felt drained and very tired. He hadn't realised that he had not actually said anything. But the man decided to talk, anyway.

"I'm actually from the country," he said. "I came into town today to buy our New Year presents." He lifted a paper carrier bag which had been hidden from Paul's view. "That was a bit of luck, because I met you."

That, Paul realised, was only the preliminary. There was more to come. He waited.

"I am a farmer," the man carried on, but he was by now immersed in his own thoughts. "In fact, I own the farm, although I am no longer sure of my title anymore. I don't know how long my family have owned the farm, actually, and I am not sure if I am going to give in easily when the government takes it over, or breaks it up. But it will happen, I'm certain of it." There was no bitterness in the voice, just resignation. "In any case, I no longer have much cash, really. My savings have been practically frozen, and the bank rations what I can take out from my own account. Still..."

This, Paul thought, was more of the prologue. At least, it was helping to calm Paul's inner turmoil. Ordinarily, he would have asked the man what he actually wanted, if it could be done without offending the spirit of charity. Today, however, it did not seem to matter. It would, he supposed, be charity just to let the man ramble on. It seemed that he needed to, that he needed an audience. Then he looked round at Paul.

"I need a priest. We need a priest."

"Isn't there one where you live?"

"No. There never has been one. There was one in the next village, though, and there was a small church there. The priest served the villages roundabout, and he used to come every Sunday on his motorbike to say Mass, or to conduct marriages and baptisms." He stopped again.

"What happened to him then?" Paul could hazard a good guess.

"He was taken away by the PLA. Three months ago." He added bitterly: "We didn't even have Mass at Christmas!"

Paul thought of Tientsin. He had been so tempted to stay. Maybe he should have, but he couldn't be sure.

"We, the Catholics in the villages, need a priest. We'd like to go to confession. We'd like to hear Mass. And… I want a priest to marry me," the man said quietly. Then he told the story.

His wife had died a few years ago one winter when the Japanese had taken practically the whole crop from his granaries, and the family faced starvation. He then found work in Wuhan, for his village was not far from the city, and he would only arrive home late in the evening, when their son had already gone to bed. His wife always had his dinner ready for him, and he was always surprised at how much food she managed to put on the table.

"Aren't you eating with me?" he used to ask her.

"I've eaten, with Bao," she would say in reply.

"You know what happened, Father," the man said, miserably. "She starved herself to feed me and our son. But by the time I realised what was happening, she was too far gone. She died. And it's my fault for being so blind… I killed her."

There was a long silence after that. The man slumped into the seat. Then he shook his head and sat up.

"That," he said, "was another matter. There was a farm-owner in the next village, a friend of mine. He also happened to be a Catholic, with a wife and also a son, like us. A year ago, his tenants accused him of exploitation, the usual lies. It didn't matter that he had built the district a hospital and founded and staffed a school at his own expense, though I have to admit he was a strict landlord. They shot him, like that man in town today, and confiscated his land and his house. So I took his wife and his son in to live with us. And now I want to marry her."

In spite of his initial hostility, Paul was beginning to be moved. He had to be a good man, he told himself. Being good, he reminded himself, had nothing to do with it. He was not there for the 'good'. However, he was still unwilling to commit himself again. One thing would lead to another. Surely his priority was to get to his monastery?

"Can't you get married in a church in Wuhan? Surely there must still be some church open with a priest?"

"I wouldn't go to him!" There was utter contempt in the words.

Paul was silent for a moment. This was another matter. He really did not know what to think. He would soon have to work the question out, and it would not be easy doing it by himself.

"The Sacraments will still be valid," he said.

The man turned round to look at him. "You are not one of *them*, are you?"

Paul did not answer. Instead, he said, "I'll come with you. Lead on."

The man went to the ticket office and bought a return ticket for him to the first village down the line to the south. "My name's Pei," he told Paul while they waited for the next train. "Pei Shunchang. Gabriel's my baptismal name, and I didn't take a new name for my Confirmation."

They left the train at the sort of village which did not distinguish it from a million other plain Chinese villages. Apart from the fact that his own home village was somewhat larger, Paul might, if he had been dropped into it in the middle of the night, have had some excuse for mistaking it for his home. There were the usual courtyard houses of different sizes, a temple with a paved area in front of it used for communal threshing at harvest time, a school nearby. It was not until someone spoke to him that he would have known he was no longer in his home province of Canton. Unsurprisingly, Pei led him to one of the larger houses at the far end of the single street which extended at right angles from the railway station.

He was greeted by two thirteen- or fourteen-year-old boys, both of whom looked at him curiously. One of the boys was very obviously Pei's own son. The lean years had probably left their marks on him, for he was thin and not entirely healthy-looking. The other boy seemed to have escaped the lean time, and he was more robust and had a better colour. Pei's son took the carrier bag from him and carried it across the courtyard into the house.

"Where's your mother?" he asked the other boy.

"She's in the kitchen making dumplings and the New Year cake."

"Tell her I've brought a *shenfu*."

The boy disappeared into the house.

By the time the two men arrived on the threshold, the woman was also coming from the rear of the house into the front room, where there was a blazing fire in a brazier. One of the boys shut the front door as hosts and guest met in the middle of the room. The woman was a few years younger than the man, and Paul reckoned that she would be about the same age as himself. Like many people, she would only wear the universal blue suit in public. She was now well if plainly dressed. In her middle thirties she was still attractive, although her face showed the scars of the experiences she had been through, and she looked a little older than she ought to do. However, she had the appearance of someone who had once exercised authority. She was introduced as Elizabeth and came to shake his hand and, again, he had some difficulty discouraging her from falling on her knees and kissing his hand. People, Paul reflected, never used to do that before. That used to be reserved for bishops. It was a new custom which had grown up in the last couple of years. The danger to the church seemed to have raised the status of a priest!

Word must have been passed around, for early next morning people began to arrive: old, young and babies. Pei informed him that he had vetted these people himself. He was, he said, well aware of the danger to the priest.

"They're all safe, Father," said Pei. "We occasionally meet, about once or twice a month, to say the Rosary. And so far, nobody's informed on us."

Pei and Elizabeth were overjoyed when Paul told them that he would celebrate a wedding Mass for them, as they had both been married at a Mass, rather than in a shortened form of the marriage ceremony, in their first marriages. They were a little surprised when he asked them for some of their china for use in the Mass, and from the expressions on their faces he gathered that they were wondering if the Mass was going to be canonically legal.

"I have no chalice, you see, but I can assure you that it's all legal," he laughed. The dark mood which had gripped him when he missed the train was beginning to lift. He found the wedding Mass in the missal, which he had had very few opportunities to celebrate: people did not usually get married in a Cistercian monastery.

The Mass was preceded by the Sacrament of Penance, when practically everyone wanted to confess. The Nuptial Mass itself was a simple occasion, and there was no dressing up. He was glad when he saw the contentment in the eyes of Pei and Elizabeth, and he joined the family and the guests at their celebration afterwards. Then, some time in mid-afternoon, he rose to leave.

"Father," Elizabeth said. "It's the New Year in a few days. Won't you stay at least until it's over?"

He thanked the family for their invitation. The lunar New Year was very much a family occasion. It would have been all right with Matthew and Susannah, who were old friends. It would have been all right in Tientsin because he had his own independent space, and Chun and Lingyi were, almost, more than friends. But with Pei and Elizabeth, it was different, and he would feel an intruder.

"Thank you," he said. "I must be on my way."

When Pei found that they could not persuade Paul to stay, he went into another part of the house and came back soon afterwards with an envelope in his hand.

"Then," he said, "you must accept this."

When Paul was back at the village railway station, he opened the envelope and found that the donation had been generous. He consulted the ticket office, and found that he could travel another hundred miles or so nearer to Canton. But then, it would leave him, again, practically penniless, without money to buy food or pay for a bed. On the other hand, he could backtrack to Wuhan where he could find some accommodation for the next week or so, until the immediate New Year celebrations were over.

Instead, he started walking south. He could not understand why he did this; he had not planned to do so. But he could not bring himself to going back to Wuhan – not just because of Mang; he could not stand the idea of waiting for something to happen, which would have been the situation if he went back there. At least, when he walked, he later told himself, he was doing something, and he was on his own, and he was able to collect his thoughts and work out what he would do next. There were still two or three hours of daylight left, and he would be able to cover a fair distance, ten or twelve miles, maybe more, if he really concentrated on his walking.

This was his first journey on foot since he had arrived back at Yang Chia Ping more than two months before, and he enjoyed it once he started striding out again. The cold, even the January cold, never bothered him, and, southerner though he was, he had been inured to much colder conditions in the north. What he must do was find shelter before nightfall. He was not sure that there were no wolves on the prowl so far south.

Just before nightfall, when lights began to show in the windows of houses he was passing, he found what he had been looking for: a temple. Most of them, even if they were in use, were never locked, and this one, which was on the edge of a village, was open. He found a space behind the altar, and there, wrapped in the blanket Lingyi had given him, he went to sleep with the acrid smell of burning incense in his nostrils.

For the second time since he became a monk, he overslept. There was sunlight on the wall above him when he opened his eyes and his watch told him that it was past seven, and when he stood up, rather stiffly, he discovered that someone had come in while he was still asleep to put fresh joss sticks into the sand in the brass bowl in front of the Buddha. It showed, he smiled to himself, that he didn't snore. Or maybe the person was kind-hearted enough to let a sleeping beggar lie, as he had been taught. He went to the back of the temple, which shielded him from the road, where he said the Office he had missed.

He found a cooked-food stall for his breakfast before he went on the road again. People in the villages he passed were making their preparations for the New Year. Strips of red paper with blessings on were appearing at doorways, and lanterns were hung. Some people were cleaning and tidying their houses in anticipation of the festival, and shops and stallholders were doing a good trade, as far as he could judge, in seasonal goods. At least the New Order, which seemed to be anxious to break the hold that the traditional family and kinship system had on the life and the mores of the nation, had not decreed against this most family-orientated festival of the agrarian lunar New Year.

The road, he knew, would be busy for the first couple of days with other travellers, on foot, on carts or on charcoal-burning buses, most of whom were returning home for the seasonal festival, and it would be busiest in the afternoon on New Year's Eve. There were also lorries and other goods-carrying vehicles making last-minute deliveries. But, then, paradoxically, he found solitude in this constant, often busy, stream of humanity and machinery. Few travellers spoke to him, and he was never obliged to speak to anybody unless he chose to, aside from the occasional wordless greetings he might exchange with them. And, also, for the first time in three months, he was truly on his own. What he appreciated, as he had already discovered when he walked from the labour camp to visit the ruins at Yang Chia Ping, was how little his privacy was invaded by other travellers. He felt at peace, and the good weather helped too. No one bothered him when he was moved not just to say the Office, but to sing quietly to himself sections of the psalms as well. Other travellers did look at him, but there were, they concluded, bound to be many strange people about.

However, there were also darker moments – for that fearful march from the monastery to Mu Chia Chuang was indelibly embedded in his memory – when he seemed once more to be walking with Father William, or Brother Andrew, or Father Chrysostom on the way to their martyrdom. Where possible, he sought night shelter in temples. Once or twice he slept in barns. Both these amenities he often had to share with other itinerants, many of them misfits, like himself, he supposed, who had previously found it difficult to fit in under the Nationalists who had not bothered with them, and who now found it even more difficult to fit in with a regime which sought to exterminate all deviants. Paul often met the same people on consecutive nights, and, brief though the acquaintance was, he found a sort of camaraderie with them. Some had tried to rob him, but he was a light sleeper, and the would-be thief quickly fled into the night, sometimes leaving something of his own behind.

The bangs and explosions of firecrackers on the three days of the New Year scarcely disturbed him. He did not know how many days he travelled, nor how many miles he covered. His mind had set an automatic course southwards, following the railway line if it was visible, and keeping the morning sun on his left if it was not. Several times a day, a train would thunder past in his direction, and another one going the opposite way. Then, one day, he noticed that the landscape had changed. He was no longer walking on the level. He was slowly climbing into the foothills of mountains which crossed his path. He discovered that he was also running out of money. He must look for work to fund the next stage of the journey.

At about midday, travel-stained and unshaven, with a three-day stubble on his face, he came to Shanglin, a medium-sized town perched on the slope of a hill, its grey-blue houses with their black tiled roofs descending in untidy tiers to the main street, and then spilling and cascading downslope on the other side. The noonday sun lit up most of the buildings with highlights on their roof ridges. A couple of modest two-storeyed inns stood on the periphery. Perhaps, he thought, he might be able to afford to stay in one of them if he could find work. A gentle uphill walk, past buildings which grew from two to three storeys, brought him to a busy market in the extensive town square. Behind a screen of horse chestnut trees which lined the square were shops, and he found the office that he had been looking for. There was, he had anticipated, bound to be one in any fair-sized town. 'Town Offices and Workers' Co-operative', the sign above its door read. He pushed the door open and went in.

There were four clerks, all busy at their tasks under the watchful supervision of a portrait of the great Chairman Mao. There was no counter to which he could go and wait for attention, so he stood by the door. One of the clerks looked up almost immediately and beckoned. Paul went over to him and explained his need. The man listened courteously.

"What sort of work do you actually want?" The man studied him more closely than he had done up to that point. He then consulted a list. "There are very few clerical jobs at the moment."

"I don't particularly want a desk job," Paul explained. "I only want a temporary job. A labouring job will be just fine."

The man consulted another list. Then he looked up. "There isn't anything here either. Sorry. Maybe if you go on to the next town…"

"How far's that?"

"Ten miles?" the clerk asked the man at the next desk. "Is it about ten miles to Liangshu?"

His colleague nodded.

"Yes. Ten miles."

The other man came over. "There is one job that's still open.

Some of the applicants turned it down."

"Right," said Paul's clerk. "There are actually two vacancies, it seems. It's roadsweep and nightsoil remover. It's on a weekly basis. That is, you get paid on a Saturday. So, if you start today, you get half a week's wages on Saturday. And you start this afternoon." The man looked up. "Can you?"

Paul took the job. The clerk took him to the back of the building and introduced him to a big, hefty man. "Your new assistant."

Paul found that his boss was called Hsu, and he headed a gang who had the task of sweeping the roads once in the morning and once in the evening, including clearing up after the daily market closed at six in the evening. Every fourth day they also had to clear up after the larger market which drew farmers from the countryside around. Surprisingly, the local branch of the Party had not interfered with private enterprise. At least, not yet. In addition, the men, and the women, of the gang had the task of collecting nightsoil from the front of houses in areas allocated to them. The occupants, his boss explained, had the responsibility of leaving it out before the collection. "That," Hsu explained, "is at six."

"People leave as soon as they find another job," Hsu said, helpfully. Then he added, "What was it you used to do before?"

"I've worked on building dams, up north," he said, and left it at that.

He was not due back for work until just before six. So he went to one of the two inns he had seen on the way into the town. He had given one of them as his temporary address, and so he booked a room there for a night, which he could scarcely afford. But, he reasoned, he would be paid on Saturday. And if he wished to save for his onward journey, he must find somewhere cheaper.

The work, he found, was not particularly onerous, although the smell of the nightsoil clung unpleasantly to his clothes throughout most of the day. In the monastery, they'd had the opportunity to wash and change into fresh clothing before attending to other tasks.

Now, he had no such facilities. After the first night he found lodgings with a family, which would allow him to save something from his meagre wages.

By Saturday, he had developed a routine. He was free between the morning sweep and the evening clearing up, but he hated spending the time in the company of his fellow roadsweeps. Their incessant chatter, after the first day, was driving him out of his mind. So he stayed outdoors, or spent some of the time watching the traders in the market place, which he quite enjoyed doing. And he was there, on the morning of the second Saturday, after he had recited None at about midday.

The prospective shopping crowd had thinned, and most of them had gone home or to a teahouse for something to eat. The traders, too, were relaxing, and many were eating their own lunches. Then he noticed the couple who had a small stall at the end of a row of vegetable sellers.

This couple, he concluded, were not in danger of making a fortune, certainly not if their only items for sale were winter cabbages – though they certainly looked good – and a few perennial herbs. In fact, it would be a miracle if they made enough today to feed themselves. Paul looked at the man. He was older than himself, quite a lot older, actually, and Paul guessed him to be about fifty or fifty-five. The woman was considerably younger, perhaps about thirty or thirty-five. Although both had obviously been exposed to the weather, Paul did not reckon that they were labourers. The couple's hands were too unscarred for that. In fact, his own Cistercian hands were rougher than theirs. Paul also wondered whether they were father and daughter, but he concluded that they did not treat each other like parent and child.

The woman took out a small bundle from a basket under the table, and the man felt behind his chair and brought round a thermos flask. This was their lunch, as Paul saw when the bundle was unwrapped. Then amazingly, and as far as Paul could judge unconsciously, both started to raise their hands to their foreheads. There was only one meaning to this gesture. The man caught Paul's look and stopped, and gave the woman a vigorous nudge, which caused her nearly to drop her sandwich. Both of them stared back at Paul.

Paul might simply have ignored them, pretending not to have noticed the incipient sign of the Cross. Instead he went over to them. He actually thought of making the tracing of a fish on the table but decided that it would be over-dramatic, and in any case would look false. And perhaps they would not understand what he was trying to do.

So he said, softly, "Don't worry. I'm one of you."

The couple looked relieved.

"This," said the man, "is a happy and auspicious day. We'll close shop, and would you like to come home with us?"

The woman nodded and smiled a welcome. Paul was not expected to be on duty for a few hours yet, and he accepted the invitation. The lunch was packed away again and Paul helped to carry the unsold vegetables.

Some of their fellow stallholders called a farewell to them.

"What, dad? Are you going already? Business wasn't very good this morning, was it?"

"You'll do better tomorrow."

They seemed to be a popular couple.

Soon, they turned up a narrow, paved lane which led from the main street as it made a gentle ascent up the hill from the market place. The lane twisted round a number of houses decorated with the usual, customary blessings and images of gods and spirits, and then it turned into a dirt road. This led, after about half a mile, up to a long building which in times past might have housed pigsties, or at least the pigsties at Yang Chia Ping had looked like that. On the far side of the building was a fence which enclosed a well-tended vegetable garden. After having been shown into the house with much courtesy, Paul discovered that the interior of the building was nothing like a pigsty. Nothing like it at all, he thought. Much labour had gone into making it habitable. Wooden partitions had been erected on the top of the low walls which divided the three sties, converting the space into three small rooms with a corridor running past them. The walls had been whitewashed, and the floor had been planked over. One of the end rooms served as a living room, and there were books on some homemade shelves which confirmed Paul's conjecture that the man had not originally made his living with his hands. There was also a radio, but Paul guessed that it was not working because there was apparently no electricity. On a hook suspended from the ceiling was a paraffin lamp.

He was invited to put his rucksack in a corner of the living room. Then he was shown to a seat by the dining table placed against the back wall of the small room, and tea was offered. The woman, in the meantime, was putting away the vegetables which they had brought back from the market. A crucifix and a framed print of Our Lady of the Seven Sorrows hung on the wall in the corridor, but they were visible only from inside the house.

"I had a picture like that once." Paul decided to open the conversation.

"So what are you?" The man was much more direct. The woman watched Paul with interest.

"Have you heard of Yang Chia Ping, north of Peking?" Paul asked.

"Can't say I have, really," the man replied.

"I have," said the woman. "It's a big monastery, isn't it, of a silent, contemplative Order. The Trappists. That's it. Something terrible happened there, a couple of years ago. Yes, we heard about it."

Paul noticed that the woman did not include the man in the first-person plural pronoun. The man gravely nodded his head as though the memory of something he had once heard was just returning to him.

"I think I get it now," he said. "Didn't Pius XI mention it in one of his encyclicals in the twenties, I seem to recall, as an example of contemplative prayer needed to back up the work of the active clergy... or something like that?"

"That's a bit before my time." The woman smiled. Paul was beginning to be drawn to her: she had a sense of humour. The man was a much more serious character, perhaps somewhat humourless. Then she returned to the topic. She looked keenly at Paul for a couple of seconds, and then said, "You wouldn't be from Yang Chia Ping, would you?"

Paul smiled to himself. He had hoped to find out what these two were first, and now he was being invited to reveal himself, while he still knew nothing about them.

"Yes," he said.

"So it did happen, didn't it, this terrible thing?"

There had been no difficulty telling Mrs Chang and Matthew and Susannah about the martyrdom, because they had all of them been closely involved with the monastery. The only detail which he held back on was the killing of the five monks in the snow. His own mind could not cope with that yet. With Chun and Lingyi, somehow, he had found it more difficult to be forthcoming, and at first he told them only a skeletal account of the story, although after they had become real friends he had also told them all that he and his brothers had experienced, again with the same reservation. This time, there was a marked reluctance, as though with every enquiry, he had to dredge deeper and deeper into himself to bring up the answers, and the answers also hurt more. But he told the story. The suffering of Yang Chia Ping, and Father Seraphin, Father William, Brother Roch, Brother Andrew – and all the others – deserved to be known and remembered, and these people perhaps also had a right to know. So, as the afternoon wore on, he told his story again, all save the massacre on the hillside. However, there was such an interest, in fact, that lunch – already deferred – was forgotten, and although his audience noticed the gap in his tale, they did not query him.

Silence fell at the conclusion of the story, which he chose to end with his return visit to the ruins of Our Lady of Consolation. The woman had shown great interest in the courage which Mrs Chang showed, and the man had questioned him closely on how he had celebrated Mass without the normal bread and wine.

"Imagine! She was the only person throughout who was brave enough to defend any one of you! Did she die from the beating?"

"No," Paul reassured her. "She regained consciousness before the end of the trial. I met her again when I went back to the site of the monastery four months ago."

"So you were able to find communion wafers for use at Mass?" was one of the man's questions. "It must have been difficult."

"It was. But I almost always managed to make my own. It wasn't difficult, even if the end product wasn't as smart-looking as the ones the nuns made. On the other hand, don't you think that Our Lord would have used just ordinary bread, and rice wine too, if he had been Chinese rather than a Hebrew?"

"Ah!" His host wagged a finger at him – it was almost like a theological disputation in a seminary. "But the Chinese weren't the chosen people."

Paul nearly shouted, "Touché!"

"Now, tell me," he said, looking from one to the other, "who, or what, you are." He was beginning to have an idea as to what the man, at least, had once been.

"I was from this town, originally," the man said. "I went to the minor seminary in Wuhan, and then the major seminary, and was ordained for the diocese. I was, however, transferred to another diocese, and I was parish priest for more than twenty years in a village on the Yangtze. Downstream from Wuhan, almost halfway to Shanghai. The People's Liberation Army came, about eighteen months ago, and turned me out of the church and put me on trial. Like what happened to you, a lot of Catholics were pressurised into giving evidence against me, but what really surprised me was that they let me go. Some of those on trial with me were shot." He paused; the memory obviously still affected him. "They asked me if I would repudiate the authority of the Pope, who, in their eyes, was merely a foreign ruler, and I said no. If I had, they'd have let me go back to my parish. Some of my friends did go back to their parishes. But I didn't, and, like you, I was told that I mustn't work as a priest again. There was no one I could go to; the bishop was in prison. So I started to come back here."

"He begged his way," said the woman. "So did I, and we met in a village about a week's walk from Wuhan."

"Anna," the man spoke before she could resume, "was a sister in a convent in Hangchow. The sisters ran a hospital, but they closed it, and the sisters were all turned out of the convent without any money."

"Most of the sisters went home to their families, somehow. I came from the mountains around here, and so I decided to beg my way. I was starving and ill and sleeping in a doorway when Leo found me, and he spent two months taking care of me." There was love in her eyes as she looked at him. "We had no idea then what the other one was."

They travelled together, and begged together, and eventually arrived at the town. Leo had no family anymore, but an old friend of his father let him have a disused farm building and a generous piece of land next to it.

"You've done marvellously well," Paul said.

"We've been lucky, so far," said Anna. "Thank God."

Leo nodded agreement, but said nothing.

"You may have guessed," he said after a short while, "that I no longer live as a priest." He put his hand over Anna's. She watched Paul defiantly.

"We're not sorry," she said. "We feel no guilt. It's a matter of survival."

Paul thought it was more than just that. There was love, a great love between these two, born out of the sharing of hard times and great suffering. Why should he be expected to condemn? God surely wouldn't. He would marry them, as he had done Pei and Elizabeth – how long ago was that now? – if they wanted him to. He had a case, he was sure, for regularising the relationship between Leo and Anna.

Anna forestalled his plans on their behalf by posing the question herself.

"Will you marry us, Father?" she asked. "I realise that in normal circumstances Leo should have asked for laicisation."

"Of course."

And so he blessed them and afterwards accepted their invitation to stay overnight.

"Thank you," he said. "I'll have to sweep the market place first, though."

"Are you working your way to Hong Kong then, Father?" Anna asked later as they were having their evening meal.

"Well, I was on the train to Hong Kong when…" He told them the story of Mang. "So I'm walking the rest of the way, until I find work somewhere and save up enough to go on the train again."

"Would you consider staying with us while you are in Shanglin?" Leo let Anna ask the question. "You can have this room. We'll rig up a bed somehow. It's no trouble, and we'd very much like you to."

"On one condition," said Paul. "You must let me share in your work."

"That, in fact, would be ideal for us. With your expertise in farming, you can advise us about what we should do. And you will have a share of the profits, if we make any, to help you on your way."

Paul found it hard to turn down the offer, and so he didn't.

Providence did have its ways with one.

# SEVEN

The worst of winter was now past, at least so most people in Shanglin said, or hoped, although it was still some way from the advent of spring. The more than occasional and intermittent blasts of icy winds from Siberia were a frequent reminder that even if spring was not far behind, there was some life in the old winter yet. Paul was conscious of these reminders in the converted pigsty at No. 84 Third Lane, which stood on its own, the nearest house being at least fifty yards downhill on its left, and which commanded a superlative view of the countryside around and the approach road that rose from the north, making its gentle but steady climb towards the town. Those in the area who were farmers and who had been fortunate enough to find work in more prosperous towns during the cold, lean months now returned to the district, and those who had stayed home shook off the lethargy of the winter season. In spite of the chill, the high, reedy sound of the children's bamboo pipes echoed round the hills again, together with their shrieks and cries as they played among the impassive cattle or cackling geese that they were supposed to be tending. Other, less fortunate children dreamed of the outdoors in front of their school books as their teachers droned on about... all manner of useless things, or so at least some of the children thought, even in this brave new world of the People's Republic, under the watchful eye of the great Chairman. Adults, too, were not slow to respond to this prelude to spring. Divested of their thick, inconvenient padded winter coats and fur-lined hats, they looked and sounded more cheerful and good-natured. The expectation of spring, Paul reflected, did do something to people, especially when times tended to be monotonous and hard.

So life was definitely returning to Shanglin. Originally a walled town, the stronghold of some robber baron, it straddled a busy highway into the mountains that were the watershed between the huge Yangtze system and rivers that flowed into the South China Sea. Then, inexplicably, the robber baron disappeared, but the town retained its importance as a local market. It had not, however, escaped the craze in the years between the First World War and the Japanese invasion of replacing the old, often not very exciting or attractive, with the new and functional, which in the case of Shanglin was simply ugly. Here, it seemed, was a town that had been in some danger of forgetting its history.

Paul's work left him with a great deal of free time, occupied as he was only at the extremities of the day. He was at liberty to do as he wished between times, and most of his fellow roadsweeps had a second job, some even a third, during the middle part of the day. Paul did not feel such desperate need for money. Besides, he was committed to Leo and Anna. He spent a lot of his time helping Leo in the vegetable garden, while Anna manned the stall in the market place. Leo was in fact a good gardener, a good judge of his market, and was able, with his originally slim resources, to invest in the right crops. He was an instinctive but effective market gardener, and although Paul was able to offer a certain amount of technical advice, there was not much that really required great expertise – which, Paul was at pains to explain to Anna, he did not possess.

"I'm more of an engineer," he said, repeatedly. "At the monastery I did all my farming chores under supervision, although that didn't stop me learning a few tricks."

"You're only being modest," Anna said in response, every time. And she would not be convinced otherwise. She always made Leo consult Paul, which Paul was afraid might one day be carried too far.

There was a lot of digging to do, and Leo and Paul worked out plans for reorganising the garden, planting new crops and creating more variety, so that they could produce for the market all the year round. And then, one morning, Paul watched his friends lay out their stall with a new product. Eggs!

That was because one evening, as they were having their meal, Paul had made a suggestion. The only new idea, he told himself ruefully, that this farming expert had.

"You know," he had said, almost casually, "we could think about having hens. They are easy to raise, and they don't need much attention, from what I can remember of chicken-raising at the monastery. And they don't depend on the weather as vegetables do."

"Eggs!" Anna enthused. Then her face fell, and she looked at Leo.

"An excellent idea," said Leo, and then he spread his hands. "But we haven't the capital. Seeds and fertilisers we could manage, and we did. But hens are a different thing altogether."

That night, Paul counted the pennies he had been accumulating for his train or bus fare, or just subsistence on the next stage of his pilgrimage. In addition, there was the remnant from the money which Matthew had given him as well as from his wages from his work at China Steamships. He had spent practically nothing from his wages in Shanglin apart from what he insisted on paying to Leo and Anna in rent and for food. Although what he had did not amount to much, the next day he invested part of it in hens and chicks, and while Leo and Anna were at the market he also managed to build a coop and a chicken run from the bits and pieces he had been able to collect from the town dump.

"I bet you've spent everything you saved in the last few weeks. You shouldn't have, you know, Paul," Leo said with mock severity.

But Anna voiced their feelings more seriously. "Thank you, Paul. But I agree with Leo: you really shouldn't have."

It was no great hardship, he thought. It only meant that he'd have to stay on in Shanglin for a bit longer, that's all. In the meantime, the garden flourished and the pennies were beginning to be put in a biscuit tin, very slowly, a few coppers at a time, but the important thing was that they were starting to be able to plan for the future seriously. Meals began to be more than just plain boiled rice supplemented with plain boiled vegetables, and there were occasionally bean curds for variety. He wondered if that was how his pioneering Cistercian predecessors at Yang Chia Ping had started. A Cistercian monastery had to be self-supporting and self-sufficient. So also Leo and Anna had to be. Even more so, because there was no one else they could appeal to in case of dire trouble.

"The money in the tin," Leo told him several times, "goes two ways. Right? Half of it goes to you and the other half to us."

"No," Paul said firmly. "It goes three ways. There are two of you and one of me."

As he had done in Tientsin, he kept to a monastic routine as far as he was able. He had been away from community life so long now that some of its minor aspects were becoming rather hazy, but the routine and the recital of the Office were the reminder that he was not alone, that everything he did was shared by and with his Cistercian brothers wherever they might be. His free time during the day enabled him to say the Office at almost all the right times, and he was mostly able to keep the hours of the Night Office. Then, one night, Leo came into his room. He found Paul sitting up in bed.

"Are you all right?" he asked solicitously. "I thought I heard groaning, and I thought you might be in some sort of pain."

Paul was startled by Leo's voice. "I'm all right. Thanks. I was only..."

"Oh, I ought to have known. Saying your Office. Well, you fellows do take it seriously! We secular priests had to say the Office, as you know, but we never took things so drastically!"

Thereafter Paul took very good care to say the Night Office in silence. But, in fact, Leo had not been far wrong. He had woken from a nightmare where he dreamed that he had been detailed to take food to Father Chrysostom who was in solitary confinement in the pigsty, and he was overcome by the smell and the filth of the place. In the dream he was desperately trying to clean up Father Chrysostom before the guards discovered what he was doing. Then he woke up, and he thought he might as well stay up for Lauds.

On the first Saturday night after he had moved in with Leo and Anna, the former asked him as they were clearing up after supper, "Are you saying Mass tomorrow? And can we come?"

Paul still had the communion wafers which Peter Shen had given him from a vast store at Sacred Heart in Tientsin, and he also had half a bottle of communion wine from the same source. He had said Mass each Sunday when he had been walking, and when and where he could without attracting attention. Twice he had said Mass under a tree before dawn on the side of the road. The privacy he had enjoyed when he was in lodgings had also provided him with opportunities to perform his priestly functions.

"Yes," he said. "I say it at about four, and in any case, I've got to say it then, because there's no Sunday rest for a nightsoil collector!"

"Four?" said Leo. "We'll be there. Do you want candles?"

They settled on a couple of oil lamps since they could not afford beeswax candles, not in those early days.

So they attended his first pre-dawn Mass at 84 Third Lane that Sunday, and thereafter, he returned to the habit of saying Mass every morning, and Leo, and sometimes Anna also, came.

If he had been tempted when he was at Lungchuan, and again in Tientsin, to say with St Peter *Lord, it is good to be here*, he was most certainly tempted to say it again, in this converted pigsty, in the friendly mountains south of the Yangtze. Canton seemed a million miles away, and Hong Kong on the other side of the Milky Way. As long as the authorities left him alone.

Years before, when he was learning Greek with the small class of young monks at Yang Chia Ping, they had to read the Iliad and the Odyssey. He was fascinated by the way in which both tales were told.

He was mesmerised by Homer's description of characters and places, and the vivid telling of battles and individual combats. Although the Iliad dealt with the anger of Achilles, he grieved for the Trojans. He was taken along by the enthusiasm shown by his teacher, an old monk who died the year he was ordained. The Odyssey appealed to him just as much, and it was Penelope who touched him most deeply. There was the story of the land of the Lotus Eaters, where man, after tasting the seed of the plant, forgot his past, his future...

Later, when Paul thought back to this period of his sojourn at Shanglin, he wondered whether he had indeed not eaten the seed of the lotus. His excuse, as ever, was that he had a contribution to make to those around him. He then realised that life would have gone on even if he had never been around. But now, he told himself that he was getting soft and self-indulgent. Otherwise missing the train at Wuhan would not have shattered him so. Certainly the hell that followed those early days of July two and a half years ago had not affected him in the same way. He knew that he needed the discipline of the monastery.

He had done another thing since had had settled in Shanglin. He had been unable to be rid of a guilt feeling about Peter Shen, even when he himself had been in deep depression. It was on his behalf that this ordinary but brave man had got into trouble. He also worried about Mrs Shen: it was supposed to be the shepherd who suffered for his sheep, not the other way round. One afternoon he wrote to Chun, hoping that it was not going to be the shepherd causing his sheep more trouble, for he could not be certain whether the post was going to be officially tampered with.

He waited ten days, but finally Chun's reply came.

"Dear Weishung," it read. "I really thought that you had already got *home* to Hong Kong." The word 'home' was a pre-arranged code, but not the way Chun had written it, Paul mused. "They released Mr Shen, much to Mrs Shen's relief, two days after you left. It seems that Mr Shen was unable to provide any of the information about a certain priest which the authorities required."

Then Chun seemed to have decided to throw caution to the winds. "What the heck!" he could almost imagine Chun say. In spite of the totalitarianism of the state, most people still believed in the incorruptibility and inviolability of the postal service. Paul himself was not at all sure if it, but it was obviously impossible for the authorities to check all the mail. So Chun carried on, *en clair*, one might say.

"They did not spare him, much, in spite of his age." Paul was by no means surprised; he remembered only too vividly how old Brother Bruno, and Father William, for example, had been treated. "They made him kneel for hours on the floor, without water or food, and beat him at intervals. But Mr Shen did not tell. Then they brought him home, scarcely able to stand and his back a mass of bruises. They came back the next day and closed the church and threw Mr and Mrs Shen out of their flat in the rear of the rectory. They had this pile of furniture and chests and other things standing on the pavement outside the church. And this was three days before the Chinese New Year! It was absolutely barbaric!"

Chun would have used a stronger epithet if he had been speaking on the telephone.

"I was at work and did not know, but someone told Lingyi right away. In fact it was the man from the cooked-food shop – so it couldn't have been him who gave you away! Lingyi organised a couple of people, went down to the church and brought them and their stuff back to the house. They are now living in your old room, and they have their meals with us. Mr Shen wanted to give you back the money you gave Mrs Shen. He needs it more than us, he kept saying; he has a long way to go. Did I do right in refusing to take it back? I thought then you must be safely out of the way, *at home*. Anyway, the church is still closed, with these official seals across the doors. Just as well: they keep thieves away. The priests still haven't come back. It seems that they are so stubborn they refuse to become patriotic (this seems to be the new term, now, applied to priests and bishops who co-operate with the government), and are in prison waiting to be re-educated. Some of us are beginning to go to Mass at St Thomas's. Have they become schismatics, then? Or heretics? I can never tell which is which."

That, decided Paul, was a question he was determined not to answer, when he wrote to Chun again. The fact was that he did not know all the answers to the question.

"Shiyu and Suhan both missed you, and for a few days kept asking when you were going to come back. I told them that you had your own home to go back to. We have a group of about twenty people who meet in one another's houses, once every two weeks, for a meal and to say prayers, usually the Rosary. There is a rumour that the government is cracking down on these prayer groups now, but we haven't actually heard anything definite, and we'll carry on for as long as possible. Lingyi is well, and she misses you, just as I do."

Chun went on to inform Paul that he had also told Mr Wang that he was well, and Mr Wang had asked to add his greetings.

"I told you he was a decent man," Chun reminded Paul.

This was one load that had been taken off his mind. At least Peter Shen and his wife were free, as far as there was meaning to this term under the new Republic, and well taken care of, for the time being. He prayed earnestly that Chun and Lingyi had the wisdom to be circumspect. Martyrdom in the Roman Empire might seem a glorious thing, but when it happened to one in the middle of the twentieth century, there was little glory and a lot of pain. He would not recommend it to anyone with family responsibilities. He began to worry about Chun and Lingyi.

He received another letter at the beginning of April, during Easter Week. This one was rather bulky and had come by registered mail, and so he had to go down to the post office to collect it. The man at the counter gave him a curious look when Paul showed him his identity document. He didn't like the scrutiny; often it set alarm bells ringing in his brain. But this time the man smiled and handed him the letter. By the handwriting on the envelope, he thought it was from Lingyi. His hands shook and fumbled badly as he tried to tear open the letter. He was half convinced that Lingyi had written to tell him that something disastrous had befallen her husband.

It was indeed a letter from Lingyi.

"There is a sudden increase of business at China Steamships," it said, "and Chun is up to his neck in work. Everybody there has had to work overtime the last ten days or so, and Chun has never been home much before nine in the evening, all tired out. So he's asked me to write and send you the enclosed."

He opened the second envelope, pinned to the letter for security. Lingyi, Paul recalled with a smile, was always careful. Inside this envelope was a bundle of notes.

"Mr Wang reckoned he owed you a month's wages, but he couldn't send it on to you as you had left no forwarding address. He's now asked Chun to do that for him. The money includes the Chinese New Year bonus which was also due to you, Mr Wang told Chun."

As Chun said repeatedly, Mr Wang was a good man.

"Nothing much has happened since Chun wrote to you. Mr and Mrs Shen asked me to send you their best wishes, and they are also anxious that you do not worry about them, as they are in, as they say, good hands, which is quite flattering. They also say it's time, really, that you got *home*."

Paul wrote back immediately to thank Lingyi, enclosing a shorter letter to Mr Wang which Chun could deliver for him. He then made the short walk downhill to the post office.

It was almost time for the clearing out at the end of the day, and so he went to his by now usual place under the tree on the edge of the square, behind the little stall run by his friends, to wait. And also to think. He now had the money to get him on the train to Canton, and even to Hong Kong. He could leave immediately – at least, at the end of the week – and be in Canton the next day. However, he still had work to do here, to finish the jobs he had started with Leo and Anna. Perhaps, then, he should give himself another two weeks. He owed it to them, not least for giving him shelter.

The traders were finally packing their things away. He gave Leo and Anna a cheery wave. "I'll see you back at home." And he and his mates began the task of sweeping and clearing out the enormous amount of rubbish which was left at the end of the market. Eventually it was done, and with the lengthening of the days there was still light as he made his way back up the hill to the house.

Anna had supper almost ready when he got back. He took the opportunity to have his daily wash from the tub of water behind the hut. Another thing he had got used to during his years in the monastery was washing in cold water, whatever the weather. Chun and Lingyi used to worry about him catching cold or pneumonia, but now Anna was beginning to get used to his ablutions behind the building. She just made very sure that she did not go round the back while he was at it.

"I got another letter from my friends in Tientsin," he said when they were sitting down to the meal.

"Are they all right?" Anna asked, half anxiously.

"Oh, they're all right. Nothing wrong with them. Well, I've been sent some money, a month's back wages plus New Year bonus from my old boss."

A small cloud descended.

"So you'll be leaving us soon?" Leo said. It was more of a statement, really.

He took a short while to frame his answer. "No. Not yet." But they had noticed his hesitation.

"Look, Paul," Anna said, "if you're staying because of us, please don't. You have done enough for us, and we are most grateful. Sooner or later, you have to be on your way again."

Leo put down his bowl and his chopsticks the better to emphasise his point.

"We'd rather you went later than sooner, as you know. You're helping us such a great deal, as Anna said, and not only in our market gardening. But you have to go some time."

"No, Leo. No, Anna. There are still things to finish in your garden. Besides, I owe such a lot to you. Another two weeks, maybe... that is, if you don't mind my staying on."

Their faces creased in smiles. For good measure Leo thumped Paul heartily on the back. "We're glad you're staying on for a while longer. We'd have missed you terribly if you had decided to go now."

A couple of days later, while Paul was again at his usual spot on the edge on the square, something unusual, really unusual, caught his eye. It was a man in a black soutane, talking to a woman, who, with her bulging basket, had evidently been shopping. The woman was incidental: it was the man. Paul thought he was either very foolhardy, or very brave, or very sure of his position. Leo, who was not more than twenty feet away, looked back at Paul, inclining his head in the direction of the figure in the clerical garb.

"I thought they'd closed the church," Paul said at supper.

"They had," Leo said. "Father Fang must have come to open it up again in the last couple of days."

"You know him?"

"Indeed I do. He's an old friend. We went through seminary, minor and major, together. He was one of the best of our year." Leo stopped, to think, it seemed. "Well, he must have come to some sort of understanding with the government, then." He stopped again.

Paul detected a certain inflection, and if it did not sound quite like condemnation, there was certainly disappointment in it. Was it not ironic that someone who had clung to his principles should end up abandoning his priesthood, although, under the circumstances, who could blame him, whereas Father Fang, on the other hand, having compromised, was able to continue in his ministry? In the days when he had been trying to survive the marches, the public trials and the labour camp, if he had had the leisure to think about the matter of what amounted to the question of juring priests – which, if he was not mistaken, had elsewhere most recently arisen when the French Revolution had attempted to control the clergy – he would have unequivocally come down on the side of orthodoxy. But now, he was not so sure at all of his stance on the matter.

Leo addressed Anna. "Well, I think that we ought to invite John Fang to a meal one day quite soon. It'd be awkward if we ran into each other and he found out that we'd been living here all along. What do you say?"

"He's your friend, as you say. I don't know him at all. Well… it's up to you. Though I hope you won't spend the evening arguing with him."

Leo was amused by the suggestion that he would start an argument with Father Fang. "I really don't have a position to defend, do I? It's like the pot calling the kettle black, as the English say." He turned to Paul. "What do you think?"

"Oh, no. I'm staying out of any argument you get into with Father Fang. But I'll certainly meet him, if you wish me to. Actually I'd quite like to," he added after a short pause.

"Right. So, it's settled then. I'll see if he has time for us next Sunday."

When Paul got back to 84 Third Lane after his evening sweep on Sunday, he found Father Fang with Leo and Anna. Father Fang was in one of the two chairs, and Anna was in the other. Leo was seated hunched up in the settee which served also as Paul's bed at night.

They all stood up when he entered, Anna going into the kitchen to see to the food. Leo made the introduction.

"Father Fang," he said. Paul shook hands with a slight, urbane and obviously educated man. "He's only just arrived, a minute before you did. Liang Weishung, from Canton originally, who is our partner in this market-gardening business, and our house guest." They had agreed that it might be wise not to reveal Paul's identity for the time being.

"Canton?" said Father Fang. "I was there many years ago, just visiting. I couldn't understand a word people there said! But there's a theory that Cantonese is the original language of China."

"That could well be true," Paul said. "A lot of the old poetry, really old poetry, can only rhyme if read in Cantonese, I'm told."

"So it's we who are the barbarians! What I meant to say was, that you speak Mandarin without a trace of an accent. Have you been long in the north, then?"

"I lived in the north for something like sixteen years or more."

"Oh, where, if I may ask?"

"Peking. Near Peking."

"Mr Liang's an engineer," Leo said. "He trained at Peking University."

"You must be good," said Father Fang appreciatively. "What do you build?"

"Oh... I've built roads and a dam."

It was clear to Paul that they were politely trying to size each other up. Leo had said that this man was 'the best'. Paul tended, at this brief initial encounter, to agree. This man, he felt instinctively rather than rationally, was a good priest, a good shepherd, one who cared for his flock.

Paul was curious whether Father Fang wondered why a qualified engineer was now working as a roadsweep and nightsoil collector. But he was even more curious as to how Father Fang had reacted to Leo's revelation that he had ceased to be a priest and was now married. If, indeed, he had been shocked, he was disguising his thoughts very well. However, the priest also had a position to explain, and Paul believed he knew what the explanation would be. If he had been a secular priest, he would have been in the shoes of either Leo or Father Fang now. It was just pure luck that his position was not so ambivalent.

Anna announced dinner, and Leo pulled the folding circular dining table from the wall and Paul helped to lay it. Anna then insisted on changing places with him, so that she was now sitting with Leo on the settee, although it was not particularly convenient for getting to the kitchen when she needed to. It was probably her way of making the situation plain to the visitor.

Leo decided to tell his side of the story first.

"Anna," he said, "was once Sister Anna of the Congregation of the Holy Name, a congregation of Chinese nuns. They ran a hospital at Hangchow. Anyway, when the PLA took over the city, they threw all the nuns out and closed the hospital, and Anna had to find her way home. She had no money... and so she begged her way."

Anna then took over, and repeated the story she had told Paul. "Leo found me starving and ill in a doorway, and stayed to take care of me. Later..." She caught Paul's eye and realised that she had been unwittingly on the point of referring to him by his baptismal name. "Later, we got married."

Father Fang was unruffled by the story. "Then I wish you both a happy life together."

"Thank you," Leo said. And then, as if to forestall anything Father Fang might be tempted to even think, he added, "We were married by a passing priest." He made an effort not to look at Paul.

Father Fang raised his eyebrows but made no comment.

The story then went back to the beginning when Leo had stood trial for his life and had then been released.

"I was given a choice. I could either stop working as a priest, or the government – or the PLA which stood for government then – was quite willing to allow me to return to my parish if I would repudiate the authority of the Pope and his power to appoint bishops in China, and give my allegiance to a bishop appointed, or at least approved, by the state." He then said lightly, not looking at his old friend, "This was too much to take, and so I came home. And I met Anna."

What he said might have sparked off a debate, and Leo would have launched into a detailed exposition of the Papal position. It was nothing new between the two men. As two of the most promising philosophy and theology students at the seminary, they had frequently been set by their professors to defend opposite poles of a thesis. Anna, however, had warned him not to sacrifice friendship for a debate, and so he merely added, rather lamely, "It would have caused a schism in the Church."

For a few moments, the only sounds in the room were those of the quiet clatter of chopsticks on bowls and plates.

"I still think," said Leo stubbornly, avoiding Anna's eye, "that without the Pope, we will not be the Catholic Church."

Silence resumed for an uncomfortable moment. A charge, indirect though it might be, had been levelled against Father Fang by his old friend. He had to speak.

"Don't you think, Leo," he said quietly, "that our flock deserves some consideration too?"

Leo looked up from his food, inviting him to continue.

"A man may do what he considers right out of selfishness, worrying overmuch about his own... salvation."

Leo's eyes hardened, and Paul saw Anna quietly lay a hand on his arm, and he said nothing.

"I agonised over the question for a long time, several months, in fact, while they kept me at this re-education camp. Conditions weren't pleasant, and there were no other priests there – I think they did it deliberately, so as to prevent us from conferring, or plotting, as they might call it. The question which came to the top of my mind every time was: what were we ordained priests for?"

He paused to let his point sink in.

"I" – Father Fang emphasised the personal pronoun – "I believed, whatever else others might believe, that I was ordained for ministering to Christ's flock, to use a stilted and rather highfalutin expression. To serve them, in fact. My commitment was to God's people, to teach the ways of salvation, to offer Mass and to administer the sacraments to them. What use am I to these people if I am unable to do all these things? Popes, cardinals and bishops had to come very much second in these considerations. People need the sacraments to *survive*."

Paul was watching Anna. Her concern was that Leo might be hurt. Who was this old friend who came to inflict pain... as if he had not suffered enough! But Father Fang had become oblivious to his surroundings.

"At least I am ministering to the Catholics of this area. I may not be able to talk about religion outside the Church. I may not be able to preach the Gospel to non-believers. I may not be able to go into schools, or open our own schools... or visit the sick in hospital or those in prison... and I must not criticise the government... but, at least, I am doing something."

Did he then mean that Leo wasn't, Paul wondered.

He suddenly turned to Paul. "What do you think, Mr Liang? I take it you are a Catholic, too?"

There was agony and uncertainty in those eyes. In a way, he was on his Via Dolorosa, too, Paul realised, and he felt sorry for him. And here were two old friends, who were trying to avoid hurting each other, but whatever they did, they were doing just that. And each, too, was looking for absolution. It was Anna who understood what was happening.

Paul shook his head. "I think nothing," he said, gazing at the empty dishes on the table, for they had finished eating for a while. "I do not want to judge. I'm not here to judge. I... I... cannot judge."

Perhaps the Church would disintegrate under the juring priests and eventually disappear. Perhaps, on the other hand, the Church would one day thank them for keeping the essentials of the Faith alive. Who could predict?

Father Fang was back with his own thoughts again. "Whatever you think, don't believe that we are at all secure, or that we are free from... harassment and persecution. We survive by the grace of the Party, whose policies towards us, as well as towards other Christian Churches, are as variable as the wind. We walk on a knife's edge, and there are some of us, I have heard, who have gone back to prison.

It's not easy, either, to face the hostility of some of our own people who regard us as traitors, apostates and Judases."

There were tears in those words, Paul thought.

Silence descended again. Anna got up to clear the table, and Paul rose to help her. As he followed her into the kitchen with a handful of bowls and plates, he heard Leo say, quietly, "You must do as you think right, John. We must not judge each other, for friendship's sake."

In the kitchen, Anna turned to look at Paul. He laid a hand on her arm and said, "It's all right. They are old friends. They will not deliberately hurt each other."

"That's exactly what I am afraid of," she said. "Not deliberately."

The two were already talking about other things when he and Anna returned to the room after washing-up.

"Actually, you know," Father Fang was saying, "there has been, surprisingly, little of the activities of the more fanatical elements of the Party in this area. Properties are still mostly in the hands of private individuals, and there is still a vast amount of private enterprise."

"Yes. My own market-gardening effort is a case in point. In other places, I would have had to join a co-operative if I wanted to sell my stuff. At the beginning, that might actually not have been a bad thing for us."

Leo then indicated Paul. "Things are a little different now," he informed Father Fang, "thanks to Mr Liang here."

Father Fang was intrigued. "Yes. I heard that you are a market-gardening expert as well. You are a man of many parts, Mr Liang."

Paul gestured self-deprecatingly. "I was interested in self-sufficiency." Out of the corner of his eye, he saw Anna smile a secret smile.

"Will you be staying long, do you think, Mr Liang? Leo told me that you might be moving on soon."

"A couple of weeks. Three, if necessary. I only stopped here to find work as I needed money to finance the next stage of my journey home."

"To Canton?"

"Yes," Paul said.

A while later, as the guest rose to leave, he asked his hosts, "Shall I see you at Mass on Sunday?"

He got no answer. Instead, Leo said, "You are welcome any time you have a moment to spare or when you need company."

The three of them stayed up late that night, conversing only spasmodically. For some reason, the discovery of the presence of Father Fang in Shanglin had cast a shadow over them. Paul sensed that, of the three, Leo felt most uncomfortable, threatened even, and whatever Leo felt, Anna reflected. Ancient friendship and shared religion were no longer guarantees of loyalty, it seemed, in an atmosphere poisoned by distrust.

"We do envy you, Paul," Anna said at one stage. "You have a destination to go to, and when you get there, there will be security. We have nothing." She looked round the room to emphasise the point. "Apart from this... Nothing."

"Besides," Leo said, "even if we did get to Hong Kong, for example, what sort of work are we going to be able to do? I wouldn't even know how we are going to make a new start. I believe we are caught."

Mid-April nights could still be chilly, and Leo fetched an old paraffin heater. As the room warmed up, Anna asked Paul, "You are going soon, aren't you?" She, or Leo, had asked the same question only a few days before when he told them of the money he had received from Mr Wang. His going must weigh heavily on both of them. It might even feel like desertion.

He gave a facetious answer, in an attempt to lighten the gloom which had become quite oppressive. "You're not thinking of driving me away, are you?"

Before either of them could protest, he continued, "As I said before, it will be another two weeks. Believe me, I find it very hard to think of leaving you two."

And Paul thought how blessed he had been with the people he had met on his long pilgrimage.

\*\*\*

Paul watched them come. It was early afternoon. He was working by himself among the vegetable beds, as he often did while Leo and Anna were down in the market square attending to their stall or to other business, when he happened to look over the fence. The day was sunny and clear, and he commanded a long view of the shallow, broad valley as it rose to the town. The road leading to it followed a straight line before it became concealed at the foot of the first forested spur. Thereafter, it followed the shape of the contours and wound into and out of view until the last quarter of a mile or so, when it became straight again before it reached town. But by then, it was hidden behind the houses lower down the slope. It was never a very busy road, although there was always traffic, both lorries and buses, and there was also the occasional military vehicle. It seemed that most people never found a reason for stopping at Shanglin.

Paul would not have noticed them if the sun had not glinted off the windscreen of the leading vehicle while it was still a long way off, on the straight stretch before it came to the hills. Even then, there was no particular reason why he should have paid it any notice. But he did, somehow. This leading vehicle was followed by two others at fixed intervals, so that they made a convoy of three. Then, as they drew closer, something else caught his eye. Over the cab of each of the lorries – for such they were, Paul concluded, by their outline – were flying red flags or banners, so that the convoy was in fact a procession. What, Paul wondered, was the big occasion? He was intrigued. However, he returned to his work.

A short while later, the indistinct noise of loudspeakers was carried up to him from the market square. He was no longer intrigued, or curious. He had a very good idea what the noise conveyed. He had been through it himself. This was the same noise he and his brothers had heard as they were led from the monastery building down the path leading to the front gate beyond which the crowd was waiting.

"Courage, mon frère," Father William had said. Paul needed it, even now.

It was happening again, all mixed up, in a sort of slow motion like he had once seen in a cinema when he was at university! He couldn't quite remember whom he had gone with. Probably Margaret. He put the weeds he had been clearing out of the cabbage beds into the bin in a corner of the garden, and the hoe he had been working with in the house. Then he changed into his shoes, locked the door and proceeded down the lane to the square.

The first sight he had of the square was always the tops of the trees. During the time he had been in Shanglin the trees had always been bare, and he was able to see through the leafless branches into the market. Leo and Anna would be on the right at their stall, out of sight. Straight ahead, across the square, he would first see the stalls belonging to Mr and Mrs Tien, a comparatively prosperous and contented couple, and old Fei, a garrulous and sometimes querulous widower of many years who had a small farm down towards the plain to the north. How he had always managed to drag his stuff up the long, even if gentle, climb on his overladen bicycle had puzzled Paul, who had got to know him because he bought the hens from him. Then, as he came down the lane, the stalls on both sides of these two would come into view. Today, however, he found to his mild surprise that the familiar view had become obscured by a screen of young, green leaves which, unnoticed by him, had sprouted on the bare branches in the early spring.

When he had descended to the level of the square, he at last saw. The three lorries were parked on the far side of the market, but the Tiens' and old Fei's stalls were no longer in their accustomed places; nor were those that made up that side of the square. Amid the din of loudhailers and shouts of protest, those which had not yet been cleared away were now being taken down. The same was happening to the stalls that occupied the centre of the market. Unlike some other places Paul had known, Shanglin did not appear to take too kindly to the fanaticism of the Party. But in fact, not everything was taken away, for the stalls on three sides of the square were allowed to stay up. Then two trestle tables were moved to the centre of the vacated space, and a number of chairs or stools were being placed behind them. Some of the red flags were taken from the lorries and planted behind the trestle tables... This was the big occasion. The stage was being set. The show trial had come finally to Shanglin, which had strangely, perhaps through an oversight of someone, so far been spared.

He looked for Leo and Anna. They were standing behind their table, their goods packed away in the baskets in which they had been brought that morning. Leo, who had been through it, too, was tense and white. Anna looked frightened and concerned, and kept casting worried looks at Leo. Paul made his way behind the crowd to them and laid a hand on Leo's shoulder. Leo turned round to look at him, unseeingly, Paul thought. Anna smiled at him nervously.

The uniformed young man had, it seemed, organised the stage to his satisfaction. He now raised the loudhailer to his lips, and turning towards the tarpaulin-covered lorries, by which his similarly uniformed comrades, most of them with rifles slung on their shoulders, were standing, he called:

"It's ready. Bring them out."

One of the men undid the rope that held the end flap of the tarpaulin down to the tailboard of the middle lorry, and two of his friends unbolted the tailboard and let it down.

"Come out," one of them ordered.

A man in perhaps his forties, his hands tied behind his back and his arms pinioned to his sides, practically fell from the lorry to the road. He stumbled as he hit the ground, but was able to regain his balance. A second man, somewhat older, trussed up in the same way, followed. He landed badly, and limped to stand beside the first man. Three more followed.

Paul glanced across to Leo. His eyes were closed. He could not bear to watch. Either he could not relive his experience or it might be because he could not see his own experience visited on someone else. Possibly both. Paul felt like that too. Anna, on the other hand, watched with fascinated horror, as she imagined what the outcome was to be.

Paul hoped that they might be able to slip away, as they were on the edge of the crowd. They might be able to circle round to where Third Lane debouched on to the square quite close by. He glanced behind him. One of the uniformed youngsters was standing in front of the entrance to the co-operative office, and although he was not watching them, any movement away from where they were would draw his attention. It seemed that the organiser of the show was determined to ensure that everyone was to participate and witness justice done, because there were others posted behind the crowd. Paul waited. There might be a chance.

The show started. The accused were made to kneel before the bench of judges, who consisted of the leader himself and two of his followers. Witnesses were brought from the third lorry.

"Yau Szetso, of the village of..."

Now was their chance. The young man had moved away, and the short distance to their street was clear. There were, in fact, other people on the move, who wanted a better view of what was happening in the middle of the square. Paul tapped Leo and Anna on the shoulder, and they edged away. They made it to Third Lane without, they believed, attracting attention, and walked home in silence, in a sombre mood. But they were not able to escape it entirely. They were pursued by the sound of the loudhailer, although the words were indistinct, and even when they got home they could still hear it, as one could hear waves advancing on the shore, and receding. But at least, it seemed to Paul, the response of the people of Shanglin to the afternoon's proceedings was muted, for he could hear no shouts, no cheers of approval. The trial judges had failed to whip up popular feelings. Had he stayed, he would have heard nothing, for they remained silent, sullen and perhaps shaken. Here in Shanglin, it appeared, the shock tactics of the Party fanatics made very few converts.

The three sat numb in the sitting room, immersed in their own memories and fears, and for Anna the shock was not the less for it being her first experience of an exhibition of such a travesty of justice.

"What will happen to those men?" Anna asked.

"I don't really know," said Leo. "I don't want to think about it."

Anna looked at Paul with the same question in her eyes.

"If they are really lucky, they'll be released." Like Leo, he nearly said, "They may be found guilty of whatever they're accused of, and get sent to a punishment camp. They sometimes call them re-education camps, or sometimes more honestly, labour camps. They're all more or less the same things. You get beaten for no reason, you get strange, unheard-of punishments, also for nothing. And then, if you are really unlucky, they shoot you."

Towards about four in the afternoon, they heard shots. They were flat, small sounds, no more menacing than the popping of a cork where they heard them.

"Three," Leo said, more to himself than to the others.

"Do you realise," Anna said after a while, "we've left our things by the stall. They're still there."

"You two stay," Paul said. "I'll bring them back after the place is cleared."

He wondered if the roadsweeps were required to take away the bodies. He found Hsu.

"Nobody's said anything. But we're not touching anything, not until that lot clear away the mess they have made. Look, I've been a Communist for thirty years, but I am no bloody murderer. So we're not cleaning this evening, nor tomorrow morning either, except for the nightsoil."

The whole gang of the roadsweeps were there, looking towards the centre of the empty market place where three bodies lay on their faces in pools of their own blood. One of them, judging by his clothing, was the first man who left the lorry.

"So I'll see you all back here tomorrow morning."

The sweeps dispersed. Hsu beckoned Paul back. "Your friends left their stuff behind. I've got it put away in the yard. Perhaps nobody's noticed it."

Paul looked at Hsu gratefully. "Thanks," he said.

A black-robed figure approached the bodies, knelt beside each one, and poured water over their heads.

"That's the new *shenfu*," Hsu said, watching Father Fang. "He's a brave one."

The following morning, however, the bodies had disappeared. Someone had come in the night to take them away. No one knew whether that was merely an act of disposal or if it was an act of real mercy. All that remained were congealed pools of blood on the cobblestones of the square. Hsu got his team to wash them out.

The market returned, but only slowly, as the stallholders were uncertain whether there was going to be a repetition of the proceedings of the previous day. The centre of the square was left empty; those who usually occupied it were unwilling to pitch their stalls where so much violence had been enacted. Shoppers, too, walked round the spot where the three men had died. The market was subdued, and there was far less banter than was normal. Gradually, however, as the day progressed, a measure of good humour returned and by the evening one might be forgiven for thinking that nothing unusual had happened just over twenty-four hours earlier. But Leo and Anna did not open their stall that day. They could not bring themselves to return to the market the next day either. Paul was no more willing, but he had a job to do even if he did not need the money anymore.

Just before noon on the following day, however, the lorries returned, with even more red flags flying from the cabs. Their arrival was greeted with sullen stares and low mutterings. This time, however, there was no show trial, but the business of the market was interrupted, again, by the young man with the loudhailer.

He had returned to harangue the population of Shanglin. He performed his lecture at the top of his voice, which frequently cracked with an emotion few of his listeners shared. He had noticed, he told his audience, the reluctance and the unwillingness of the people of the town to co-operate wholeheartedly with the punishment of the guilty ones two days ago. That was not how things should be. The citizen of the new People's Republic should do his best to eradicate all that was evil in the old, feudal order and visit the representatives of the old order with just punishments for the crimes they had committed against the people. It was the duty of the townspeople to bring forward any person they suspected of such past evil-doing so that he could be dealt with. He himself also had a list of the people he needed to 'deal with'. Anyone with information on anyone else should come to him. He had come, in fact, to clean up the town.

He installed himself in the Town Offices and Workers' Co-operatives, displacing the normal workforce. People with legitimate business at the town offices were either turned away or were invited in to be interrogated about other people in the town. When what was happening there became known, the building was avoided; it had seldom been so empty and poorly frequented since the town offices were set up many years ago. However, the roadsweep gang, who had their own entrance at the rear of the building, retained free access to the room where they kept their equipment. The somewhat smelly condition of the room had possibly discouraged association with the roadsweeps.

However, either there were informers, or the young man with the loudhailer really did have a list. There was whispered confirmation the next day that people had been taken away in the night. The town offices continued to be occupied for the next few days, and there was news of more disappearances. The news and the rumours totally demoralised Leo and Anna, for Leo was convinced that he was going to be part of this cleansing process, because he had been a Catholic priest, even though he had been acquitted in a public trial, and even though he was no longer practising as one.

"They're going to have it in for me," he told Paul several times as they worked in the garden. "Don't tell Anna. She'd worry."

Paul was not entirely sure himself that Leo was wrong, and he knew that Anna was already worrying. But he had to say something to alleviate the anxiety.

"Surely, they won't do anything to you again. They let you go."

"Now, tell me. Are *you* secure? They released you. Do you think they won't arrest you again on some trumped-up charge?"

Paul saw the force of the argument. He consumed the few remaining communion wafers he still had, and the tiny amount of communion wine that still remained in the bottle. The bottle he broke up and disposed of in the town tip. He did not quite know what he ought to do with St Bede, the à Kempis or the missal, and he certainly was reluctant to get rid of the latter.

The town returned to normality after a few days. The town offices were vacated, and the lorries were no longer parked on the side of the square. The Tiens and old Fei and their neighbours set up their stalls in the accustomed places again, and even those who had been unwilling to use the centre of the market now seemed to have forgotten their reluctance. Leo and Anna, too, returned to their stall.

It had been nearly two weeks now since Paul had decided to leave Shanglin, and he had delayed his departure chiefly because he wanted to complete the current tasks in hand. Now, as they were coming up to the end of the week, and Leo and Anna seemed to be settled into a routine – and in any case, Leo was a perfectly competent gardener – he thought it was time to give notice to Hsu and the town offices. Then he would be off the following weekend.

The Friday that followed was a day like any other, and Leo and Anna seemed to be having a good day, judging by the little that was left of their stock when Paul went down to his usual place to watch the stallholders pack up and leave.

"You've done well," he called to Leo and Anna, "it seems to me."

Business had recently been better than they had dared hope two months ago. Leo nodded and Anna smiled.

"Yes," she called back. "Why don't we eat out tonight? We'll wait for you to come home first."

"That would be great," Paul signalled back, for with everyone packing away and calling to friends and shouting to others, the square had become really noisy.

Leo and Anna moved away, and Paul turned to go to the rear of the town offices for his equipment – a tub, a large bamboo broom and hand brushes, with which he could both sweep and scrub. Someone had already brought out the dust cart. They might have another ten minutes to wait for the square to clear completely, but there was always somewhere that they could start to save time.

"Right," Hsu told his people a while later. "It's finished for another day. See you all tomorrow."

The tops of the trees glowed orange and gold above the darkening shadows in the square. Paul could see the sun set behind the purple mountains in the west, and today the eastern sky was still pale blue with wispy clouds streaming diagonally across it. The beauty of the scene stirred him, and he thought of the Compline hymn: *We pray thee, O Creator of all things, before the end of the day, that in Thy accustomed mercy, stand guard over us.* Well, He has stood guard over us, he mused, all three of us, and not just at night, the last couple of months. Before he left Shanglin, it would be appropriate to say the *Te Deum*.

# EIGHT

He rounded the last of the town's houses where the path led up towards No. 84, still, as he had expected, bathed in the last golden light of the setting sun. But there indubitably was something very wrong this beautiful evening. The first thing he noticed was that a section of the garden fence beyond the house had been flattened and was lying in the lane. And then he saw that the front door was hanging askew on its lower hinge, and there was stuff from the house in the lane. There should be smoke from the chimney, for although they were going to eat out tonight Anna was forever making soup, which to her was a panacea against all ills. However, the sky above the house was blue and empty. He ran.

"Leo! Anna!" he called.

The interior was in darkness. He peered through the open door into the living room. The settee had been turned over, and his bedding scattered on the floor. The rucksack which he kept under the settee was lying to one side, empty. The next room, which had been the kitchen, was also in a mess, with earthenware pots and bowls smashed on the floor. The sole aluminium saucepan that Leo and Anna owned had probably been used as a weapon and lay dented on the stove. The only things untouched were the bamboo chopsticks. He went on towards the last room, Leo and Anna's bedroom, and on the way found the crucifix that had hung on the wall of the corridor lying broken on the floor, as was the picture of Our Lady. This room was in a similar disarray to the other two, and someone had used his bayonet, or sword, on the cotton quilt. Tufts of the material were floating about the room, settling on scattered clothing on the floor.

There wasn't much point asking who would do such a thing. He, like almost anyone in town would, knew only too well. But there was no time for grief. He must find Leo and Anna.

He went into the allotment. Apart from the broken and trampled fence, there did not seem to have been much damage done, at least to the crops. The chicken coop, however, had been smashed, and the large birds had been taken away. The tiny chicks that were left were running about, apparently quite at a loss. He went behind the house. Anna was sitting on the wet ground by the water tub, leaning against the wall, her head raised as though to catch the dying sun on her face and her eyes closed. It was obvious that she had been struck on the left side of her head with a heavy object such as a rifle butt. There was a bruise and a cut, but it did not seem to be deep, and the bleeding had stopped. She had come to the tub to wash off the blood, and streaks of blood and water were still running down the side of her face. There were no other external signs of injury

"Anna." Paul knelt by her and called her name softly. She heard, for her eyelids flickered, and then slowly opened. She moved her head round to look at him, wincing at the pain. There was recognition, and she made a little nodding movement.

He helped her up, supporting her as she got on her feet. He was a little surprised at how light she was. He walked her back into the house and seated her on one of the stools which had survived the destruction. He then tore up one of Leo's shirts, and using the saucepan as a basin, cleaned up Anna's head wound and bandaged it.

"Are you hurt anywhere else?" he asked, but Anna seemed not to have heard.

"You've got to get into some dry clothes," he said. "Can you manage it?"

Anna nodded but made no move, and closed her eyes again, looking as though she were going to go into a sort of coma. Paul watched her for a minute, and then started towards her room to fetch the quilt before he remembered that it was now useless. So he picked up the one he had been using and wrapped it round her. He set up the bed again in her room, and returned to her. He hesitated for a long moment, then he undressed her and put her to bed. Anna had in fact, he discovered, taken more than the blow to her head, but it seemed that no ribs had been broken.

The sun had by now set, but it had only been about half an hour since he had detected that something was wrong on his way home. He remembered seeing that the paraffin lamp looked undamaged, and managed to light it. There was still rice in the earthenware urn under the stove, and he cooked a rice porridge which he flavoured with salt and cabbage that he dug from the garden.

The three of them had planned to eat out tonight!

He fed Anna, still wrapped in the quilt, straight from the saucepan. She made no effort at all to help herself and appeared to have lost the will to carry on, but she allowed herself to be fed, which Paul thought was a good sign. Afterwards, she lay back inert. Paul sat by the bed and watched her until he was certain that she had gone to sleep. He had to have help. So he took a chance.

He sprinted down Third Lane, across the square and down the hillside on the other side of the market place to the Catholic Church. By the light in the window of the presbytery, he saw that someone was in. He hammered on the door.

However, the person who answered the door was not Father Fang.

"Is Father Fang in?" he asked urgently.

"He's at Mr and Mrs Liu's," said the old lady, who was obviously the housekeeper. "They're at No. 23 Cherry Street."

Paul did not know where Cherry Street was. It was not in the area where he had the responsibility for collection of nightsoil, and it would be futile to try to find it in the dark. There was only one thing to do.

"Could you please ask him, as soon as he gets back, to go to Leo's house. He knows where it is. Tell him it's urgent. Very, *very* urgent!"

He made the old lady repeat the message. Let's hope, he thought to himself as he sprinted back to the house, that Father Fang wasn't making a social call that evening, because then it could take all night! Anna's even breathing told him when he got back that she was still asleep. He blew out the lamp, sat down and continued his watch. He mouthed the words of Compline, but at first his mind refused to think. The words, however, did get through when he came to the hymn which had sounded so comforting barely… two and a half hours ago? He went on doggedly and finished with the accustomed *Salve Regina.*

As the night advanced it became really chilly, and he could feel the cold draught through the half-open front door which he had not been able to shut properly. However, he was so exhausted that he actually fell asleep. He dreamed of Father William again. He was kneeling in the middle of a market square between the old priest and Brother Andrew, their arms bound to their sides, and he kept wondering why Andrew had no shoes. The crowd around them were gesticulating angrily and menacingly, and he was very afraid, because he knew that they were all going to be shot. Then the old priest leaned across to look him in the eye and tapped him on the shoulder.

"Courage, mon frère."

But it was not Father William tapping him on the shoulder. Someone else was shaking him, and it was Father Fang.

"What's happened?" he whispered.

The two men moved out of the bedroom so as not to disturb Anna. Paul lit the lamp and its weak light cast big fuzzy shadows on the walls and the rafters.

"I don't know," Paul said. "Anna hasn't spoken since I found her. I can have a good guess, though." He did not need to tell Father Fang that Leo was missing. Paul was sure, too, that Fang had a very good guess as to what had befallen his old friend.

"Why don't you get some sleep?" Father Fang suggested. "I'll keep watch."

"Thanks. We'll take turns. Call me at about two." He would normally wake at two anyway. He wrapped his overcoat, which had not been damaged, round himself and went to sleep, squatting in a corner of the sitting room.

Father Fang had dozed off when Paul woke up to relieve him. Anna was still breathing evenly in her sleep and Paul watched until daybreak. To judge by her moans and movements, he was convinced that her sleep was no peaceful slumber, but that might well be nothing compared to the shock which would come when she woke to remember what had happened the night before. He roused Father Fang at a quarter to six.

"I've got to go to work," he said. "Don't go before I come back – I'll be as quick as possible."

Nightsoil collection was a lengthy business. After collecting it from the various houses, he had to take the smelly tubs of human waste to the town's communal septic tank half a mile outside the old walls, and after that it was his responsibility to sweep the streets of his area. This morning he hurried over that. But is was still nearly half past seven before he finished. However, he did not go home immediately. Father Fang would have to wait.

Paul waited for Hsu to finish his own round. Fortunately he came into the depot only ten minutes after Paul.

"You know my friends, the couple who have a small stall over there?"

"Oh, yes? The gentlefolk-on-their-uppers, we call them." He took a real look at Paul. "Something's happened to them."

Paul told Hsu what he knew.

"So." Hsu rubbed his perpetually unshaven chin. "You are thinking it's that young whippersnapper with the loudhailer?" He added carefully, "I wouldn't say you'd be wrong."

Hsu had to have influence in the Party, or he would not have attained the position of supervisor of the town's sweeps. But he was certainly a decent man. "Do you think," Paul said, "that you could find out where they've taken my friend?"

Hsu continued massaging his chin, his eyes on the cobblestones. "I'll do what I can. I'll come to you when I've got some news."

"You know where I live…"

Hsu nodded.

"If we're not there, we should be in the Catholic Church down the hill, on the other side of town." He watched Hsu for his reaction, but the latter showed none. So often the mere mention of a Christian church had the effect of a red rag waved in front of a bull.

"By the way," he said, "I was going to give you my notice. I was planning to leave for Canton after next week. But now, I may have to stay."

"I shouldn't worry. Forget this notice nonsense. Nobody keeps to it anyway. Go when you are ready. Just tell me the day before, and I'll get you the wages we owe you."

He got home to find Anna still in bed, but awake, and sobbing. Anything was better than the wordless grief she experienced the night before. Father Fang was still at his post, waiting patiently for the weeping to end. Paul boiled some water to make tea.

"They were waiting for us, and their lorry was in the lane just beyond the house," Anna told them, calm again outwardly. Both men saw the anguish behind her eyes. "There were, I think, five of them, including the man with the loudhailer."

When Leo and Anna sighted them, they had already demolished a portion of the garden fence and broken down the front door; others were presumably wreaking havoc inside.

Leo strode forward, ahead of Anna, really angry.

"What the hell are you doing to my house?" he bellowed. He flung one of the men into the lane, and was going for another when the two who had been in the house came out and knocked him to the ground. Anna dropped her basket of vegetables and rushed to help Leo but she was swept a side. She went into the house and came back out with the aluminium saucepan in her hand and hit one man over the head.

"He went down like a sack of rice," she said, and Paul was glad that she was beginning to show emotion again. She was almost exultant. "I thought for a minute that I'd killed him... and I was glad. Damned glad."

Then two men came at her with their rifle butts. They hit her on the shoulder and the ribcage, then the blow to her head laid her out. By the time she came to, they had gone.

"And so had Leo." She made as if to cry, but found the strength to control herself.

"Did they say why they'd come for Leo?"

She shook her head. "Nobody said anything. They wouldn't have to justify themselves, would they?" she said bitterly.

After a while, Father Fang said, "You can't live here anymore. Why don't you come down to the presbytery? You can stay until you've recovered, and then you can decide what to do."

Paul told her that Hsu might be able to find out where Leo had been taken.

"And he's coming here with his news?" Anna asked.

"If we're not here, he'll go down to the church."

Anna thought for a little while. "No. Suppose Leo comes back?"

She would not be persuaded otherwise. The two men did their best to put the house right again, but it was really a hopeless task.

"You will try to get her to come down to the presbytery, won't you, Mr Liang?" Father Fang said, as they were straightening the sitting room.

"This will depend on Hsu. If he can bring us definite news as to where they've taken Leo, Anna will probably come down. Otherwise she'll want to stay here, just in case he gets back."

Not that that was likely.

Father Fang sent up some food and pots and pans and eating utensils during the day, as well as another quilt. Anna wanted to get up, but Paul managed to persuade her to stay in bed.

"Look, Anna," he said. "You may think you're all right, but when you get up, that head wound is going to force you to go back to bed very quickly."

Hsu came just before Paul was going off to report for work that afternoon. They had taken Leo to another town about twenty miles west before sending him on to a labour camp at a place called Paisha in Kwangsi, to the south-west, not far from the border with French Indochina, Hsu told them.

"Why did they do it? How can they do a thing like that?"

"Look, missus," Hsu said gently, "they said that your husband had been given the wrong sentence when he was tried before. Now, they say, they're rectifying the mistake."

"So what should he have been condemned for?" Paul asked.

Hsu shrugged his shoulders. "For being an uncooperative *shenfu*." Then he was really curious. "He *was* one, wasn't he?"

"Yes," Paul said. "He was."

Then Hsu did a really kind thing. "Why don't you stay with the lady this afternoon? I'll see you tomorrow morning. Right?" Then, as though embarrassed by his deed of kindness, he walked off rapidly down the lane.

That night Anna got out of bed and hunted round in her room.

"Can I help?" asked Paul.

"I'm looking for our biscuit tin," she said. "I'm going to Paisha. That's the place, isn't it?"

Miraculously, the tin had not been tampered with, and the savings were still inside. Anna counted out the money on the floor, putting it into three piles. Then she sat back on her heels and shut her eyes. "It won't get me very far, will it, Paul?"

"But what will you do in Paisha, Anna? You don't even speak Cantonese, as they do there."

"Oh, I can sew, I can work in a hospital, I can do laundry... and you, Paul, will teach me Cantonese in a week."

She looked at the money on the floor. "And I'll walk there." She looked up at Paul, her eyes flashing in the light of the oil lamp between them. "I love him, Paul."

A week later, during which they accepted Father Fang's hospitality, Anna had learned to say "Paksha" instead of "Paisha" and many other things besides. Both Paul and Father Fang had tried to convince her that she should wait another week, but she would not be persuaded, and so Paul took her to Changsha to put her on a train to Liuchow.

"From there, if I'm not mistaken," said Paul, "it's another couple of hundred miles to Paksha. You'll have to ask your way from Liuchow because I don't know it, but you should have enough money to get you to Paksha."

"You're a good man, Father Paul," she said, giving him a long hug before getting on the train.

He could not help remembering Margaret. She and Anna would be about the same age. On his way out of the station he stopped by a rubbish bin to tear up the envelope which had enclosed Mr Wang's money to him. Most of it had gone on buying Anna's ticket to Liuchow and there wasn't much left now.

In any case, *he* would have to walk to Canton. He did not want to stay on at Shanglin any longer. But first he must retrieve St Bede, the à Kempis and the missal from behind the chicken coop back in Shanglin. He must also say goodbye to Father Fang.

\*\*\*

The walk took two and a half months. All in all, he enjoyed the journey. There were times when he did nothing much more than stroll along, and there had been periods of hard walking and a great deal of climbing. Occasionally, he was offered lifts, and once he rode on a coach carrying Party members from one town to another. Everywhere he could see evidence that the Communist Party was tightening its control on the country, but he was surprised how seldom he had to show his papers. When he did, there was a lot of poring over his release papers, and suspicious glances cast in his direction. Once he was asked to prove that he was indeed Cantonese, heading for home. So he spoke Cantonese, for almost the first time in fifteen years. Often he had to break off from walking to find work to make money for the next meal, and sometimes he paid for his lodgings with work, which usually meant washing dishes and fetching water from a well.

He tried to sleep in empty temples when he could, but when he could not find one in which to pass the night, or when it was too cold to sleep in the open, or when it rained, he had to use inns. The trouble with sleeping in the open or in temples was that, with the advent of warm weather, even at high altitudes where one could freeze, mosquitoes were ubiquitous, and several times he had been driven to seek refuge in inns where he had instead to contend with bedbugs. Of the two, he could not decide which was worse, but by and large he believed that mosquitoes were slightly preferable. Also, as he had discovered previously, he frequently had to share his night's free lodgings with fellow itinerants, and once an old man who had spent most of his life on the road told him how to deal with mosquitoes.

"Draw a circle on the wall," he said, demonstrating how with ash from his cigarette, "and all the mosquitoes in the building will settle in it for the night."

"What makes them do that?" Paul asked.

"You'll have to say this charm which I'll sell you. Interested?"

There were other stretches of the road through the forested mountains which were infested with bandits, who, according to what he was repeatedly told – often with much relish – dealt with people who had nothing to offer by cutting their throats. He always took the precaution at these times of travelling with a large party, where possible, although numbers were obviously no complete guarantee of safety. Fortunately, luck seemed to follow him. In any case, all that was now behind him.

Eventually, he reached Kukkong, a railway town, familiar to him as a train stop when he had travelled between Peking and home. He was almost entirely out of funds. He failed to find work on the first day, and had to resort to begging, which, although he had always been prepared to do it, proved to be a novel but totally debilitating experience. He did not think that he would willingly do it again. He then found work as a dishwasher in the kitchen of the busy railway restaurant, which was in reality more of a teahouse. They gave him board and a diminutive wage, and he had to sleep on a bench at the railway station. On the third night, someone in a railway official's uniform ejected him from the station, but when he told him that he worked in the restaurant he was allowed back in, but was told that he must not *lie* on the bench. By then it was almost time for him to get up for the Night Office anyway.

What he made in Kukkong was sufficient for him to buy food for the next few days as he walked south, almost all the way downhill now, to the lowland around Canton. On the way, he found work as a casual labourer on a collective farm, picking vegetables and being paid by the weight of the vegetables he picked. He worked hard for three days, and then moved on.

All that, too, was behind him.

He was now sitting under the shade of a tree in the blazing noonday sun at a table by a wayside foodstall, sipping the tea that had come with the simple meal of fishballs in noodles which he had just finished. There was an assortment of people around him: country folk with bags and suitcases who were travelling on foot between villages; passengers, less encumbered, who had been let off their buses for a lunch break; and others who were travelling in sedan chairs also taking their meal break, the chairs with their long poles parked under the shade. There were lorry drivers, and there were bus drivers. There were sedan-chair carriers and there were porters of goods. All were eating, drinking, smoking, chattering away and making new friends.

Paul, however, had no inclination for polite banter. His eyes were on the skyline of the city he had taken two and a half years to reach after he left Mu Chia Chuang. It had also been more than six months since he had left Tientsin. His interim destination was still distant. It was no more than a dark line in the noonday haze in a sea of yellow ochre, the colour of the ripening rice, with islands of dark green woods and the slate-blue of village rooftops. But, he said to himself, he was going to sleep there tonight. And, just to make sure, he was going to get on that bus there, the No. 35, under the tree, when it continued its journey to the provincial capital. He had made sure of that by buying a ticket from the driver. He took another sip of his tea.

He had decided to take the bus into Canton because he did not want to get lost in the maze of unfamiliar streets on his way to the centre of the city. Much as he called Canton his home city, there were areas that he did not know at all well. But the bus would take him to a part that he did know, and he would work his way out from there. This bus ride was another luxury which would reduce him to near penury, but whatever he did, he would be penniless by the time he got to Canton.

He smiled to himself. How many times in the last twelve months had he thought about money? Should he have worried about it so much as a monk, dedicated to, among other things, the spirit of poverty? Well, he decided, people with no financial problems spoke about poverty. The really poor worried about money for the next meal. All the time.

The bus driver then finished his lunch, and, not particularly concerned if his passengers had finished theirs, announced the imminent departure of his vehicle. Some of the passengers hurriedly gulped down the last mouthfuls of their food, others cursed, and still others were already at the bus. Paul slung the rucksack on his shoulder and gathered up his other bundles. He had not acquired any additional baggage during his walk, but the weather, turning from spring in the temperate mountains to summer in the subtropical plains, had made him carry his thick, cold-weather clothing. He had been tempted several times to leave this behind, but decided that it would be unwise to do so. It was quite a change from the freezing ride on the back of an open truck which he and Brother Andrew made... how long ago?

He found a place on the bench in the rear of the bus. Travellers on foot had not seemed to mind his scruffy appearance, and he had been able to make friends if he wanted to. On the bus, his fellow passengers gave him one long, suspicious look, and made sure that they gave him room. All except a toothless old man who was probably too blind to notice how he looked. He came and sat next to Paul, nodded a smile, and started to light up the first one of at least ten cigarettes he smoked on the journey.

"Come far?" He made the first move, as the bus pulled out of the shade of the tree it had sheltered under. He offered Paul his packet of cigarettes.

Paul put his hand up to decline the offer. "I've come down from Hunan."

He had found to his surprise when he arrived in Kukkong how easily he had slipped into his native Cantonese, which he had not used since he entered the monastery, except on very rare occasions when there had been Cantonese visitors, for being the only Cantonese in the community he was always assigned as their guide and interpreter. Then there was the coaching he had given Anna, but that was a different thing altogether. This was amazing, he told himself. And oddly, he would not be speaking in Mandarin again until he arrived at the monastery in Hong Kong. And, who knows, the community might in fact have learned to speak Cantonese. That would be something to look forward to! Although he would not need to speak much again, when he rejoined the community, except when he was in contact with visitors and people from the outside.

Not long now.

The bus wound its way round the countryside through practically every village north of Canton. During the journey he heard the old man's life story at least twice. He had been a small farmer, Paul learned. He also learned that he had five sons and two daughters. Two of the sons had died fighting the Japanese. Another one had died fighting for the 'evil' Nationalists.

"They were bad people." They had simply come to his home and taken all three away to join their army. "Didn't ask nobody!" Then he swore. And now between himself and his two wives, his two remaining sons and their wives, and the widows of his dead sons, they had to bring up all his grandchildren."

"And how many would that be?" Paul asked.

The old man spent the next ten minutes counting them out by name, and then he got completely confused.

"How about your daughters?"

"Oh, they were married to the same man in the next village when they were fifteen, and I never saw them again." He added, "They did write though, twice, to their mothers."

A while later, he suddenly said, "You don't sound like a Hunanese!"

"No, I'm not. I didn't say I was."

And then, as they stopped in a village square, the old man pointed to some dark stains on the ground. Paul knew what they were.

"They had a trial of the local landlord and his family here a week ago. They were all shot." He added after a short pause, "He cried like a pig before they shot him."

"Were you there?" asked Paul.

"Of course," the man said. "I wouldn't have missed it for anything."

Then a while later: "You know I had five sons and two daughters..." It started all over again. The conversation would have been interesting if it had not been so repetitive.

The old man eventually got off at the last village before they entered Canton, and Paul began to recognise landmarks. The city had not altered much since he had seen it last. There were the same three- or four-storey buildings, some plain and others grandiose, as one drew towards the centre. But a lot of the commercial and business buildings had changed. Like in Tientsin, the old foreign names had disappeared, as had a number of Chinese ones, before the arrival of the Communists. There was evidence of civil war damage, too, which had not been repaired or pulled down. He learned later that there had been no battle for Canton when the Communists approached, and all the damage had been caused by the retreating Nationalist troops. Buildings had been blown up, and bridges destroyed, in an effort to delay the PLA's advance.

By and large, he understood, the people were not entirely sorry to see the Nationalists go, but Communists were not famous for generosity and magnanimity in victory, and although certain people had argued that they had not imposed any overtly drastic measures on the city itself, what Paul had heard about retributions carried out on old foes convinced him that Canton was not going to be a particularly safe place for him if the local Party decided to begin random identity checks. Leo's fate was too recent in his memory. Anna should have got to Paksha by now, and he wondered if she had been able to get in touch with him.

The bus got in to the central bus depot at about four in the afternoon, only fifteen minutes or so late, but that was enough to make him miss the connecting bus to his home village, in theory an hour's ride away. He caught the next one, half an hour later, and as he watched the road from his seat on the bus he found that he still knew every inch of the way. There had been two wars since he had left home, but he was still able to predict the appearance of every tree and every house round unsighted bends.

But the question was whether his family were still going to be there, in that rambling old house with its three courtyards. Four years ago they had talked of moving to Hong Kong... and if they had stayed, would his father have survived the purges which must have taken place in the villages? And how would his mother have coped?

And then, after fifteen years, would anyone recognise him? Perhaps it might be better if they didn't. Well, he would know very soon.

He got off on Main Street. The grocery store was still open, and out of curiosity he entered it. Old Mr Poon was no longer bustling round the shop. In his place was a younger man, and he halted with surprise as he recognised old Mr Poon's son, a primary school friend. He looked up to watch Paul suspiciously, without any sign of recognition. His expression told Paul plainly that he wanted no beggars or itinerants in his shop. Paul looked at some tins and came out again. There wasn't much point renewing old friendship.

He followed the familiar walk up Main Street and the first side street to the old house. He could see that the house was still there as soon as he turned the corner. From that distance and that angle he could detect no change. As he drew near, however, he saw that the big wooden front door was open, and the main courtyard had become a communal area. The one house had apparently been turned into a commune, much like the one which the community was taken to see from Yang Chia Ping and of which their gaolers were so proud. He walked in, sure that no one was going to challenge him. He wandered through all the three other courtyards and found, as he had expected, that every room opening out to them was now occupied by a different family. There were only women in the compound, sewing and darning and doing other chores, and children tumbling about on the flagstones, and he guessed that the men had not yet returned from work. Like his old friend the greengrocer, most of them watched him suspiciously.

One of the women seemed somewhat less hostile than the others. He decided to approach her.

"Can you tell me if the Leung family still live here?" he asked.

"I don't know any Leung family: we've only been here a couple of months." Then, raising her voice, she called: "This gentleman is looking for the Leung family who used to live here."

"The Leung family!" a woman called from a corner of the

courtyard. "They went away, three or four years ago, it must be. They sold the house to the family who owned it last."

"Do you know where they moved to, miss?"

The answer was a shake of the head. "Ask at the shop," she suggested. "He ought to know: he's been here all the time. Most of us are new here, you see."

No help for it. He had to go back to the shop. His old friend appeared even less welcoming than the previous time.

"Do you know where the Leungs have moved to?"

He was given a thorough scrutiny. Then, "They moved to Hong Kong almost three years ago... lucky, we all believe, for the old man." He then looked hard at Paul again. "Who are you?"

Paul ignored the question. "Did they leave a forwarding address at all?"

"Yes." The man reached for a thick ledger on a shelf and opened it to a marked page. "You have to tell me who you are before I give it to you."

"You don't remember Leung Waihung, do you?"

He did. "So you are!" he said, all suspicion fallen away. That night, Paul did not sleep in Canton after all. For his board and lodging he gave his friend and his family an edited account of what had happened to him since he left the village for the University of Peking.

"There are lots of Party activists in this area at the moment," his friend warned him. Paul noticed the backward glance before the information was given. This backward glance seemed to be becoming a national habit, even if those present were one's own family.

He returned to Canton the next day. In his pocket was a three-year-old address for his family. His old friend had proved to be a true friend after all. He had to find a job before he could continue his journey. His friend had fitted him out with some decent clothes and a pair of nearly new shoes, and the village barber had been called in to give him a haircut and a shave. He had discarded his well-worn rucksack finally for a small suitcase. He had been reluctant, however, to throw away his winter coat.

"Look, Waihung," his friend had said. "You don't need it now, in the middle of summer. You'll be able to afford one when you find your family in Hong Kong. Winter's a good four months ahead yet."

He'd had to agree.

He was now reasonably presentable again. With the money his friend had given him, he was able to stay in lodgings for a week or so while he worked for his train fare to Hong Kong and to have something left over so that he did not enter Hong Kong totally destitute. He hoped that he would be able to find the monastery easily. That is, he prayed, if they were really in Hong Kong rather than in Taiwan or elsewhere. He found modest lodgings with an old couple just outside the centre of town and deposited his suitcase in the tiny wardrobe, but he was careful to retain his personal documents. Then he went out to look for work.

There were a number of clerical jobs advertised on the windows of various business establishments, but he did not want those. These jobs were all on monthly terms. He wanted to be able to get away as soon as he was financially independent. He was fortunate. He found a cleaning and tea-making job at a branch of the National Communications Bank, which certainly was an improvement on nightsoil collection. However, he was not due to begin until the next morning, and so with most of the day to spare he decided to explore more of the once familiar city.

As he had discovered on his way in, practically all the old landmarks were still there. It was no hardship therefore to find his way about. The Cathedral of the Sacred Heart was shut, and so were several other Catholic churches in the city. The small foreign community at Shameen had disappeared but it was impossible to find out who now occupied their spacious houses. Party high-ups, possibly, he guessed. On the edge of this area were the ruins of one of the bridges which the Nationalists had blown up, a once beautiful bridge, the destruction of which had alienated not only the locals but also the foreign residents who were still in the city. The force of the explosion had also destroyed a number of houses nearby. All that was left of some of them were precarious ruins which looked as though they might collapse at any moment.

He was now sitting looking at one of them. He was safe enough here, almost a street away, in the shade of a tree, one of a row that lined the bank of the river. He watched a group of boys go past him, one of them holding a football. It reminded him that this was also the middle of the school summer holidays, time for football and basketball and rowing and... all sorts of delightful things. They led his attention to the ruins, jagged bare walls overlooking a pile of seven- or eight-foot-high rubble. The ruined Chapel at Yang Chia Ping had looked something like that, he thought. The difference was that the Chapel walls were still solid, while these looked as though they would sway in a breeze. Then he spotted three children, younger than the ones with the football who had passed him, playing hide-and-seek in the ruins.

Hadn't their mothers warned them not to play there? he thought.

One of them, a boy of about ten, was 'it'. He was the one, wearing a white shirt as well as a red scarf, obviously an enthusiastic youngster who would one day rise high in the Party, that first drew Paul's attention. The second boy was wearing the universal quasi-military blue jacket, and the third child was dressed like the first, but without the red scarf. The first boy was leaning against a wall, his head on his right arm, and Paul could hear him counting: "Twenty-two, twenty-three, twenty-four..." The boy in the blue jacket was hiding behind a large pile of fallen bricks, while the other boy had gone behind the far wall.

Paul did not know what caused him to look up. The house had once been a three-storeyed apartment block. The roof had collapsed and brought all the floors down, and the debris on the ground floor was made up of this fallen material. Most of the sections of walls that were still standing tapered upwards, except one which extended into an overhang on what had been the second floor. By some miracle, this had managed to defy the laws of gravity for the best part of a year. Now, however, it decided that it could no longer sustain this feat.

Paul watched in horror as the overhang slowly broke away, loose bricks cascading directly onto where the first child was still counting. Then the falling brickwork dragged the rest of the walls down to land in a dense cloud of white dust. The child behind the rubble had also seen the collapse of the wall, and screamed. He had the presence of mind to run away, but he did not run far. The dust cloud caught up with him and enveloped him. Paul, however, could see his faint outline. He was still on his feet, but bending over and coughing.

Even before the main bulk of bricks hit the ground, Paul was sprinting up the street towards the ruins, yelling at the top of his voice to attract attention. Out of the corner of his eye he could see people coming to their windows and doorways, drawn more by the noise of the falling building than by his desperate shouts. He was stopped by the dense dust cloud. He knew roughly where the child was, and he realised that he had to be able to see if his efforts were to be of any use. He waited, and was soon joined by a crowd.

"Is there anyone underneath?" the first man who arrived after him asked.

"There were three kids playing here," Paul said. The cloud was settling, and the top half of the boy in the blue jacket was clearly visible now. His eyes beneath the film of white dust were red, and although he was opening and closing his mouth, no sound came. He sat down in the road. "That's one of them. One went behind the building, and there's one under this lot..."

"There were always kids playing in these ruins," the man said. "Mine did until I stopped him."

The crowd began to chatter. Paul raised his voice.

"Has someone called the... Fire Brigade?" he asked the crowd in general. Was there still a Fire Brigade, he wondered. Or perhaps it was now called something else?

"They're not very good answering distress calls," said the first man. "For one thing, they're horribly undermanned... after a lot of their officers were liquidated for graft and corruption and for failing to perform their duties satisfactorily in the old days. Isn't that right?" he asked another man. This one shrugged, unwilling or unable to commit himself to an answer.

By now the dust had settle sufficiently for the new devastation to be visible. There was a small mountain of debris where the child had been. Paul started to clear it, and he was joined by several other men, while others passed the bricks out of the way. An ambulance arrived, and the crew joined in the rescue work, but it seemed that they all preferred to take orders from him.

They cleared the top layer of the debris and found that a large section had fallen and landed in one piece at an angle against the wall at ground level.

"Maybe," an ambulance man said, wiping the dust and the sweat from his face with the back of his hand. "Maybe..."

They cleared some more bricks away to discover a cavity created by the angle of the fallen section, the base of the wall and the ground. It was no more than two feet high, but hope rose. The senior ambulanceman reached in.

"I've got him," he said.

They cleared some more of the debris away to enlarge the opening, and were soon able to see a pair of child's hands lying in the dust. The ambulance man pulled gently. "I hope he's not trapped or pinned down further in," he said.

Fortunately the child was not pinned or obstructed in any way, and slowly and carefully he was pulled out of the hole. He was unconscious, but he did not seem to have sustained any visible injury. They put him in the ambulance.

"There's one more," said the ambulance man, "I understand?"

He looked round. Someone pointed at Paul.

"I saw him go round the back," Paul said. By now perspiration was making dark streaks down his whitened face and staining his shirt.

"I don't like it," said the ambulanceman, looking up at the sections of wall which were still standing. "Bugger it, why doesn't the Fire Brigade come?"

One of his men said, "Someone reckoned there had been another fallen building on the other side of town."

"Hm," said the chief. Then he found that Paul was no longer by his side. "Don't you go in there!"

But Paul was already round the back. Most of the ruin had fallen inwards, and he found the third child lying at the foot of the wall, also unconscious, knocked out possibly by a small lump of cement lying by his side, but still breathing.

"I've got him," he called, as he picked up the boy.

And that was the last thing he knew.

# NINE

Margaret was standing at the open window of her second-floor flat on Robinson Road, a long, quiet, mainly residential street which ran almost levelly, hugging the contour of the mountain, halfway between the Harbour and Victoria Peak, and looking out on a vista that she knew well. In front of her and to her right across the road was Wah Yan College, the Jesuit college, two buildings that clung to the steep hillside. Boys in blue blazers were arriving, some in buses, and a few in cars, but most of them on foot, before the morning bell rang at nine. The college gate on the road would then be manned by one of the Fathers who would be taking the names of latecomers. Slightly to the left was the narrow, short flight of steps that led to one of the gates of her old school, the Sacred Heart Convent School, generally known as the Italian Convent after the nationality of the nuns who founded it. Her parents had bought the flat because it was so convenient for her school, and it had remained in the family, with an old servant and his wife as caretakers when the family was not staying there. Before she returned less than two years ago, the flat had been more frequently empty than used, and Margaret had wondered if she should sell it when she eventually returned to America. But her mind was now made up. She would keep the flat.

Below the two neighbouring schools, across all those rooftops and not too far away, was busy Hong Kong Harbour, and then Kowloon, bathing and glistening, this late winter morning, in the bright sunlight, and beyond that, the Kowloon Hills, blue and purple in the distance. She did not, however, see any of those things outside her window. She was aware of only one thought in her mind this morning: it was coming to an end. Again.

It had all begun that summer day in Canton, a year and a half ago.

*** 

The Canton General Hospital was busy. Perhaps it was not much busier today than other days; it always seemed to be so. The first serious cases were brought in early that morning. There was a fire in an eastern district of the city and the Fire Brigade brought in eight victims, all members of the same family, who were suffering from second- and third-degree burns. Two of the children had subsequently died. The condition of the other six was stabilised, but it was not clear how many of them would eventually survive. Later in the morning, the police brought in a busload of accident victims. Fortunately, it was only actually half a busload. The passengers had been travelling from the country and the bus had driven into a ditch and overturned. Two of the victims had suffered multiple fractures and had to be detained, but the rest were treated and discharged. After lunch the Fire Brigade brought in some more casualties. One of the new, postwar blocks of flats had collapsed, and the injured were mainly women and children who had been at home; most of the men were at work.

The number of admissions was in actual fact not by any means exceptional for a city hospital, and the material resources of the hospital were not being stretched. There were plenty of beds still, which could be filled, and with great foresight the hospital administrators had laid in a large store of medical supplies which were still in use, and orders which had been made abroad, from Hong Kong, for example, were still being delivered. No, materially, there was no shortage. The problems that faced the hospital lay in another direction.

The Communist Party had unhappy memories of Canton. Twenty or so years before, its members had suffered a thorough purge at the hands of the Nationalists, and the streets literally ran with their blood. There were daily executions in the waste ground outside the city. In general, the city's sympathies were with the government of the day, for which certain people now had to pay. In a country in which frequent unrest made it difficult for the poor to survive, it was no surprise that the people viewed rebellion with hostility. It was perhaps for this reason that the new government's treatment of the city reflected its history once they had taken it over little more than a year ago. Old scores were settled, and some that were by no means old. And the best way to settle scores of any sort was, as Paul and the Cistercians had experienced, to encourage certain disgruntled members of the community to point fingers. It did not matter whether the accusations could be substantiated or not.

Fingers were pointed at a large number of local officials and people who belonged to the wrong background, and the innocent suffered with the guilty. The staff of the General Hospital was not immune in this settlement, and though no doctor or nurse had been imprisoned or executed for crime, some had been dismissed from their posts or downgraded, which resulted, for example, in surgeons being made lavatory cleaners. People were being persuaded of the truth of the adage that it was necessary to break eggs to make an omelette.

The result of the persecution of the medical profession was that the hospital saw the departure and emigration of half of the best-qualified and most experienced doctors and senior nurses. They knew that they would not have an easy time in Hong Kong, where their qualifications were not recognised, and that they would have to take on jobs which did not reflect their abilities and qualifications unless they passed stiff examinations in a strange language. However, the majority of them were hoping to make it to America, where they believed that they would be better treated.

And so, today, the hospital pharmacist was kept extremely busy. There was a constant stream of demand for drugs to deal with the emergencies – in casualty, in the wards, in the operating theatre.

And, then, there were the normal requests. But at last, the in-tray was empty of chitties. That was no guarantee, of course, that there wouldn't be more before she was due to come off duty in half an hour. Only another fortnight of this, thank heavens!

In fact, however, she should not have been at this job at all. The Party had, six months ago, found that she had come from a decadent bourgeois background, had gone to the wrong school in the wrong place, and – even worse – had qualified in her profession in the land of the nation's arch enemy, America. She was sacked. Two weeks later, when she was in the process of making ready to leave the country, the hospital had begged her to return, with the blessing of the Party.

"All right," she had said reluctantly. "Until you find a replacement."

The blessing, however, in spite of the insistence of the hospital, was grudging, and she was made to feel it. So she finally decided to leave. In any case, she had returned to Canton only because her mother had been terminally ill, and with the latter's death, there was nothing to hold her there. Eventually, they agreed to let her go. And so, there was now only another fourteen days.

It was her custom, on her way in as well as on her way out of the hospital at the end of her shift, to look over the new patients' admission cards at reception so that she had an idea what special drugs she might be required to prepare. This afternoon she stopped by the receptionist's counter as usual.

"Off now, Miss Siu?" the receptionist said, pushing over the pile of new cards. "Quite a lot today, a few pretty horrific." She must have been referring to the family of fire victims.

Margaret nodded, quickly glancing through the top cards. Nothing really out of the ordinary.

"They brought in three more to Emergency about twenty minutes ago."

Just then a nurse came through from Emergency. "One's being

discharged after he's had a rest and when the parents come to collect him. The other two are being admitted: they're both unconscious… concussion, knock on the head, we think." She put the cards on the receptionist's desk. The receptionist passed them over to Margaret. She read the children's cards first.

"Cheung Yuenpang, aged nine," Margaret read. She turned the card over. "He's being discharged. He was able to tell you his name?"

"Just a bit of shock, really," said the nurse.

She looked at the second card. "No name, aged about ten. He's in a bad way, isn't he?"

"We're trying to find his parents. One of the crowd at the scene thought he knew the kid."

Margaret picked up the third card. "Leung Waihung, aged thirty-eight. I knew a Leung Waihung once," she said.

"He's apparently from these parts," said the nurse. "A village just outside the city. His papers said so. I had a look."

Margaret thought for a moment, and then asked, casually, "Have these two gone through admission already?"

"They're being taken through to their wards now."

Margaret looked at the card again. "Chungshan Ward," she read.

She tried not to hurry as she made her way to Chungshan Ward. This was a ward with eight beds, and the new patient had been put in a bed by the entrance, nearest to the sister's desk in the aisle. The ward sister was just saying, "Put a couple of screens round the bed."

She looked up and saw Margaret.

"Could I have a look at him?" Margaret asked.

The sister mistook her concern. "He's still unconscious, and we hope he's going to come round soon. He actually looks worse than he really is, I think, with that saline drip. Apparently it's all bruising rather than anything really serious. He should be all right once the swelling goes down, and if he comes round." She sounded anxious. "He did take a knock on the head, you know."

"I once knew someone by that name," Margaret explained. "I

wonder if it's him."

The sister pushed aside one of the screens for Margaret. "There are lots of scars on him," she continued. "Poor man. Look at his wrists, with the weals right round them... and there are others you can't see under his clothes. Whatever did they do to him!"

The patient's head was bandaged, and a saline drip was fed into his arm which lay on top of the blanket. The weals on the wrists were there, very much in evidence. The face below the head bandage, fortunately unbruised and unswollen, was definitely familiar, a face she could not forget. Older and leaner, and more weatherbeaten, it was Paul's face. But what was he doing here, in Canton?

The sister heard the sharp intake of her breath. "Are you all right, Margaret?"

"Yes, I'm all right," she replied.

"Is it your old friend?" the sister asked.

Margaret nodded.

"Do you know where his people are?"

"They left Canton a couple of years ago. I don't think he knows where, though. I'll get a bite and then I'll come back... if you don't mind."

The ward sister did not mind, and Margaret dozed that night on a chair by Paul's bedside, waking every time his breathing changed rhythm and volume. She took his hand in hers and held it most of the night, and wondered what had caused the scars round the wrist. Then at dawn she went home to shower and change before returning to the hospital for her shift.

"Tell me when he comes round," she made the ward sister promise.

It was four days later, and he was still drowsy and kept drifting in and out of consciousness. There was not much chance of talking to him, but she spent her free time at his bedside.

It was late morning on the fifth day when the telephone rang in the pharmacy, and she was told that the patient had woken up.

"Come now," said the sister, "if you can." There was an urgency in her voice.

It was, however, nearly half an hour before Margaret was free. The sister was waiting for her at the entrance to the ward. Margaret could see that the bed was still surrounded by screens, and a doctor was with Paul.

"He's awake," the sister said. "But he's apparently lost his memory. He can't remember his name, or where he is. Well, the doctor wants to see you. He thinks maybe you can help."

But the worried, scared eyes that met hers showed no recognition.

"Do you remember me? It's Margaret."

This made no impression. The eyes that looked back at her were querying, and then he said, "I don't think I know you..." Then the agony of concentration. "I can't even remember my name!"

"What do you remember about yourself?"

The patient shook his head, then discovered that the movement was painful, and winced. They showed him the papers he had been carrying in his pocket.

"You are Leung Waihung. These are your papers. And this is your Peking University degree diploma."

The patient shook his head, winced again, and then, reluctantly: "If you say so." *So I am an engineer... What did I build?*

The doctor began to doubt his patient's identity. What if he had actually stolen someone else's papers?

"Look, doctor," Margaret said firmly. "I know him. I knew him for four years. We were at Peking University together." She nearly added, "He was my boyfriend."

If necessary, she could show them a photograph of herself and Paul in front of the Chaplaincy. Faded and brown now, she still had it.

"All right, calm down. Breathe deep. Now let's try again."

It was hopeless.

"Where have you been the past week?"

"Does Yang Chia Ping mean anything?" This from Margaret.

"Try to remember: when did you come back to Canton?"

"Think of a word. Does it mean anything?"

"Hasselbach?"

"Look at your wrists. Where did you get those scars?"

*Yes! Where did I get those scars?*

The patient's memory appeared to be a complete blank, although he seemed to have retained all his physical and mental faculties and skills and motor movements. He had everything but his memory. And the only psychiatrist who had been on the hospital staff had been hounded out, and had long left Canton for Hong Kong and the United States.

At last, after more than an hour, they gave up.

"Don't worry, Mr Leung," said the doctor. "Give it a rest now. We'll try again tomorrow."

"Is his amnesia permanent?" Margaret asked anxiously.

"Most patients, it seems, do recover their memory eventually, but I wouldn't know."

She returned to see Paul after her shift had ended. He looked up when she entered the ward.

"Did you say you knew me?" he asked.

She fought for control, and said, "Yes, Paul."

He was puzzled. "You call me Paul. I'm a Catholic, aren't I?"

Margaret nodded. "You're a Catholic." She wondered if she should tell him more.

"I thought as much. You see, I prayed after you people left this morning. Interesting, isn't it, that I should forget everything, and yet remember to pray."

"So you know what being a Catholic means?"

He ignored her question. Instead, he said, "Do *I* know you?" When she told him that he did, he said, "Tell me how I got to know you."

She told him about that first Chinese New Year party at the university Chaplaincy nineteen years ago. She could see his rapt attention, and the superhuman effort he was making. But finally he told her that what she had said had stirred no ripple in his mind.

He looked at her for a long moment.

'I'm glad I knew you. I was lucky to have known you." Did he wonder if there was anything more than just being fellow students?

Margaret could see that he was beginning to be resigned to his amnesia because he said, "I'm tired now... Shall we please stop?" But his eyes were beseeching, and she promised to return.

She prescribed herself a sleeping draught. She could not afford to lose another night's sleep, and she had to keep herself in good form for his sake. And that night, she made plans for both of them.

Paul's bruises were healing, and the swellings were going down. They had long disconnected the drip, and he showed a healthy appetite. In another few days, he would be discharged. Margaret went to see the director. The result was that it was agreed that Paul was to be discharged into her care when he was physically fit to leave hospital.

At the beginning, she had fought to put him out of her mind, and in time the last glimpse of him from the window of the train as it pulled out from the railway station on its journey to Hong Kong began to fade. For a time, she did almost forget him. America, and Ann Arbor in particular, was a totally new experience, and she was kept busy at her studies, and after she had finished the course, there was her first job with a Midwest pharmaceutical company.

Then there was Ralph Zachs, who had been a fellow post-graduate student, who besieged her with flowers and chocolates and tickets for concerts with the Chicago Symphony Orchestra, and she knew that it would lead to only one conclusion. Then with hostilities first in China and later in Europe, and war clouds over the Pacific, Ralph proposed one evening after Elgar's Cello Concerto.

"There will be war very soon," he said in preamble, "no matter what anybody else may say."

She had meant to say yes, but something held her back, and Ralph went to war promising to raise the question again when he returned. He did, twice, when he came home on furlough. And then he was killed on D-Day on Omaha Beach. His parents never forgave her. Ralph had been an only son.

Then, not long after the end of the War, her mother had fallen ill, and she had come home to Canton, fully aware that she would be caught up in the aftermath of the Civil War. And now, here again, was Paul, whom she had not expected to see again, ever.

She looked in on him several times a day, whenever her duties permitted, and when she was not on duty she spent long hours with him. She could see that he was pleased with her attention and it was transparent that he was looking forward to her company. She wanted to talk to him about making plans, but it was difficult to talk about the future with a man without a past.

She asked to see his personal papers, and they were passed on to her, as she was now officially regarded as his only 'relation'. There was his identification document, which, apart from his name and age and his place of residence when it was issued, gave little useful information. The name of Yang Chia Ping, she had seen, elicited no response. In fact, he didn't even know where it was. He was surprised that he had been as far afield as Peking, but when Margaret spoke Mandarin to him, he was well able to respond without any effort, and that, too, astonished him.

"So, you see," she told him, "you did live in the north."

He closed his eyes and tried to remember, but failed.

In addition to the degree diploma, there was the document which was issued to him when he had been released from the labour camp in which the commandant confirmed that the person in question had paid his full debt to society. The bearer was reminded that he must produce this document together with his identification paper when he applied for work or for benefit. It was apparent that Paul hadn't used this much.

So Paul had been in prison, pretty obviously because he was a monk and a priest; Margaret knew that many priests were. But that probably did not explain why he was in Canton.

Then she found two letters in the same envelope. The first one she pulled out was signed with a woman's name: Lingyi.

"Don't be an idiot, Margaret," she told herself.

It was, however, Chun's letter which finally gave her a clue. "*Home* in Hong Kong." That seemed to explain a lot of things.

She tried the names Lingyi and Chun on him. Neither succeeded in jerking his memory. She sighed. And he only nodded when she told him that he had probably been on his way to Hong Kong to join his family.

Did that mean that he was no longer a monk?

Paul's discharge from hospital coincided with the termination of her own notice as the hospital's pharmacist. She brought him her brother's old clothes, which smelled of mothballs and fitted him badly, but, she told herself, they weren't the universal blue cloth suit.

"Are these my clothes?" he asked.

However, she noticed that his confidence returned on the short journey to her house, and by the time they arrived, there was little to reveal that he was a man without a memory. He was worried that he was going to be so indebted to her, someone he scarcely knew. In the mean time, he had the courtesy to accept her charity with grace. She hoped that he was on the way to becoming the Paul she had once known.

"You're being very good to me. I'll try to pay you back one day," he said at dinner that night.

"Paul," she said, "I once knew you as well as your family. This is the least I can do."

That night, she recalled, she was awakened by the noise of something heavy falling over in Paul's room. She switched on her bedside lamp to read the time on her watch. Three o'clock.

"Sorry I woke you up," he said when she got to his room. "I woke up and couldn't get back to sleep, and I got up in the dark and knocked the washbasin stand over. Sorry."

The next morning, he told her that he thought that there was something which he ought to be doing when he woke up, but he could not remember what it was.

"Why would anybody be wanting to get up at three o'clock in the morning?" he mused aloud. "I was waking up early in hospital, too."

Margaret should have remembered, for the ward sister on night duty had told her the curious hours he kept.

The next evening she outlined her plans for both of them. He was, however, reluctant to leave Canton. More accurately, he was reluctant to go to Hong Kong.

"There's nothing for me there," he said.

"Look, Paul." She decided to be plain. "With your amnesia, you will not last very long under this government. Besides, your family's probably in Hong Kong. We'll try to find them there."

He then changed the direction of the conversation. "What's so bad about this government?"

She looked hard at him. "It's bad." She nearly added, "How do you think you got all those marks on your body?" but refrained from doing so. She was also tempted to tell him that they had probably put him in prison for nothing, but he would not have understood.

*If I was in prison, was I a bad character?*

Two days later they left Canton on the eighty-mile journey to Hong Kong. There was some urgency in their departure. The Chinese government had been concerned with the brain drain which was taking place, though of course they would not admit to themselves that it was their treatment of their own people which was causing it, and there were plans to stem the tide of emigration. At about the same time, the tiny British colony of Hong Kong, with its four hundred square miles of territory, was afraid that it was going to be swamped if the tide was not checked. Both governments were therefore rumoured to be contemplating the institution of border control. Margaret, with her American passport, would have no trouble, but Paul might find himself stopped at the border. She had some anxious moments when the train stopped just before it crossed Lowu bridge into British territory, and there was a great deal of activity from the Chinese border guards as well as from Hong Kong's border police.

"The train used to go straight through," she told Paul. It was apparent that both sides were serious about erecting border control.

At last, however, the train was allowed to cross into Hong Kong, and they, like most of the other passengers, alighted at the terminal at Tsimshatsui on Hong Kong Harbour.

Margaret took Paul's arm as they walked down the platform towards the exit. Paul turned to smile at her.

"You know, I was going to claim that you were my husband if they should query your entry," she said.

"You couldn't," he said. "We don't have the same name. And we don't have a marriage certificate."

"Well, many Chinese couples keep their own names, and we could have been married in the War and the record been destroyed in an air-raid."

"Clever girl." Paul squeezed her hand on his arm. Definitely the old Paul.

Margaret might have realised that if she had told the Hong Kong immigration people that Paul was a Cistercian monk, he would have had no trouble entering the colony! But she did not know it then.

She installed them both in the flat on Robinson Road. The old servants at first looked at the oddly dressed man whom their mistress brought with her with a certain apprehensive curiosity, but when they realised that this was the same young man she had brought home years ago in Canton, their apprehension disappeared. In fact they were grateful for his presence, for otherwise Margaret would have immediately returned to America.

On Sunday she took him just down the hill to the Cathedral to Mass. She watched him as he automatically and unconsciously made the monastic obeisance instead of genuflecting. Later she went up with him to receive Communion.

"So you have become a Catholic, then?" he said as they stepped out of the church into the covered porch. Then he said, puzzled, "Why did I ask you that?"

There was something in the depth of his memory that was waiting to surface, but try as he would, he could not reach it. He raised his eyes to see Margaret watching him.

Unfortunately – or was it fortunately from Margaret's perspective? – the recall proceeded no further than that. Margaret got in touch with the doctor whom her family consulted when they were in Hong Kong. He put her in touch with the specialists. Paul saw four of them, two just once and fairly briefly, the other two several times in long sessions over the course of the next three weeks. They also made an effort to trace his family, but neither telephone calls nor newspaper advertisements brought any result.

"It's no good, is it?" he said one morning, referring to the medical consultations and tests.

"As the doctors said," Margaret replied, "it takes time. Your memory will come back one day."

"Yeah, if you say so." Then, after a long silence, he said, "You know, I've been thinking things out a bit. I'm healthy, and I'm all right, really, apart from not being able to remember anything about myself. I'll find a job." When Margaret did not say anything, he carried on. "I don't know when I learned English, but I've been listening to the radio and I can understand what they say. I can write it, at least I think I can. And I can say things in English as well, but not fast, maybe not correctly. Do you think I can get a job... in a business firm or a bank, Margaret?"

She thought for a moment before replying. "Do you remember anything about engineering?"

"I never thought about that."

"I know someone at the university," she said, "who might be

able to help."

That night she handed him a pile of books and notes. "This is final-year material. See what you make of it."

She scarcely saw him for the next four days. Then, at dinner on the fourth day, he said, "I know most of the stuff. There are new things, but nothing drastically advanced. And" – he hesitated before telling her – "there's a job in the *South China Morning Post* I'm interested in."

He showed her the advertisement. They were building a dam at a place in the New Territories called Taai Laam Chung and the firm which had the contract for its construction wanted replacement local engineering staff. Paul thought the pay was marvellous.

"Six hundred Hong Kong dollars!"

Margaret did not want to disillusion him: it was only one hundred American dollars. She helped him to draft the letter of application for the job, as it was obvious he had not done it before, and he was struggling with his English as he had foreseen.

"You have to tell them how good you are, and how well you were trained," she said, as she worked the name of Professor Hasselbach into the letter. "If Hasselbach thought you were good, then you must be good."

"Right," he said.

Three weeks later, he was asked to attend an interview. He was in a mild panic then.

"It's my spoken English," he said.

"You understand everything they say on Radio Hong Kong, don't you?" she said. "So just keep calm. And take your time about saying things."

There were a large number of candidates, and the interview was tough, but Paul carried it well, and got the job. He had to live on site, but had Saturday evenings and Sundays off. Although he rang Margaret every evening, she worried about him during the first week, and the flat felt empty without him. In the meantime, she had decided to relinquish her original plan of returning to the United States. She could not leave Paul while he was in this condition, and she felt responsible for him. Besides...

She shook her head to ward off the incipient thought. The fact was that she had never been able to forget Paul, and that probably explained why she had not been able to marry Ralph.

She, too, got a job, as pharmacist at Queen Mary Hospital. And she bought a car, a little Austin, to get to work in.

One evening she went across the road and knocked on the door of Wah Yan College. The door was opened by one of the college's servants.

"Could I see one of the Fathers, please?" she asked.

"Anyone in particular?"

"I'm trying to trace a Jesuit Father I used to know in China, fifteen years ago."

The man thought for a moment. "You may want to see Father Cotter, then."

She was shown into the parlour, with its polished wooden floor and leather armchairs. A large print of Turner's *Stonyhurst College* hung on one wall, and there was an inexpertly arranged bowl of flowers on a coffee table in the centre of the room. Five minutes later, a white-haired, keen-eyed and spare-looking man, in the distinctive winged cassock of the English and Irish provinces of the Society of Jesus, entered the room. He extended his hand.

"What can I do for you, Miss Siu? Would you have some tea, or coffee?" He pressed a bell by the door, and when the servant reappeared, he gave the order.

"I met a Father Liu while I was at Peking University in the early thirties. I'm anxious to find him because there is something which I believe he is in the best position to help me with."

"Peking... He was with the famous Hasselbach, eh?"

Margaret nodded.

"Well, Father Hasselbach died in 1940. Sorry, but that's not what you want to know, is it? Father Liu came through here in 1948 on his way to Australia. He's attached to the Australian province now, and is working in the Chaplaincy, if I am not mistaken, at Melbourne University, looking after Chinese students there. I hope I am right."

"I was half hoping that he might be here," she said in a small voice. There really was no reason why she should, but somehow she had.

Father Cotter saw her face fall. "Is there anything I can do for you... anything I can do to help?"

She told her story, a little haltingly at first. Halfway through her recital, Father Cotter took the cup of cold coffee from her hand, rang and ordered more, and when it came, took it at the door from the servant who had brought it. Margaret received the second cup gratefully.

"I think he was put in prison, and from the marks on his wrists and his body he was badly treated and beaten, because I'm convinced he was a monk. But he doesn't remember. Tell me what I should do," she said at the end. "I think he is far too dependent on me, although he doesn't realise it, and I don't want him to be."

There was a long silence after that, but at last the priest stirred.

"Quite a story," he said. Then he looked up at her. "You still love him." It was partly a question, and partly a statement. "Yes. You still do. Imagine, after fifteen years, you still do."

There nothing she could say to that. So she kept silent.

"You realise that there isn't an awful lot I can do to help you, or Paul. You have to make up your own mind about it."

She nodded. "Yes. I know that. But... talking to someone about it helps. I hope."

"So he's working on the Taai Laam Chung project. When did you say he started? Is he happy at it?"

"He started three months ago. He lives on site, and only comes home on Saturday afternoon, and he's off again on Sunday afternoon. He seems to be happy with the work. It seems that he is being recommended for some sort of promotion already." Then she added, "I miss him terribly."

"Do you think he's... in love with you, too?"

She took time to answer the question. She remembered the time when he got his first 'pay packet', and they had gone out to celebrate. "I believe he is. He's so much like the old Paul I used to know... apart, that is, from his diffidence, which is new. And that's the problem. That is, if he's really in love with me."

Father Cotter waited.

"I would marry him if he asked me. Can I marry him, legally, Father?"

"Would anything I say make any difference, Margaret?"

She shook her head. "It might do. I don't know. And then, if he recovers his memory and finds that he's been... trapped into marrying me. It doesn't bear thinking about."

"I wouldn't call it trapping. But I see what you mean. Now, may I tell you something before you go on? It has a bearing on this case."

"Yes, Father."

"There is a Cistercian, or Trappist, monastery in Hong Kong. It's on Lantau Island, and it was founded about three years ago by refugee monks who had escaped from China, but I don't know if there are any of them from Yang Chia Ping. I believe they're all from another monastery called Notre Dame de Liesse, or Our Lady of Joy. They haven't completed their buildings yet, and they are still living in temporary shelters."

"And I can just take Paul there and tell them: here's one of yours; you can have him back!"

"Paul won't thank you for doing that either," the priest said seriously, ignoring her sarcasm. "In any case, they probably don't know him."

Margaret remembered something. "I found a letter written to Paul by someone in Tientsin. He referred to Paul being 'home' in Hong Kong. Do you think that he had been left behind, and was making his way to the monastery here?"

"It's a possibility. Do you know what happened to the monks at Yang Chia Ping?"

"No."

"One of our Fathers has been interviewing some of the monks and is in the process of writing a pamphlet or an article on the martyrdom of Yang Chia Ping. It seems that this is what happened..."

Margaret was now getting a fuller picture of what Paul must have gone through. Am I going to lose him a second time, she wondered.

Then she found that Father Cotter had been speaking to her. She was starting to become angry.

Father Cotter was trying to be helpful. She could, he supposed, petition for a dispensation and for laicisation, for Paul to be released from his monastic and priestly vows. But, much as she wanted Paul, she had to agree that this step was going to cause problems. And it was perhaps questionable that one would abandon a life for which one had suffered so much.

She would just have to wait.

Then Paul bought a car with an interest-free loan from the construction company. She was really surprised, as he had not given her any inkling at all.

"It's only a used Ford," he said, as he showed her the interior. "We're a two-car family now!" he added proudly.

"I didn't know that you were taking driving lessons," said Margaret, as he drove them to Deep Water Bay on the south side of Hong Kong island which was more of a cove, guarded by two rocky headlands, with a quiet, short beach. On the right, as one looked out to sea, was one of the famous follies of Hong Kong: a replica of a Scottish castle clinging to an almost vertical cliff. One could only, however, look from the outside, as the castle was not open to the public.

"Well... That was meant to be a surprise." He grinned at her.

In the depth of Hong Kong's subtropical winter, there were not many people at Deep Water Bay. They found a place to sit down, right under the battlements of the mock castle, and they were happy with each other's company. Then Margaret had a thought.

"Let's go to Aberdeen," she suggested. Father Cotter had told her about the Regional Seminary, which was run by the Jesuits, where they sang Vespers at four on Sunday.

"See how Paul reacts," he said. "Just ask for Father Rector. Say I've sent you."

This building stood on what was apparently an island overlooking Aberdeen Bay, a stretch of enclosed, crowded, busy water with narrow entrances. Most visitors to the seminary were ferried from the quayside in the sampan provided by the seminary, but one could also approach it by a long, seldom-used causeway a mile or so before one got to the fishing village. Father Cotter had obviously briefed the Rector about them, and they were treated like honoured guests, and were shown round the compound and the building. That afternoon they were two of the eight lay people who attended Vespers. Margaret watched Paul during the Office, but he showed little reaction.

"I like the music," he said afterwards. "We could come back another time, if you fancy it. Did you know Father Rector?"

They did return several times, and Margaret herself appreciated the experience, but it had no effect on Paul.

The trouble in fact was that Paul was not being tempted to a celibate life. Although he knew he could not make long-term plans, his thoughts were full of Margaret.

*** 

Spring came, and then it was summer, and Paul seemed to be accepting the fact that he was as he was, and was content. One weekend in August, they celebrated their first anniversary in Hong Kong.

"We have nothing much else to celebrate, have we?" he said. "So we may as well celebrate this!"

"There's your promotion, you seem to forget. They appreciate your work."

"Ah, well. That's nothing much, really."

They had dinner at Chantecler, a Russian restaurant in Kowloon. It had been clear to Margaret from the very beginning that Paul had not forgotten his European table manners, which he could only have learned in the monastery. Paul himself seemed to be totally unconscious of the fact. Anyway, it was very late when they made it back to Robinson Road. They let themselves into the flat without waking the servants, and Margaret switched on the table fan for it was a particularly hot and airless night.

"Do you want a drink?" he asked her.

"Yes, please," said Margaret.

He went into the kitchen and poured them both a glass of water. She held out her hand for hers. She did not get the glass. Instead, he took her in his arms and kissed her. She hesitated for a fraction of a second, then put her own arms round his neck and kissed him back.

They stood together for a longish while, then she stepped away.

He said nothing. It was plain that he was asking, "What's wrong?"

She shook her head. No. There was nothing wrong. She kissed him again, briefly this time, and said, "Good night, Paul."

She lay awake a long time, and she knew that he was finding it difficult to get to sleep as well.

He returned to the subject a week later. "I was going to ask you to marry me, but I thought I had no right to, until I knew, really knew, who I was, and what I had been doing all these years. And when I do ask you," he went on after a pause, "you'll say 'yes', won't you? That is, if you haven't already said 'yes' to someone else."

Yes. Yes! And there won't be someone else. She did not say it aloud. Instead, she took his hand in hers. Anything she said would be inappropriate. She just had to help him to recover his memory, for his sake as well as her own. But, in spite of doubts, they moved even closer to each other. Margaret felt that she was being carried along, but she was content... even happy. It did seem as though Paul really had no recollection of a life in which he had spent fifteen years.

They were getting to know Hong Kong well, and they drove everywhere in his Ford, or her Austin. They spent a lot of their time on their favourite beach, Deep Water Bay, and sometimes they went to Clearwater Bay in the New Territories, and when the weather grew too cool for bathing, they went walking. They would go up Victoria Peak on the Peak Tram, and climb from the station to High West, a narrow spine of a ridge from where they had a view of the harbour on one side and a vista of islands on the other. From the end of the ridge they would look down on Queen Mary Hospital where Margaret worked, and then descend the precipitous hillside to the hospital from where they caught the bus home. At other times, they would walk the quiet path from the Peak to Pokfulam reservoir and then on to Aberdeen before taking a bus back. It was very much, Margaret thought, like the days when they were in Peking. But she was the only one to remember them.

One day, as they were negotiating the slippery, grass-covered ascent of High West, he suddenly stopped and stood very still, his forehead furrowed.

"Anything the matter?" she asked him.

"I seem to have done this before. Slippery. And wet. And I seem to be carrying something. Heavy."

She watched him. "We've never come up here in wet weather."

He shook his head. "Never mind. It's gone."

"Did you ever go out with a girl?" she asked him later as they stood leaning against the wind which was blowing from the south, and she was sheltering behind him.

"Not that I can remember," he said. "Wouldn't you know?"

She did not answer.

"Did I go out with you?"

In answer, she put her arm through his. She was dying to say 'yes', but thought that would be unfair. He looked at her but said nothing more.

On another occasion, he said, "What horrifies me is that I'll wake up one day and find that I am already married."

"Do you feel as though you may have been married?"

"No again! At least I don't think so."

Margaret paused, then said:

"You might have been a monk."

"An interesting thought. Wouldn't you have known?" The tone was serious.

She decided on evasion. "Don't forget that I hadn't seen you for fifteen years."

"That's true."

She was not sure if he was really satisfied with her vague reply. She went to see Father Cotter again.

"So Paul hasn't changed?"

"Not really, Father."

"How long has it been now?" asked the priest. "Two years?"

"Sixteen months, close enough," she said. "But the situation is getting unbearable for both of us. He's being noble, and yet I can see it hurts him when I seem to be putting him off."

"Then... I wonder if it's time to initiate the canonical process of dispensation and laicisation," said the priest thoughtfully. "You may wish to go to the Trappists."

"They won't let him go, surely."

"You could well be wrong there. They have no claim to him, as you may know already. Besides, what use is Paul to them as he is? If they have him, assuming he is handed over to them, he's no willing monk. Frankly, they'd rather not have him. Anyway, why don't you go and talk to Father Prior? There are processes of having him released from his vows."

Margaret thought long over it. "Yes. I'll go and see him after Christmas. It's only another month to go."

Then Paul asked her if she would like to go to a Christmas Party. It had been organised by the construction firm for its employees, and was to be an all-night, glittering affair at the prestigious

Peninsula Hotel.

"You'll have to wear a ball gown and I've got to get myself a formal suit. And we can steal away to Midnight Mass at Rosary Church up the road and then return to the ball afterwards." He had it all planned.

Margaret was in fact very pleased, not because they were going to the ball, but because, junior though Paul was in his job, his abilities and his merits were being recognised. He was asked only because they thought well of him in the firm. She mentioned the ball to one of the almoners at the hospital, whose husband was connected with the Taai Laam Chung project.

"Congratulations, Margaret. Your man's on the make, because they don't ask just anybody."

And yet, it was sad, she thought. She would almost, she began to realise, have preferred to see him in an unbleached white woollen habit and open sandals.

It was a good Christmas Ball. Margaret thought Paul looked elegant in his dinner jacket and bow tie, and she was in a black ball gown she'd had especially made for the occasion. She had never been inside the Peninsula, and was suitably impressed with the grandeur of the place, although she believed that they had overdone the Christmas decorations. They were greeted by the chairman of the firm as she entered the ballroom on Paul's arm, although it was quite obvious that the august person had very little idea who Paul actually was. But Paul's immediate boss was standing by the chairman, and he gave them a genuinely welcoming smile. Paul was introduced to his wife.

"Brenda, this is Paul Leung, a very promising engineer. He did his training at Peking University under Hasselbach, you know."

And Paul introduced Margaret to his boss and his wife.

"Welcome to the inner circle, old man," one of Paul's English colleagues clapped him on the shoulder. "And this charming lady is...?"

"Margaret. And this is Piers Ireland."

Margaret decided that she did not like Piers Ireland.

"You'll want a drink," Piers said, stopping a waiter with a large tray full of glasses.

"We're teetotal," Paul said rather abruptly, taking two glasses of orange juice, one for Margaret and one for himself. "For the evening," he added under his breath.

They circulated, and Margaret met many of the people Paul worked with, some of whom she liked, while others she detested. Which, of course, was only normal. However, she was pleased that most seemed to be friendly, and Paul seemed to have been able to get along with nearly everyone. The only exception, it was obvious to her, was Piers, who quickly became far too merry, and the charming and elegant woman he had come with, who was evidently his wife, eyed him all evening with alarm and concern.

Paul was as poor a dancer as she remembered, and after a couple of near disasters, they decided to watch instead. They slipped away at half past eleven, and a taxi deposited them at Rosary Church. They had come too late to find a seat, and had to stand in the nave, looking totally incongruous in their formal wear. However, they were not the only ones, for there was a European couple in the same predicament. They had obviously escaped from another party somewhere else. The Mass was celebrated by three priests, resplendent in gold vestments for the occasion. The choir performed both Plain Chant and polyphony, and the congregation was spared a sermon because otherwise it would have made the Mass too long. Although she had modestly covered herself with a shawl, one of the priests looked at Margaret's low-cut and off-the-shoulder gown with scarcely concealed disapproval when they went to Communion, but he forbore to say anything. It was Christmas, after all.

They were back at the ball after Mass, and Margaret made a determined effort to improve Paul's dance technique, but soon after the crowd began to thin. By three, both of them thought they had had enough.

The cross-harbour Star Ferry ran an all-night service on Christmas Eve, and they were back in the flat soon after four.

Margaret headed for her bedroom, but Paul stopped her.

"Margaret," he said, "will you marry me?"

***

School was starting. The few boys who had not managed to arrive before the bell were stopped at the gate and the priest on duty made a big show of writing their names down. The little boy at the front of the line, Margaret could see, was almost in tears. One of the older boys behind him tried to look nonchalant. On her left, a group of girls, nervously giggling, crept out of sight down the steps to the side entrance of the convent school. Nuns, she remembered, were worse than priests with recalcitrant offenders, and she pitied them if Mother Filomena was on duty, and then she remembered that good nun must have gone to her reward by now. In any case, the road was quiet again, and she remembered the feelings which that brief question on Christmas day aroused in her. Four months before, he had promised to ask the question again if... She had not expected it to be so soon. She might, perhaps, have been praying that it would not be soon.

She remembered the room that early Christmas morning. They had switched on the lamp on the piano when they came in, and its light lit up the cards on the sideboard as well as the decorations on the Christmas tree on the other side of the room. He had untied his black bow tie on the way up the stairs so that the two ends hung down the two sides of his collar, and she was on the point of taking off the silk wrap she was wearing.

***

"Margaret, will you marry me?"

She looked at him, and there was no need for words. There was in her an indescribable mixture of emotions all clamouring for recognition. But outwardly she was calm, showing no sign of the turmoil inside.

He looked back at her, and nodded.

"When?"

"A few days ago. Monday last week."

"A week ago. No, eight days ago." For it was already Tuesday, Christmas Day.

"Yes."

"I'm... glad. Very glad. Congratulations." She should have been really happy, but all that she felt now was numbness. "How... how did it happen? Had it been coming on gradually? Or..."

"It might perhaps have been coming on gradually all the time, but everything suddenly, as it were, fell into place last Monday."

He told her.

He had been at the base of the wall of the dam to inspect one of the drains. These allowed the stream to discharge its water until the work was completed and they were ready to start filling the valley behind. As he looked up at the dam, even he was impressed with and awed by the enormous height of the structure which he had been helping to construct. He then looked round him and for the first time realised that the only parts of the surrounding hills which would not be submerged were the bare hilltops – everything else would disappear, which, he told himself, was a pity, in a way. Out of curiosity, he started walking upstream and came to one of the small tributaries that emerged from a narrow valley on the right. He followed the smaller stream, and found himself in a narrow gorge, with the sides rising almost vertically into the pale December sky, and here, where the sun did not reach, it was chilly. Then suddenly, the valley widened, and he found himself in a circular clearing, and at the end of the clearing was a long, low building, with a door at one end. It was a pigsty.

This should no longer be here, he thought to himself. It should have been demolished, but someone had overlooked it.

"I don't know why it was missed out. In any case, I went to check that there was nobody there."

The sty was divided into three stalls, and although the roof was still intact, the interior was full of debris and dead leaves; but it was dry, as it had obviously not been used for a while, and any smell of ordure and animal feed had long disappeared. Something then began to tug so insistently at a shutter in his mind that he gasped. And then the shutter opened.

"That was what did it. The pigsty. I saw the converted pigsty which Leo and Anna lived in." His mind reached further back. "And Father Chrysostom was made to live in one as punishment for his stubbornness, not clean and empty like the one before me, but one with the pigs still in, and wet with filth and smell."

He saw the incomprehension on Margaret's face at the mention of the names. He'd answer her questions later. He went on. "Terrible things, really terrible things, happened at a place called Mu Chia Chuang."

She went to sit down in the sofa. "You want to tell me…" But he was sidetracked by another strand of his memory.

"I only survived because they wanted somebody to build a dam, you know. There was Andrew, too… Brother Andrew, but he died in an accident later. Poor Andrew."

She couldn't, however, help smiling at the irony and the coincidence of it. That's why they thought so highly of him here!

"It was an illusion, of course, what I saw last Monday, but it was an illusion which brought me back to reality. And my memory."

"You could have called me in the evening, and you didn't say anything during the weekend when you came home, Paul." It was almost a rebuke.

"No. I'd been planning it for tonight."

He certainly did not want to tell her that he suddenly realised that he had, again, come to the crossroads, and the decision this time was going to be even more difficult than the one he had made all those years ago. He lay awake almost all that night. He could not bear the thought of losing Margaret again... the physicality of her feel, her touch, her smell, on top of his obligation to her. He had left her once; could he leave her again? The loss of her was going to create a void which he knew would be hard to fill. But the pull the other way was equally strong, and he began to resent it. He could just walk away. But could he, really?

*Father, if thou wilt, remove this chalice from me.*

He finally drifted off when the eastern sky began to pale, but by then he had made up his mind.

"One of my colleagues told me about the monastery on Lantau, and I took a day off during the week to go and see Father Prior. He said he remembered me from a visit he made to Yang Chia Ping, and he welcomed me to his new community."

Paul told the Prior that that was not what he had come for. He had come, he said, to ask advice about dispensation from his vows.

"He said he would enquire, if that was what I really wanted. Come back after Christmas, he said, and he would have news for me."

"Why?" the Prior asked after a short pause. Paul explained.

"He said again that I should come back and see him after Christmas. He must have been hoping that I'd change my mind."

She was quiet when he told her. "Do you know," she then said, "I was going to petition after Christmas for you to be released from your vows." Events had beaten her to it. For her, it was a pity, she thought. It was a disaster!

They looked round at the sound of shuffling feet.

"Oh, you're back," the old servant said. "Do you want me to get you anything?"

"No," said Margaret. "Sorry we woke you."

They waited until his bedroom door closed, and then turned round to face each other again.

There was a pause. Margaret knew what was coming.

"I am whole again. Margaret, I am asking you to marry me?" He nearly added, "As I promised."

She went and stood by the window, looking out, her back towards him. The city below her was dark now, and it was still another two hours before dawn. But the ships in the Harbour had been dressed for Christmas. She turned round to face him, still without saying a word. If she said 'yes', she knew that they would have a future worth sharing for both of them. But it was not as simple as that, and so she did not know what to say. More accurately, she knew what she had to say, but was resentful about saying it. However, she had to say something. It might as well be the truth, or as much of the truth as possible.

"I love you, Paul. There's nothing I want more." He started to come towards her, but she stayed him at arm's length.

"I almost swore that I wasn't going to lose you a second time."

"Were you badly hurt the last time?" Paul asked. She did not reply, but he saw the answer on her face. "I'll... I'll make up for all the time that we have lost."

She looked into his eyes.

"No, you won't, Paul. I do not doubt you love me as much as I love you – in fact, I know you do – but you are also committed to someone else, someone I cannot compete with. You'll wake up at two o'clock every night, feeling guilty, perhaps, that you are not saying the Night Office. Every time we go to Mass, you will imagine yourself up there at the altar. And you'd feel happier in your monk's habit than in this ridiculous suit that you are wearing! No, Paul." It hurt as she said it.

She saw the agony in his eyes. He started to say something, but she would not let him.

She went up to him and kissed him, lingeringly and tenderly. "No, my love, my dearest love. I won't marry you."

"You can also be cruel, Margaret," Paul said quietly. "The trouble is, I can't remember the Office any more. I tried to say it, but apart from the opening responses, the words just didn't come back."

There was another piece of news which he had wanted to tell Margaret, but the events of the night had quite driven it out of his mind. However, he told it at breakfast.

"Father Prior told me that my father had gone to the monastery to look for me," he said. That had been two years ago, when the family were staying in Hong Kong waiting for their American immigration applications to be processed. "He had read about the monks' arrival in Hong Kong in the newspapers. And he was disappointed that I wasn't with them on Lantau. But he left them the family's forwarding address in America. And later, he wrote from America to the monastery to give them their permanent address."

"And you kept that from me as well! You know how anxious I've been about you finding your family."

"Well. I couldn't reveal one without revealing the other, Margaret."

"All right. You are absolved."

And so they had something else to celebrate in addition to Christmas. Later she took his arm when they were out for their walk after lunch, and he smiled and pulled her to him as she reached up to kiss him.

And, slowly, and in detail, he told her all that had happened to him in the last four years.

"That day at Mu Chia Chuang," he said, and he realised that this was the first time he did not have to force himself to tell someone what happened that day. "They tied up Father Seraphin, Father Chrysostom, Brother Alexius, Brother Roch and Brother Eligius and led them to the hillside just outside the village. It had snowed the night before, quite heavily, and their footsteps made no sound as they were led away. And on that hillside they were horribly butchered, as we worked out afterwards. They made each one of them lie down with his head on a rock, and then... crushed the skull of each man with another rock. When we were taken to see them, there they were, all lying with their crushed heads on their rock pillows."

He was silent as in his mind he watched their blood-stained bodies on the blood-stained snow, and Brother Martin breaking down, and Margaret saw him wince at the memory. Then he wrenched his mind back to the present.

"I'm convinced that I escaped the same fate only because they were desperate for an engineer to rebuild some dam which they had themselves destroyed."

He told her how Father Simon had encouraged him to get away, and how he managed to take Brother Andrew with him.

"The monks I met afterwards in Peking told me that Father Simon and five others were killed in the same way soon after I left… I really don't know how anyone could do a thing like that. Not once, but twice. Did the second time make it easier?"

They were both silent for a long while, he with his memories, and she understanding and finally accepting that there was only one path he could follow.

He said goodbye on Boxing Day, pleading that he had plans to check over before work restarted on Thursday.

He did not come home the following weekend, but turned up on New Year's Eve for the small party which Margaret was throwing for a few of the friends she had made at the hospital. After he had been away for the second weekend, the servant asked whether Mr Leung had moved to his own flat.

"Yes," she said. Which, in essence, was true enough.

He rang to ask her if he could come for the weekend in the third week.

"Of course, Paul," she said.

He came that weekend, and he also came the following weekend, which happened to be the Chinese New Year.

"Do you remember that first time we went to the Chinese New Year fair in Peking?" she asked him as they made their way to the fair on Hong Kong island.

"How can I forget!" he laughed in reply. "We'd only just met, and you were angry with me."

"Yes. For being prejudiced and pig-headed."

"You must admit I've got better since then!"

Later...

"I gave my notice," he shouted into her ear as they jostled their way through the crowd. "Mr Stansfield, you know, my boss whom you met at the Christmas Ball, couldn't understand why I had to leave, even after I'd told him about my amnesia."

She shook her head to indicate that she hadn't heard what he said. So he repeated it later when they found a relatively quiet corner.

"I really fail to understand your reason, Paul," Mr Stansfield had said. "Will you reconsider..." His eyes suddenly lit up. "Why don't you ask your superior to let you come and work for us during the daytime?"

Paul replied that he doubted if his superior would allow it.

"So you're definitely going back to the monastery?" Margaret asked, linking arms comfortably with him, and clinging to him for warmth, for the night was cold. But also for memory. "I was wondering if you might be having second thoughts."

He looked at her and did not say anything, and she turned away to escape the look. He then said, "You are right, you know. I am a monk, and there's nothing else I can be. But I am still sorry that you turned me down this time."

\*\*\*

He came out of his room and found her as she had been the last ten minutes, standing motionless by the window looking down on an empty street, for the priest had withdrawn from his post by the school gate. She heard him, and turned round.

"Aren't you cold, standing by the open window?"

"I needed to clear my head," she said. "I didn't sleep very well last night."

"Ready?" he asked after a short pause.

"Yes."

"Are you sure you want to come? You don't have to, you know."

"Yes." She smiled. "The least I can do for you and for myself is to deliver you to my rival!" She was only half joking. In doing so she hoped that she would perhaps feel then that a part of his life would always be hers. Was that irrational, she wondered.

A taxi took them to the ferry. And through most of the hour-long crossing to Peng Chau, they sat in silence. Then he stirred to look at her.

"When will you be going to America, then?"

"When I've worked out my notice at Queen Mary. Another six weeks." She smiled. "I seem to have been making a habit of working out my notice recently."

"You'll be selling the flat?"

"No. I thought about it, actually, but old Shun and his wife need a home, and I'll come back on visits." She then grinned and said, "Shall I come and see you?"

"That will make me very happy, Margaret."

They got off at Peng Chau, a small pancake of an island off the much larger Lantau. Then they looked for the monastery's boat.

"It's gone off to the monastery with a load of building stuff," a local boatman told them. Then he said, hoping to earn a little extra, "It may be a long time. I can row you across if you wish. It's twenty cents each. Very cheap." But they preferred to wait for the monastery's boat.

At last the ancient motor boat which had been a gift to the monks from a local benefactor returned and they took the short crossing to Lantau. From the pier a steep path, between heavily forested slopes, rose up, but the hilltop which the monks had cleared and the monastic buildings were hidden from view round a bend. After they rounded the bend, they saw the still incomplete Chapel which the monks were building themselves. Straight ahead was an enclosure surrounded by a wrought iron fence in the middle of which was an archway, also of wrought iron, and beyond was the temporary main building of the monastery. Work would only begin on a permanent building when the Chapel was completed. On the semi-circular arch were the familiar words of welcome: "Pax Intrantibus."

Peace to those who enter, Margaret translated to herself.

Paul turned to face her. "Goodbye, then. I haven't actually thanked you properly for the care you have taken of me in the last two years. It was remiss of me."

"Don't exaggerate, Paul. It was one year seven months and three days, including today." She put her hand out for him to shake.

"Goodbye, Paul," she said.

They shook hands formally, as they had done all those years back, at the Jesuit Chaplaincy in Peking.

He stepped through the archway, holding his small suitcase. And Margaret could swear that Paul had undergone a definite if indefinable transformation. She turned to go back down the path to the pier and the monastic boat and therefore did not see him turn to watch her when he arrived at the main building.

Then he knocked on the door.


FINIS

# A HISTORICAL NOTE

There were two Reformed Cistercian, more popularly known as Trappist, monasteries in China in the 1940s. The older one, Our Lady of Consolation, which was founded in 1883, was in the mountains north-west of Peking, and its daughter house, Notre Dame de Liesse, Our Lady of Joy, was south of Peking. In 1947, there were seventy-seven monks, including five non-Chinese (European and Canadian), in Consolation, and about sixty monks in the second monastery. Between July 1947 and February 1948, the monastery of Our Lady of Consolation, which was in an area held by the Communists, was destroyed and the monks underwent extraordinarily cruel suffering at the hands of the Communists. Thirty-three of the community died of the ill-treatment and some of them were brutally murdered. While most of the younger monks were released, only four of the eighteen priests, it seems, survived.

The monastery of Our Lady of Joy was also closed and the community dispersed. Twenty of the community managed to make their way to Hong Kong to refound their monastery in the wilds of Lantau Island in the Colony.

There are still remnants of both monasteries in China today, according to news which has filtered through to Hong Kong. It seems that the monks are not just content to survive in their small groups, but are, in spite of their age, actively trying to resurrect monastic life there. The name of Our Lady of Consolation has not been deleted, but is still on the active list of the Cistercian community.

In this tale, the list of the names of deceased monks in Chapter Three is that of real persons who died between August 1947 and February or March 1948, starting with eighty-two-year-old Brother Bruno. Maria Chang, who defended Father Seraphin (and the fictional Father Paul) in the trial in the Chapel, was a real person, although apart from the name little is known about her, and there seems to be no record of what happened to her after her imprisonment in the monastery. In addition, Dom Alexis, Abbot of Consolation, was a real person. So was Dom Paulinus Li, the Prior of Our Lady of Joy and later of the monastery on Lantau Island; he was in Peking in 1948 before he went to Hong Kong. In reality, no monk from Our Lady of Consolation made it to Hong Kong. All those who got there were from Our Lady of Joy. Li Tuishi, who was perhaps chiefly instrumental in the destruction of the monastery and the ill-treatment and deaths of the monks, was also a real person. Again, nothing else is known of him.

Paul, Brother Andrew and the other characters in the tale are fictional.

I have referred to the monastic community as monks, rather than make a distinction between *monks* and *lay brothers*. The term *brothers* is used to refer to fellow monks; monks who are priests are called Fathers, and those who are not are Brothers. With the Cistercians, *Dom* is a title reserved for the abbot and the prior. Chinese people always call monks and priests by their surnames – Father Leung, Brother Yau, for example. In this book, however, since I am writing for English readers, I have followed the less formal custom of calling them by their title and Christian names. I have also used their baptismal names for most invented characters in the story for the sake of convenience.

# ACKNOWLEDGEMENTS

For the account of the destruction of Our Lady of Consolation I have drawn heavily on a section of Thomas Merton's book *The Waters of Siloe*, which was based on notes taken by a Jesuit priest, Father McCarthy, from Brother Joachim, one of the monks released by the Communists, in St Vincent's Hospital, Peking. I have also made extensive use of an extract from a booklet written by Father Raymond, *Trappists, the Reds and You*, which is a first-hand account by Father Stanislaus Jen, originally from Our Lady of Consolation, who escaped from Our Lady of Joy to Peking and then to Hong Kong, and who also supplied a map of the environs of Yang Chia Ping. The Yang Chia Ping map in my book is based on Father Jen's map. For all these, my grateful acknowledgement and thanks.

In addition, I wish to thank Father Benedict Chao, Prior Emeritus of the Trappist Monastery, Lantau Island, Hong Kong, for supplying the account written by Father Stanislaus Jen. I wish also to thank Brother Theophane Young of the same monastery for so patiently answering my questions, and for critically reading the manuscript and pointing out the mistakes in it. Not least, I wish to thank Brother Herbert, OSB, Turvey Abbey, Bedfordshire, for his encouragement.

My thanks must also go to my publisher Janet Weitz and her team, Jo James, Eric Waring, Mark James and Simon Vickery, for their encouragement and their indefatigable efforts on my behalf. Special thanks go to my editor, Wendy Toole, for so painstakingly editing my manuscript, and my publicist, Tabitha Pelly, for her work.

And, of course, my thanks to my wife Irene for her interest, encouragement and support.


Mark Cheng
Bedford

Lightning Source UK Ltd.
Milton Keynes UK
UKOW03f1910151013

219130UK00013B/222/P